SWANSONG

SWANSONG

Kerry Andrew

JONATHAN CAPE
London

1 3 5 7 9 10 8 6 4 2

Jonathan Cape, an imprint of Vintage Publishing,
20 Vauxhall Bridge Road,
London SW1V 2SA

Jonathan Cape is part of the Penguin Random House group of companies
whose addresses can be found at global.penguinrandomhouse.com.

Copyright © Kerry Andrew 2018

First published by Jonathan Cape in 2018

penguin.co.uk/vintage

A CIP catalogue record for this book is available from the British Library

ISBN 9781911214229

Typeset in India by Integra Software Services Pvt. Ltd, Pondicherry

Printed and bound in Great Britain by Clays Ltd, St Ives plc

Penguin Random House is committed to a sustainable future for our business, our readers and our planet. This book is made from Forest Stewardship
Council® certified paper.

For my little brother, Daniel

Come all you young fellows
That handle a gun
Beware of night rambling
By the setting of the sun

1

My breath is the loudest thing. And a thundering in my ears like a war drum.

On the evenings when rain and sun are tangled up together, I relive it. As if it were the first time.

The thundering is my bones, thumping either side of me, arcing strangely. The ground bumps and blurs and the sea-loch tilts, slipping away far below. My tongue curls in on itself and there's that strange cry, brassy and elastic. It is mine. Me.

I am a girl, and I am flying.

Then, as always, a fisting blow. The pain in my breast. The ground see-saws.

Heat and sorrow and blood.

My heart, made metal.

I will always be a girl, flying.

A bird had been hit. The tarmac was pale and furry.

More roadkill. On the way here we had driven past rabbits in various states of squishiness, two foxes, and a badger – huddled up as if just having a kerbside snooze, except I'd looked back and seen the great marbled gash in its head. No corpse this time though, just an explosion of feathers, like the road had coughed them up. I took one, tawny and black-striped.

There was a jeep awkwardly parked on the verge up ahead. No one was in it but the lights were still on, and when I lifted one headphone off I could hear the engine's sleepy, constant growl. Maybe the bird had done the driver in, landing one for the wildlife team. Cut to badgers and otters cheering, waving flags. I walked around to the side of the jeep and my heart belted me in the throat.

A man in a puffer jacket, sitting on a tree stump. A mass of feathers in his hands, and in the feathers something bright pink and purple and glistening. It was turned upside down, wings hanging outwards. Fluffy legs. The speckled head was tipped back, small black beak open, near-orgasmic. Red eyelid, pillar-box red. His hands were stained red.

He was – *taking it apart.*

I jerked back and almost fell, putting a palm out onto the bonnet. 'Sorry.'

His mouth moved a little and I turned and walked away very quickly, my music raging in my ears, waiting for bloody fingers to encircle my neck. Don't look scared. Don't run.

My breathing didn't return to normal until I shut the front door. All the way back to the house, I had waited for the jeep to cruise by and stop just ahead of me, was planning my made-up ju-jitsu moves and wishing I had pepper spray, but not a single car had passed. I sat very close to Lottie for an hour in front of the TV, Tyger on my lap. Mother–dog panic aversion therapy.

His thumbs had been in the bird. I'd seen bone, sticking out, and blood and maybe an intestine. God. Had he hit the bird on purpose? If I'd come by a minute later would he have been chewing on its liver? The man's eyes had been wild, tar-coloured. It was as if all of him had been drawn with a heavy pencil lead – hair, beard, the movement he'd made when he saw me.

Lottie, her eyes on the screen, murmured something about apprentices and power heels.

The feather was still in my closed palm. I kept seeing the bright red swipe above the bird's eye. Horror Movie Red. The wings, questioning fingers. A black tail like a broken fan, lots of it smashed into the road.

This place was not right. This place was *dark*.

*

Dead. Not dead. I stood at the window, fingering the feather in my pocket.

Rain again. Our first proper day on the west coast, further north than I'd ever been or ever cared to go, before, and it had done nothing but rain like a bastard. Scratching itself with a penknife onto the glass, idle but insistent. Slipping among the layers of the tune I was listening to, making loads of little extra hi-hats, filigree beats. Getting into my brain, folding in with the words.

Dead.

I ran my nails along the edge of the feather.

Not dead.

And back the other way, the fronds separating, little gaps between them like the one in my teeth.

I'd come here to get away from the dark. From the thin, serrated line of fear I felt when I swallowed. From the words, hurling themselves round and round my skull like bumper cars.

He might be dead. He might not be dead.

'Polly?'

I turned from the window and took a headphone off.

'I said, did you want some tea?'

'Yeah. Thanks.'

I'd only gone into London because Stef had insisted that he would make everything better. *Come be my hag, u lil deadbeat. ILL RESCUE U.* Everything had gone wrong. A cascade of mini fuck-ups falling like dominoes behind me. Fuck-up One: my brain going into meltdown and me becoming the worst student in the year, maybe in the whole English department. Fuck-up Two: finding distraction in the valiantly jerking crotches of a few boys, including my housemate's boyfriend. Fuck-up Three: moving back home early following housemate shitstorm, but still paying rent on my empty room. And then Fuck-up Four: running to Stef, my real friend, and doing the thing that made all previous fuck-ups seem like something on CBeebies.

We'd gone dancing in Dalston, me wearing Stef's pork-pie hat and totally surrounded by gayboys, and Stef, with one of his classic, chipped-diamond smiles, had picked up this Spanish boy. He was cute, in a high street, touristy sort of way. Earnest head-nodding and peering at the coins in his cupped palm at the bar. A total drugs virgin – as far as we could make out with his Catalan and our half-arsed Spanglish with French bits mixed in – something we both found completely hilarious before force-feeding him an E.

4

We hardly prised his jaw open, but there was a hefty dose of cajoling. And faux-whimpering. And acting out that he was a wuss with street entertainer-quality mime. The night was hard and bright and brilliant until he had an epileptic fit at the bus stop. He went jump-cutty, like frames of him were being missed out. And we ran away. Just freaked and legged it, with him juddering there on the pavement, his head next to a load of scattered bits of fried chicken. We ran. Left him.

The next day, sober and pale, we'd gone back to scraps of chicken and a strange, sulphuric smell. And, right beside the overflowing bin, the 'I heart London' badge that had been pinned to his bag the night before.

On the train south, I'd held an *Evening Standard* on my knees, unbelieving and hollow, looking at the compact report of a man in his early twenties who had been taken to hospital in East London and was fighting for his life after being found alone on the street. I hadn't told Stef. And we hadn't talked since.

I put my forehead on the conservatory window and felt for the feather again. He was dead. Or he was not dead. If he was dead, we had killed him. I had killed him.

And now I was here. Where everything was greener and greyer. The fag-end of nowhere. Not much evidence of the new fighting spirit, you know, Scotland for the Scottish, Labour out on their arses. The sky looked smeary, as if someone had wet a tissue, wiped at it and just made it ten times worse. Who the hell could *live* here, miles from anywhere? Yodellers. Meditation experts. People wanting to practise their thousand-yard stares. I sat down and dug my toes underneath Tyger. He shifted and slumped his head onto my foot.

Lottie brought a tray in, spoons and milk and sugar as though we were in a Georgian salon and not a conservatory infested with wicker. My mug had a cartoon lipsticked fish on it and the words 'Master Baiter'.

It had seemed like a good idea at the time. The only solution. The further away I was, the less I'd have to think about it. Initially, I'd said no thanks to Lottie, but after two days of shitting myself, taking the train a few stops into town to get the free paper and speed-reading it with a lump like a gimp's ball gag in my throat, I changed my mind. Green, grey escape route. Quick getaway. Lottie hugged me hard in the kitchen at home and said that we were going to have a real catch-up, quality time together, a laugh.

I had stood alone on the deck of the five-minute ferry to the bit of mainland just over the water, looking at the little gobs of spit flecked on the loch, wanting to add my own, feeling us pull further and further away from humanity. You couldn't believe that anything was beyond that line of hills, just an aching void of mizzling sky. Everything had gone soft focus. Well, no one would ever be able to find me up here. I was being swallowed up.

Lottie sat down, sighing too loudly, her smile too wide. When I didn't give her one back, the laughter lines were chased away underneath her chin and up to her ears. She raised her eyebrows at me instead and tipped her head on one side. I shifted my headphone off again.

'You're not going to be like this the whole time, are you?'

I shook my head and picked up the milk jug.

Dead. Not dead.

The cottage was owned by someone that Bev and Adam, her old London friends, knew. He was away for a couple of months in South America catching really big fish and comparing them to the length of his dick, probably. Tucked away off the village road – you could just see the roof from the driveway gate, AN EALA BHÀN written in blue paint on the paddle of an oar at the top – it had been pressed deep into the ground with a giant thumb, bending sopping pines and tropical-looking palms down towards it. Everything was wet and spongy. You could probably leave an imprint the depth of your calf in the grass.

My room was at the far end of the house. Baby-pink flower noodlings on the bedding, NHS-tight. A shiny chest of drawers in the corner, a mirror with a studded frame on top. And a white orchid with black-green, rubbery leaves on a small table between the twin beds. All it needed was a crucifix on the wall and my get-thee-to-a-nunneryness would be complete.

A single window faced the garden, full of ferns and plants that looked like they were dancing at a rave – arms up, ecstatic. You could just see a dark corner of the loch behind the branches at the edge of the lawn, past the bleak misery-memoir sky.

The guy who lived here seemed to be into angling, big, fuck-off mountains and pints that made him red-faced and greasy-looking. His interior design skills were seriously lacking. The living room was a disaster of clashing colours – salmon-pink sofas, tangerine rug and blood-coloured shagpile. There was an exposed stone wall, a tiny telly up on a bracket, and a cabinet full of mismatched glasses and retro cameras. The bathroom had an impressive patch of mould in the top corner. The outside slowly working its way in.

The small study next to my room was probably meant to be private. It smelled woody and a bit like fermenting apples. There was a desk, a beaten-up leather chair and more over-exposed photos of the owner with his arms wrapped round massive, spent fish and a dirty grin on his face. The night before I had slid open the top drawer. Fountain pen, collected business cards and a tin of Mint Imperials, which rustled softly when I shook it.

Angling, mountains, pints – and weed. Loads of lovely weed. I decided that this guy wasn't so bad after all and slotted the tin into my back pocket for a rainy day. Which, conveniently, was every day.

We got a drink in before the imminent welcome party dive-bombing by Bev and Adam. The hotel was a mile away, at the near end of the village, some little boats docked low in the loch beside it.

So this was going to be my den of iniquity. More pine panelling than you could shake a stick at, a log fire, swords on the wall, and a carpet that looked as though it had once been the kilt of some giant Highland man with thighs you couldn't get both your hands round.

I worked out my Sex Order as we took a table in the corner. Sex Order had always been Stef's game. Wherever we were – pub, gig, tube carriage, school playground back in the day – we'd chart all the guys, deciding that if you had to sleep with all of them, no vetoes, who'd be your first choice all the way down to the last, the ickiness factor getting higher. I'd be incredulous at some of the men that Stef would have at the top of his list. Thick necks, black fingernails, workboots, guys with uneasy smiles and hair sticking out of their collars.

Sometimes we'd agree – pink jeans and a big afro, say – and Stef would graciously announce that I could have him first. At one of the townie pubs back home it happened for real – a quiet boy with a scar above one eyebrow and tattoo sleeve of Japanese fish. We all did some MDMA in the loos and somehow I was sitting on the toilet cistern and he was kneeling on the seat, the sleaziest thing I'd ever done. After getting some air outside I had come back to see him and Stef sloping off together, Stef with a big grin on his face, rubbing his thumb at the corner of his mouth. I don't know who was more surprised, me or the boy.

From then on Stef had joked that we were Sartre and de Beauvoir, Fred and Rose West. Shouted it to me as we hung on to the shoulders of the Spanish guy in the scratchy little club that night. Two cats and a mouse.

Dead. Not dead.

My skin prickled and I shivered enough to prompt Lottie to glance at me. I wasn't allowed to think about it. Scotland. It would be OK because I was in Scotland. Green and pheasanty land.

Slim pickings here on the Sex Order front. Last had to be an oldish dude nursing a dark pint of something and looking at an ancient brick of a phone with a magnifying glass. Tufts of hair spiralled out around his ears, like he was trying to keep a load of wind-blown clouds under his cap. Then maybe the guy in the corner with the handful of grubby ginger beard, poring over leaflets with his wife or whoever. I imagined him carefully discarding his waxed jacket, unhooking the thin frames of his circular glasses from his ears and shoving that beard into my crotch. Yuk. A guy in his thirties at the bar wasn't too bad – Jesus, who was I kidding? His hair was too long, swept back in gross City-banker style, a bit paunchy and hairy. He'd probably have been Stef's numero uno. I touched the tip of the feather in my pocket. The weirdo I'd almost fallen on yesterday wasn't here, thank God.

The barman came out from the kitchen with pies and chips for Wire-rims and wife. He was my age or near enough, quite skinny, in a T-shirt made to look like it was spattered with black and blue paint. I went to the bar.

9

'What can I get you?'

Good hair. Somewhere between grey and blonde, densely curly on top and really short on the sides. A healthy amount of spots, but he was still cute enough.

'A glass of red and—' I held on to the rail and stood on the step, peering at the bottles behind him. 'What vodkas have you got?'

'Um, nothing fancy.' He showed me the selection. Of two.

I pulled an exaggeratedly disappointed look.

He tipped his head up at me as he poured Lottie's wine. 'You on holiday?' His accent had a lazy little loll to it.

'Sort of. Housesit–revision thing.' Slash escape route from possible murder scene.

'Oh yeah, whereabouts?'

I told him and he nodded. It was probably one of those places where everyone knows everyone and the names of everyone's partners and children and dogs and their birthdays and favourite colour and deepest, darkest perversions.

When he asked how I was finding it, I hesitated for slightly too long. 'Is it not good enough for you up here?' He feigned indignation, very badly, a dimple appearing next to a load of spots.

I bit my lip with a grin and looked away. 'Um. Just very – sedate.' Plus the occasional fierce-eyed creep, bird carcass, etc.

'It doesn't have to be.' He flicked his eyes up to mine and down again, quick as anything. They were a mixture of bright-blue and grey, a properly confused Scottish sky.

I moved some barmats around. 'No?'

'No.'

I squashed my eyes at him a bit. Yep. Doable.

He was a student in Glasgow, a year younger than me, bless, and back at home in the next village west of here, popping down for exams at some point. There was a blotch of red on his neck as I typed his number into my phone.

Lottie had her chin in her hands when I sat down again and a look on her face like she'd just seen me ride my bike down the road for the first time. She'd never seen me in full flight, lap dancing arse-first into a row of boys, or telling the guy in the offie that I'd give him a blow job if all the change I'd emptied out onto the counter wasn't enough for the beers. I picked up my book and wrapped a hand around my glass.

'Are you not going to talk to me, Polly?'

I held up my book. 'Reading.'

She gave a small, tight sigh, combing out her curls and letting them spring back. I wished she'd stop being so bloody overexcited. What was she expecting? Some sort of epic mother–daughter romance, the two of us arm in arm in – *knife* me – National Trust souvenir shops and up evil windy hills.

I crossed one leg over the other and hung my hair over the pages, sneaking a look at the barman, who seemed to be making himself very busy drying glasses.

'Maybe there'll be a lovely Scottish man for me, too.'

I looked up then. 'I'm sure there will. How about him?' I nodded at the old guy in the corner, now crouching so far over his phone that he looked almost asleep.

Lottie shoved me with her elbow. 'Fine. *Read*.'

'Soaking up the atmosphere?' Fraser was dumping a bag into the bins.

I was leaning against the wall outside, staring at my phone and its extreme lack of messages. Not from my housemates, who would never talk to me again, probably. Not from Stef.

'Something like that.' I sighed and bashed the back of my head against the wall, counting off the glittering sights of the rest of the village, dark shadows down the road. Shop. Café. The End. 'What do you *do* around here?'

He joined me, hands in his pockets. 'What do you do when you're home?'

'Go out. Go shopping. Eating. Go to gigs. Galleries. Look at stuff. I mean – there's just so much more *stuff*.' I tucked my phone away and passed him my beer. 'What do you do for fun?'

He took a swig. 'I don't know. Same as you. Just with less *stuff*. Used to ride dragbikes at the quarry but my mate's brother lost a leg so I decided I'd best stop. I run. Shoot a bit. And,' he looked over at me, 'get fucked.'

I gave him my best smile, fished out the mint tin from my pocket and opened it.

Fraser leant over. He smelled faintly of tobacco and deodorant. 'Magic.'

The door slammed behind us and the old tufty-haired guy lurched out. He mumbled something to Fraser, before peering at me and crooning something. It sounded like the sort of song that minstrels off their heads on mead would have sung about a thousand years ago while everyone threw cabbages at them.

I held my bottle up at him and he turned and walked along the lochside, still singing. 'People are bloody weird up here,' I said.

'Speak for yourself.'

'I can almost entirely guarantee that people do not take birds apart on the side of the road in Surrey.'

A knot in his forehead. I told him what I'd seen last night, a rough artist's impression of the guy. Jeans. Beard. Late thirties, maybe older. Eyes like hurled knives.

'Dunno. Could be – there's a guy who lives a few miles away. Off-grid a bit. Proper fuck-up. You shouldn't get too close.'

'Yeah, well, I kung fu-ed him to death already, obviously.'

He grinned. 'I've got to get back.' He pushed himself off the wall with a foot and looked at me, suddenly a bit shy. 'Do you want to come to the hotel up the road tomorrow night? I'm playing there.'

'Playing what?'

He scratched behind his ear and looked at the ground. 'Fiddle.'

'Really?'

'It's probably not the kind of gig you were hoping for but ...' He gave the slightest shrug and squinted towards the loch, another little slap of red behind his ear.

Cute.

Adam was a certified fucking A-grade perv. He hadn't stopped looking at me in the rear-view mirror on the drive over yesterday and now, at ours for dinner, he was performing the not-unadmirable trick of simultaneously leching at my thighs and smiling genially at an oblivious Lottie. Bev needed nothing more than two sips of wine and a forkful of the fish pie she'd brought over to start gossiping about everyone they'd ever known between them. It all made me want to jam my eyes down violently on my upended fork.

Lottie had known them both since I was small. She used to work for Adam's architectural firm in London, before he and Bev decided to up sticks and move to the edge of the known world. Then, after she'd split up with Dad, she'd started doing interior design for friends and gradually built up enough clients to have her own business. It meant that we had a bit of a scrapbook of a house, covered in samples of wallpaper and fabrics, and the bathroom was a patchwork of paint smudges in Leafy

13

Cottage and Summer Coulis and, I don't know, fucking Field Mouse. But I liked it, and liked how the house would transform from year to year, turning its colours slowly. It had its own seasons. Unlike this place, which seemed to just have one.

'How's uni?' Adam asked, drumming his fingers on the table top in some sort of self-consciously calculated math-rock rhythm.

I was just finishing a fairly heroic draining of my wine glass and made a sound somewhere between a hum and a cough.

Lottie threw a smile at me. 'Polly's my star.' She squeezed my hand and picked up the sea salt. 'She's brought enough books to start a library.'

I wondered when would be the best time to tell her that I'd totally failed my second year, lost all my friends, killed someone.

The olds had started settling down with whiskies in the ski-lodge vibes of the conservatory, Lottie turning the lamps down low.

I picked up a wine glass and stayed standing. 'I'm going outside.'

Lottie squinted up at me. Her cheeks were feathered pink and she'd just stopped going on about it being glorious here. And heavenly. And wild. And freeing. 'Now, darling?'

'Yup. Just going to have a look.'

'Keep an eye out for the pine marten,' said Adam. They'd got Lottie insanely excited about seeing what sounded to me like a draught excluder with teeth.

Their voices reduced to a low simmer as I shut the back door. I heard 'She's not quite' and 'Good to have a break'.

*

14

Nearly eleven and still not totally dark. I could just about see the loch's tapered beginnings over to my left, before it stretched and got swallowed up by the hills and the rain on its way out to sea on my right. I imagined plucking the loch up like a big, porny silk sheet, leaving a load of fish flailing on the mud floor.

The moon was out, the exact shape of my thumbnail when I bit it off, gnawing a perfect seam. It had got a lot colder. At least it wasn't raining any more. I pulled my hoodie round me and put my fists under my armpits, standing there in the squelchy grass. With the glow from the conservatory and a line of stubby little lights sticking out at the edge of the beds, the garden looked like a theatre stage, over-real props curved inward towards the lawn. Waxy near-black leaves cut out and stuck on.

Well, this was the place to get some work done. It was completely bloody silent. Maybe I should just think of it as a really wide, green prison, apply myself, like the guy does in Shawshank, read all my books, re-write all my essays, boom, done.

Lottie knew something was up, I could see it. She was looking at me like she wanted to smother me in kittens and pillows and candyfloss but was too afraid that I might wallop her. But I couldn't tell her. I couldn't tell anyone. I kept envisaging the boy, strung up to a load of drips, a big tube shoved in his mouth, eyes closed. A police officer waiting at the edge of his hospital bed for him to wake up. A mariachi band in a hot, dusty Mediterranean town – did they have those at funerals? Or tango or flamenco or something. Dead. Not dead. Fuck.

I held my wine glass up to my chin and breathed in the sweet gloomy stickiness. A taste the same colour as the shadows.

The bottom corner of the garden blurred into woodland that led all the way down to the loch. Pine trees were massed in front of me, not wanting to let me pass. I wandered a bit closer.

A tiny noise to my left. Something between a soft click and a rustle. This garden would do what an old house did, creak and bend and whine. I took a step forward, onto mud and sticks, and listened.

The wind fluttered against my neck. The sky had slipped into a sort of night without my noticing. I dipped my finger in the wine, put it in my mouth, and as it came out there was the noise again, a few metres ahead of me in the trees. *Rustle-click.* A drop of wine loosened from my finger.

Maybe it was a pine marten. Maybe my ankles were about to get ripped off by a two-tone rat. I started to feel like I was being coated in the darkness, layer after layer patiently obliterating the light from my back, my neck. Or maybe it was a person. A local. I fingered the feather in my pocket. That guy—

'You're not spooked by the dark, are you?'

I practically fell over in fright. 'Fucking … fuck.'

Adam was a few paces away from me, further up the slope. My neck feeling weirdly heavy, I stalked past him towards the conservatory and stood with my back to it. Held my thumb up to the moon, closed an eye and angled my hand so that it sat perfectly on top.

He came and stood next to me, and leant in a little. 'You smell nice.' He hadn't even inhaled.

I'd sweated rain all day. Rain and guilt. 'I really don't.'

A faint, far-too-confident smile hung on him. Jesus. Well, it was clear as a bell now. He wanted to finish what he'd started two Christmasses ago down at ours, outside the downstairs toilet – a hand on my arse and his tongue making slug trails on my ear lobe while Lottie and the others bawled out 'Fairytale of New York' in the living room. I'd had an experimental, Smarties-coloured mixture of party booze and a pill and would have probably happily licked the banister. Bev had come out, hooting, and he'd been off me, quick as a flash.

He seemed unruffled and looked out towards the loch. 'It'll be fun having you up here.'

I drained my wine, clumps of sediment on my tongue. Bev and Lottie's voices bubbled away behind us.

He spoke quietly. 'Feel free to, you know, drop in, if you're at a loose end.'

'What for?' The only loose end I'd want would be a generous noose for me to shove my head into.

Adam still didn't face me. 'Whatever you like.'

He made me want to scratch at his mouth, graze him. 'Yeah.' I studied my nails. 'I don't think I will.'

'Shame.' He clapped a hand suddenly on his neck and looked at his palm, then went for my hand. I whipped it back, but he just took my glass and held it up.

'Another?'

I watched his back as he went inside, whistling an unrecognisable tune full of air.

I know the ways of the wind. The air. I am part of its song.

The wind has strong arms that lift me up above the hills, and I travel over water bright as new pennies. I fly and I fly.

Once I was a girl who grew up here, in a house overlooking the loch. A girl who walked, feet scudding against leaf-mulch, who danced, who dreamed of leaving this place. Who fell in love with a boy.

Now the feathers come in and out. I am one single feather, a fine comb. I am many feathers, burrowing into my own snowdrift. When the days are at their lightest, I am almost myself again. The girl I once was.

But whatever I am, I'm always waiting. Waiting for you to hear my song on the wind.

As the light grows longer in another summer, I finally see a way that it can be done.

One day, you will know I'm here. One day, my love, you will join me.

2

An ear-splitting sound in my head, a girl's scream mixed with a brass band, then somehow my long breath was louder than any of it. The pillow felt damp. That wine had left bruising colours on the inside of my skull, just above my eyebrows. I lay looking at the single orchid flower, small pale petals veined with purplish threads underneath three bigger, pure-white ones.

At first, I thought that the windows were fogged up with condensation and wiped them with the curtain lining, but it made no difference. A mist was hanging so close that you couldn't see the end of the garden.

I wandered through the house, imagining it closed off from the world. A soggy biodome. No one would be able to see me if I couldn't see out.

'Polly.' Lottie was stock still at the kitchen door in her dressing gown, one arm wrapped round herself.

There was a deer in the garden. A smallish one I think, Ugg boot-coloured, with a white shock of tail quiffed upwards, standing right in the middle of the lawn. In the mist it looked porous, a pointillist painting. A tremor went through a back leg and its ear twitched, slowly and perfectly, like the Queen waving.

My shoulder was touching Lottie's. Neither of us budged. The deer brought its neck down and nibbled at the grass, each tiny movement graceful, almost lazy. I didn't know how those anorexic ankles could hold all that deer up. At ballet classes when I was six, I would try to stand *en pointe*, clinging onto the pole for dear life, my legs a blur. I wondered what it would feel like to touch it, just on the rump there, the short, dense fur under my palm.

And then it was as if all along the deer had been attached by a thread to someone we couldn't see. In the time it took to blink, its head went up and it disappeared, tugged away, becoming mist and trees.

Lottie gave a shiver and looked down. 'My tea's gone cold.' I was standing dead still. She rubbed my arm like I'd just returned from a lengthy expedition to the Arctic. 'Did you sleep?'

'Bit hungover.'

'I'm so glad you're here.' I opened three cupboards on a biscuit mission. 'We'll be all right, won't we? Just do your own thing. We've tons of time, so you just say when you want to do something together, or if you want to be on your own, or—'

My sigh cut her off. 'It'll be fine. Just ... relax.'

One for you Polly. Dadx

If I hadn't known any better I'd have thought someone had been kidnapped and was being horribly tortured, probably with chainsaws and jaw-clamps and mace. But these were just the videos my little brother liked to send when he was away, especially when he was excited. His face was pushed right up to the camera, and he was screaming and blowing spit bubbles. His eye loomed towards the screen like an orbiting planet, voice alien-distorted, before Dad said 'Benji, that's enough now' and the video stopped abruptly.

It would have been a bit much with him here. Good for Lottie to take a breather. And he liked it at Dad's new place. When we dropped him off this time, Benji had wailed and pulled my sleeve, until Dad reminded him that the camp they were going to had a climbing wall and he'd be sleeping in a tree house. Dad had said he liked my new hair and he and Lottie exchanged a look, the one they always did these days. Like the other one was going to hit them really hard.

My eyes kept straying from my book. I was rubbish at concentrating at the moment. Had been for months – permanent brain-freeze. The words were like flotsam, slopping up against each other and off the page. All that quiet, and *sky*. It was more distracting than a whole load of people jumping up and down and shouting my name through megaphones. I put on my boots and stepped into the garden.

The mist had lifted a little but there was still a clamminess to the air. How could it be almost June? Everything was covered in gauze, a gauze that wrapped itself round and round my ears and face, blanketing out the sounds I should have been hearing – old school Balearic trash-beats and shrieking and puking, probably. Me and Stef had talked about doing a last-minute thing – Magaluf or Ibiza, cheap-as-chips apartment, skin-smacking sunshine. Until we ran.

The cottage owner was obviously into his gardening. Labels, written in a tiny, coiling hand, hung from the plants and read like name tags for a posh girls' boarding school. *Storm lavender. Mauve nepeta. Osmunda regalis.* Even in the mist, the garden was insane with colour, the lawn hyper-green and glossy.

I wandered to the edge of the garden, to where the noise had come from last night. It felt like a cut-off point, where

21

the stylised, fairground mania of the garden stopped and the wild started. This must have been the way the deer had gone.

There was a half-arsed path where the leaves had been stamped down, but I couldn't see any hoof prints, not that I really knew what to look for. My boots left double puddles. A few last-gasp bluebells keeled over and low ferns tickled my calves. The ivy on the trees made me think of Lottie twirling her hair round a finger in front of her computer. I stopped for a second, listening for that noise again, but there was hardly even a breeze.

The path disappeared into a guttering stream. I began to pick my way down it, standing on the stones not darkened by water, some covered by cardigans of moss. One stone got me. My foot skidded straight down into the shallow water and my ankle right-angled. I swore, a lot. Kept going.

After a bit the stream broadened out and turned the colour of cider. I had to put my hands on rocks and grab at over-hanging branches, moving in a rather less graceful way than that deer. It had practically levitated. I could see more of the loch by now, a slick swipe of it.

The stream thinned again and I came onto the shoreline. It was a pointed, muscly stretch of rock, curving back into bays on either side of me and out again, a pattern that repeated and repeated. Each bay was tiered like a trifle, working downwards from grass to pale stone to darker rock and loads of stringy, dark green seaweed, the sort of stuff that would clutch at your ankles and pull you under if you stepped on it.

The loch was pencil-lead grey. It made me shiver. I tried to imagine it as one of Lottie's paint samples on our hallway wall: Loch Grey. Fucking Miserable Loch Grey. The whole place looked pretty unhappy – I wanted to take my sleeve to it again like I had at the window this morning. I should have been sprawled next to Stef, looking at a sea and sky so bright it hurt.

Bev had warned us about the midges. The plague of the summer, she'd said, making them sound biblical, leaving us a bottle of some cheap-looking moisturiser that she swore by. It smelled of the claggy cold cream stuff that I used to stick my fingers into at Nanna's. And here they were, an extra dash of seasoning to this shitty scene. Loads of them, polka-dotting the air in front of me. Gross.

I sat down on a stone just where the grass stopped, a dry prickle on my thighs, and got out the mint tin. There'd been half a pack of baccy in the desk drawer too, and a few Rizlas. The weed smelled dead pure and lovely.

I made a little joint, heavy on the weed, lit it and picked up my phone. If I messaged Stef and tried to sound normal maybe he would actually reply.

Wanna come up?

There was a weird band of mist in front of the hills on the other side of the loch. I picked up my book and whacked a few midges about. 'Right, motherfucker.'

My phone buzzed.

UP 2 SCOTCHLAND babyp?

He was talking to me, then. And had read my other message telling him where I was going. I typed back *Come uuuppppp* and ran my hand over my book cover. *Romantics, Rebels and Reactionaries.* I wondered which one I was. None of the above.

NOOOO TAR

Stef, on the other hand, would have bloody loved hanging out with the three Rs, swearing copiously in various European languages, acting out fairy tales in various states of undress, and merrily mixing laudanum with belladonna and cayenne pepper and brandy while making violent proposals of marriage to inappropriate ladies. Well, maybe not the last bit.

Its very ... spacious ... & ... ummmm ...
MAN COUNT
Small. SCOTTISH
Small & scottish = NONO
Yup some are small. All are Scottish. And white

Stef would roll his eyes very slowly over this place as if it were an extremely unsexy guy he had to talk to. He'd squeal a bit at the mud and run his fingers along every surface in the cottage. Charm Lottie into buying us rounds of drinks in the pub and flirt with anything he could find. Oh, what did I know – he'd probably love it and become a fucking deer-stalker or something.

ANY FOR MOI
Plenty BEARDS
On me way;) lolllzzzzz

But I knew he wouldn't be. Who were we fucking kidding. I wasn't sure if it would ever be quite the same between me and him.

Stef had spent a year and a half at uni in Derby trying – mostly unsuccessfully – to turn troglodyte football players. I had missed the hell out of him, stuck on my own nondescript, IKEA-lite campus. *Dis place is dead anyways*, he'd messaged, before stalking off to East London where he'd proceeded to become the centre of everything. The centre of his flat, which had a red handprint on the wall in the kitchen that I always hoped was paint, and mysterious draughts coming from every-where. The centre of the bar in Dalston where he worked, dressed in one of the oversized vests that showed off his old heart-operation scar, shouting at everyone as though he were their husband and their lover and their doctor and their mayor.

And the centre of Kingsland Road, which felt like the centre of London, which felt like the centre of the world. Everything seemed to cram in around his heat.

I'd stayed with him for two days, got my nails done – leopard-skin – had the ends of my hair bleached pink, hung out by the canal and played pool with some skanky guys who seemed to think the world of Stef. I slept on the sofa and his housemates would wake me up with kisses and coffee in filthy cracked cups. I never wanted to leave. Until the Spanish boy. I couldn't understand why Stef was ignoring me – *it*. He didn't know what I knew, about the guy fighting for his life, but still – I'd always thought his shrugged-shoulders, *que-sera-bitches* blitheness about everything was a bit of an act. Maybe not.

This weed had a tang to it. Definitely not homegrown. It flicked at the back of my throat and my pulse was starting to go all '90s tribal drumtastic. I let my mind turn to wet cement, imagined it being smoothed out, a trowel going over and over it methodically. And I was working on smoothing the loch down too, erasing every contour, when I saw something in the water.

Ten metres out, further along the shoreline, under the surface. A white shape. I was sure it hadn't been there before.

It looked like a shirt or a pillowcase – except they would float right on top, wouldn't they? Maybe it was a seal. A dolphin. That would be amazing, to see a dolphin arc out of the water, like my own flipping private Disney movie. But it just stayed there, not moving, and surely seals and dolphins liked to swim around a bit, unless they were dead.

I stood up into a cloud of midges to get a better look. It was as if a patch of mist had got itself in the wrong place, under the water instead of over it, just hanging there. I thought of clothes again – a sheer dress. It lingered. As I craned my neck, my eyes hit a pole sticking up on a larger headland further east, a way off.

Except it wasn't a pole. It was *someone*. A person, standing dead straight, looking out on the loch. Looking out at me.

I almost tumbled off my rock. Another look. Maybe it was a scarecrow. Yeah Polly, a scarecrow without arms and no field to take care of. And scarecrows didn't *move*. It – he – moved. Fuck. I turned, quickly, and ducked in among the trees, the loch's eyes on my back, the *person's* eyes on my back, imagining Stef still lounging there on his elbows, laughing, shouting 'Come baaaack, you slag!'

My ribs were tight. Jesus, that was fucking creepy. It was him. The bird guy. It had to be. He'd been watching me, I swear. His arm had come up. How many guys like that could there be in a place with more trees than people?

By the time I got up to the cottage, my legs were soaked, and bits of the wood – leaves, moss, mud – were stuck to my bare calves. Two of my leopard-skin nails had come off. Little white flowers behind my eyelids every time I blinked.

And I remembered my book, still there on the rocks. Arse.

Once, I sat on the rocks. The day we met properly. Do you remember?

I was looking for stones to skim. The best ones, delicate as bone china, barely registering in my hand. I would never be able to do them justice and they'd be lost forever, like those wishes that people kiss on coins and drop into wells. So I would drop them into the pocket of my skirt and place them on top of each other on my windowsill.

My column of wishing stones. Somehow I thought that if it fell, my world would fall too.

That morning, I'd found four stones when you appeared beside me. I knew your face, but not well. A year older than me, and we'd never talked. Is this any good? you had said shyly, opening your palm. I'd pretended that it was and let it fall into my pocket with the others.

You came at the right time. A door opening, a rulerful of light.

The column never fell. It was taken down, after I died. Since then I have had only one wish for all the stones I could ever pile high. For you to hear me.

All this time, no one has heard me. Least of all you.

Now though, I think someone can.

Keats Madeline

The internet would write one of my essays for me. If the wifi ever worked.

Coleridge Christabel Madeline compare

You just had to rewrite everything to avoid the plagiarism software. Piece of piss.

Christabel Madeline virginity

Come on, ancient wifi of death.

'Their behaviour even disrupts gender roles' could just become 'the actions of both characters challenge gender stereotypes of the period,' blablabla. Online thesaurus to fill the gaps, sorted. Copy and paste was for dickheads.

Some seriously dark videos here, once you got past the stuff about Keats – but the word 'virginity' would do that. Nothing I hadn't seen before.

Sherlock Watson gay sex. Yeah. Bit more fluffy, though the wifi was spluttering its final requests. I might as well write to the porn mafia and ask them to make a whole new badly lit movie with BBC lookalikes than wait any longer.

The rest of the day was a mushy haze of eating and sleeping and wifi resuscitation attempts. Doors banged a few times and Tyger barged around. I picked my remaining nails off and had a bath, freaking out when the water ran brown. Outside, the rain gave everything the look of an old home video.

God, what was I going to do here? I wasn't a fucking Girl Guide. I was going to get *paler* – my legs would be the colour and texture of budget frozen chicken by the time the month was through. Maybe it was time to get heavily into writing epic Romantic poetry, stalking the hills in worsted skirts, Byron and Wordsworth trying to keep up with my dramatic strides and flourishes of penmanship. I wondered if there was any opium lying about. Maybe I should have stayed down south, faced the music.

I looked at my watch. Still hours until I was meant to meet Fraser. Time for some more porn.

*

There was a tap at the door and a man's voice. Adam was leaning against the wall in the hallway. All he ever seemed to do was *lean*.

He looked past Lottie to me. 'Evening, kiddo.'

It was stupid not having a car up here. You couldn't get anywhere on foot unless you had legs of steel. Lottie had said that she wanted to live simply, but it wasn't as if she was wandering around in sackcloth planting seeds, and Luddites definitely didn't have a specially developed remote control thumb or need help from their daughter in working out the finer points of tweeting to their fifty-two followers.

Lottie had told me to text Bev and ask for a lift to the pub. She kept calling it my *date* and looking very meaningfully at me.

'What are you doing here?' I said.

Lottie's head turned sharply at my tone of voice.

Adam smiled. 'Bev's got tied up. I said I'd take you.'

I bet you fucking did, I thought, imagining Bev lashed to the radiator with a pillowcase stuffed in her mouth.

'You are an extremely special and lovely person,' Lottie said, picking a loose thread from the shoulder of his jumper.

He leant a bit further towards her. 'I *know*.'

*

'This music all right?' Adam was battering his forefinger on the steering wheel along to some kind of stabby jazz with manic, dislocated beats.

If I really concentrated, the hills to my left blurred, as if someone was painting them with a roller, some bits lumpy and sticking, other bits glossily smooth. A garbled mix of brown and yellow and green. 'It's your car, you can play what you like.'

He continued tapping, irregularly. 'So, what's happening tonight, then?'

I put my arm next to the window. 'Some music.'

'Didn't take you for a folkie.' The drums started fizzling. 'Ah,' he said, after a bit. 'Fraser.' He took a considering breath in. 'He's a nice boy.' There was the slightest emphasis on the last word.

Oh, just fuck off, I thought. The loch had a lavender tinge to it. 'What animals do you get in there?'

Adam glanced towards the water. 'Fish – skate, mackerel, that sort of thing – birds, obviously, though not so much in it as on it. Apart from cormorants, and shags.'

For God's sake. 'What?'

'Shags,' he said, more definitely, and cocked an eyebrow at me. 'Diving birds.'

Oh. Twat. 'What about anything bigger? Like seals or something?'

'Sure, you get seals coming up, the odd porpoise. Not normally right up this end, though.'

I trawled my brain for nature documentary scenes, when I'd try and see past Benji who would sit a foot away from the screen, trying to click his tongue like a dolphin. 'Nothing like – I don't know, a manta ray or something.'

'Mmm.' The sound was low and drawn out, as if he was taking it very seriously. 'Don't think so. Why, what did you see?'

I was beginning to feel stupid. 'Nothing. Just – probably nothing.'

He looked over at me for far too long. There was a heady smell of something, cinnamon with alcohol mixed in. Jesus. He was wearing cologne. Maybe it had been him over on the loch, spying on me like the colossal reprobate he was, hoping I'd take my kit off and sunbathe. I gave him dead eyes until he turned to face the road again.

Fifteen minutes later we'd reached a little bay with a small hotel on a hill. It had a conservatory running all the way along the front and the picnic tables were dark with rain. I unclicked my seat belt.

'How are you getting home?' The permanent lines on either side of Adam's mouth looked as if they had been made with a penknife.

'I'll work it out,' I said, thinking that I'd happily wank Fraser off in exchange for a lift if it meant not doing this again. I had practically suffocated on the aged pheromones floating about in the car.

He sat looking at me. 'I like your hair.' One corner of his mouth curled up. 'It's like you've leant over a paint pot.' And then he bent over and got me, a hand on my jaw and his stubble on the corner of my mouth. When I stayed rigid, he came away an inch, his finger still behind my ear.

'Yeah. Don't do that,' I said.

Adam made a small, sighing sound from behind a closed mouth, as though a needle had just perforated his stomach, and dropped his hand. He tried to rearrange his face back to its usual slantiness. 'On you go, then.'

I slammed the door as hard as I could.

*

31

This place was a bit swankier than the local one, white walls with deep green-blue window frames, slate floors, whiskies stacked neatly up on a high shelf. There were three rifles lined up on the wall and fishing rods and baskets and other crap.

Fraser was talking to a couple of younger teenagers, one so acne-infested she looked like she'd been sprinkled with dried chilli flakes. He leant his forearms on the bar as he greeted me. 'Found it all right, then.'

'This better be good.'

'Piss off. It'll be what it is.'

I grinned and let him get me a drink.

Folk time. Fraser sat on the other side of the room with a guy in his forties and a skinny girl who was sixteen or seventeen. They put their heads together and I wondered whether they were talking about me until, without any preamble, they began to play. Fraser jammed his fiddle under his chin in the way you'd hold a phone to your ear while eating, and the guy, who had scoured cheeks and a Saxon T-shirt stretched over an impressive belly, began opening out a huge accordion on his knee. The girl just had a little tin whistle, and she and Fraser launched into a tune with the accordion heaving away underneath. The few people in the bar stopped talking for a bit and looked at their glasses, before picking up where they'd left off. The brown leather seats gave off a roasted smell.

They seemed to be playing to themselves, really. As though it were simply another conversation. The girl tugged her tin whistle to the side, her mouth dragging outwards. The way the accordion player pulled out the folds and pushed them in again made me think of those chest expanders that were used by men from the 1920s with handlebar moustaches. Their tunes just went on and on, notes unspooling. You got lost trying to follow them.

There was a smattering of applause as the players got up. At the bar, Fraser put his hand on my back and introduced his bandmates. Becca reminded me of a bedraggled crow. Her hair was very long and straight apart from an irregular fringe, and she wore tons of black eyeliner, even more than I would ever lash on. You could have snapped her dull white wrist like a bit of Kendal mint cake. She nodded at me without making eye contact, her shoulders up around her ears, hands in her pockets. I turned on my best glittery smile and talk-show host chat and aimed it over her head to Fraser.

A guy tapped him on the back and Fraser held up a finger at me and disappeared. Becca was scraping her nails along the bar.

'Um, do you want a drink?'

'Coke. Ta.' Thanking me was clearly as bad as swallowing acid.

Of course – she was under the drinking age. 'Oh yeah, I forgot, sorry.'

She scowled and took out her tin whistle, gripping it tightly at both ends. I watched Fraser chatting to the guy in the corner, both of their heads down, and tried to think of something else to say. Becca glared at the beer mat as I slid her Coke over. She didn't look like she needed any more caffeine.

I pointed to the door. 'Gonna get some air.' Before you stab me with that fucking thing.

She nodded viciously, her knuckles going white.

*

33

After several gulps of lung-lacerating Scottish air, I came back inside to find Fraser playing on his own, staring fixedly at the table. He made me think of a seagull hanging out on the wind, calling stroppily.

Becca sat down and the fiddle swayed around the whistle, sometimes joining it on the tune, or straying on to gently see-sawing chords. Neither of them ever looked at the other. It was like a desperately shy eighteenth-century courtship. Finally, Gray, who'd called me pet and excreted sweat and beer, great big man smells, sat down again and stacked up bricks of notes on his accordion. I got out my book – I didn't think they would mind seeing as no one else was paying any attention.

Once they'd finished I headed outside and looked at the loch. There was a word in Swedish, untranslatable, Adam had said during our first dinner, for the road-like reflection of the moon on water. Tonight, it made milky puddles in the shallows. A cobbled street.

I lit one of the two slim joints I'd brought.

'That smells promising.' Fraser was there with his fiddle case.

'Who said I'm sharing?'

We leant against his car, more grey than white and with a dent in the side that made it look like bashed-in skull. A shuffling figure came towards us.

'See you, Becca,' said Fraser.

'See you later,' she said to him in her tiny, cracked crow-voice, scurrying past.

'See you, Becca,' I shouted at her back. She half turned before scurrying on faster.

He elbowed me gently in the side. 'Don't be mean.'

I laughed. 'I'm not.' I watched her disappear, a black bird folded into the night. 'She doesn't like me.'

'She doesn't like anyone much. Or pretends not to, anyway.'

'She blows nicely on a tin whistle though.' I raised my eyebrows at him. 'Has she blown on your tin whistle?'

Fraser dug me in the ribs again, making me giggle. He scratched the back of his neck, shaking his head, and took my joint off me.

The two teenagers he'd been talking to earlier sloped past and said bye.

'You're popular,' I said.

He just shrugged and grinned a bit.

'So, that was nice.' He looked over as if he was expecting me to make a joke. 'It made me think of heather. And whisky. And shortbread. And putting my hand up a big man's kilt.'

'Yeah, go ahead, take the piss why don't you.'

I did my best cute smile. 'Why d'you like it?'

He passed the joint back to me, exhaling. The smoke came out in a feathery plume. 'Dunno. Just always done it. Nice tunes. They stick in your brain. And ...' He put his hands behind his head, unclasped them and brought them forward again. 'I don't know, they're old songs, from before you and me, or my ma, or my grandpa. They've lived.'

'You're sweet,' I said.

He turned his head to me, pulling his eyebrows together, brooding-vampire style. 'Sexy, you mean.'

Nice try. I nudged his calf with my boot. '*Sweet.*'

Clouds had collected behind the moon. A big, powdered wig.

'Need a lift?' he said.

*

I sat him down in the conservatory with a beer. Lottie was still up when we arrived, squinting through her specs at my laptop, her hand lolling in a box of chocolates. When she saw Fraser, she leapt off the sofa with a beam, pulled her dressing gown tighter around herself, grabbed Tyger and made a massively embarrassing, whirlwindy show of disappearing.

He stood up and went to the window. All you could see were the garden's dull disco lights. I silently rated his arse against all other recently studied arses until he came and sat back down, then stretched my legs out right next to his, just touching, and sighed very loudly.

He looked at me. 'That weed's fucking strong.'

'Just the way I like it.'

A sound in his throat, somewhere between a cough and laugh as he brought his beer bottle up. 'What did you do to your tooth?'

My tongue was up there again, playing with the chipped edge. 'I got into a fight. With a boy. Over a pogo stick. I hit him with it and he hit me with a scooter. In the mouth.'

Fraser scrunched up his face in slow-motion, as if watching it happen. 'How old were you?'

'Oh, you know, eighteen,' I said.

He grinned.

I tangled my foot up between his legs. He rubbed the condensation on the neck of the bottle with his thumb. I was quite enjoying how coy he'd got.

He turned. 'Can I kiss you?'

I tried very hard not to laugh. Failed. 'You don't have to ask.' Fraser blushed and looked down. 'You'll just have to lunge at me and see if I try and hit you with anything.'

He put his elbow on the back of the sofa and leant in. I bit his lower lip not entirely by accident and let him come at

36

me some more. His hair had the texture of an itchy woolly jumper. The kiss was getting a bit washing machine-like so I grabbed the nearest thing – an angry, out-of-proportion bronze buffalo on the table next to me – and pretended to whack him with it, just to get him to take his tongue out. He'd gone all sleepy-looking, like he'd just woken up.

I moved closer, slinging my legs on to his lap, and Fraser's eyes darted over to the door.

'What?' I said.

There was a red patch on his neck again, like someone had given him a slap. 'I should probably go. I'm feeling pretty wasted.'

'You can stay here if you want.'

He took in a lungful of air and his mouth went goldfishy. 'Thanks, but – another, yeah, another time.'

I thought of Lottie finding Stef in my bed when we were fourteen and trying to give us a hippie agony aunt talk over cups of tea. 'She won't mind.'

'No, it's cool, my da needs the car first thing,' he said. I carefully slid my legs back off him. 'What are you doing tomorrow?'

I shrugged. 'What are you doing?'

I got a few more kisses out of Fraser in the hallway and on the driveway before he left. The stub of the first joint was on the table. I picked it up and put a handful of Lottie's chocolates in my pocket on my way back through the house.

The whole garden was rustling. Different layers of it, a blanket of fast-whirring sounds and louder, intermittent ones on top. I stood in my tights, feeling the soft clutch of the grass and thinking of Fraser and Becca and Gray's instruments weaving around each other.

I wanted to know what the real darkness felt like. I wanted to *wear* it. I turned the garden lights off and let it envelop me. It hardly made any difference when I shut my eyes. There were a few lights over on the other side of the loch, making morse code signals, but otherwise it was just me and the darkness – and the wind, making everything rustle. My curl of smoke was erased like chalk on a blackboard.

I shut my eyes again, crushing a strawberry cream against the roof of my mouth, its cheap taste – the Claire's Accessories of confectionery – all mixed up with the peaty greenness of the weed. When I opened them, my tongue halted, stuck in the chocolate.

A little cloud was there.

Three metres to my left, head height. Bizarrely low. At first I thought it was the last puff I'd exhaled, but I had watched that disappear. Hadn't I? And it was whiter, too. I waited for it to dissolve, but it hung there. It just – hovered.

It was like a tiny, lost raincloud. Some peculiar Scottish micro-climate thing. I took a couple of steps forward, thinking I might put my fingers in it, and –

It moved. The cloud shifted away from me, as if trying to stay out of my reach.

My hands went cold. Every single one of the hairs on my arms rose up.

I turned very carefully, went inside and locked the door.

3

My bedside light was still on in the morning. I rolled towards the switch and something crumpled under my head, a loud, crisp sound. There was an orchid flower on the pillow. The petals were as dry as paper – the fine, textured stuff you get in art shops – and pinched and caramel-coloured in a few places.

I lay on my back and held it in front of my face, twirling it from the stem between forefinger and thumb. Underneath the petals, three more small ones were pressed close together and, as I prised them open, the whole flower came apart in my hands.

My mouth seemed to be full of mushrooms. Ugh.

I messaged Stef. *Semi-cute boy alert*

Yeah, Fraser was nice. I wanted to attack his face with a kebab skewer and do those spots in, but we've all been there. He seemed to veer between having a bit of swagger and suddenly going eyelashy and bashful. It was sweet.

I raided the cupboards for biscuits and my phone went. *SHAG HIM*

At least Stef was talking to me if I kept it non-murdersome. *Aye aye capn;)*

*

Two missions.

Mission Number One: five thousand motherfucking words. Using my actual brain. How hard could that be? Prof Handley had given me two weeks to get my essays in. After that, she'd said, giving me a frowny hamster look, she wouldn't grant me the luxury of marking them. Fair enough. Liza was all right. She seemed to see beyond my sullenness even though I had mostly proffered her turgid, sub-A level crap and nicked ideas from Lewalski without crediting them. I'd written the first attempt on the night before the deadline, chasing a skinny line of speed and some ProPlus with energy drinks so sugary I couldn't chew anything the next day.

I touched the burnt orange tip of my dead bird feather – grouse, I'd looked it up – to my nose. It was beautiful. And weird that it was from something so extremely dead. I imagined an ancient Japanese man dipping his brush in glossy black ink and painting these undulating lines on it, swirls unique to this feather alone, and when the ink had dried, carefully inserting it back into the bird, which was whole again. The elastic squeak of the shaft penetrating taut skin. The calligrapher sitting back, satisfied. Until the benign-guru face was replaced with the dark one of the guy I'd seen on the road that first evening and the shock on it that had almost matched my own. Birdkiller.

Mission Number One aborted in favour of Mission Number Two: to rescue my book without ending up part of a low-budget fashion shoot entitled 'Decomposing Forest Waif'.

It was a lot brighter today, but damp as anything still – the grass had a glitterball glimmer to it. I needed my sunglasses just to walk straight. Birds bleeped away, mobile phones with different ringtones. Apart from that, not a single sound. I felt as if I had to turn my ears up to try and catch a breath of anything.

I had nicked some navy blue wellies from a cupboard, way too big, so I was rocking three pairs of socks, two lots over my knees. Sexy. I splashed my way through the coppery water this time, slipping and sliding my way down the stream, invincible. Yeah, fuck you, stream. The loch, when I reached it, glinted like a watch catching the light.

I found the rock I'd been sitting on the day before. The book wasn't there. I scouted around, lifted up a couple of stones, wondering if I'd somehow emerged in a different place, but you couldn't really go wrong following a stream. I'd expected the book to be sodden, the pages all stuck together, and having to blowdry it back to life, but at least to *find* it here. Maybe a great big bookish golden eagle had snatched it and was sitting in a nest turning corners over with its talons, disagreeing with Butler's take on anti-intellectualism. That was one of my essays fucked then – I'd written tons of notes in the margins. I lit a joint and sat down.

The loch was making quiet slurping sounds on the seaweed, like a drunk old man blowing kisses. I looked for a floating book being used as a raft by a frog or something. And as I did, a tingle swept up my throat.

There. The white patch was there again. Further down the loch this time, though nearer to the shore. The light was different today and the patch looked brighter, more textured. Maybe it was closer to the surface.

Joint in teeth, I began to climb round the stones by the shoreline, following them back inland towards the trees and out again to the next ridge. Slow work. I had to lean on the higher rocks, dried seaweed making bubble-wrap pops under my hands. There was a green, heavy smell, like overcooked

41

broccoli with a whole salt-shaker accidentally emptied onto it. I grazed my knee against a rock and jabbed my palm on a mussel.

Judging distances was obviously not my superhero skill – I'd moved fifteen metres or so and the patch didn't seem any closer at all. Bastard. I clambered further round to a bay with a thin-lipped smile of beach, put a foot down and sank two inches, yelping and wobbling and falling forward, wrist-deep, into Polyfilla mud. Brilliant.

Hand coated, I did a stupid skipping walk, like long-jumpers do just before they take off, over the rest of the beach and got up onto a boulder. I couldn't see the white patch at all now. Maybe the angle of the sun had changed. Or it had just been a reflection of a cloud. I stood on tiptoes. Crouched down. The loch had an oily skin to it, the film you get when you make proper chicken stock. *There* – floating, like a flat, shredded piece of chicken breast. Except more shimmery.

Suddenly, there was a splash right in the middle of the patch and my heart caught, a little hook going right into me. Ripples spilled out and all at once the water was only black. As the ripples widened, a grey mist began to spread from that point, unfurling slowly, just above the surface.

The loch was alive. Alive and breathing.

It was too far to scuttle back round the rocks the way I'd come. I headed straight inland and walked very fast on pine needle-matted ground, the trees crowding in. The road would have to be up here eventually. God, everything looked the same. I had no idea where my joint had gone.

There was a big cleft, a sudden drop cut into the slope, veering round and pushing me further in the wrong direction. Further away from the cottage. A dribbling stream at the bottom made me think of Benji when he'd had one of his freak-outs. If he'd been here, I'd be charging after him pretending to be a knight or something. Benji wouldn't have been scared. What was wrong with me?

I seemed to have been walking for ages. The ground was getting steeper, becoming lumpy, and I had to use trunks and branches to pull myself up to the next slope and the next, my calves tightening. The trees leant in heavily, looking like they might topple forward and crush me to death at any second. I'd lost all sense of where I was.

A dry-stone wall up ahead. I levered myself onto it, swinging my legs over. My feet touched something – a plastic yellow car, big enough for a toddler, grass growing through the windows and two snails on one tipped-up wheel. The bottom of someone's garden, a long one, with a proper lawn I could walk on.

I jumped down, the backs of my legs feeling as though they'd been battered with gigantic chains. A big, plain house sat further up, its windows opaque. The back door was open. I kept to the inside edge of the wall, running my nails gently along the stones, my head down.

A little girl came out, white-blonde hair and a Spiderman T-shirt, doing an erratic, hopping dance. She stopped dead when she saw me and put the fingers of one hand into her mouth. I gave her a small wave and went to climb back over the wall.

'Georgie, do you want your toast or—' A woman had come out of the back door. I was straddling the wall like a first-time horse rider. 'Can I help you?' Her voice suddenly scraped of warmth.

Nothing for it. 'I'm really sorry, I got lost coming up from the loch,' I said. 'I'm so sorry.'

She came stalking past the girl towards me as I manoeuvred myself ungracefully back onto the lawn.

'Could I go through your garden to get to the road?'

Her nostrils flared slightly. The weed. Her eyes were lasers. She gave a small, tight nod. 'This way.'

I followed her to a side gate. Her earrings were black and white dice with silver stars dangling underneath. A tattoo of some soft-focus leaves peeked out from her neckline.

She turned round, giving me those eyes again. 'Next time, follow the loch to the village.'

I answered her with multiple *yeahs* and *sorrys*, thinking, well, I would have done if the water hadn't been scaring me shitless.

Spidergirl was still standing in the same place, sucking on her fingers, eyes big as bowling balls. The loch sliced into slivers by the trees behind her.

I think of you as the sky spills onto the loch, stirs itself in. I float on it, stick my neck down. There are pockets where it's saltier, pockets where it's warmer. Pockets where trout clump together, or where mussels open and shut like the clasps of purses.

The loch collects shadows of birds. It collects clouds like laundry rolled over an arm.

It collects me. I am sheets and old-fashioned petticoats, drifting. A white shirt tugged in the wind.

I was always drifting, dreaming. Time waits for no man, and no bloody girl either, my uncle would say, rapping me on the backside for standing on the porch caught up in my own thoughts. He had lots of sayings.

But I shouldn't speak of him. Not to you.

Essay splurge with mild online distraction and a soundtrack of rain. 'Romantic poet porn' drew a blank, apart from a pretty diverting article about Byron and Shelley's free-love tendencies, a hundred and fifty years ahead of their time.

This soon morphed into playing a game on my phone in which I had to infect the whole world with a contagious disease. Mine was airborne and starting to spread.

I messaged Fraser. *Hey fiddler*

I watched my plague cross the Atlantic and fuck up America.

Whats up

China's government had fallen.

Fancy hanging out then?

I was now more infectious than HIV.

Yeah cool free later, maybe 4?

☺ Where?

Perfect. Zombie apocalypse.

The rain had stopped. Tyger was looking up at me as I picked up my bag, a tiny whine coming from him like a radio frequency.

'No, Tyger.'

He attemped emotional blackmail, wandering around, sniffing the skirting board and looking back at me occasionally, his eyes going all melty.

'You won't like it.'

He froze.

'I'm going to see a *boy*.'

His tail twitched hopefully.

I dug my toe into his flank. 'You're a wuss. You'll want to come home after half an hour.'

He sat down on his back legs and put on his best sticky-toffee-pudding face.

I picked up his lead. 'I'm taking Tyger!' I yelled to Lottie. A muffled response floated back from the living room.

'Now that's service.' I got into the passenger seat, Tyger in my lap. 'Do you mind a threesome?'

'As long as he likes drinking.' Fraser was wearing a T-shirt with triangles all over it. Some bleepy drum and bass was pulsing away, like a wardful of faulty hospital equipment.

'He said he'd only come if I brought vodka,' I said, kicking my bag so that it gave a low gulp. The cupboard in the study had yielded a pretty good bounty. Brooding behind the more usual selection of spirits had been dusty bottles of Kahlúa, fruit liqueurs and a ginger wine from before I was born.

'In that case' – he put his fingers behind Tyger's ears – 'all right, fella.'

Tyger practically leapt out of my arms to give Fraser his feather-duster-in-the-face greeting.

'Tyger, you're supposed to be my bodyguard,' I said in a stage whisper as I pulled him back, my face in his fur. 'You're not supposed to give him *tongue*.'

Fraser made a slight snort at the back of his throat as he put the car into gear.

'That's what *I'm* supposed to do,' I whispered even louder, sneaking him a look.

His dimple defeated a couple of spots.

I'd requested Fraser take me somewhere cool, resigning myself to the fact that the word would probably be taken in its more traditional sense and I wouldn't be going to a gallery opening with a free oyster bar. We drove up into the hills, the road getting skinnier, me blasting a brief but very rocking Polly-mix through his speakers. You could probably hear the thumping three mountains away.

The car crunched to a stop on the gravel. There were no trees. Up ahead the road curved lazily into the hillside, which had sections cut out of it, the shapes too perfect to be natural. Smaller paths spun off and round, like a Scalextric track. I could imagine Fraser and his mates snarling about on their bikes, high on cheap whizz. Thistles and yellow gorse were sprinkled among the dull, bleached colours.

We walked. Mines made me think of riots and Margaret Thatcher and David Peace novels, but Fraser said it was all minerals up here, not coal, and that these days you just got groups of collectors coming up occasionally. Little troops of rock nerds armed with tiny hammers and hard-ons.

Fraser was in his foundation year as an engineering student, a *proper* degree – when the real zombie apocalypse hits and everyone goes all survivalist, my knowledge of Keats's contribution to modernism isn't going to really cut it. He started talking about tunnels and bridges and the Harry Potter viaduct not far from here, his hands curving.

'But yeah, a lot of them are connected. There's mines up there and over there' – he pointed in the direction of the mountain and to the pale hills further west. 'And you've got engine shafts this way and then levels going along.' He sliced his palm down and across. 'Me and my brother used to go down some of the tunnels, try to find how it all linked up.'

I balanced on one leg on a giant, dark-red wheel, broken in two and laid flat on the grass. 'We're not allowed to be here, are we?'

'No.'

I grinned at him. 'Sick.'

*

48

We sat with our shoulders touching and a mini-headphone each, passing the vodka between us. A bird circled overhead, letting out small cries the same shape as itself, fine curving strokes. Cream-coloured stone streaked the black rock. I ran my finger along it and let my boot rest against Fraser's trainer.

Tyger was at the end of his lead, pissing on a rusty milepost – the lettering sunk into the metal, the distances ambiguous. I pulled him in, poured vodka into my cupped palm, and let him sniff it. His tongue came darting out. He gave a garbled snuffle-cough, and lapped some more.

'You, Tyger, are a dog after my own heart,' I said.

'Why's he called that, then?'

'My little brother. His mind works in a different way.'

It had taken me a while to see that Benji wasn't like the other kids his age. I'd assumed all toddlers were like that, me included. I hadn't known that children didn't usually jam their knees against the skirting board, banging their heads on the exact same area of wall until they were hoisted away to the sound of the neighbours pounding back. I hadn't known that children normally talked more by the time they were two and didn't just scream so loudly that dogs in the next town were probably chewing off their own paws. I hadn't known that children didn't normally look blank when their own name was called, or find cuddling tortuous. But my ears were trained to the conversations Lottie and Dad had downstairs at night, and I began to understand. The long minutes of low murmuring would give way to sudden bursts, dropping to almost nothing in the middle of a word, like someone turning the volume up and down on them.

We got on to vodka dares, downing a capful if we failed our challenge. Fraser had already sung, extremely badly, and I'd flashed him, which hadn't made him blush in the slightest. I was almost disappointed. He was definitely a lot less inhibited without a roof over his head.

My turn again.

Fraser nodded to a distant mound. 'You have to go underground.'

'I can go underground,' I said, offhand. 'I *am* underground. I'm my own subculture.' I stood up, wobbled slightly, and stamped off to the brow of the hill, dragging Tyger behind me.

On the other side was a man-made archway and a gate with rust like eczema. The stone swelled around the metal. Beyond that, nothing but serious, no-holds-barred darkness.

'You want me to go in *there*?'

Fraser shrugged, nonchalant, and put a hand on my shoulder. 'Not if you don't want to.' He leant over me and took the vodka bottle.

'It's locked, anyway.' I pointed to a padlock the size of an orange.

He rolled his hand into a fist and bashed the top of it. The clasp clanged open and the lock thudded to the ground.

'Oh. Bollocks.' Tyger sat on his back legs huffily as I tied him to a log. 'Back in a sec, little man.' I bunched his cheeks between my palms. 'Tell my family I love them.' He coughed at me and looked the other way.

Fraser pulled a slim torch from the pocket of his jeans.

'So *that's* what that was,' I said with a killer smile, and opened the gate.

The tunnel was just a few metres long before it turned a corner. Metal frames held the roof up, with older wooden struts in between. It looked sturdy. Sort of.

'Turn left.' Fraser's voice, and Tyger's bark eddying around it. 'You don't have to go far.'

My mouth had a chemical dryness to it and matches were being struck in my stomach. Should have eaten more at lunch.

I couldn't see any minerals. I'd been expecting a treasure chest of blinding, sparkly rocks, an adventure playground for a Russian oligarch's wife. But it was just stone, black and damp, with a smell that made me think of changing for gym in Year 8 after lunchtime in the rain. No bling at all.

The tunnel narrowed. Fraser called my name and the sound splintered. God, I was scared. The whole thing could come down on me and I'd have my own rubble coffin. There'd be a memorial service on the hill, Fraser's head bowed, Tyger in a bow-tie, Stef with my name freshly tattooed on his neck, Lottie weeping in the drizzle, Dad holding Benji's hand, explaining quietly that Polly wasn't here any more while Benji did his elephant-stamp into the ground. Maybe it would be karma. I deserved it, after what I'd done.

There was a tiny, dripping sound, the pock of a serene table tennis match. I stopped to listen, the dark shrinking around me. I held my breath and the drips seemed to stop and that was more scary than anything. I turned to hightail it out of there, and a hollow caught my eye. An opening.

Oh, fuck it. Two fingers to the funeral. It was just *rock*.

The archway opened out into a cave. This felt different. Warmer, somehow, even though my cheeks were clammy. My torch spread pale butter on the walls. On one side there was a curved lip of rock, cool and smooth, perfect for sitting on, and marks scratched on the wall, nothing you could really read. I felt like I'd disturbed something – like people had been hanging out here and had scarpered when they'd heard my

51

boots tramping down. Shreds of their shadows, their smells, lingering in the air.

The light caught a small shape above my head. A dark, solid object tied to a thin pole by a ribbon that had maybe once been red. I could have cupped it in my hands. Standing on tiptoes, I tapped it with my fingernail. A quiet, metallic clank. It looked very old.

A heart.

'Thought you'd fallen down a hole.'

A lung-smash of fear and relief all at once. 'Jesus fucking – *Fraser*.'

He was looking around, the vodka bottle dangling from his fingers. 'Not been in here before.'

'How long's this place been here again?' I asked, taking the bottle off him and having a massive, panic attack-soothing swig.

'Dunno. Three hundred years or so?'

A lovelorn miner, covered in rock dust, making trinkets for his sweetheart in the dark.

'It's definitely your turn now,' I said.

Fraser was running his hand along the scratchings on the wall and flicked two fingers to his temple, as though I was his sergeant major.

'You can't distract me by being Indiana Jones or whatever.'

He twisted round. 'Who said I'd forgotten?'

'Fine. Dare you to strip.'

The torchlight gave his face a waxy glow. 'Oh, it's like that, is it?'

'Yup.'

'It's pretty cold.'

I handed him the bottle.

52

He took a regretful in-breath. 'Can't do much more. Not if I'm driving.'

'Oh well,' I said, with extreme brightness.

Fraser grabbed me and kissed me with zero shyness. Damp walls, damp air, damp tongues.

I tugged at his jumper. 'Right. Off.'

He brought it, along with his T-shirt, over his head. I shone the torch at him. Ribs. Nipple ring.

His stomach flinched from the light. 'Sooner do this outside, really.' He glanced at the walls. 'Bit creepy down here.'

I put the torch under my chin and glared at him.

'I'm not trying to get out of it,' he said, laughing, and I followed him back out of the cave.

The dull Scottish sky seemed as bright as a desert. I took his T-shirt and jumper off him. They were warm.

He looked around. 'Better not be any mineralogists around here.'

'Ah, they'd love it. Getting their rocks off.'

'Ha ha.'

I hooked a finger in the belt-loop of his jeans, and pulled him towards me a step. 'Come here, you.'

'Where's your dog?'

I looked at the log. 'Fuck.'

I called out for Tyger. My voice sounded more and more ridiculous, each repeat of his name sprouting wings, heading over the horizon on a one-way ticket. Fraser, who had dressed again, came back from the archway, shaking his head. We looked everywhere, all the places we'd been and further. It didn't make sense. Tyger was a complete sissy, the most pathetic dog in the history of the universe. He practically cried when he saw a cat. He *always* stayed put when he was left outside a shop, simply because he was absolutely terrified.

We looked for an hour, and then we sat and waited. He had to come back.

At the rescue home, Benji had wailed into Lottie's crotch at every new cage until Tyger's. A scraggy mixture of Havanese and, who knows, a dormouse or something, and the first one to look at Benji and not bark. Benji had pointed at him and said 'Tiger.' Wrong on all counts, but Tiger he remained and I changed the spelling, thinking I was being well erudite.

A mist was coming down.

'Polly. I'm really sorry. I have to get the car back.' Fraser gently took the vodka bottle away from me as I was taking another gulp and it splashed down my top. 'Why don't we come back tomorrow?'

'Fuck tomorrow.'

I couldn't speak for the whole journey back. Fraser put some music on and turned it off again. I thumbed the soft teeth of the feather in my pocket and rested my head against the window.

He parked up outside the drive. 'Want me to come in?'

I shook my head. 'Best not.'

When I told Lottie, her face lost its softness.

'What do you mean?' she said, looking past me up the driveway.

I tried to explain, leaving out the trespassing and the tonguing, but I could see straight away that she blamed me, utterly.

'You went to a quarry. Illegally. And let him off the lead.' Her fingers dug into her upper arm.

'No. I tied him up.'

'And went … ?'

'Just went exploring a bit, just having a—'

'Right, Polly.' She leant forward, inhaling, and gave me a look of disgust and crushing disappointment wrapped up together. 'You've been drinking all day.'

I let her have that one. 'We're going back tomorrow. First thing. As soon as it's light.'

She lowered her forehead into a palm as if she was doing a yoga move, before bringing her face up again. 'Maybe I should be calling the police.'

'I don't think they come out for lost dogs.' My voice was trying to burrow underground.

Her fingers were digging into her other forearm. 'I don't know what to say to you.' She turned.

Fraser wasn't at the bar yet. The landlord gave me a wink with my change and went back to the football. I propped my cheekbone on my hand and peeled the corner off a beermat.

'Never mind, eh, lass?' A man over in the corner was addressing me. He had a birthmark over one side of his face that made it look like someone had chucked red wine at him.

'What?'

'Never mind, eh?' He nodded to my glass. 'You've a drink, a coat, and the sun's given you freckles. Can't be that bad.'

I smiled a non-smile.

'There you go.' He sat back and turned the page of his *Daily Record*.

Dead. Not dead. Tyger was wandering around the quarry with his mopiest face on. Tyger was nothing more than a floor mop at the bottom of a shaft. *Distant deeps.* Or suspended mid-air, his lead a noose. *Its deadly terrors.* I'd killed him. *In the forest of the night.* I was getting good at killing.

55

'Not once was nerve lost.'

The birthmarked man was holding a half-length pen between his fingers and had newspaper ink on his forearm. He was looking at me expectantly.

'Sorry?' My beer mat had shed both sides of its print. 'Oh. I don't know. I'm no good at those.'

He gave a grand, gracious shrug. 'Me neither.' Felt hat, a long plaid coat, and a finely striped scarf the colour of old-fashioned sweets. He looked like he was off to a West End play.

The look Benji would have when we picked him up and he saw that Tyger wasn't in the car with us – a plastic doll face, someone slowly pressing their thumbs in. *Water'd heaven with their tears.* Fuck.

'Dog returns as a deity.'

My head came up sharply. 'What?'

He smiled at me and read it out again, as if he was on stage at the Globe. 'Dog returns as a deity.'

I tore up the last of the beermat. 'God.'

'Ah. You're a sharp tack, too.'

I felt like crying. The beermat had become a heap of curling shreds. I gathered them with the edge of my palm, my own snowdrift.

The door opened and though I didn't look up straight away, I felt the air change just slightly, a subtle quickening. Like the wind had come in.

A man, tall and roughly sketched. The man with the bird. Except it wasn't a bird in his hands this time. It was Tyger.

I blurted his name and stood up so quickly that the table tilted and my vodka fell off, the glass rolling halfway across the room. Tyger twisted out of the man's hands onto the floor and ran through the spilt drink towards me, his lead trailing.

I scooped him up and put my face in his fur. 'Where have you *been*?' Tiny manic tremors shot up and down his legs.

The man had a hand in the pocket of his jeans, awkward, as if he didn't know how to stand up properly. I was sure he recognised me.

'How did you – where did you find him?'

'He found me, I think.' He looked vaguely behind him. 'Up in the hills, west of here.' He sounded like he needed to cough, clear his throat.

'Oh my God. You are unbelievable,' I said to Tyger. He licked my ear and whimpered. I fingered his collar. 'Did you call the number?'

'No one picked up. Thought someone might know here.' He glanced round and I saw then how uncomfortable he was.

The landlord had the heels of his hands on the bar, thick forearms bulging. He tossed the man a small, slight nod and there was a light in his eyes, but not much. I saw the man register the nod and peek from under his eyebrows at the rest of the room. The couple in the corner were pretending not to watch. Crossword Guy was leaning back with a strange look on his face, proud and sleazy and waxen. His hand was crumpling a page of his paper.

The man swallowed, hard, and spoke to the floor. 'Take it easy.' He turned.

'No, wait—' I took a step towards him. Everyone was still looking at us. 'Can I buy you a drink or anything?'

He snapped his eyes to me, two dark stabs. 'No, you're all right.' And he left.

*

I walked down the road clutching Tyger like a brand new designer bag.

'Where did you go, you crazy fucker?' He was still quivering, little sporadic spasms. 'Did he torture you?' There wasn't a mark on him, just some mud caked in the pads of his paws. 'Did he mess with your mind?' I imagined him tied to a chair, his straggly belly fur all over the place, torchlight making white orbs of his eyes. 'Or was he nice to you? Did you get doggy treats?'

Tyger wiggled round in my arms and licked my neck. He smelled of vodka and damp earth.

'Yeah, very sexy, Tyger.'

A white car passed slowly. Fraser's. It stopped just ahead and I ran, as much as you can run with a limp, wet beanbag in your arms, and bumped up to the passenger window.

'Look!'

A woman was sitting there, looking faintly alarmed, her head turned to Fraser, who was in the driver's seat. They had the same nose. She wound the window down two inches. It was the woman whose garden I'd climbed into.

'Hi – hello, sorry, I just wanted to show, um, Fraser—' I hoisted Tyger up and he scrabbled slightly at the slanting bit of the window.

Fraser bent his head. 'This is my ma.' He sounded more polite than normal, like he was wearing a tie.

Her smile didn't quite reach the middle of her cheeks. 'Jeannie Robertson.'

'Hello! How are you, hi!' Ouch. Telesales operator greeting.

'And you are?' She glanced at Fraser.

He didn't quite meet my eye.

'I'm Polly.'

'Polly … ?'

Just Polly, I thought. 'Vaughan.' From Redhill, four A levels, two bronze ballet medals, little brother, does a mean spag bol with chorizo, always first on the dance floor and last to leave, broken home, serious lack of friends, shit at English, abandons people dying on the street, loser.

Her earrings were like the old coins you might dig up in an archaeological hoard, so worn that you couldn't see the runes or kings or dragons. This was the point when she was supposed to say, 'A pleasure to meet you, Polly,' or, 'So *you're* the lovely girl Fraser's been telling us so much about.' Instead, she just gave me another tight-lipped excuse for a smile.

'Yeah, anyway, got to get him back.' I began to wave Tyger's paw at them and then thought better of it.

Fraser grinned at me guiltily as his mum wound up the window.

I had never done a meet-the-folks thing, not for anyone. Mostly because I'd not had a single relationship that lasted longer than a month. Enough to find out how useless they were in bed or how gloopy they were – flowers and fluffy Disney animals once, seriously – or, the other way round, how completely wet and munterish I was.

It hadn't exactly been an auspicious first go. Still, she hadn't given me much to work with, looking at me like I was a smear of birdshit on the window, and Fraser had done me no favours. Whatever. I didn't care. Tyger was my boy. We basically snogged all the way home.

I set him down in the hallway and he looked up at me uncertainly.

'Go on then, scrapper.' I nodded at the living room door.

He scuttled in and there was a cross between a horrified scream and orgasmic sigh. Lottie came out with Tyger doing lizard tongue-flicks at her earlobe. 'You didn't go back there in the dark?'

I thought about claiming all the credit, being Superhero Dog Finder of the Year. 'A guy brought him to the hotel.'

Her look was more gentle. Forgiven, just a little.

It had been weird in the bar. Saloon doors in an old Western squeaking on their hinges. Big tangles of tumbleweed scratching past. Maybe everyone knew about him. Maybe they called him Birdkiller behind his back. The local nutjob.

A message from Fraser. *Glad yr dogs back. Come 2 mine 2moro? X*

The dark, scuzzy patches under his eyes had been like a crap go on those old Etcha-Sketches. He'd been taller than I'd thought.

Another message. *My house. Not quarry mine ;)*

4

I stared at the screen, my entire body seized up. Everything except my heart.

Police are appealing for witnesses.

With the wifi chugging away as if somewhere, deep below the house, slaves in chains were turning some colossal wheel to make it work, I'd lain on my bed and googled the words I hadn't typed since arriving in Scotland. Just to see. If nothing had been reported then he was fine. He'd gone home to Barcelona and got on with living the rest of his life. Not dead.

And now I was wishing I hadn't. In a coma. Traumatic brain seizure. His wallet had been stolen. His *wallet*. No ID. Police appealing for witnesses. Dead, dead, dead.

I carefully brought the laptop screen down and went to the front door.

Lottie poked her head into the hallway. 'I'm going to buy some cake ingredients this afternoon. It's been ages since you've made any of your treats.'

I put my boots on.

'Where are you off to?'

'Out.'

'Want some company? I've hardly seen you.' As if I'd been off rock-climbing up mountain ranges rather than lying on the sofa eating waffles with maple syrup and watching sappy cookery shows on telly. She'd obviously forgotten the Tyger thing enough. 'I want a Polly Day. Soon.'

I shut the door behind me.

It was misty again. Monochrome. The trees were smoke trails rising up from the ground. I headed west, wandering in the middle of the road, waiting until cars were right on top of me before idling over to the verge. One guy in a pickup truck with a pyramid of thin logs in the back yelled something unintelligible at me, but the rest just slowed, waiting for me to shift. I could probably have amassed a train of cars, my own funeral procession. Or his.

Dead. Almost dead.

The road curved inward and the trees on my left fell away, revealing a long bay full of boulders I'd passed in Adam's car before. By the loch, the rocks were studded with dried, peach-coloured barnacles, sharp enough to pinch the underside of my thighs. I let them dig in and took deep, furious drags on my joint, feeling the weed bloom in my lungs. Out here there was a brightness to the mist, like a torch behind a sheet.

I stacked some slim stones in my palm and sent the first one into the water. It careered off at an angle, sinking quickly. The second hopscotched along five times. My third one scudded once and disappeared.

Dad was the champion in our family. We used to hold competitions on holidays at the big lake in France, when we were all still together. He was like a choreographer, making the stones pirouette or do light, tripping footsteps. He'd cele- brate the epic ones – ten, even twelve – as if a Wembley crowd were roaring around him. Benji would just lift up the biggest stone he could find, stagger to the edge and heave it in, before screaming as if he'd just caved someone's head in and it was blood all down his front, not lake water.

The Spanish guy had been almost completely quiet, short-circuiting on the pavement. There hadn't been anyone else on the side street when it happened. Just us. The thought of him lying there, someone coming up, taking his wallet from his pocket – a wave of disgustingness rolled up from my gut and I hunched over my knees, retching, failing to puke. As if the words wouldn't even come out. I'm sorry I'm sorry I'm sorry. Please don't be dead.

Manslaughter. That's what it would be. It sounded worse than murder. The slaughter of a man. A man, slayed. A boy with his rucksack on both shoulders and some pretty amazing dance moves, once he was high.

God. The loch seemed to be rising. Each lurching wave bringing it higher, rearing up, and I was underwater, suspended in a slow, floating death dance. Salt packed into my throat.

Jesus, the weed.

I was clutching one last flint. Focus. It had a subtle sparkle, the remains of a glitter dust pot tipped out onto it. A sawtooth edge and a very sharp point. No good for skimming. I put it to the inside of my wrist and drew it along one of the creases in my skin. The crease deepened and went pink. A little harder. It made a chalky line and I felt a faint, thin pain. I kept going. Tiny beads of blood appeared. A dark river blossoming under ice. I sharpened the point on the boulder beneath me and made two more lines parallel to the first, going over and over them until I hissed.

When I finally looked up, the mist had completely vanished, the sky now breezy and blue and nonchalant, as if it had been like that all along and I just hadn't noticed. In front of me, the water was scuffed silver in places, stretched taut and black in others, and there were white patches everywhere. Shit. White patches. My chest clogged up. But they were just clouds.

I looked back down at my wrist. Three lines. I could do a fourth and put one more across the lot of them, jail-count style. And cut open all my veins, bleed out right there, with no one for miles to take me to hospital, see how I liked it. I licked the tip of my finger and wiped at the blood, making a smeary square.

The dry seaweed was rattling. Really loudly. Just one cloud was reflected in the water now, flowering like a jellyfish. I tilted my head up to the sky, a wide swipe of glassy blue. Wait – no clouds. Not one. Nothing to make that—

I stood up, looked for the white patch.

The water was silver and black, just as before. For fuck's sake.

I stomped along the boulders, destroying as many barnacles as I could. They made a sound like chips being deep-fat fried. This maddening, trapping vastness made my ribs tight. Maybe a prison cell would be better.

He wasn't dead yet. If I never looked it up again, he would never be dead.

I needed to pee really badly. Too much coffee. I climbed over the low chain slung across the opening of a little dirt road. Maybe I'd find some sexy forestry type wearing only dungarees and wiping sweat off his forehead with grimy knuckles to distract me. No chance. There was a big digger in among the trees, the colour of English mustard and streaked with rust, its windows long-since smashed. More recent vehicles had churned up the mud on the path, leaving thick tyre marks filled with pools of caramel-coloured water. Damp logs were stacked in triangular piles and there was a smell like a Christmas overload, warm and oily.

A few of the trees by the track had a piece of white tape tied around their slim trunks. I found myself looking for the next one, and the next, as I climbed higher. On either side of me the ground rose up, uneven and luridly green, the scratchy trees huddled together. I jumped a ditch and landed on moss so soft that I almost trampolined back up again.

And squat. These outdoor pissings would put some definition in my thighs. Though I needed to work on not dribbling on to my boots next time. I kicked the used tissues under a few leaves and went further into the dark tree hush, wondering how far you could get before being completely surrounded by pines with bark like the backs of crocodiles and this crazy, squashy floor. Every time I took a step my foot got swallowed up.

I lay down, sank into it. Princess and the pea stuff. The smoke from my fresh joint wound its way up among the branches as I tried to ignore the numbness in my wrist. Moss was in my ears, on my cheek. I could lie here until it totally soaked me up and no one would ever know where I'd gone. My own mossy coma – the way to avoid everything. One day some hiker would come upon a strange lime-coloured thing that wasn't quite human or flora, all splodgy and fronding and faintly female-shaped.

The moss was the best pillow ever. Caffeine hadn't even made a dent. The vertical oblongs of silvering light between the trees at the top of the hill looked like doors if I narrowed my eyes. And that one—

Wait.

Between two of the silvery doors, there was one much shorter tree on the horizon. Human-shaped. Like it might be wearing a hat. Christ. I sat up and looked again. It wasn't moving, not even an inch, but the other trees were taller and thinner. This was lumpy, smaller and rounder at the top. It could have been a person, standing dead straight. Shoulders, a neck.

The pines creaked, a slow, scraping sound.

Move. I got up, my ankle slipping, grazing my hands on the trees. I half skipped away and hit a new footpath. Euro house beats were going in my chest. My clothes were sticking to my arse and back. I began to feel a bit stupid. A man with a trilby? A film noir detective wandering the woods seventy years too late? Yeah, right, Polly. I slowed down.

There was a sound. A rustle and a click, somewhere in the fog of the trees beside me, like I'd heard on the first night in the garden. Every blade of grass was still. Every leaf, every branch. A scrap of white plastic ribbon hung limply on a skinny bough. The wind was finding its way into *something*. I kept tramping down, trying to ignore it.

There it was again. I couldn't quite tell if it was following me or I was following it. What sort of animal made that noise anyway? I waited for some killer chipmunky pine-squirrel to leap out at me, all teeth and claws and ear-splitting shrieks, a weird Scottish Z-movie, but it never came.

My boots now caked in mud, I chose the right hand path at a fork, aiming for the pale grey of the loch between the trees. I swear that rustle was still there, every time I stopped listening for it. Everything smelled heady and damp.

I looked down the path and stopped dead. Someone was coming towards me. A long coat and scarf, blood-coloured spatters on his cheek. The man from the bar. Red-top cryptic crossword man. He had one hand in his pocket and the other held a walking stick with two short, polished antlers on the top.

His face opened as he saw me. 'Not much for you down there, I'm afraid, lassie.'

'OK.' I stopped and pulled my phone out, looking fixedly at it as he passed me, pretending that I knew where the hell I was going, pretending that I had five thousand friends to urgently communicate with, pretending that there was reception, before idling forward.

When I turned, ten paces later, he was in the same place, his body twisted to watch me as I went down the hill, his hand still in his pocket. When I next snuck a look back he was heading up the path in the direction I'd come, the lower end of the walking stick pointing ahead of him every time he lifted it, as if he were at the head of a parade.

The path continued on the opposite side of the road, becoming a steep grassy bank that led down to the loch, further along than I'd been before. Half a bay, seaweed like discarded wigs in the water. A black and white bird with a long, neon-orange beak flew low, making little rape alarm calls.

One large stone stood out. It wasn't mottled and baggy-looking like the others. It sat upright, on its own, in a way that didn't seem possible, facing out to sea. When I got closer, I could see that it was glossy, polished black, the shape of an egg sitting on its smaller point. Two long sweeps of pearly white on it, like crescent moons back to back. I ran my finger along the rough texture of one moon and then along its twin. Three very thin stripes of the same jewelled white ran around the whole stone. It was attached, though I couldn't see how, to a base of more jagged rocks that were nestled in among the others. It was a sculpture, a marker of some kind.

I felt ridiculously tired. I jiggled around in the stones until I found a way to fit with them, and looked at the cuts on my wrist. Drying already. I couldn't even do *that* properly.

Midges gathered above me. God, they were fuckers. I put my jacket over my face.

A trail of burn-water gurgled near my ear. There it was. *Rustle-click.*

*

'Ow. Fuck.'

'Sorry.'

I had one hand in a bag of kettle chips and the other – with three plasters on my wrist – around Fraser's neck, my foot lodged between his legs. His palm was underneath my thigh and his other thumb was on the remote control of the film we were definitely not watching at his place. He was attempting to perform some sort of deep-sea rescue mission in my gullet, but it was all right. I could almost forget.

I pulled away and picked up my beer. 'What's that?' I nodded up to a picture of a red shield with three white wolves' heads, tongues wagging. It was only when Fraser had texted me his address that I realised he didn't live in the house with the garden I'd climbed into. His mum child-minded that little blonde girl, and Fraser's family lived instead on the most residential street in the village, which wasn't saying much.

'Oh. My da's into all the family history, clan stuff, you know. That's the shield of the Chief of the Robertsons.'

'What do the words say?'

'I can't pronounce it. Don't speak Gaelic. But it means "Fierce when roused".'

I snorted and almost spat my beer on him. He put his fingers into my sides and I squirmed away, disentangling myself, taking a slug of Sambuca to wash it down. 'Where's your loo?'

He pointed, gave me a salty kiss and turned up the sound again.

I leant back round the doorframe and jabbed a finger at him. 'I will be back for you. You are totally going to get *roused.*'

It was all set up, really. He'd invited me round. I'd shaved my legs and had a condom in my pocket. If weed wouldn't blot everything out, maybe some earnest humping on the sofa would.

I opened the bathroom cabinet. Nothing too seedy. Witch hazel and Herbal Essences and plasters and tweezers and expensive de-wrinkling face cream – no matter how poor you were, every middle-aged woman could afford that. Earrings with curving silver shapes and the number three on them in a glass bowl.

The front door bumped.

'Yeah, OK, in a minute.' Fraser was sauntering up the stairs, holding my bag, as I came out.

I could hear his mum say something about fishcakes. Arse. Time to be mega-head-girl Polly again. Except it didn't quite seem to be the time. Fraser waved his fingers in the air, the way Lottie did when she had just painted her nails and the taxi was already outside. He did it again, a small, flapping gesture, and reached past me, opening a door and shunting me inside.

'Back in a sec,' he said in a whisper, slinging my bag in after me.

*

69

It was the classic student-back-at-home bedroom, full of left-overs deemed not cool enough to take to uni. Old DVDs, posters of bands who were so hot right about two years ago and a few shitty airport crime novels. Single bed. A map of the world with pins stuck in it. Folders and books and a hefty laptop stacked in the corner. All quite unnervingly tidy.

Blurred murmuring mixed in with the telly downstairs. I pulled my skirt down over my thighs in front of the mirrored wardrobe and tried to look like I hadn't been eating Fraser's face off. Jesus, what did I care? I should just go down there. There was something about her, though. As if she'd put a hex on me.

I lay on the bed and wondered about getting naked and hiding under his creased duvet. Forget the niceties and just crack on. My lips were sticky, liquoricey.

The door opened. Fraser shut it behind him quietly and turned to me. 'She was not supposed to be home.'

'Never mind.' He wasn't coming over. I stood up and pushed him back against the door, putting my tongue behind his teeth. Might as well give as good as I got.

He held on to my wrists and pushed me away a little. 'Polly. We can't. Not here.'

Talk about changing your tune. Five seconds ago he'd been making jokes about me and the green-haired lesbian in the dumb film we were watching. 'So? You're not *fifteen*.'

'I know, but – I promise you, she'll kill me.' I raised my eyebrows and he dropped his shoulders and looked at the carpet. 'She's dead religious. She hates me working in the bar but I need the money.'

'What, no sex till you're married sort of thing? Fraser' – I looked at him with oodles of pretend sympathy and lowered my voice – 'have you not had *sex*?'

He squirmed slightly and looked away. 'Aye, of course I have. Shut up. Just – not here. Not now.'

Excellent. I liked a challenge. 'Are you a God-lover too then?'

'No. Just, you know, on Christmas and that, to keep her happy.'

'Aw.' I did my best pious look and turned it into a fluttery-eyelashed, whimpery puppy thing that also shouted *I want sex*.

'Stop it.'

'How will she know? Unless, you know, you bark like a dog when you come or something.' I opened my mouth and he put a hand over it, and then clamped his lips on me instead. I was practically falling over laughing. 'All right, fine, fine, I'll go.' I picked up my bag.

'No ...' He grabbed my hand and looked at his bedroom window.

I made him go first. No way was I going to fall through the roof and land arse over tit in the hallway if he wasn't going to crash down with me. Fraser sat on the windowsill and took my hand to help me through. I bashed my forehead on the frame. Jesus. We crept over the flat porch roof and he crouched down before levering himself onto the lawn using one hand, as if it was a specialist Olympic sport. He'd definitely done that before. Wiggling forward, my skirt totally riding up to my crotch, I leant down and he just about got me around the waist and I fell into him, almost taking us both out.

Being a cat-burglar fugitive was quite a turn-on. I kissed him, teeth clashing, and ran round to the back of the house. The booze had sluiced my brain, sugar and acetic loveliness. Fraser appeared and I slammed him against the wall and kissed him again, my hands under his T-shirt. He was breathing my name and swearwords into my mouth and trying to get me off him at the same time. I got my fingers to his belt buckle and knelt down in the gravel and his hands were in my hair and he was still hissing at me but I carried on anyway, and pulled him out.

Light flooded the garden and there was a squeak of a door handle. A woman was there, looking at me with her son's cock in my mouth.

*

When I was nine, I climbed up to the tall diving board in our local swimming pool, having thrown a strop at Dad, who'd said I wouldn't like it. I got to the edge and vomited, ten metres up, a waterfall of sick that caused swimmers to shriek as though they were being murdered.

At the Year 7 disco, Bryn Hannaway planted both hands on my cheeks and delivered a kiss worse than a goldfish dying on my face. I broke his nose and had to write a letter of apology and mow his lawn for the summer.

At thirteen, I was besotted with a lanky footballer two years older than me who wore an Afro comb in his hair and walked like he had a limp. I made him a Valentine's CD of sarky chart rock and stoned-sounding hip hop tunes, ruining it all by ending with James Blunt. After that, Olayemi laughed behind his cupped hand every time he saw me for the rest of the year. As did all his friends. While singing 'You're Beautiful' and miming handjobs.

Getting locked out of a German exchange dorm wearing only my pants and a pair of fairy wings. Flashing my arse at fresher's ball. Letting a PhD student shag me because I was

72

too drunk to care and her throwing me a coming-out party before crying in a corner of the English department. Trying to drag the driver of the student bus out of his seat so I could take everyone home.

None of these came close.

I lay in bed, replaying it over and over in my head, dying a little more inside each time. Fraser had dropped me home without saying much, apart from an occasional, agonised 'Fuck'. I hadn't said much, apart from an occasional 'Fuck' in reply. His mum had said nothing at all, just walked very slowly back into the house, shutting the door carefully behind her. I'd heard the key turn in the lock, like the neck of a bird being broken very precisely.

Very very very sorry x

I typed it four times, and deleted every one.

*

Hot sex

On my bed, laptop open. No more googling the bad stuff.

Hot sex threesome

Laying low seemed like the best course of action. I finally helped Lottie with her website and watched the rolling news with Tyger as a pillow – suddenly finding East European civil unrest and the stock market incredibly interesting while I chewed my nails to obliteration. My phone kept shtum. Another friend lost, in record time. I was such a dick.

Hot sex threesome boy girl girl

Boy boy girl

The videos were always the same. Dead-eyed girls seeming unfazed by alarmingly cocked, hairless men. This one was at a swimming pool – hopefully one with a lot of chlorine. And the girl pretended to love every skin-slapping minute of it and made sounds like the presenters did on *Great British Bake Off* when they tasted gossamery cream cheese icing on a courgette and lime cake.

Still, it got me off.

Lottie knew I was down, though with the saintly conviction that I was stuck on my work – I carried round a pen indented with teeth marks as a handy prop – rather than because I'd been caught in a scenario that you'd get berated by Jeremy Kyle for, in addition to being a potential tourist-killer.

She put a hand on my forehead and I tipped the pen in my mouth up at her like it was a thermometer under my tongue. 'Come to the bar. Let's have roasts. I'm buying.' She always bought.

Oh God, who cared. If I was down south, I'd march up to Stef's door and fucking make him talk to me. If Fraser was at the hotel, then he could punch me in the face or whatever he needed to do, and I could feel very noble and bruised and martyr-like while eating crunchy brussels and salty gravy, holding my chin very high. It was nothing.

I rolled off the sofa.

Fraser was rubbing the rim of a glass with a tea towel when we came in. He rubbed it more intently when he saw me.

I put my palms flat on the bar. 'Hello.'

There must have been a lot of lipstick on that glass. 'Hiya.'

'How are you?'

He didn't look up. 'I'm all right.'

Great. I'd ruined everything. Back to a possible fuck-count of zero and nothing more to do than research epilepsy comas and shred my arms with stones. 'How's … your mum?'

Fraser shrugged and put the glass on the shelf above him. 'I wouldn't know. She's not really speaking to me at the moment.' I made a sound like a terrified pirate and he leant a hand on the bar, finally looking at me. 'She'll come round. In about a hundred years.'

I thunked my forehead into my wrists. 'Oh God.' I peeked through my arms to find him grinning at me bravely, like he'd just come out of battle unharmed. 'I am *really* sorry.'

'No matter.'

No chewing lamb with a throbbing jaw necessary, then. He kept his grins coming from behind the bar and Lottie winked at him and me conspiratorially. Yeah, she wouldn't be doing that if she'd seen my Highlands-porn crime scene last night.

Fraser came to clear our plates. 'There's a pool table next door.'

Lottie put her palms up. 'I'll leave you two to it. I think the last time I played was in 1991.'

I shut an eye at him. 'Only if you don't mind being totally destroyed.'

He smiled.

Fraser knew the boys in the pool room, two fourteen-year-olds with a high-energy, grungy thing going on, as if they only listened to emo-metal while writing mopey, coded whining in their diaries and wanking off to anime. Finn was Becca's little brother, just as pale, but twenty times as talkative.

He motormouthed on at us while we played – I gained a wine-pumped confident streak and delivered the promised destruction – and took the pool cue off Fraser. 'I'll show Polly how it's done, you able-bodied loser.'

Fraser crossed his arms and angled back against a shelf, shaking his head mock-ruefully.

Finn's left arm was shorter than his right, I noticed, and more spindly looking. His hand was curled in slightly, like he was cupping a ciggie away from the wind. When he leant over the table the back of his hand rested on the felt. He slotted the pool cue between thumb and palm and deftly potted a red, talking all the while.

'So, you know she was always a bit of a bitch, mate, yeah? And she hated me, she marked me down on purpose, definitely, and she made me and Devo sit at opposite ends of the room, like we're five. But it just made us worse, right, and Dev's like, real good at making stuff, he's like Dr Frankenstein or something, white coat stuff yeah, and I helped him make a smoke bomb at home – it's like, made out of sugar and potassium nitrate, you sort of cook it up, right – and he brought it into the classroom and when she dissed him, which he knew she'd do and she did, he started talking about cursing her, that he'd do something she'd really regret, you know, and all the others are going what? Shut up, man, and he works himself up into it, you know, stands up, and does this hilarious like, magician hand thing yeah, and lights it, and this great big brilliant cloud of smoke starts going up, and he'd put stuff in it to make it go purple, and everyone starts screaming and running out of the room, and he's laughing like, I don't know, like he's some evil nemesis or something and I'm pissing myself in the corner, and when it all clears yeah, there's just us two in the room and the smoke alarms are going off, and she's like, standing there with her arms folded like, totally unimpressed, and Dev's got like, three weeks of detention for it, and he totally took it for the team, you know, didn't say I had anything to do with it, so now I owe him. Big time.' He potted the black. 'There you are, Polly.'

76

I'd been leaning on my pool cue the whole time. 'How the hell did that just happen?'

A middle-aged guy with a baseball cap poked his head round the door and caught Fraser's eye.

Fraser pushed himself off the wall with a foot and headed to the door. 'Back in a sec.'

Finn nodded at my pool cue. 'Shall we get you going on that, then? I'll swap hands if you like.'

After another arse-kicking by Finn, but at least one in which I put two balls away, I went outside. Fraser was standing a little way off, a blue-grey cloud rising from him. Twilight Fag Blue. A car was just leaving.

He took a double-drag in when I joined him. 'Hiya.'

I nodded and we stood facing the loch. 'What's with you and all your friends?' They hung around him like he was catnip.

Another drag. 'I dunno.'

I jammed my hands in my pockets. 'Sorry again.'

'Don't worry about it.' Rain began prickling my nose, subtle as an itch. 'I've got to go down to Glasgow for a couple of days.'

Invite me, I thought. I could remind myself what shops were, see real live actual people of maybe a few different shapes and sizes and sorts, we could go clubbing, I could finally sleep with you. The unspoken invitation dwindled in the air long enough. 'Yeah? What are you doing?'

He exhaled. 'Some exams.'

'Testing you on how to build big fuck-off bridges that turn into skyscrapers?'

'That sort of thing.'

Yep, he totally wasn't inviting me. 'Good luck.'

'I need it.' He offered me the cigarette. I shook my head. 'Not been revising much.' He leant over a bit, enough to nudge my elbow.

I put my hoodie up and tucked my hair away under it.

'Fancy a party when I get back?'

'Yeah?'

'Just a wee one.'

I nodded. There were only so many nights watching moody-yet-sexy forensic scientist dramas with Lottie that I could take.

'Finn'll look after you, if you want. He likes you. He doesn't talk to everyone.'

'Lucky me,' I said. I wasn't shagging a fourteen-year-old. That was below even me. Though maybe I would, just to spite him for not taking me to Glasgow.

'Fraser.' The door had opened behind us and the landlord, Haimie, was there. 'You are working tonight, pal, aren't you?'

Fraser dropped the cigarette and swiped it with his toe. 'Sorry, mate.' He turned to me, hesitated, before quickly pulling me in towards him, a hand at the base of my back, and giving me a nice, tongueless kiss. 'Catch you in a few days, then.'

*

The afternoon sun flashed white on the conservatory window. I swear the loch had a costume change every time I looked out. Today, it had folds in it, turn-ups on jeans. There was a little pale triangle over to the right. A boat, one person in it. I found a monster pair of binoculars.

The edges of the garden were startling and gargantuan, and I could see all the detail on the loch now, its zigzagging lines. I cruised around until I found the boat. The back end seemed to slope straight down into the water, but no one was flailing about on there. A man, dark-haired, head bent, something in his hands. He was reading.

It was that guy. With the bird. With Tyger. This time it definitely was. He was wearing the same dark blue sleeveless puffer thing he'd had on when I first saw him.

It was a bit much to expect to actually *see* the words from here, even if they were superhero-vision-strength binoculars. I wondered what it was. *To Kill a MockingGrouse*, or *I Know Why the Caged Pheasant Sings*. Maybe *The Curious Incident of the Dog in the Highlands*. *How to Stay Afloat and Influence People*, ha ha. And then a thought came – maybe it was my book. What if he'd taken it? Swiped it from the rock? *The Book Thief*, then.

My arms ached. You could totally take someone out with these bad boys.

We met on the rocks and from then on it was you and me. You'd pick twigs and leaves from my hair. We'd drink beer and take each other to the places we loved.

You visit them all the time now, and I follow, a little wake, a rustle of feathers.

The hollow in the oakwoods, which was always damp, even when we put a blanket down. Surrounded by leaves the colour of wet foxes. I tuck up in high branches there and listen to the scratch-language of woodlice, to the loudness of birds.

The singing sands, where we swam in the sea on the days when it was green-grey and almost warm. The small, dumpy lady who lived there would bring us cups of hot chocolate and look out to the horizon as she talked. You seemed to like her. Maybe she made you think of your ma, before she was ill. I think I came at the right time for you, too.

Rock to woods to sea-salt. I move at the pace of clouds.

I drift after you, to the place we liked best. A place no one knew but us. Dark, hushed. Scratching our initials into the stone with your penknife, after our first time. I told you that I'd never done it and you said you'd not done it much either, and your smile made me feel safe.

The place where I left my heart.

'You have got to be kidding me.'

Finn was sitting on a moped, and the moped was making a sound like a lion cub with a chest infection. It was a cross between a motorbike and the squeaky old shopper that Lottie liked to zigzag down to the market on. One of the handlebars was extra-long, a plastic bar strapped on with loads of gaffer tape, which Finn was leaning on. He was still in his school uniform. Jesus.

'Say hello to my stallion,' he said.

I folded my arms. 'Are you even old enough to be driving one of those?'

'Yeah, course.' He pursed his lips at me. 'Near enough, anyway. I've been driving it for two years. My da got it from an auction. It's an antique. Got to get around somehow.'

Even better. An *ancient* moped. 'Have you got a helmet for me or something?'

'Naw. They're for diddies.' He wasn't wearing one either, his black hair tucked behind his ears.

'Christ.' I got on behind him – there was just about enough room, though I had to bring my legs right round his.

'Tuck in, gorgeous,' he said, and put his foot down.

Finn had asked where he could take me in the pub the night before. I'd told him I would accept nothing less than a hot beach and cocktails, preferably served by a highly attractive man wearing nothing but very short shorts. Finn stroked his chin with his stronger hand and said he'd see what he could do.

Now I was just worried that he was going to attempt to seduce me with a bag of groceries down his trousers. We cruised through two villages and onto an even smaller single-track road with flat, boggy land stretching away on either side, and tons and tons of sky, the clouds all whipped up into a

TV chef's best egg whites and moving fast. If we reached thirty miles an hour, the moped started to sound as if it might fall apart underneath us, but even when we were going slower the wind rashed my legs and my hair went to strips of leather. Finn let me have a go, too, on the dead straight bit, my sleepy brain trying to cope with the hand-and-foot thing. He had a little portable speaker attached to the front, so we wound along the road to skinny-sounding guitars and bursts of screamo mixed in with the jagged engine hum. Rock and roll.

The road got smaller and bouncier – I'm sure Finn was aiming for the potholes just so I'd have to grab onto him a bit tighter. We parked in a deserted yard with a sign saying CARPARK 50P and a tiny shed with blackened windows. He strolled off round a corner past a couple of squat houses. One was made of corrugated iron and painted green, babygrows on the washing line. There was a metal barn at the end and a massive, dark chocolate-coloured bull looking at us from behind a gate, its lower jaw working.

Finn turned round at the crest of the road, putting his arm out as if showing something off. I caught up with him. The tarmac shelved right down into the sand, which was pale grey and clogged with mounds of seaweed. Chunky rocks were darker at the bottom where the sea had been, and a low hill rose up to the north. A painted wooden rowboat lay on its side, partly filled with yellow water, and a much larger sailboat was perched on its stand in the sand.

'Yeah. This is not a beach,' I said.

'Course it is, darlin'. Best one there is.' Finn prodded the ground with the toe of his cheap biker boot. 'Sand.' He nodded ahead of him. 'Sea.'

Also pale grey. Scottish Seaside Bleak As Fuck Grey.

'And, hang on.' He rummaged in his bag, which had inky markings all over it just like the biro tattoos of band names and reptiles he'd drawn on his weaker forearm. 'Cocktails.'

I looked at the plastic Coke bottle he'd thrust proudly in front of me. 'What the hell's in there?'

'Try it. Concocted just for you.'

'Better not be a smoke bomb.' The lid hissed. It smelled of the stuff you'd buy in the Body Shop if you were twelve. I raised my eyebrows.

Finn screwed his mouth up. 'Archer's. And lemonade. And mango juice.'

'Yum.'

'I dunno, it's what my mum drinks. A girl drink. All girls like that sort of thing.'

I snorted. 'You definitely need to meet more girls.' I tried it anyway. It was very sweet. The drink – and his chivalry, really, even if basically there was a ten-year-old inside him busting to get out.

'So …' He gave me a ridiculously lascivious look, up and down. 'Got your bikini on under there?'

'No.'

'Oh well, just take a photo of yourself for me later, then. With or without.'

'Fuck off, Finn.'

He grinned at me and wandered onto the beach, his swagger slightly awkward, his left arm swinging a little.

I drank my glorified perfume oil and had a look round. Finn said that the local beaches had been used for Second World War training and that you sometimes found unexploded bombs and chunks of metal sticking out of the sand. Yep, you didn't get that in your Malaga resort. The seaweed was like used latex-wear from an S&M basement party. The sand was really grainy, still visibly shell-like. Milk teeth and bracelet charms.

Maybe you got white patches here, too – though the sea was much shallower than the loch, guttering out over the sand for ages. I was climbing onto a fat rock to get a better view when I heard a shout from Finn. He was jogging towards a short, elderly lady who was coming down the ramp, giving her a one-armed hug when he reached the edge of the beach. Snatches of their voices caught and twisted on the wind, swooping kites. They headed up the road away from me, the woman walking jerkily from side to side, Finn loping next to her.

I hung out on my own for a bit longer then retraced my steps, grinding my heels into the sand, letting it make that munching sound. Finn wasn't anywhere. Maybe I was walking back on my own, then.

'In here, darlin'.' He was behind me, sticking his head out of the door of a long caravan that rested on piles of stones. Cocky little shit.

His grandmother was a potato-shaped woman dressed in thick green and red. Finn introduced me as his girlfriend, which made me glare at him until he said it was a joke. The caravan was incredibly warm and everything was furred and textured, itchy tapestry cushions on the benches and ragged towels hanging up to dry. Heat stains blackened the wall above the hob and there were photos on loops of string, including of Finn, and Becca with her tin whistle, looking slightly less mercenary than I remembered.

Finn was blathering away about his actual girlfriends, of which there were many apparently – I didn't believe that for a second, though maybe it didn't take much up here and his stupid skin-and-bones moped got all the lassies a bit damp down below.

His gran put a chamomile tea in my hands and sat down opposite me. 'So, what's your story then, Polly?' Her voice had a doll-like quality to it.

'She's looking for love and she's just in denial about having a younger man.' Finn was walking around, jiggling his arms.

I slurped at the tea. A noseful of steaming hay, old flowers, sweat.

'She's actually a spy and she's found you out at last, Gran-gran.'

'Oh, you,' she said to him, still gazing at me. Her face was incredibly lined, deep gouges like some of the mountains had around here, even though she was probably only in her late sixties. A red and black bandana saying 'Trinidad and Tobago' swept her hair back off her face. 'Everyone has a story.'

'Um, I'm up here with my mum, and doing some work and that.' There was something about her calm that I found slightly unnerving. A gentle sea-sway all of her own. And it was like she could see through me, to my bones. Hear them rattling with guilt.

'When did you last come?' she asked me.

'How do you mean? Oh, no, I haven't been here before.'

'Yes, you have.'

I sat up and looked at her. She had spoken so surely, as if she'd said that I was a girl, or that my hair was brown. 'No, I – this is the first time I've been to Scotland. Except I went to Edinburgh Festival when I was little with my folks.'

'No.' The word was like a long bubble blown from a wand, wobbling in the air. 'You've been here before.'

The table was sticky. My cup made a sucking sound when I lifted it. 'Yeah, I don't think so.'

She didn't say it again but just continued to look at me, not quite smiling, her eyes soft and curious. They were blazingly green, sun-on-the-sea stuff. She seemed to be waiting for me to say something else. I swiftly asked Finn about the last girl he'd mentioned and off he went, talking about skirts and paper birds and trying to make lip gloss out of PVA glue and cherry liqueur. The windows fogged.

'*Gran-gran*?' I asked as we walked back to the still-deserted car park.

'Yeah, she says she's the best of the two, so she should get double the name. Gran One hates her.'

'Is she, you know ...' I tapped my temple. 'Is she all right?'

'Yeah, course she is. Sharper than anyone. She can tell you the names of every king of Scotland and the year they were on the throne. She can do it backwards or forwards. And she knows all the types of submarines they used in the war. She's mint. Do you mind if we go quite fast? I've got maths homework.'

I thought about the lines around her chin and on her cheeks as we chugged homewards, seeing them in every burn that cut through the bogs.

*

'Darling, is this yours?' Lottie was holding a small, flat wooden box.

I'd practically been asleep against Finn's bony shoulders by the time he dropped me off. It wasn't just the weed. And the drink. There was something in the air up here, like it was infused with Temazepam. My limbs moved more slowly. My brain, too. 'Don't think so. What is it?'

86

'Well, I really thought it must be. I mean, you're doing the Romantics, aren't you? It was down by the loch.'

She put it in my hands. Pale wood, slightly pockmarked. There was a tiny cut-out triangle at the edge. I put my finger into it.

Inside, the box was lined with dark green plastic, the type you might use for a ground-sheet. And there it was.

My book, the one I'd left on the rocks.

5

'Yeah, so my da was having a right hissy over it and ma was like, no way you big bastard are you coming back in here looking like that and my da said like what? and she said you've got your trousers round your ankles man, you've pissed yourself and you've got pie on your face and he sort of like, crashed to his knees and started crying and going but you're my WIFE and ma was like, not tonight I'm not and slammed the door and I said to her you're his Wife of Pie and she tried to belt me round the—'

I looked over at Fraser. 'Tell me we'll be there soon.'

He smiled, chewing gum, his eyes on the road. 'Not so far now.' He turned up the music.

We'd been driving for twenty minutes and already Finn had packed every square inch of the car's air with words, shouting in my ear behind me as the music got louder. At least on the moped he'd been in front most of the time. Becca sat opposite him, scrunched in the corner, her forehead against the window.

She had scowled at me at the top of the driveway as she got out of the front passenger seat, by which point Finn was already halfway through a story about cat torture. With my book back, I'd arse-whipped myself into action for an afternoon and actually written some real-life words of my own before Fraser had picked me up. We'd taken a single-track road on the other side of the loch, going higher and higher into hills that had taken too many steroids. The sky was blissing out. I didn't know where we were headed – Fraser had said it was a surprise.

His small upper arm muscles curved out of his T-shirt – blue, white and red, like a French flag – his wrists resting on top of the steering wheel. It was nice to see him again. He said his exams had gone all right. I didn't ask after his mum.

The clouds were hot pink by the time we stopped in a lay-by under some fir trees. I couldn't see anything resembling a rave venue. Maybe we were having a campfire party, like scouts. Really, really drunk, stoned scouts.

Fraser pulled out a couple of rucksacks from the boot and handed one to me. It clinked.

'You'd better not be taking me somewhere to kill me.'

He turned round to face me and walked backwards down a track, his bag slung over one shoulder. 'Best place to do it if I was. No one'd ever find you.'

We walked a couple of miles along a path that got narrower and muddier, the light just beginning to dissolve. Finn stormed along in front, shouting that he should have brought his moped, he'd have got there in no time, and Becca trailed behind us, probably muttering crow-spells under her breath at me.

Fraser led us up to a small stone building that looked like it had just fallen from the sky. Why else would it be there, in the middle of all these blank hills? Bothies were apparently there for people passing by, shelter for the night. Walkers and campers. And us, he said, giving me a bit of a grin as he kneed open one of two wooden doors.

89

It wasn't exactly a festival tent, but it was quite cool, I guess. The stone walls were partly plastered in gunky cement and the roof sloped down to a flimsy wooden table along one side. A couple of candles were jammed into wine bottles next to the sort of salt and pepper shakers you get in greasy caffs. Makeshift bunk beds at one end and a fireplace at the other. It was freezing, colder than outdoors.

Fraser bent down by the fireplace and started piling some of the short logs in. 'People always leave stuff here for the next lot.'

Finn jumped up to grab the wooden poles that hung horizontally over the fire and one of them came away in his hand. I tried to imagine what this room would smell like if you had the clothes of damp, sweaty walkers drying on them, too. There was already something stale and off-green in the air – maybe the ghosts of stinky dead ramblers who'd done one mountain too many. I bashed open the top of a beer and sat on the side of an armchair upholstered with an unconvincing leaf design.

The fire took the edge off the skin-chill, licking around the firelighters that Fraser had brought with him. He turned to me, looking quite proud.

'Yep yep, man make fire, very hunter-gatherer, very *masculine*,' I said.

'Be nice or you're not sharing my sleeping bag,' he said.

Finn had set up his mini-speakers and started playing some terrible, snivelly emo shit.

'That is not how this is going to be,' I said to him.

He turned it up. 'Screw you, darlin'.' He began bouncing up and down.

Beer turned into vodka turned into ancient ginger wine turned into Fraser opening his hand to reveal four little chalky pills the colour of a ten-year-old girl's first eyeshadow set.

'Where did you get those?' I asked, taking a powdery blue one.

He scratched his nose and grinned. 'I have my ways.'

Finn came bounding up.

'God, don't give *him* one,' I said.

Turning. The low clouds were turning into the hills and the hills into the clouds, each nicking colours from the other. I wanted to eat the clouds. They looked like cookie dough.

Hands were on my shoulders.

'I really, really like cookie dough,' I said, leaning back, feeling a cheek on my ear.

'Cookie dough's inside,' said Fraser, twisting me round gently and leading me back to the door.

Finn was the best dancer in the world, or the worst. Becca had her own tightly quivering thing going on, as if she were disagreeing with someone very, very strongly, her limbs occasionally exploding outwards, but her younger brother – you couldn't fault his conviction. I think Stef might have taken him under his wing, whether Finn liked it or not, with moves like that. And then we would have run away, killed him. Finn, lying on the pavement, spit thinning at the side of his mouth.

'Don't die, Finn,' I said, holding his crooked hand in mine.

He looked quite pleased for a second. 'I'm never going to die!' He shouted it twice more, before running around the room.

Fraser pulled me towards him for a completely out-of-time, filthy grind. There would be no mums up here, or wayfaring dogs, or anything else.

Lips on my ear, and my mouth. Hands slotted between my pants and my hips. I thought about biting his tongue. I should probably have just told him I didn't like it as much as he seemed to, but part of me didn't care, and I let him swirl around my teeth. Didn't bite.

Time went fuggy. It zipped by, or maybe it billowed, like a parachute. The fire strobed. Fire-disco.

There was a disembodied cry outside. Rising.

I prised my limpet-mouth off Fraser's neck. 'What's that?'

Fraser lowered my head back down. 'Dunno.'

Again. A sort of *yowling*.

'I don't like hyenas,' I said, tugging slightly on the neck of his T-shirt.

He detached my fingers. 'It's not a hyena.'

I let him take my hand and lead me to the door.

The sky. God. It was so dark now, except that the moon was the brightest and most amazing thing ever. Someone had used a pipette and dropped milk and oil, all marbled together. Bang. Stars too, loads of them.

Becca was standing at the edge of the grass before it dropped away, her chin in the air, howling. A small, soaring sound, like the movement of a heavy bird leaving a tree, down then up, up, up. And – I swear I heard it – the hills answered her back with their own tiny, tripping howl. I'd caught her earlier, retching our crisps and chocolate dinner up into a bit of bog, her fingers in her mouth. Maybe she hoped the moon would suck it out of her instead.

The night sky swiped and tilted and curved, turning us really slowly. Turning. I put my hand up into it, trying to touch the stars, daring to get as close as I could without burning, not quite reaching. When I blinked there were more, just for a millisecond, ten times as many.

There was a tug on my other hand. I looked at Fraser. 'I totally need to pee,' I said in the sort of voice that would normally say 'You are very beautiful', or, 'This is the most magical night of my life'.

When I came back in, he was walking towards me, hands in his pockets, head bent. Something between his teeth.

I plucked out the little square of plastic and tapped his nose with it. 'Don't really want an audience,' I said in his ear.

'What audience?' Fraser nodded to the armchair in the corner, where Finn was curled up, one arm slung over his head, his mouth loose. Becca was still outside doing her banshee-wolf thing.

'You asked for it.' I pulled him towards the corner.

Sleeping bag sex. Awkward. Hilarious, but awkward. I was fifteen again, trying to work out where everything went. Joey Crawshaw, dyed-black wavy hair and painted black nails and breath like cinnamon chewing gum and dried chickpeas. That little blitz of pain and making him stop really suddenly, convinced that it was the wrong place entirely because it hurt so much. He'd had dark blonde hair on his stomach and texted me twelve times the next day but I was too embarrassed to reply. Me and Stef would fool around but our hearts weren't really in it and, frankly, he was rubbish. 'You've got all the wrong bits, love,' he'd said after a while, squeezing my breast unceremoniously like it was Play-Doh and feeling for my crotch. 'Need a bit more *here*, not here.'

Fraser stopped. 'Hang on,' he said in a whisper, and started yanking at the zip of the sleeping bag on the bottom bunk. He was half lying on top of me, trying to undo it, getting his feet stuck.

I put my hand over my mouth.

'Shhh,' he said. 'No giggling.'

We rolled over onto the ground mat, the sleeping bag sliding over us and catching under his knee. My thighs were definitely going to get splinters. And my elbows.

There was more shushing and more unzipping of things and a lot more giggling. My head felt like a honeycomb. And then somehow we'd managed it, and everything was cute and slick – and still, to be honest, a bit wrong, what with an unconscious fourteen-year-old in the room.

Becca was standing there in the doorway, dead straight, looking at us.

'JesusFuckFraser,' I said.

He stopped inside me and looked up.

Becca just stared, her face glowing blood orange. 'There's a man outside.'

Fraser shifted his hips and I tried to be totally bloody normal about the fact that we were having a conversation with someone while having sort of static sex. 'What do you mean?' he said.

'There's a man. Outside. He's coming in.'

Fraser looked at me, his nose next to my cheek. Blinked. 'Um, right. OK.'

Do you remember how we lay underground, blinking at each other? I would tell you about the rocks that men cut out of the dark. I know them all.

Corantee, Clashgorm, Bellsgrove. Places bruised by air and water. The sound of rocks, shifting. Ancient pressure. Liquid, hardening.

Around me, time is strange. I get stuck in its folds. Seasons, too. Autumn might stretch and stretch, or the leaves rash and redden and fall in a blink. Sometimes the snowdrifts bank up at the pace of a breath. I bask in summers, as summer as we get up here, or miss them completely. And I would curse them, then — another season gone. Another season in which I hadn't talked to you. Made you hear me.

The one I wait for, over summers and winters.

I was cut out. A bullet is lodged in my breast. Just here. An acorn-shaped jewel. I wear it, a heaviness that weights me unnaturally. An awkwardness, like a fishbone at the back of the throat. A tiny fleck of grit under an eyelid. A mineral speck.

Even cut-out rocks can speak. They speak in colours. You have to know how to turn them, just so, until you can see it. The gleam.

They speak in light. Perhaps I can too.

To her.

A yellowy shimmer on the long wall opposite the door. Growing brighter. Maybe the moon was coming in.

Or a man.

He stood just inside the doorway, blowing on his hands and stamping his feet on the stone, a torch as big as a rugby ball under his elbow. 'Christ on a bike, it's cold up here at night, eh? My fingers are falling off.' His voice was slightly too high and loud for the room. He flung his fingers downwards before blowing on them again. 'All right, fellas?'

He definitely didn't seem like the man in the moon. He was in his early thirties and had a shaved head apart from a wide stripe of hair a centimetre long in the middle. Quite short and probably pretty keen on the beers. I had just put my hips back down on the bed after pulling my shorts up. Becca had shuffled into the corner and was squeezing the wax of a candle between her fingers.

Fraser stood in the middle of the room, his hands in his pockets. 'All right, mate.' I could sense all of us wondering the same thing. 'Have you walked here, then?'

The man was looking about. 'Aye, 'course. Nice set-up you got.' His eyes grazed over the fire, up to the roof and, I swear, from my crotch down to my ankles.

Fraser had said something about the rules being that anyone could come in and you had to all bunk up together, but he hadn't suggested for one minute that someone would actually come.

He didn't look much like a walker. They all had Gore-Tex and super-grips and breathable hoods and toggles. This guy was wearing shiny grey tracksuit bottoms with electric blue piping, white trainers and, I could see as he unzipped his jacket, a matching tracksuit top. No rucksack or anything.

'You weans having a party up here, then, eh?' Most of his vowels were turned inside out, a proper Glaswegian. He sat down and leant his elbows behind him on the table. Becca moved away from him to the furthest end of the bench.

'Just hanging out,' said Fraser. He was standing tall, being the grown-up among us.

'Nice one, fella, nice one.' He looked at me again. And at Becca.

I slid the sleeping bag over my knees. The pill was making my brain tick. There was an uncomfortable silence, apart from the spattering fire, and Becca, scuffing her toe on the stone.

The man huffed loudly and stretched.

'Do you want a drink?' asked Fraser. 'We've got beer and vodka.'

Shifting forward, the guy lightly pounded one palm into the knuckles of his other hand. 'Naw, man. I'm off the cheeky stuff. Just tea for me these days. Red, green and white. My personal trainer's put me on it. Got any hot water?' He rose abruptly and looked in the cupboard by the fire. 'Oh aye, I'll boil some up.' Pulling out an old-fashioned black kettle, he took some of our bottled water and glugged it in, before hooking the kettle on the pole above the fire and standing watching it. 'Like being in the Middle Ages or something, no?'

The strip of his hair went all the way down to the base of his neck and was flecked with grey. A sort of toilet-brush Mohican. He didn't seem to have the slightest idea that he might not be particularly welcome. Or maybe he just didn't care – it was hard to tell. He came over and shook Fraser's hand and mine and told us his name was Rocky. Maybe it was the raccoon look he had going on.

He craned his neck down at Becca, whose hair was hanging in front of her face. 'You OK under there, sweet cheeks?'

Becca continued to give the floor utter evils, her finger in the wax.

He wandered round, looking at the very little there was in the room. Finn was still sound asleep in the corner, one knee up against his face.

Rocky picked up Finn's phone and started scrolling through it. 'Got any Tamla Motown?'

Fraser glanced at me, very quickly, with a derogatory grin. 'Don't think so.'

'Shame, that. Best music there is, that and a wee bit of Northern Soul, maybe.' He caught me biting my lip at Fraser. 'Come on, you're not telling me you don't like some of that. Gladys Knight, Diana Ross. Smokey Robinson.'

'No, there's nothing wrong with any of them,' I said. 'We're just into more – they're just a bit old-fashioned.'

'Old-fashioned my arse. It's a fucking sight better than this shite.' He sounded sharper, just for a second, before he spoke brightly and high again. 'Kids these days, eh, you don't know what's good music, all this bleepy buzz-buzz crap, it's got no soul.'

'I guess we're just different, then. I'm sure some – kids are into it.' I spoke in my best soapy water voice.

Rocky muttered something. Using a filthy tea towel, he picked up the kettle from the fire and set it down on the table, gently hooting and shaking his palm out. 'Naw, it's fine, I'm just jeebin' you.' He took a mug from the cupboard and slipped his fingers into an inside pocket of his jacket, his voice calm and easy again. 'You just don't have proper basslines, harmonies, I don't know, it's like all the stomach's been taken out of it.' He carefully opened out a crushed square of tin foil and held up a tea bag by its edge. 'It's what tribes in Africa drink. Cracking stuff. Good for your insides.'

That accent. Like the words had been knocked about with a spade on the way out.

We stayed in our positions, looking at the fire or the floor. Fraser in the middle of the room, standing. Me sitting on the bed with the sleeping bag over my legs. Becca as close to the end of the bench as she could be without falling off. A tune with aerosol-can sound effects was rattling tinnily and slightly too loudly, the cartoonish rapping beginning to sound idiotic. The party had died on its arse. A popped balloon, limp plastic going everywhere.

Rocky slurped his tea and sat back. 'What are yous lot on, then?'

Fraser made a bad attempt at looking completely blank. 'How do you mean?'

'Come on, you're not just on the bevvies.' He looked round at us all. 'You're blazing away, especially this one.' He leant over to pinch Becca on the arm and she flinched, darting out of his reach.

Fraser knelt down in front of the fire. Rocky fixed his eyes on me and I stared back. There was a small dark patch, a bruise or a birthmark or something, on one of his cheekbones. How the hell were we going to spend the entire night with him here? It was just embarrassing.

He suddenly spoke more loudly to the corner. 'All right, pal?'

Finn had woken up and was just beginning to uncrumple himself from the chair, rubbing his eye with a knuckle. He looked at Rocky, confused, his cheeks bright red. 'Hello.' He looked at his sister, and at me, and at Fraser.

'Pills, then? Got any cheeba on you? You can't leave me all sober on my own. Come on.' His *own* and *on* sounded the same and were both dragged out, as if he was talking to a bunch of toddlers.

99

'Peps,' said Fraser quite quietly, his head only half turned, pissed off.

'Nice, nice,' Rocky nodded. There was a pause. Fraser didn't move. He didn't have any left. And I sure as hell wasn't giving my weed up.

'You can have mine,' Finn said, getting up and reaching into the pocket of his jeans. He looked at me guiltily. 'I didn't have it yet.'

'Very generous, pal, very generous.' Rocky took the pill from him and held it up to the fire. 'Haven't seen one of these in a bit of time. These spare ones, then, Fraser?'

For a second I didn't quite realise what had happened, but I knew that something had. Fraser, still fiddling with the firelighters, seemed to go stiff. He stood up very slowly with the tongs in his hand and turned to look at Rocky. And then I realised. He'd never told Rocky his name. None of us had.

The fire seemed to shrink very quickly and draw all of the sounds in the room in towards it. Rocky was looking at Fraser totally casually, as if nothing had happened.

'How ...' Fraser didn't finish his sentence, taking one swallow and opening his mouth. The dry click in his throat was like a tiny piece of wood snapping.

'There you go, pal,' said Rocky, putting his cup down on the bench beside him and interlocking his fingers over his belly. 'You getting there? You cottoning on?'

What the hell was happening? He – he *knew* him. Fraser was beginning to look pale.

Becca had stopped scuffing her feet. Her finger was pressing very slowly into a bit of molten wax that had pooled on the table around the bottom of the wine bottle.

'You and me have a mutual friend,' said Rocky. 'Though he's definitely more my friend than yours right now. Know who I'm talking about?'

Finn, Becca and I looked at Fraser. Fraser nodded.

'You owe Badger some money.' Rocky had a neutral, almost placid expression on his face.

Fraser's shoulders sagged very slowly. 'Yeah. Yeah, I know, I'm sorry, I messed up a bit on the outgoings.'

'Sorry doesn't cut it, big man. You're three days late and that's three days too many. Badger doesn't do debts.'

Fraser was swallowing again, several times. 'Yeah. I know. I'm sorry.'

'You don't know, otherwise you wouldn't have done it, would you?' Fraser didn't say anything. Rocky rubbed a palm on the top of his scrubby hair, back and forth. 'What are you, economics student?'

'Engineering.'

'You do a bit of maths in there, I bet.'

Fraser nodded again.

'To be honest pal, I don't even have my Standard and I could fuck up the numbers less easily than you've done. I'm not sure I believe that story. I think you've been keeping a wee bit of dollar-dollar back for yourself, maybe for this one.' He nodded at me. 'Don't blame you for being a bit fanny-struck, she's quite fit, but all the dosh in the world's not going to do you any good if you're floating somewhere down the loch, is it?'

I sucked in a breath. He couldn't be – this was – my heart was jump-starting.

Fraser put his hand out, brought it back and covered his ear, and put it out again. 'OK, now look man, I'm really sorry, I just – made a mistake, honest.'

Rocky stroked the stubble on his chin. 'I'm just saying, pal, if you owe my man money, what happens is this. He gets very, very annoyed, and he calls me up, and he sends me to find you, and I go trailing round the city looking for you, and coming up here on the fucking train with the hill-bunnies, and getting the fucking minibus which goes once every two days, till I get to the bar from *The* fucking *Shining* and find out where you're off to, and you know what? It's a lot of bloody effort for a wee shite like you and the scrap of cash you owe him, so I'm thinking it might just be best to knock this one on the head, because I'm not coming all the way up here again like a fucking charity rambler.'

Suddenly Becca was in the middle of the room, darting in front of him, almost dancing on the spot. 'Fuck off! Fuck off!' She made a jerking movement, like a featherweight boxer might do.

Rocky didn't move a muscle from his position on the bench, eyeing her curiously. 'All right lassie, no need to be like that, hen.'

She jumped forward again, shrieking. 'Just go away!'

His hands remained clasped in front of him. 'It's just banter, just business talk.'

'Becca,' I said, trying to sound extremely calm.

There was a small whimper from Finn in the corner.

Either she hadn't heard me, or my saying her name made it worse. Becca leapt towards Rocky, stretching past him to the other wine bottle and candle. In one quick movement, she had grabbed the neck of the bottle and was tipping it upside down, taking a step back, her elbow up, and aiming for his head.

Too late. Rocky's movements were light and deft for such a bullish-looking man. He stood, reaching behind his back.

There was something in his hand – he grabbed Becca by her other arm, elbowing the bottle out of her grip, and held it near her head.

A gun. A small one, but a gun. The wine bottle rolled along the floor and got caught at the end of the bench. The candle had gone out.

Rocky tipped the back of the hand that was holding Becca towards him. 'You got wax on me there, hen. That stings.' A splodge of white shone above one knuckle.

Becca had gone rigid and was breathing through her nose very heavily, like a horse. Wax had caught on her sleeve, a long dribble of it. Fraser had hardly moved the whole time.

'Let's just calm the fuck down,' said Rocky. 'All right?' He thrust his head down at Becca. She gave a tiny, very tight nod. 'All right?' he said to me. I'd stood up when Becca had moved.

'Yeah, yeah, definitely.' I tried to think what hostage mediators did in films. I couldn't think of any films. Ever.

'OK, now I'm just going to sit down again and hold onto you, you little daftie.' He sounded like a surgeon, going through the incisions he was going to make. They sat down side by side on the bench with aching slowness, Rocky's fingers still gripping Becca's elbow, his gun still pointing at her neck. 'And turn that shite off, will you? I can't concentrate with that fucking tin-can bollocks going on.'

I went to Finn's phone. My hand didn't look like my own. Someone else's forefinger was swiping through, pressing stop. The music was sliced off in the middle of a word.

'Please don't kill my sister,' said Finn in a very small voice.

'I wouldn't be thinking about killing anyone if this numptie hadn't tried to do one over on the boss. Fucking eejit.'

'It won't happen again,' said Fraser.

'It won't happen again, no. It won't happen again because you're going to go to Glasgow tomorrow and pay Badger like you were supposed to three days ago, and I'm never going to see your spotty-arsed face again, am I?'

'No,' said Fraser very quietly. The tongs still dangled from his fingers.

'What?'

'No.'

Rocky looked around at us all. 'What have you got on you?' No one spoke. He pointed his gun at Finn. 'You. What you got? Cash? Pills?'

'Um. Nothing. Just what I gave you. I didn't bring anything, apart from my speakers and my sleeping bag, and some crisps, 'cause I don't drink that much but I get hungry, and my ma says—'

'OK, pal, don't need your life story. You—'

I saw the barrel. The barrel of the gun he was holding. 'I've got – I've only got twenty quid on me. You can have it.'

'Naw, somebody's been smoking puff in here.' He pointed the gun towards my bag. 'What's in there?'

It wasn't the time to be disagreeing with him. I knelt down, fished out the mint tin and handed it over. He put his arm around Becca, swapping the gun to his other hand. It hung idly down by her shoulder. He flicked the lid open with his thumb and held it to his nose, then closed it, manoeuvring it into his trouser pocket.

Rocky looked at my knees and my belt and my breasts. 'Maybe I should just have a sooky off you and all.' He squeezed Becca in towards him. Her hair completely covered her face. 'Be better off with the one who didn't try to bleach me, eh?' he said to her.

My mouth dried up and I looked carefully at Fraser. His eyes had widened ever so slightly.

No one said anything.

Rocky sighed. 'Give us your twenty, then.'

He made Finn pass him Becca's bag so that he could rummage through it and Fraser got his wallet out. Like we were sorting out a bill after dinner.

'Right.' Rocky stood up, finally letting go of Becca, and put the gun into his waistband at the base of his back. He eyed us all, shaking his head. 'You fucking kids, man.' He came and stood in front of Fraser, chest to chest. 'What are you gonna do?'

'Pay Badger tomorrow.'

'First thing?'

'Yeah.'

Rocky remained looking at him.

'First thing tomorrow,' said Fraser, his eyes somewhere past Rocky's shoulder.

'You'd better.'

There was a moment's pause and then Rocky's head went back a couple of inches and he lunged forwards, both hands on Fraser's shoulders as he smashed his forehead into his face. Fraser staggered and fell onto the floor, the tongs clattering away from him.

'Fucking amateur.' Rocky picked up his jacket and his torch and drained the last of his tea. He stalked out, leaving the door open.

No one moved. Finn had disappeared into the chair cushions. Fraser sat on the floor with his elbow on his knee, one palm covering most of his cheek, and Becca was standing by the bench giving little involuntary shudders.

After five minutes or so I shut the door, not daring to look outside, and sat down on the bed again. The fire hiccupped.

'You're a dick,' I said quietly.

A weird mewling sound, like a wet kitten, coming from Becca. Finn went and sat her down on the bench and put his arm round her.

Fraser just looked at me vacantly. Maybe he was in shock. 'Polly.'

'You just let him do all that.'

'He had a gun.'

'You knew someone with a gun.'

'I didn't know him. I've never met him. I don't know any of the big—'

'Don't. Don't even try.'

'It was just some low-level stuff up here, it was supposed to be—'

Two stones sparked together in my stomach. '*Low level?* That was low level? Being threatened with a gun, Becca almost having her brains blown out, he bloody – *fuck* – he was talking about making me or Becca ... and you just *stood* there.' I stood up with a rush, and the whole room almost flipped upside down. 'You are so unbelievably shit.'

'I'm not – *he* was—'

'*You* were. You. You're the one at fault. How do you not see that? You're disgusting.' I stood up and shoved my arms into my jacket.

'What are you doing? He might still be out there somewhere.'

'I don't care.' I didn't look at him.

'Polly, it's dark, don't be stupid—'

'Fuck off, Fraser.' I grabbed my bag and Fraser's little torch and left.

*

Gogogo. I didn't know where I was going. Just that I *was*. As far away as I could, as quickly as I could, away from there. I was shaking and there was something snagged in my throat, bubbling up.

'*Polly!*' Fraser's voice tore through the air.

'Fuck *off*!' My words sounded ridiculous out here, a gash in the hills.

I began to run.

6

The light swung. The path appeared and disappeared. Around my feet, the grass was spiky, vicious. Night was everywhere, great big punches of blackness being thrown at me, and stones on the path appeared high-focus and terrifying. After a while I stopped and looked back, shining the torch downwards. I could still see the stamp of light from the bothy's one window.

Mountains and darkness and me. My breath was loud and coming apart. Not a single other sound. Any second now, something was going to loom up and grab my jaw and rip at my face and stick its tongue into the gaping hole of my throat and chew on my guts and—

An orange light. Blinking. I'd thought that I had to go further up and head left, but that looked like a road over to my right, a long way off. A forestry vehicle, or an AA van maybe. Ahead, a path came off the main one. We must have come from there, before. I swerved, walked in the direction of the little light. Ran again.

The path got narrower. Zigzagged. Didn't feel quite right. I backtracked and went in the other direction. That dwindled to nothing too, the grass getting higher and higher. Shit. I shone the torch on my footprints and went back, veered a different way. I started to sing to myself. *She's up all night till the sun, I'm up all night to get some ...* Breathy, quiet, the words sliced up. I stopped again, looked. Three stamped-down paths, and none a proper one. Fuck. I was making my own maze.

I made myself turn around, one slow, full circle on the spot. The sky was less heavy than the hills, rinsed just once. And there—

A pale light, not orange, bobbing like it was on a string. Far away on the hillside. Another torch. If I could see it, then it could see me.

I didn't care about the path any more. I took off, straight ahead, through the grass.

Each bootstep made a horrible, slurping sound. A moorland flesh-eater. I aimed for the higher mounds of grass, but my foot kept going straight down into mud. Water seeped into my heels. If I dared to glance behind me there was the light, bouncing along. It was him. Rocky. He'd waited out in the dark. And now he was trailing me. I mean, how had he got all the way up here on his own anyway? He wasn't a normal human. He had powers.

The bothy was long gone, sunk into the mud. Once or twice the light – always just behind me, right up on the horizon – seemed bigger, and high in the sky. A second moon. Or it was down in the grass again, smaller, much closer, like a lost firefly. Following me. Or I was following it. Maybe it wasn't a torch. I didn't trust my eyes any longer. Cold, spongy air filled my mouth. My lower legs were soaked.

Something sharp on my shin. I let out a scream that somehow had no sound before realising that I'd walked into a boulder. God. I was so lost, and freezing. Tears came, finally.

Somehow, it was less scary with the torch off. I could see the backs of the hills, just, and stars, blurred by clouds in places. *We've ... come too far ... to give up ... who we are.* My pulse was pumping in my fingers, my lips. I would stay here, just for a bit, in the dark. On this stone. No one would know I was here, so no one would come. Still as a stone, like the one I'd found on the loch beach. Upright, and not supposed to be there.

I thought of the Spanish guy again, lying in an East London hospital bed, Homerton, or the one in Whitechapel – I'd looked them up. What was it like, being in a coma? Was your brain a stone, or your whole body? Noise crashing around you like a tide.

Still as a stone. Me, and him.

There was a buzzing in my ears, like tissue paper in a draught.

If Rocky came then he came. I'd just have to take it. This would be payback.

The night was assuming the blackest of blue tinges, as if the horizon were a lid being lifted. The stars were tiny and amber, a skyful of blinking car lights. The road was up there. I was the wrong way up. My breath stuttered.

Slowly, I began to tell the clouds apart from the hills. The strange, bobbing light was to my right, very faint. It had stopped when I stopped. Like it was waiting. But I couldn't see anything that went with it, the dark line you'd expect if someone were standing there. Maybe he was lying down, holding the torch up.

Colours appeared. The intensely bottle-green trees, and the silver sky. Pale Dawn Relief. Not-Dead Green. Light began to emerge between things, too, between the knee-length blades of grass, the fine-toothed top of the forest. Beads of dew on the branches of the single bush next to my boulder, a well of light curving in the bottom of each drop. There was the low, woody rattle of a bird and I wanted to track it down and hug it to death.

Light between things, but no longer over *there*. It had gone. Faded completely, along with most of the stars.

There was something else too, newly defined by the dawn, right down at the bottom of the hill. A small, dark square. I had thought it to be a large rock but now it looked too perfectly angled. A cardboard box.

Or a house.

The last star was smothered by a mink-grey cloud. My fingers were part stone, my legs raw with cold. God, I was thirsty.

I began walking towards the half-light.

Maybe it was another bothy. There was a dull gleam – the roof of a car. No, a jeep. I stumbled down towards it, feeling a fresh wash of fear. There was something creepier about the possibility of it being inhabited than abandoned.

The darkness seemed to be peeling away from the house. It was small, single-level, with a corrugated iron roof that made me think of war shelters, and a chimney at one end. Two wooden sheds a little way off. In front was a thin river choked with rocks. It came down from the hill to the side and curved away on the flat, bending out of sight.

Pieces of plastic tubing, spiralled wire and iron bars were scattered around, alongside stacked-up bricks and an upended wheelbarrow. Something that looked like a speed-boat engine was up against the back wall, with a pipe snaking from it.

Rough tyre grooves in the grass by the jeep ran up the hill, parallel to the river. I could just follow the track. It would have to lead to a road. I shut my eyes, put my face in the air. Prayers of thanks to every god ever.

By the side of the house, beer bottles were lined up and filled with rainwater, shallow at first and almost full by the last one. The walls were made of jumbled stones, some big slabs, some slim and slotted in at all angles.

Who *lived* here? God, maybe it was Rocky – no, he'd come from Glasgow, and had sounded as if he'd sooner jam his own gun down his own throat than hang around here. I moved a little closer, squelching. I'd ruined my boots. There was a pair of jeans draped over a plank of wood leaning next to the front door, which had green paint curling up at the bottom. Heavy curtains piled up against the two small windows, with one tiny gap. I took a peek. It was dead early still.

'There's not much to steal, you know.'

I whipped round, grazing my palm on the stone sill. A man was walking towards me, the dawn light behind him, hands jammed in his pockets, a woolly navy-blue hat down to his ears. I'd walked from one stupid thriller into another. Probably a slasher movie. Oh God.

'I'm sorry – no, I'm not trying to ...' I straightened up, my voice high and tight, backing into the wall. 'I'm really sorry. I'm totally lost.'

'Aye, you must be.' He stopped a couple of metres from me. It was the man who'd found Tyger. Birdkiller. Fuckfuckfuck. He scratched the back of his neck, a rasping sound louder than it should have been. 'It's normally quite hard for people to find this place.' He lifted his chin slightly and looked along his nose at me, one eye crumpling up.

I shifted my weight to my other leg and sneaked a look at my grazed palm. There were two little lines of raised, pale skin below my thumb.

'What are you up to out here, then?' he said.

Past him, the hills were moving like low, migrating animals. 'I was at a bothy, up – quite a way up there. With some people. There was, like – there was a party. Sort of.' My voice didn't quite sound like mine. I looked back at him. 'It went a bit wrong. There was a guy and he came in from nowhere, I don't know how he could have known, but then he was just *there*, and it got messy and he had, I know it sounds stupid, but he had a gun, a small gun, but a *real* one, or at least we all just assumed it was a real one, I mean you didn't really want to ask and he was really, really scary and – God, I thought we were all going to get *shot*, and—' I gulped a big, notched breath.

He was eyeing me quietly, patiently, like I was reading him the bus timetable. 'Do you want a cup of tea?'

The words tripped out of him so lightly, all consonants – the skimming stones on the loch. Nausea was starting to hover uncertainly in my chest. I squinted up at him from under my fringe. He probably wasn't going to rape me and stab me to death. I was so fucking cold. I nodded.

He walked past me and opened the door. 'Come on, then.'

It was a house with an identity crisis. One large room, stuff everywhere. Nothing seemed to quite fit or hold together.

The floor was just concrete with some rugs chucked about. A fireplace was roughly made with three thick pieces of blackened wood, maybe old railway sleepers. There were matchboxes stacked like Jenga pieces on top. Books were piled up on the floor on one side and logs on the other. A bag of coal.

There was a bed on a wooden mezzanine at one end, high in the eaves of the roof. A thin metal ladder rested against the wall next to it, and a couple of lanterns hung underneath.

I loitered at the door while the man busied himself at the kitchen end, his back to me. Shelves were crammed full. Bottles of spirits. Jars of screws and nails. Vinegar and ketchup and tins. Stained pans. And more books, shoved into any space left. There was a rusty-looking oven on legs, a table and a stone sink with a crack in it.

'Do you ... Do you live here?' I was shivering.

He was getting teabags from a box and his arm stiffened slightly, before taking two out. 'Aye.' The word was rigid.

'No, I just mean – I didn't know if maybe you just stayed here sometimes, that you had somewhere else ...' God, I sounded ridiculous.

He turned round and leant his palms on the sink behind him. 'This is it.'

I'd normally say that it was *nice*, that I liked the curtains, the twisted wire picture frame that held a photo of my mate's toothy baby cousins, but – I came in properly and looked around for something.

'I like your rug. Yeah, your rug's nice.' A sheepskin – you saw them in all the village shops here – ancient-looking, like it had come off the back of a really raggedy, pissed-off old sheep.

He looked at me, surprised, and like I was an idiot, and nodded. He handed me a chipped brown mug, the same colour as the tea he'd made.

There was a chair that seemed to have been assembled from an old bench. Its back was fashioned from criss-crossing rope, strung on the frame like an Inuit snowshoe. The seat cushion was a blanket, folded up.

I sat down on it. Queasiness swirled in the base of my throat. 'Do you have any sugar?'

He picked up a dirty, crinkled bag from one of the slatted shelves below the sink and passed it to me, along with a dessert spoon. God, he didn't say much. I dumped a glen's worth into my cup, trying to stop myself shaking.

A family of cacti stood on the table like a bristly version of the three bears. The little lumpen baby was set low in the pot, covered in fine white spines as if spritzed with frost. The big fat daddy had a ridged back sprouting dark orange spikes. And the rubbery middle-sized one had two furry eyes, which were getting bigger and glaring at me.

They were definitely glaring at me.

'Um, excuse me?'

My mouth was a peat bog. I had my face in a pillow.

'You need to wake up, I think.' I opened my eyes to find him standing on the ladder, looking at me.

His bed. I was lying on his bed and had kicked the covers into bunches. And was sweating like mad.

'Oh my God.' I dragged my head up and wiped the saliva at the side of my mouth. 'I'm really sorry.' My brain felt like the underside of that sheepskin, stretched from ear to ear. 'I don't know how I—'

'You just went out. Cold.'

Had he *carried* me up here? I put a palm flat on the bed and sat up. The roof was really close to my head. I could feel groovemarks in my cheek, as if Benji had driven one of his old toy cars up and down my face. I'd left mud streaks from my boots on the covers.

He rested an elbow on the side of the bed and then removed it. 'You just stood up, and climbed up here, and ...' he looked at me simply. 'It's been a couple of hours.'

I scrunched a fistful of my fringe. Jesus.

He was looking at my wrist. 'Did someone hurt you?'

I didn't have time to pull my sleeve back over the cuts. 'No.'

'What's that, then?'

I scratched the skin above my lip. 'A bear?' I blinked at him, hoping that I looked faintly adorable. 'Do you get bears in Scotland?'

He didn't smile back, staring at me, hard, and chewing the inside of his cheek.

I flipped my eyes to the wall, to the bed, my neck beginning to burn up.

'Don't do that to yourself,' he said.

Time to go. I began to shunt over the bed towards him. He disappeared and I completely ungracefully clambered down the ladder, nearly falling off it. My head swam. The walls were angling in, tilting from the top.

'Thanks for the tea.' The words sounded far away.

He stood in the middle of the room, scratching the back of his head. 'You're all right.'

I looked up at the bed, which seemed to be tilting towards me too, turned around in a full circle, like Tyger after his tail, and spotted the door.

'Do you know where you're going?'

'I'll just follow your tracks to the road.' My fingers found the doorframe, but the handle seemed to have disappeared.

'Do you know what road it is?' His voice was getting fainter.

I put my face to the wall. It was a beautiful cool stone. It was Lottie's hand. I rolled my forehead against it.

'It's a few miles, you know.' A soft jingle. 'I'll take you.'

*

The jeep smelled musty, like wet dog. *Dead* dog. It was the sort of battered, bashed-in thing you'd take on a low-budget Kenyan wildlife tour and was spattered with mud up to the windows. It had no proper back seat. There were insects mashed up on the windscreen, collecting at the bottom like flotsam after a storm. My stomach was starting to feel really, really violent. It was boiling. Eyafjallawhatsit. The track made us jerk, limp as rag dolls, not that he seemed to notice. He kept glancing over at me. Well, don't bloody *talk* then. What was he, a monk? I opened my mouth to speak, and—

He stopped just in time. I was sick from my seat, belt still on, half hanging out of the door. That awful sound, like someone discovering their voice for the first time. I unclicked my seatbelt and staggered down, wiping my eyes and my mouth with the back of my hand.

The hills were sludgy and rippling. I did it again, punched in the gut. God, this was so completely morti-fying. I was a semi-conscious vom-machine. The least sexy thing in Scotland. I spat out the last of it, a thread of liquid spooling away from the corner of my mouth, pulled by the wind.

He was still sitting there, his hands on the steering wheel. I got back in. I couldn't think of a single thing to say that would make it any better, so just swallowed, a thin burn

coiling looped patterns at the back of my throat. Ginger and
tea and vileness. He started the ignition again.

Our house looked like the safest place in the world, soft and
warm and nestled among the palm trees. He'd blinked once,
hard, when I told him the name of the cottage, before
nodding.

The handbrake made a sound like Dad clicking his neck.

I stared at the windscreen. 'I'm really sorry.'

He gazed at the driveway and gave an almost imperceptible
shake of his head.

'Thanks.' I put my fingers on the door handle.

He nodded. 'Mind how you go.'

My legs had turned into rickety wooden stilts. I felt the
pocket of my jacket, crushing only material and tissues. No
keys. Bollocks. I knocked on the door.

As Lottie opened it, her eyes widened slightly. 'God, Polly,
what have you done to yourself?'

The jeep revved and drove away.

I pushed past her. 'Just – don't. Not now.'

A light like cymbals smashing together right in front of my
face. I got up, my skin itching. Bathroom.

Dried spit, or sick, or both, lay in a diagonal trail across
my cheek. My eyes were bloodshot and scummy. Mascara
everywhere. A living, semi-breathing Jackson Pollock.
Jackson Polly. I hung over the sink for a while. Nothing
more came, although if I could have retched shame I would
have.

Lottie turned round from her baking when I leant against
the kitchen doorframe. 'Better?' Her hands were covered in a
gooey mixture.

118

I nodded and swallowed dryly.

She looked at me as if I was a recipe she was disagreeing with. 'How was the party?'

'It was …' I went over to her and scooped a finger of gunk from the bowl. 'Interesting. Yeah. Are you making flapjacks?'

'Well, if you're not going to make us anything then I will do my worst.'

'Needs more honey,' I said and lurched back to my bedroom.

Lottie shouted after me. 'I'm glad you enjoyed yourself.'

Every time I thought of being out there in the dark, that bobbing light following me, I burrowed further under the duvet, the inside of my own hill, smelling of old earth and mulched sheep bones. I never wanted to see another light, or another hill.

My phone buzzed. I dragged it under the covers, opened my eyes just enough.

Fraser. *U ok? x*

Now he was asking. Not when there was a man threatening to mouth-rape me. What had happened up there hadn't quite seemed real until now, until this message. A fucking kiss on there, too. I saw Rocky headbutt Fraser again. He deserved it.

They weren't my friends. Not Fraser, or Finn, and not Becca. I didn't have any friends – not my housemates, who would probably never talk to me again, not even Stef, five hundred miles away in his own orbit, crowd-surfing above a load of shaved heads and shaved chests, his head arched back, yelling blissfully, trying to forget what we did.

I let myself suffocate.

Those underground jewels. Names that spark off the tongue, like faraway places. Zeolite. Aragonite. Galena. All just water and air, and yet each one different.

Woodruffite, with its charred look and firecrackle glaze. Brewsterite, the colour of clover honey. The long ice-shards of Strontianite, dirtier grains clumped on top like old sugar, my colours. I always liked white and now it's all I am.

My uncle once put a block of harmotome into my palm, cut out from the dark. It was the width of my finger and had the shine of raw silk. Sharp enough to nick, to tear, just. A twinned crystal, he said.

I always wanted to find one of my own. I searched and searched. A twinned one is special, morphing to become more stable, to survive. Sometimes the crystals pass through each other, symmetrical, like two dancers.

Like this girl, the one living in the house I once lived in. I see her and she sees me, though she doesn't know it yet.

I will make her see.

Lottie made me go for a walk. Practically pushed me out the door. The hills looked as hungover as I did, foggy-headed, sick. The village was a cobwebby drizzle. I sat in the cafe, using their wifi on my phone, trying and failing to drink a mocha. The place smelled of fried bacon and cheese scones, which almost made me puke again. Kids were running around in wellies, shouting. The clink of cutlery from the woman two tables down was like being stabbed in the ears. I read for about five minutes, my chin on my hands, the words too close. Every single one hurt my brain.

Another message. *U get home ok? x*

As casual as if he'd waved goodbye to me at a bus stop.

Through the window the sun was making the wet road spark. I went out to the playground on the green outside the cafe and dumped myself on a swing, my headphones on. Closed my eyes and let a new electronica band I'd found throb out, dry, sullen beats.

When I opened my eyes again there was a little girl standing in front of me. The girl whose back garden I'd climbed into. She was wearing a T-shirt that said DINOSAURS AREN'T JUST FOR CHRISTMAS with a cartoon of a dopey brontosaurus on one shoulder. Her eyes were as wide as a manga heroine's.

I dug my toes into the mud and put my headphones around my neck. 'What?'

She just looked at me, put her hand on the swing frame and moved the woodchips around with her Day-Glo trainer. A boy with a big bandage round his head was hauling at the roundabout behind her.

I nodded to the other swing. 'Don't mind me.'

Her hair was almost white, her eyebrows the same, something from a fantasy novel. A tiny wise ancient girl. She walked

121

slowly to the neighbouring swing, giving me a wide berth as if I were contagious or might detonate, and carefully, after a couple of goes, edged her bottom onto it. She sat very still.

'You have to move your legs, you know,' I told her.

The boy came charging up and stopped dead in front of me. His cheeks were purple and mad tufts of hair spiked upward in the centre of the bandage. I thought of the cacti in the birdman's house.

'Who are you?' he said, king of his territory.

'Polly.' I smiled at the girl.

'Polly who?'

Precocious little shit. I narrowed my eyes at him. 'Polly Eats Kids Who Are Too Nosy.'

He frowned. 'I don't like her,' he said to the girl.

I don't like me either, I thought.

He pulled violently on the chain of the girl's swing. 'I want a go.'

'No.' I sighed and yanked myself up. 'Use this one.'

Her brother kicked off furiously, making whooshing noises, and I pulled back the chains on the girl's swing. She gripped on tightly as she floated forward, the breeze lifting her hair up, white wings.

'You don't say much, do you?' I said.

Someone was coming over the road, their arms folded. Oh God. Fraser's mum. As she saw me, her pace slowed, just for a second, before she hurried up faster.

'Come on you two peskies, time to get. Your ma will be home now.' She didn't look at me.

I took two steps forward so that the girl came to rest against my thighs and she hopped off obediently. The boy made a noise like someone was driving a drill into his foot, until he saw Fraser's mum's look and slid off, mopey-faced.

'Go on, back to the car. Hands now.' The boy took hold of his sister's wrist and began to stomp off. The girl twisted her head back to me as she was dragged over the grass.

Fraser's mum stayed put, her shoulders hunched, scrutinising me.

'Hello, Jeannie!' I said, with extreme brightness.

Her lips came together. 'You're leading my boy astray.'

If I'd just taken a drink of something I'd have spat it out, sprayed her with it. I looked out onto the loch, trying to suppress a grin, put my head down and scratched the back of my neck. 'I think he's quite capable of leading himself astray.'

'What's that?' Her voice could have mined minerals.

'Nothing.'

The kids were getting further away. 'I don't think you should see him.'

'I'm not seeing him.'

'I'm *telling* you not to.'

'Fine. Whatever.' There was a faint howl. I nodded past her, where the girl was hitting the boy on the arm, over and over. 'Think you need to catch them up.'

Jeannie stalked off, giving me a final glare, a look that wanted to say *I've got you pinned. I know you.* What the hell? Yeah sure, I'm the drunk slut steaming in to deflower the lily-skinned princeling. Jesus.

I went home and ate five flapjacks.

A spatter of sound that might have been distant gunshots. I swore and sat bolt upright.

'It's just me, darling.' Lottie sat on the edge of the bed and put her hand on my forehead. Her voice was soft as a box of baby chicks.

I slowly rolled away from her and pulled the duvet up, lying very still. 'What time is it?'

'It's ten.'

Still light. 'At night?'

'Yes, Polly.' A little huff of breath, slightly exasperated.

'OK. Thanks.'

'Fraser's here.' My skull prickled. 'He's been in the wars a bit.' She sounded intrigued.

'Tell him to go away.'

'Really? Oh, I thought—'

'No. I will.' My knees landed first. I dragged my hoodie across the floor to the door.

He was standing in the hallway, looking at a framed map of the outer islands. When he saw me, he attempted a sort of half smile, half hello. The underside of his left eye had swelled and turned mauve. I pushed him out onto the driveway, shutting the door behind me.

'You didn't reply to my messages,' he said. 'I was really worried.'

I looked past him up to the gate. 'Yeah, thanks.'

'Did you get back OK, then? I – did you walk or something?'

'Yeah. I walked.'

He was nodding, unsure, not really taking it in. I could have told him I'd flown home, risen up and bloody floated here, and he would have done the same nod. 'Right,' he said. 'Wow. I'm glad you got home all right.' He tried another smile.

I wasn't having it. 'You didn't come here first thing though, did you? To check that I was OK?' I had to have a weirdo hermit rescue me.

He looked at me sidelong, guiltily, but also as if part of my brain was missing. 'I had to drive to Glasgow. You know.'

I turned away from him and looked at the light crumbling among the trees. 'Yeah, of course, because that was more important.'

'Polly, you heard what he said.'

I spun back round. 'I can't believe you were even in that shit. How did you not pay your dealer? Isn't that, like, in the beginner's manual or something?'

'I was just using it to – I was behind on my room rent.'

'How did you pay him? Where did you get the money from if you didn't have it before?'

'My brother helped me out. Transferred some.' He sighed. 'So now I owe him.'

'Not your mum, then?'

'No.'

I saw her as she stormed towards me at the swings. Her lower jaw jutting out. 'No, 'cause I bet *she* doesn't know about this, does she?'

He spoke very quietly. 'No, of course not.'

'Maybe someone should tell her.' Her golden boy, backhanding the West Highlands with all their supplementary needs.

He put a hand out towards my arm. 'Come on.' There was the faintest note of panic in his voice, though he tried to hide it.

I took one step away from him. 'You can go now.'

When he didn't, I left him standing on the mat, and shut the door very precisely in his stupid, bruised face.

7

The orchid was blooming again.

I'd watered the plasticky stalks and had woken up to find two of the buds had burst, their petals like Marilyn Monroe's skirts in that old photo. They had a whisper of a smell, something delicate and translucent, and were cool on my cheek and lips. The smaller set of petals on each flower had three jagged, deep crimson lines on each side. I held my wrist up to them. Three lines, deep crimson.

Lottie, trying to smooth the annoyance out of her voice, insisted I get a new house key. The nearest locksmith: twenty-four miles away, obviously. This was not the kind of place you could get a kebab at three in the morning, or only wait ten minutes for a taxi to anywhere you wanted. A gun in the face, midge-attack, or avian open-heart surgery, on the other hand.

We got the bus–ferry–bus to Fort William, had a new key cut, and did the sights, all one and a half of them. I watched Lottie try on oversized woollen items and drank lots of coffee. My insides hadn't quite recovered from the bothy yet. I swear it wasn't just Fraser's little pick-me-up. I kept seeing Rocky's gun lolling at Becca's shoulder, and his look when he'd said that word I hadn't heard before.

God knows how long I would have been stuck out there, lost and freezing and with all the bits of my brain slowly drifting apart like icebergs, if I hadn't found that guy's place. He'd let me sleep in his bed. I had totally destroyed his covers and he hadn't said anything about it. Maybe I owed him, even if he was unnervingly quiet and had a tendency to eat raw bird. He'd found Tyger, too. I thought of his kitchen table and pulled Lottie into a gardening shop.

We met each other at the counter, Lottie holding some psychedelic primroses she had picked up for Bev and Adam. She looked at the cactus in my hand. One stout, three-sided stem, and a bulbous top. Sort of dark and thorny. Like him.

'To keep the orchid company,' I said.

We got outside and got pelted. The rain couldn't decide which way to go, so it went in all directions at once. Lottie pushed me, near-kicking and screaming, into a camping shop, a living hell of spikes and base layers and socks that go over socks, and stood over me while I clumped around in walking boots that were like the shoes Lego people wear.

'You are buying them,' she said.

'Can't you?' I drummed my nails on the bench. 'I'm a bit brassic.'

'What about your dad's money?'

'You know, rent and travel and stuff.'

She was frowning at me. 'You're not paying rent any more.'

When I'd moved back home my story was that our landlady had terminated our contract early, was selling the place. Rather than that I'd fucked Lena's boyfriend against a chip van after eight too many Jägerbombs. 'Yeah, no, I mean, bills and that. Quite a few are only just coming in. Nightmare.' I gazed earnestly at a rail of multi-coloured cagoules. Yeah.

My relationship with my housemates had pretty much imploded after that.

She took her wallet out, shaking her head. I'd have to tell her at some point. Just – not yet.

*

Operation Cactus-Giving. I dug out an ordnance survey map from a kitchen drawer, the corners teddy bear-soft, and spread it out on the table. It was funny, looking at my soggy stomping ground drawn so precisely. The village was reduced to squares and rectangles, and the roads looked ridiculously dramatic, pink and yellow lines of civilisation cutting through the vast swathes of nothingness.

There were surprises, too. Pools hidden up on higher ground. Remains of a fort. Waterfalls. Cairns. Caves. Settings for a dozen twee fairy tales. Cute names – some in Gaelic, words that probably sounded like you were coughing your phlegmy guts up.

My blood turned to gazpacho when I found the party bothy. It was just a barely there oblong with two meandering dotted lines spinning away from it. I imagined a stick-figure version of Rocky, with a round belly and a tiny L-shape for a gun, hiding behind the little grey swipes on the map that meant rocks, his torch swaying. I still wasn't sure if it had been his torch I'd seen, in the night. What use would it have been to hunt me down? Actually, I didn't want to think about that. Part of me wondered if the light had just been my fevered, über-high imagination.

Those hills. The benign curved lines on the map gave no proper hint of what bastards they were. I couldn't believe I'd walked all over them, in the dark, and not fallen into that looping bit of river or skewered myself on one of those spiny trees. The birdman's place had been somewhere between the bothy and the road, although that left a few gaping miles to choose from. I really had no idea which way I'd gone. This map would have come in bloody useful.

I ran a finger along the road that went from the village, around the side of the loch and into the hills, looking for a turn-off. Nothing. It was strange – even half-arsed paths that you could probably only shuffle down sideways were marked on here. That was probably his river, though, a fluttering thread. Probably. Maybe I'd got it wrong. I had been a fountain of vomit, after all. Or maybe I'd imagined the whole thing and really *had* floated home.

I stuck my thumb out for a ride at the far end of the village. Didn't really feel like asking for a lift from Bev in order to deliver a quite odd present to a definitely odd man. The frostiness in the bar when he'd come in with Tyger – you could practically hear the icicles forming.

Five cars passed before one stopped, three bikes stacked on the roof – a tourist couple and their son, who had the most impressively futuristic-looking braces I'd ever seen. We chatted about the weather – I could easily dash out five-thousand-word essays on *that*, even if I couldn't scratch one together on Charlotte Perkins Gilman and the female utopia – and I attempted to sound super interested in deer sightings while watching the kid deposit a globule of snot from his nose onto the window.

They seemed baffled when I suddenly asked them to dump me miles from anywhere. The massive oak tree we had just passed, with a branch striking one of Stef's super-queeny dance poses, had given me a jolt of familiarity. I waited until they had bumped out of sight before wandering up and down the road, looking for something else to recognise. If a car approached, I looked earnestly up at the sky, the world's least convincing bird-watcher.

By a mile further up, my calves felt like they were on a medieval rack. The new boots were so heavy. My map flapped in the wind, a great big clumsy bird. Then a deep bank of forestry trees, one trailing a loose white ribbon, as I'd seen before. I wondered what that meant. Trees to chop down? Trees to save because they were just too pretty? Didn't people tie ribbons around trees in America for their sweethearts or prisoners coming home or something? Those were yellow ones, though.

In the middle of the long line of trees was a gap. Just enough, maybe, for a jeep to squeeze through, so long as the driver didn't care about it getting scratched by pine needles. There were two dips in the ground running through the trees and small, regular diagonal marks pressed into them. This was it. A track to someone who didn't want to be found.

I looked at the cactus in my hand. I couldn't just go down there, knock on his door, Jehovah's Witness-style. Please accept my thanks in the form of this extremely ugly plant. A megawatt smile. I knelt down and shoved the pot into the mud, right in the middle of the path. On a torn-out blank page from the back of my copy of *The Yellow Wallpaper* I wrote *Thanks (sorry)* and automatically put a kiss on the end, which I crossed out and tried to make into a filled-in square, which looked stupider still, so I drew little triangles around it, and then it looked like a bizarre witchy pentagram symbol. Jesus.

I walked back down the road, giving it the big thumbs-up again, my note left impaled on a few spikes. Yep, classy as hell.

*

130

Boom. One essay tweaked and in, somehow, fuelled by a packet of Jammie Dodgers and three sports drinks that tasted like neon. Liza sent back a curt *Thanks, Polly.* All I deserved, I guess.

I kept thinking about my plucky little cactus, waiting among the trees. He'd either pick it up and crush it to his chest, perhaps weeping a little, or just be extremely befuddled and kick it away. Or maybe he'd not even notice and it would be crushed to bits under his wheels – that was if he ever drove up there again, which was unlikely, seeing as he probably didn't have to cart home dribbling girls too often.

That night, I woke up to find moonlight rimmed around the petals of the orchid. A little movement, like water running down the edges. Ringing. I swore I could hear it. High and pure, someone running their finger around the top of a wet wine glass. Wind in the grass, far away. I felt like I was being tuned, sounding my own note as I lay there, dead still.

It was only in the morning, remembering, that I saw that my curtains were shut.

Water and glass and moonlight.

I sang old songs and new ones, and you said my voice was like water and didn't laugh like those girls always did at school. They called me lame-brain, and though I know I looked it sometimes, I wasn't. The letters just swapped round sometimes when I wrote them, the words turning differently in the light.

Other things sing now. The loch, when twilight comes in. Tree bark, as it grows. My bones.

You brought books and read to me, and didn't mind when I fell asleep after a page. Showed me herbs — cloudberry and vetch and bogbean, which we smoked once, making us wide-eyed and sick. You would carry me around on your back, saying I weighed less than your rifle, less than a bara brith cake, less than feathers.

Feathers.

Everyone knew that my family never had any money. But you made me feel like the shine on a mineral, the dew-gleam on a petal.

They're just jealous, you'd say. Knowing good words is more important than knowing how to spell them. Your words are beautiful. You're beautiful. And you'd pull me on top of you so that my hair would fall into your eyes and your mouth and you'd laugh and say I was snow piling off a mountain, an avalanche in summer.

Snow, falling like feathers. Feathers, falling like snow.

The weekend. I'd bought some more baccy from the garage store. Not really my thing, regular fags, but I needed something to suck on, to sear my insides. Bet Rocky had chomped all that weed by now. I should probably replace it, but the only person who could help was the last person I wanted to talk to. I stoppered my boots into the mud underneath the swings, wondering if that funny little girl might come by again. Though if she did, maybe Jeannie would too, and I would have to karate chop her face off like I should have done last time.

A sound like a baby bear growling. Finn's moped ambled by, and I watched as he did a circuit around the car park by the shop and came back, pulling up in front of me.

'All right, Polls?'

'Hey, Finn.'

He nodded at my hand. 'Give us a go on that.'

He joined me on the swings, kicking his legs out. 'You mad at Fraser?'

'Aren't you?'

He shrugged and took another amateur drag, the roll-up held awkwardly between his third and fourth fingers. I wondered what had happened at the bothy after I'd taken off. Had they snuggled up together all night, a post-showdown slumber party, nice and cosy? Had Becca wailed like a cityful of sirens?

'Good story though, eh?' His face was bright.

'Is that all it is?'

'Not much happens round here. Good to have a tale to tell, you know? Not that they believe me, at school, like.' He looked at me puckishly. 'But then I did say that I broke his kneecaps with one of them drying poles.'

'My hero.' Finn bowed, his ciggie-hand looping in the air. 'You like telling stories, don't you?' He shrugged again. 'You've always got one up your sleeve.' I raised my eyebrows at him. 'Like your many conquests, Mr Lothario.'

'They're all real.' He screwed his nose up at me. 'Some of them.'

'Mmm-hmm.'

He used his legs to spin himself round, the chain choking itself. 'Gran-gran always told good stories, still does. It's probably in my veins or something, like being allergic to stuff, 'cept I'm allergic to dust and cats and that and my da's allergic to eggs. But yeah, she's got a story for every day of the week. She used to make ones up to explain everything too, 'cause I always had questions' – I bet you did, I thought, imagining him trailing behind her on the beach, tugging on her finger until it practically came off – 'I don't know, like about how everything was made and that, and why submarines came so close, and why the barnacles like some rocks but not other rocks and stuff.'

'What were her answers?'

He unwound the swing the other way. 'That the subs weren't here for the war, that was all a cover-up. They were actually looking for mermen, because the real war was down there, under the sea, between land-men and sea-men. And the barnacles are tons of little, like, fannies, and they're all having sex with the sea.'

'Your *gran* told you that?'

'Yeah.'

I threw a woodchip at him. It pinged off his forearm, which was adorned with new biro-drawings of swords and insects with elaborate horns. 'So now you've got a new story.'

'Yeah.' He looked at his phone. 'Ah shit, gotta go.' He held the cigarette towards me.

'Keep it. It's had your scabby mouth on it now.'

Finn straddled his moped, giving me the full cowboy-at-sunset grin, fag hanging from his lips. 'Off to see a girl.' He began walking it over the grass to the flowerbeds, looking like someone who really needed to pee.

I folded my arms. 'Your sister?'

'No, a real girl. Proper one. Gonna see if I can get some naked photos. Taking her up the lochan.' He bent down and yanked out some tulips, bulbs and all.

'Is that what the kids are calling it now?'

He looked puzzled, then shocked, then extremely pleased. He stuffed the stems down the front of his trousers. 'Oh. Yeah. Totally. Later, gorgeous.'

The moped started to roll off and I felt the long day ahead of me. I stood up. 'Finn.'

He looked back.

'Which way are you going?'

I had to hand it to him for generosity. He went several miles in the opposite direction to drop me at the disco oak tree – it seemed wrong, somehow, to give away the birdman's sneaky driveway – shouting at me about the lucky lady who was going to get both those flowers and his tongue shoved in her face, and asking me about the best way to unhook a bra. Cute.

For once the sun was out, a pale, unwashed thing. Some of the grass was yellowing, giving off a dry, slightly sweet smell. I trailed up to the gap in the trees. The white ribbon wasn't there any more. Nor was my cactus. *His* cactus. There was no evidence of the plastic pot having been smashed into the ground. He'd taken it.

I imagined opening the front door of our cottage and finding a thankyou note on the outside mat in return. Sticking

135

out of half a dead pheasant. He knew where I lived, after all. Yeah, that was never going to happen. Was that it, then? He helps me out, I say thanks, he scuttles off to his hole?

Maybe he was lonely. Maybe he'd like a visitor.

I wound through the forest, my music on, the birds adding in some little turntable scratches. Dark pines yielded to a much older group of trees, their needles feathery and pale red, their trunks mottled. Occasional silver-white trees among them looked like shadows, not-quite-real things, as if they might fade if you touched them. After two tunes, the woods gave way to swathes of long, shaggy grass, the ground rising up here and there to show the mud and stone underneath. The hills were far less terrifying in daylight. I wondered where I'd been sick, adding my own contribution to the textured, marshy colours.

In your face, puddles. I could totally take them now in these stupid lumpen boots and splashed through the ones made by the birdman's tyre-tracks, my toes staying completely dry. Puddle after puddle. I was so busy aiming for them that I hardly noticed I'd crested another hill and was nearing his place.

A squat, surly block, giving nothing away. If it could have humphed and crossed its arms, it would have. The ground around it looked worn, like old upholstery. Well, I'd come this far. It felt like I'd been walking for days.

The jeep was there, wonkily parked. The curtains were shut again. Everything had a stillness, as if it were coated in glue. I thought about coughing loudly. Instead I stamped up to the door and hung there for a second.

Maybe he had a wife. A *boyfriend*. A kid who stayed some-times. I knocked. Waited. Thought about knocking again. I put my ear to the cold wood and the door opened and I jerked back, quick as whiplash, trying to look casual.

The guy's face looked like it had not long before been scrunched up into a ball and was only just starting to get back to normal. His eyes were gummy and his thick, dark hair stood up like the grass. He looked at me as if I were much further away than I was.

'All right?' He said it guardedly. Rock salt in his voice.

The words came out higher than normal. 'Yeah. I was just …' Just what? *Passing?* He'd only opened the door to the width of a hand, and it wasn't getting any wider. I pushed my sunglasses up into my hair. 'I thought I'd come and say hello.'

He peered past me into the sun and looked at me in a way I couldn't quite read, like I was a Sudoku puzzle, the hardest type, from *The Times* or something. He probably didn't do Sudoku. Or get *The Times* delivered. Coming here suddenly felt like a very stupid idea.

He took a breath in and held it, still looking at me. 'Give me a sec.'

The door shut and I thought about running away, except he'd still have been able to see me a mile up the track, my legs having turned to wet cement. The clouds were dragging over the hills like a white sheet being snagged, and a single bird, a gull maybe, wheeled underneath them, its wings tipping and turning.

Around the corner, tools lay scattered among tufts of grass. The beer bottles were still there. The one at the end of the row with the least water in gave a dull clang when I nudged it with my toe. I picked up a two-foot-long pipe, bright blue, and gently hit the bottle just below the neck with it. A sound like a bell underwater. The next one along had a slightly lower note. I ran the tube along all of them slowly, letting it bounce on the glass, and it made a little falling pattern.

He was there at the corner of the house, watching me. I tossed the pipe away and tried not to look too sheepish.

Lines appeared in his forehead. 'Did you come here on foot, then?'

I nodded. 'Except—' he followed my eyes up the hill. 'On the track this time. Got a lift to the end of your road.'

He nodded a few too many times and eyed the bottles. There was a faint, muffled sound, a whimper. First of all I thought it was the gull, or maybe a flock of them. But the whimper rose and got louder.

He saw my freaked-out look. 'Kettle,' he said, and disappeared back around the corner.

I sat on the upturned wheelbarrow, one ridge digging into my thigh. Above me, it was as if someone had pressed pause, the clouds caught mid-blur. Over to my right, the river had a nervous blink.

It was so empty out here. Way more so than at our cottage. At least there you had people close enough to help if your car battery went flat, or to hold a parcel for you, but *here* – you definitely couldn't borrow a cup of sugar from anyone. You could yell and scream all day long. About not having any sugar. I tried to imagine him doing that.

A mug appeared next to my ear. It had an out-of-focus picture of trees and birds on it, the sort of mug you find in charity shops. I smiled up at him and curved my hands round it as he stood next to me with his own cup, holding the rim with the tips of his fingers. He didn't smile back.

God, he really wasn't going to be the one to speak first. He just stood there, looking towards the river, one hand in his pocket.

'It's very quiet here,' I said.

'Aye.' There was a big scar slicing from the join of his thumb down to the raised bone on his wrist and under his sleeve. 'It usually is.'

I shot a glance up at him. That sounded like a hint. Right. I started trying to think of good excuses to leave.

He turned to me, slightly formally. 'Thanks for the cactus.' He immediately took a sip from his mug.

So he did find it. I looked at my tea, feeling a bit petulant. 'How do you know it was me?'

He took a short breath in, clamped his mouth shut and made a noise in the back of his throat that might have been a laugh. 'People don't tend to leave me plants.'

I pulled the cuffs of my jumper down to my nails and spoke to the grass. 'I just wanted to say sorry for – I wasn't really in a very good state. The other night. Morning.'

His head went up, following the flight of the bird still tumbling about. 'You haven't seen any more trouble, then?'

I shook my head, remembering the dried sick on my cheek, and the way Rocky had moved before he nutted Fraser. I didn't really want to talk about that. 'So, what do you do out here?' Besides walking around at sunrise and getting dead bird under your fingernails.

'How d'you mean?'

'I just wondered, I don't know, what you get up to.' My voice trailed off a bit.

'Just ...' he scratched the beard at his cheek. 'Getting on with living.'

He wasn't exactly dinner party material.

I looked up the track and tried again. 'How long have you lived here?'

A silence. 'Five years now.'

139

'Do you like it?'

He rubbed his thumb over his bottom lip as if wiping something off it. 'You ask a lot of questions.'

'Sorry.' I turned slightly away from him and let the heat from the cup sweat into my palms, pressing hard.

He put his mug down in the grass and went back inside. Way to go, Polly. I dipped my head to my tea. Drink it quick and fuck off.

It tasted really sweet. He'd remembered to put sugar in it.

The door opened again and he walked past me, carrying a small bucket and a khaki-green cloth rucksack with bits of wood poking out of the top. He was wearing the sleeveless puffer jacket and the woolly hat again and was halfway to the river when he stopped. For a second I thought he was stalking something in front of him, but then I realised. He was waiting for me.

I slid off the wheelbarrow.

We followed the river along the valley, my boots darkening in the damp of the high grass. He walked slightly ahead of me but seemed to hang back occasionally, just enough for me to catch up.

The river started to fatten and get deeper and quieter. It had a pale grey sheen to it, putty-coloured. Staid River. Hill Brown.

There was a wooden rope bridge across the water up ahead. It looked like a badly made kid's xylophone. Or like something you'd have to cross in a hobbity adventure novel in order to get the ring, or the gold, or the flaxen-haired girl or whatever, although you'd only be up to your waist in water if you fell in. The handrail was barely-there rope, twisted round the boards every couple of feet or so.

140

'We're not going over that, are we?' I said to his back.

'Nope.'

'Thank God. It looks like a fucking deathtrap.'

He turned around. 'I made that.'

I stopped. 'Oh.' I looked at it. 'Sorry.'

He put his lips together and carried on walking. Maybe he'd been joking.

After another mile or so, my toes starting to web together in my boots, we came out by the loch – my loch, but a different bit, with no road snaking along beside it. The grass gave way to wrinkled rocks splattered with mustard and grey – a primary school class mixing all the finger paints and going on the rampage.

'So, what are we doing out here?'

He dumped his bag on the rocks and sat down, untying it and not looking at me. 'You wanted to know what I get up to.'

The splints of wood became a sort of diamond-shaped cage, held together with dark turquoise netting. A home-made version of those baskets you used to get in Superdrug to dump all your hairsprays and nail polishes into. He wrapped a long piece of string around his hand just below the knuckles, putting it to his teeth and gnawing until it divided. The other end was tied to the top of the cage with a nifty triple knot.

The water looked deep here, with a sleazy leopard-skin print in dark blues and black on the surface. I dug a pebble out from a crevice and lobbed it in with a truly crap overarm throw, unused since playing rounders in Year 6. A hollow *gollop*. The ripples spread slowly into a massive, perfect vinyl record. A crackly version of 'Sittin' On The Dock of the Bay', maybe. Or 'River Deep, Mountain High.' Yeah – '60s soul and this place. Perfect combination.

The grooves ironed themselves out and I noticed an acrid thread of something in the air, mixed with the scent of salt and the faint, mouldy tang of seaweed. Behind me, the birdman had a small Tupperware box on his knee, its brick-red lid on the rocks beside him.

The smell slimed up my nose and down my throat. 'Jesus. What *is* that?'

He hardly looked up. 'Fish heads.'

I could just about see some off-grey fleshy triangles. Dull button eyes. Aghast mouths. A plastic graveyard for decapitated fish. Yep. He was definitely a bit disturbed. 'Um. Right.'

He picked one out with the tips of his fingers and put it in the cage. 'Lobsters like their fish rotten.'

It was as if someone had stored the foulest fish-bits for centuries and boiled them down to the most rank bouillabaisse ever, then reduced it further into a highly-concentrated essence of decrepit zombie fish hell. And rubbed your face in it.

I backed off a bit. 'That is just really – God.'

He dropped another in as lightly as a sugar cube into a bone china cup.

'Do you do this for fun?'

'For lunch.'

Maybe that's what he'd been doing with the bird that time. Though running into it with your jeep and pulling it to pieces with your bare hands seemed a bit much. Extreme Chef-ing.

I was never going to forget that smell. That was it. Stuck for life. I absolutely did not want to give him the impression that hurling my guts out was something I did every single day so turned away, putting a palm over my entire face.

'You can help with something.' He tilted his head slightly towards me. 'If you like.'

*

142

I collected a couple of large stones by a row of silver-trunked oak trees and pines, before coming back to stand next to him, trying not to breathe or look at the fish-torture porn. He took a stone from me, holding it in his hand as if assessing the ripeness of a melon, and I had a sudden flash of panic. I was in the middle of nowhere with a man I didn't know. A man who hardly spoke and liked hanging out with dead animals. I'd unwittingly been sourcing the blunt instrument for my own remote lochside murder. That Nick Cave and Kylie song. Well, I still had the other stone. I could just brain the hell out of him. My fingers curled around it.

False alarm. He carefully placed the rock in the net and put his hand out again. Scalpel, nurse. I attempted to look nonchalant as I gave him the second one and he squinted up at me in a way that might have been a thank you.

He stood, checking the netting the same way Lottie would check a cardi for moth holes at the end of summer. The walls of the cage tightened as the rocks and fish-carnage rolled together at the bottom. Giving it a slow swing he sent it into the air, the string feeding quickly through his fingers. It hit the water a few metres out with a light slap and disappeared into the black folds.

'Cool,' I said.

He secured the string on a jutting rock and picked up his bucket, striding away. Midges followed him like his own personal raincloud, not that he even seemed to notice.

They were even worse here, horrible fuckers. The anti-bug juice didn't make them scarper, just not bite. They were head-butting and elbowing each other, desperate for my attention like I was the greatest celebrity they'd ever known. I kept bashing my hands on my arms, or flailing in the air, trying to wave them away.

I was wondering what I'd done to piss him off – or maybe he was just bored of me now – when he stopped a few rocks over, bent down and made a movement with his arm like he was dealing cards, looking intently at the loch. Maybe he'd spotted a white patch. The water began to move, and for a second it looked heart-stoppingly like a mass of hair, rising, before another, smaller cage came slowly out, slanted and low in the water, as if resisting him.

I went over. No dead fish heads this time. A dark tangle of things had gathered in the corner, making clicking noises. Crabs the size of blinis shifting over each other. A shiny fish, flopping alarmingly, and something bigger on top. He picked up the empty bucket and lay down on his stomach, leaning out over the water. His shirt rode up as he stretched one long arm. A flash of paleish skin. The bucket came back up, water smacking gently against the plastic.

He shoved his arm into a circular gap in the netting and pulled the biggest thing out. It had long protruding bits. Which moved. 'Hold this for me.'

'Oh – what? No, it's OK. Thanks.'

He gave me a look that I couldn't quite suss out. 'Got to get that fish out.'

'What is it?'

'Squat lobster.'

'Doesn't look like one.' I couldn't see it tapping mournfully on the inside of a glass tank in a Chinese restaurant, or sitting on top of Dalí's telephone.

'You get more of them than the usual type here. He's quite a big one, mind.' He thrust it a bit nearer.

'Oh, crap.' I took it gingerly by the hard shell on the top, keeping it as far away from my body as possible.

Everything in me wanted to scream and fling it in his face. It was an oversized mutant prawn spliced with Edward Scissorhands. An armoured, candy-orange tail, three bent stubbly legs on each side and, in front, two really long legs – or arms, or killer pincers – covered in spikes.

It wiggled.

'Fuck.' I swivelled my wrist to look it in the eyes, which were like swimming goggles with furious, golden-glowing orbs in them. 'Hello, little man.' Its blood-red feelers waved slowly in the air at me, probably saying *Yo. Put me back in the water or I'll cut you, bitch.* 'You are really, really minging.'

The birdman popped a flapping, silver-grey fish into the bucket. 'Don't like shellfish?'

'Yeah, I like shellfish,' I said to my alien-critter. 'When they're covered with lemon or in a pie or something. I mean, he is just—' I suddenly wondered why he hadn't put him in the bucket first, before he'd gone for the fish. 'Please take him off me.' I had used up all of my nerve.

There was a faint light in his eyes as he took it back, chucking it into the bucket. I could hear it scraping feebly against the side.

He plucked out crabs between a thumb and forefinger and threw them back into the loch. They didn't make a sound. Maybe you could skim them. I watched his arm toss out, over and over. He had totally swindled me – he'd made me hold that thing on purpose. There was a tiny bristle stuck to the inside of my thumb. I plucked it out and flung my hand wildly at a midge-cloud. Bastards. Bastard.

My throat felt as dry as anything. Stupid fags and nothing else since three cups of coffee this morning. With added lobster terror.

'Um,' I said. I still didn't know his name. 'Do you have anything to drink? I forgot to bring anything.'

He looked at me with his eyebrows raised, as if he'd just asked me a question and not the other way round. His gaze swivelled to where the river churned over some rock shelves on its last gasp before the loch.

'Oh,' I said. 'Right.'

The pool foamed like a shaken-up can of Coke. I knelt down and the falling water fanned out from my hand, leaving tiny little fronds of – *something* – on my palm. I gulped some, feeling it slalom down inside me.

There was a dopey thud next to me. An empty plastic bottle. I filled it up and walked back to him, holding it in front of my nose. The water was a pale, yellow-brown and there were tiny specks floating in it that I absolutely never wanted to look at under a microscope. 'Gross.'

'Fresher than you'd get in a tap.' He was collapsing the cage.

'Tap water doesn't have insects doing synchronised bloody swimming in it.'

I definitely heard him laugh then, the tiniest, punctuated breath through his nose, as he pushed the splints together.

'I'm Polly,' I said.

His shoulders stiffened. He turned his chin slightly, eyes on the rocks somewhere near my feet. 'Hello, Polly.' Like he'd just been introduced to me at a ball. The long piece of string went around the bundle of netting and sticks. 'Jim.' He glanced at me, just enough, as if saying his name was the most difficult thing he'd had to do all day. His eyes were the colour of seaweed. 'All right to head back?'

*

It was another dead quiet walk, apart from the river, which buckled and fizzed past us, and the slop of the water in the bucket. My little toenails were digging into the flesh of their neighbours. I was walked out.

When we finally reached his house, Jim — it felt better knowing he actually had a name — set his stuff down and looked at me hesitantly. Maybe he was mulling over whether to invite me in for a mouth-watering fish supper. Or maybe he was just wondering how to get rid of me. Either way, I didn't really want to witness the death of my new crustacean BFF. My BCF.

'What are you going to do with him?'

He sniffed. 'Boil it. You just eat the tail. Crack it off.'

I eyed the track. Three more miles. Up a hill. 'I should get going now.' I took a deep breath and began to squelch over the tyre-grooves.

'I'll drop you.'

I stopped and put my little finger in my tooth-gap for a second. He was standing in front of the door, cradling the back of his head in a hand. 'It's cool. I've bothered you enough.'

'You're no bother.' His voice was so quiet and low that I hardly heard the words.

The backs of my legs felt like they'd had pieces of shrapnel inserted under the skin but I spoke super brightly. 'I think you're just being polite. It's fine. I'm getting quite into it, really.' I slapped my thigh twice, loudly. 'Walking.'

He looked at me like he was impressed at my gusto but didn't believe me for a second. 'I'll drop you.'

We bumped up the track, me managing not to puke unceremoniously, which was a bonus, until the pine needles brushed against the windscreen before the main road. I opened the passenger door.

'Polly.'

I let the belt slide up over my shoulder. Jim wasn't wearing his.

He scratched his temple. 'I don't ...' He swallowed and made a sound like he was lifting something very heavy. 'See people much. I forget.' He looked away, out of his window, and at the windscreen, and I thought he'd finished his sentence. 'How I'm supposed to be.'

There was a tiny fissure crack in the glass, almost all the way to the bottom. Like the rivers coming off the hills.

I shrugged at him and smiled and shook my head, all at once, and got out of the jeep. 'See you.'

'Aye.' He leant over and pulled the door shut.

Well, that was different. The polar opposite of my normal life. Fish heads. Communing with lobsters. Taciturn wild man of the hills or whatever he was. I hitched a lift back to the village with a man on a tractor whose patter seemed gak-fuelled by comparison, and imagined Benji hooting with delight at being so high up and trundling along so slowly.

I described the tractor, noises and all, when Lottie and me Skyped him that evening. He kept putting his finger on top of the laptop camera, like an inquisitive giant eel, and his tongue, too. A virtual Benji lick. Nice. Dad told us he'd been hanging upside down from trees and had even made a friend, a French girl with Down's, and they'd sat around together in Velcro suits without speaking a word of each other's language. I wondered if Benji had licked her, too.

Lottie hid in her wine afterwards. She felt guilty for not having him here. It was a strange dynamic without Benji pulling at hair and clothes and doing his little tuneless hum with that smile that made his face look like a walnut shell. The smile he did when he wanted to assure us that he really, really meant it. I tried to distract her with a trashy online dating site and soon enough we were pissing ourselves laughing over men roughly her age calling themselves TwilightCruiser and AdAstraAdUltra, or wizened yoga freaks, and a guy who had decided the best way to enamour himself to the ladies would be to whack up a picture of himself playing acoustic guitar while standing on a dry stone wall. In a cloak.

Lottie took a lock of my hair and curled the pink bit round her finger. 'We could look at younger ones.'

'No. It's really all right.' I pointed. 'Jesus.' *Tall, blue eyes (both of them). Openly admit that im not perfect (what man is?)*

'There's no one at uni, then?'

'Hell, no. They're shitheads. Look at him.' *Im hot as Im close to the sun. But will I melt! Nothing ventured nothing gained …*

'All of them?'

'All of them.'

I thought about Jim winding that string round and round his hand, a dark cuff of hair on his wrist, and wondered what his profile would say. It was probably up there on bagyour-selfawildman.com. *Monosyllabic glower-machine, likes gutting fish and not saying very much. Looking for woman – man? dog? – to accompany brooding silences and bird dissection.*

'And how's Fraser?'

'Fine.'

I couldn't work him out. He'd made me hold that disgusting lobster for a laugh, I swear – *did* he laugh, properly? Was that a thing he could do? – or maybe to test me. Little did he know that I had a penchant for trying out new things. Normally they involved hallucinogens or extremely bad fashion decisions – stonewashed denim-print jeggings, I salute you – but hey. He wasn't going to scare me off that easily.

'Everything's all right with you two? I thought maybe ...'

'It's all fine.'

He was pretty dark, for sure, and had all the conversational skills of a brick wall, but – that last bit. In the jeep. He'd meant that he hadn't hated me being there. I think. It made me want to dig away at him. Just a bit. A toe in the mud.

'I know this isn't your ideal holiday.' Lottie looked at the screen again. 'Oh dear.'

Ordinary Guy looking for an Ordinary Woman who is'nt full of herself or is'nt looking for the earth. Don't want to waste my time, or your's, loking for full relationship and all that comes with it.

They really needed punctuation Nazis on these things.

8

Baked beans. The locals obviously existed on a diet of baked beans, mustard, spaghetti hoops and sausages, because the shop didn't sell much else. It wasn't exactly the gourmet deli-come-artisan-bakery-come-organic-greengrocer I'd had in my head before we got up here. My favourite shop at uni was the Asian supermarket, where Lena and I would go to pick up sheets of seaweed to make sushi with, or shrunken dried plums to put in hot water with lemon, or knobbly mushrooms I faintly hoped would be magic. Lena – before she found out about chip-van-gate, before she pushed me against a wall and said *you fucked him* – would buy bamboo leaves and show me how to make killer rice dumplings and we'd stuff our faces with the lot.

Definitely no bubble tea or miso paste or ready-made pho here. I trailed my fingers along each shelf, collected every vegetable that didn't resemble a dying balloon and tried to think what they'd do on *Masterchef* if they were armed with a crap oven and really blunt kitchen knives.

When I stepped outside with my booty, the jeep was parked at the garage opposite. It couldn't be anyone else's, with those scrapes along the passenger side, as if a yeti had taken a big swipe at it. He wasn't a complete recluse, then.

I lingered outside the shop, looking at the flyers stuck in the window: 'HOME HAIRCUTS ONLY £12' and 'LOGS FOR SALE' and 'DIANE'S MEDITATION YOGA – MEETS MONDAYS'. I probably needed that last one, except the thought of some flaccid-voiced woman instructing me to put my toe in my ear made me want to hurl. At the muted jingle of a bell behind me, my eyes slid over.

Jim came out of the garage with a hand in his back pocket and I whipped my head back to the notices. The jeep door slammed. He hadn't seen me. Or he was incredibly shy. Or rude. I turned round, took two casual steps and stopped as if I'd just seen him, before sauntering over.

He wound the window down.

'Hello,' I said, dumping the bags at my feet.

'All right, Polly.' He looked at me patiently.

'Um.' I looked over the roof of the jeep to the pale sky for inspiration. 'Are you having a nice day?'

His eyebrows slanted. 'Same as most of them.'

I refused any awkward silence. 'I still owe you a drink.' A deep horizontal crease appeared in his forehead. 'For bringing my stupid dog back.'

He gave the slightest shake of his head. 'You're fine.'

'No,' I started to turn towards the shop. 'I'm right here. I'll get you a beer. To add to your collection.' God, it sounded like I thought he was an alcoholic. 'I mean – all your bottles.'

Jim turned off the engine and put his arm on the window frame. He looked faintly anguished. 'Go on, then.'

I left my bags where they were and dashed across the road before turning round. 'What do you like?'

He didn't shout, but I knew what he'd said. 'You choose.'

*

152

I came back with a bog-coloured stout and a warm Beck's and held them both up. 'Went for both ends of the scale.'

He took them by the necks in one hand. 'Thank you.' A polite nod.

I loitered. 'So where are you off to?'

'Just work.'

'Oh yeah? Where's that?'

He looked mildly uncomfortable. Too many questions again. Polly's inquisition. I was no good at judging that at all.

'Up ...' He hesitated, before shaking his head as if to tell himself it didn't matter, and put a palm over one eye. 'Forestry stuff. Few miles away.'

Dad singing that Monty Python lumberjack song came into my head. 'Really? Do you wave a big chainsaw round?'

'No.' He gave me the same patient look.

God, it was tortuous. You couldn't say I hadn't tried. 'Right. Um, OK. Have a nice one.' I bent down to my bags.

He cleared his throat. 'Come and drink the other one with me sometime, then.' The jeep seemed to startle itself into firing up.

'Cool, OK,' I said, my voice drowned out by the engine.

The bottles clanked together as he drove off.

*

Hitching was my new special skill. Putting my hair in two plaits seemed to help – an overgrown Girl Guide vibe – and less smoking probably didn't hurt. Rucksack, too. This time, I climbed up into a massive truck driven by a girl with a long tattoo of a squid coiling along her arm. She told me about the plans for her wedding to her rock-climbing instructor boyfriend in Inverness and about fixing up her powerboat, all the while hurling the truck round impossibly tight corners.

Today the sun was being drained through a broad-bottomed colander over the opposite hills, lemon and lime streams of it, widely angled. Somewhere, a clump of grass and mud was getting its fifteen minutes of fame. There was a smell like burnt caramel and the ground underfoot actually crunched rather than squelched. I whacked up my music, strident, punchy voices soaring over synths.

It had been two days since seeing Jim in the village, long enough, according to the rules, to go for my beer. One day for gays, two days for straights, Stef had always said, usually with his tongue in the ear of some boy he'd just met. Not usually a boy he'd then abandon on a cold, wet pavement at three in the morning.

Obviously this wasn't a *date* date. I just needed some serious distracting after protracted arm-wrestles with nineteenth-century feminist history. Playing Dinner Spinner on my phone, taking tilt-shift photos of the tribal tat around the cottage and browsing new music by bands no one except three people in New York had ever heard of hadn't quite done the trick.

When I emerged from the pine trees, my toes thudded into the front of my boots. There was something lying on the ground near the house. I pressed pause, quick. It wasn't some-*thing*. It was someone.

I looked at my phone. Zero bars.

Keep walking. I carried on down the hill, eyes on the prone body, never wanting to arrive but knowing that I had to. A tug in my gut, pulling me towards it. It was him, or it was someone he'd *offed*, and either way I was stumbling on a terrible scene and probably about to make it a lot worse. As I got nearer, I could see that it was definitely him – Jim, I

154

mean. He wasn't moving. His ankles were crossed, his hands folded on his stomach. There was something on his chest.

A book.

Polly Paranoia Vaughan. Really had to work on that. I couldn't even blame it on the weed any more.

I got all the way down to the house, treading only on the softest mounds of grass. It seemed wrong to disturb him when he was so *asleep*. He looked different. Less scribbled on. His head was tipped to the side, exposing scraps of beard and two raised veins on his neck. A reddish pink ear. No boots on, just socks. The book, which had a woozy picture of a rainforest on the cover, was splayed page-down.

Edging quietly backwards to a respectable distance, I sat on my jacket next to the wheelbarrow and three damp lozenges of wood. I ran my thumb underneath the nails of my other hand, flicking the little eraser flakes of dirt into the grass. Took my plaits out. Imagined Jim on a pavement in Dalston, and me sitting patiently by him, waiting for an ambulance.

Wow, it was quiet. Just you and all your maddest thoughts out here. The river made a little popping noise, like it was cracking its joints. Other than that and the wind humming against my ears, there was not a single sound. I pulled my own book out of my bag.

My brain was soupy. Felt a bit like going to sleep myself. There weren't too many midges and the sun was still winning, just about. The sky was so big. A puddle of shadow sopped slowly over the valley. It dribbled over the sheds, coated Jim, then me, and disappeared behind us.

It probably wasn't a good idea to crash out here. Might give him a seizure, finding a catatonic girl in the grass. I eyed the two sheds.

Just a little look.

Immediately, I wished I hadn't. You knew what the first one was from the smell as soon you opened the door. Ripe and hot, the stench of sweating hay. It was like a festival loo, except without the queue of people hopping about outside, the thump of the dance tent making the plastic hum. I shut the door again.

The second one had no tool shelves, or pipes, or tins of tomatoes. Inside was death.

Death in the form of a single rabbit, hanging upside down in the middle of the shed. There was a thin buzzing sound, indeterminate white noise. The rabbit was tied by its ankles with red cord to a short, horizontal wooden bar that hung from the ceiling. A spray of white tail. Long feet. Its front legs dangling as if about to clap. It felt hallowed, being in the same intimate space as something so wrong – an animal that should have been moving fast along the ground, instead suspended in the air, inanimate. I put my hand out. There was a short, loud spitting sound, and a black spot appeared on its eyeball, like a sudden growth. A fly.

In a millisecond I was outside again, my palms flat on the wood of the door behind me. That beer didn't seem like such a good idea any more. Time to go.

There was a sniff. Jim folded an arm up over his face followed by the other, clasping his elbow. I took a sidestep. He stretched and arched his back off the ground with a muffled expulsion of air.

Oh, fuck it. 'Hello,' I said.

He froze, before lifting his head through the frame of his elbows. 'Christ.'

I tried to look extremely unassuming. 'Sorry. Didn't want to wake you.'

'How long have you been there?' His voice was peppery.

'Oh, you know, *hours.*' I snuck a glance at him.

He shut one eye and squinted at the sun for a moment and I realised he was telling the time, old-school style. He sat up and looked at his hands. His knitted jumper was a murky blue, with purple and white mixed in.

I poked the handle of the wheelbarrow with my toe. 'I came for that beer. But ...' He looked creased up, face and body. 'Maybe you're beered out.'

He rubbed his eye. 'No.' The word was soft and drawn out. 'Just tired,' he said to his feet. 'I don't always sleep well at night.'

Maybe the air didn't affect you once you'd lived here a while. Unlike me and Lottie, both dead to the world by ten o'clock every night, like eight-year-olds.

'I didn't have your number,' I said. His palms were still upturned, his head down. Maybe it had just been a throwaway comment, back at the garage, anything to make a break for it. 'Not that there's any reception up here.'

He eyed me like I was something quite small but also quite dangerous. A rabid puppy. 'You can get them if you like.'

I went to the front door, pulling my skirt down over my arse.

'They're not in there.' He tilted his forehead towards the river.

At the bank, in a slight dip, water coursed around some clear plastic boxes wedged between rocks. The two beer bottles lolled on their sides in one of them, next to a couple of cans of low-rent lager and some wormy-looking apples. I peeked under another lid – a mass of leaves, some wide and ribbed dark-red, some small and stringy. Nettles, too, hairy ones.

I came back and whacked the lids off on the lip of the wheelbarrow. They made two metallic, shuddering twangs and a tiny sliver of dark blue paint fell off.

He took the Beck's from me, his elbows resting on his knees. 'Unless—'

'Oh, I'll drink anything. Is that, like, your fridge?'

He nodded.

'Your actual fridge?'

Another nod.

I sat down. My ale tasted like trampy Coke. He picked at the corner of his bottle label.

Me first, then. Again. 'Did you build this place?'

'I put it back together, aye.'

He told me, with lots of pauses for beer, that it was at least a hundred and fifty years old and had probably once been owned by a farm further away. Men would live here when looking after sheep or cattle, and more recently deer watchers used it as shelter during the summers.

He was actually more chilled out today. Maybe he was still half asleep and hadn't quite remembered to be all scratchy and serious.

'What do you do, then?' he asked.

Do. What did I do? Hung around feeling useless. Wished I lived in London. Enjoyed over-exciting my brother. Thought about sex more than I thought about love. Tried to write poetry but never got further than three words through crippling shame. Left boys on the road to die. 'I'm a student.' I tapped the mouth of the bottle against my unchipped front tooth. 'A rubbish one, at the moment.'

I got carried away. It was the first proper question he'd asked me. After he let me talk a bit about how pathetic I was, how behind I was in my work, how I couldn't write for shit or string an original coherent sentence together, I trailed off. 'Um, did you – sorry if this sounds stupid, but did you find my book? By the loch?'

Jim glanced at me sidelong. 'It was yours, then?'

'Yeah, I—' Was legging it after seeing a freak water-cloud. 'I forgot it.' I eyed him carefully. 'Did you make the cover for it?'

He shrugged. 'Didn't want it to get rained on.'

The book-whisperer. 'Did you read it?' A pair of half-moon specs on his nose, frowning and shaking his head at all my double underlinings and tiny stick-men poets fighting with giant fountain pens and boning each other.

He scratched between his eyebrows, as if trying to make the line there even deeper. 'I had a look, aye. Went a bit over my head.'

'You like to read, though.'

Jim looked at me as if I'd just announced his entire life story.

'I mean, you have lots of books.'

There was a moment of embarrassed silence, in which we were both no doubt remembering that the only reason I knew this was because I had been in his house, totally wired, dribbling and leaving mud on his bedsheets. I quickly asked about the book he was reading, which had fallen off him when he'd sat up. He passed it to me. Some sort of epic journey through an impenetrable Peruvian jungle, all hardship and face-of-danger stuff. Seemed appropriate enough.

Clouds were making the tops of the hills look frothy.

'What's it like here in winter?'

Jim tipped his beer up and wiped his mouth inelegantly. 'It can be hard I guess. You're right in its fist.'

'Do you get snowed in?'

159

'Sometimes.'

I imagined the house up to its chin in snow. 'What do you do?'

He shrugged. 'Weather it out. Get plenty of wood in, and food.' Another glug of beer. 'I'm part-squirrel.' A quick glance and a hint of a sly smile.

Wow. He'd made a joke. I returned him a full-whack grin and lay back on the grass, my arms out, trying to imagine living here. My mind would drain out of my ears, I swear – a mash-up of the Brontës, the first Mrs Rochester let loose and wandering the moors. I popped my thumb out of the mouth of my beer bottle. *Thwop*. 'Don't you ever get lonely?'

His breath ignited, followed by a long exhalation. 'Been round people a lot. Had my fill.' He got up and went into the house. The door gave a little thump.

Right. Pushy microphone-in-the-face technique again. Nice one.

A terse clatter from inside. It was probably time to leave, but there was a cementy stubbornness in my bones. He'd invited me, after all. The other day he had said that he *didn't* see people much. Maybe in a former life he'd been a taxi driver or a politician or something, and had made a Great Escape. Too bad. I imagined I was glued to the grass prickling my neck and calves. Clouds flapped overhead.

The door opened and Jim walked past me, dropping something onto the ground. A pan. He went to the shed, the bigger one, and left the door hanging open. Seconds later he came back, holding a vicious-looking weapon in one hand and the rabbit by its hind legs in the other. Its front feet grazed the grass. Without a word, he crouched down by a flat log, laid the body on top and whacked it once, hard, at the neck.

One rabbit, suddenly headless.

He was trying to freak me out. Frighten me. Well, I'd already seen it in the shed. And I'd seen *Saw VI*, too. I could watch this. Sitting up, I looped my arms around my knees, very deliberately rested my chin on them and stared intently at the decapitated rabbit, hoping it would piss him off.

Chop. One front leg. Chop. The other. Startlingly bright and loud, like rifle shots but with a slight grittiness against the bone. I thought about the cleaver coming down on my fingers. The tail came off, a streak of shit on its underside.

'That's one big rabbit,' I said, trying to ignore my curling stomach.

'It's a hare.' Jim gave me a darkly amused look as he flipped over the body. He pulled a small knife from the pocket of his jeans, unfolded it and sliced into its crotch, working upwards.

There was a glimpse of a coiled mass, an impossible amount of it. He pulled it out in one swift, stringy pile and I almost retched. It was the marine life of your worst nightmares. Alien spawn. Sausage-sized maggots. A greyish kidney and a deep red jelly-wobble coming with it. Its liver.

Jim held the hare up for a moment, his arm high, and gave it a shake, like a wet umbrella in a porch. A few drops of blood made flat clicks into the pan.

He put his thumbs in. There was a shock of mauve-coloured flesh and the fur loosened, really easily. I had thought you might have to slice at it, but Jim was just rolling it off. Its torso was so long. Pink and purple legs with a PVC shine.

Jim made an occasional nick with his knife, the skin snapping as he pulled it. The underside of the fur was brazenly white. I remembered being stuck halfway out of a too-tight jumper-dress in a changing room in Topshop, Lena and Jen and Alice hysterical and taking photos of me on their phones while I swore at them and banged blindly into a rail. TopshopTopshopTopshop. If I thought about Topshop, I wouldn't throw up.

A quick, cricking sound and suddenly it wasn't a hare any more. The whole thing came away and he dumped the coat to one side, next to the head. Its soul had been sucked out. It wasn't in the fur, or in the gleaming, taut carcass remaining, which was the kind of colour you'd slick on your lips if you wanted to look vampish, and was marbled with paler parts that must have been fat.

It turned in his hand. Oh God, there was still stuff hanging out. Glistening. Indecently red, a red that no one should ever see.

Jim held the carcass by its legs in one hand and put his other hand into the middle of it, like a magician whose rabbit-or-hare hat-trick had taken a really sick turn, before bringing his fist back out, clenched and oily. He dropped the contents into the pan.

I stopped looking then. That was about as much as I could take. A bit of white fluff drifted past me. No wishes on that stuff. 'So you're going to eat that?'

He flashed a look at me, eyes as spiky as holly. ''Course.' He nodded at the pan. 'And them.'

'Did you shoot it?'

'No. Don't do guns. Wire traps. It's fairer.' His hand was treacly-looking. 'It needs washing.' He gazed towards the river and I realised what he meant.

I didn't want to wash it. I wanted to roll up under a duvet and apologise to every animal I'd ever eaten, maybe open a sanctuary for traumatised bunnies and do some high-profile anti-fur campaigns.

'Sure,' I said.

*

If I didn't look at it, I'd be OK. If I imagined that it was made of wood and plastic, a slightly macabre model for an art show or medical lecture, I would be fine. I strolled to the bank, super carefree, and knelt by the river. A thick smell packed into my nostrils. I glanced down, just for a breath, at the stretched, sinewy red-death-thing, and stuck it out into the water, leaning my other hand back on the grass.

A desperately sharp pain, like I'd been knifed. A wasp, a big one, was vibrating on the flesh of my palm below the thumb. I leapt up, brushed it off and started swearing. A lot. Uncreatively. The hare was lodged in between rocks and mud.

Jim came over, frowned at the ground, and stamped, hard and definite. He eyed me. 'You OK?'

Distilled acid. A laser beam. An acid-infused laser beam. I clung onto my wrist and swore louder, my eyes thistling with tears. Jim watched me, saying nothing, which just made me feel worse. Like a stupid, pathetic child. He picked up the hare and walked away.

I'd never been stung by anything in my life. God, it hurt so much. A thousand times worse than an injection. Searing, vicious pain, like a white-hot needle being drilled into the bone. It made me dizzy. I couldn't believe a tiny little fuckshit like that was making me cry. And he'd just gone and left, as if seeing me upset was too much for him, which was ridiculous given that he'd just annihilated a fluffball bunny.

I was rooted to the spot, wondering what to do, my hand between my thighs. I wanted to put it in an ice pack, or a bag of kittens, or both. Fuck. Maybe I was really allergic. Like, *death*-allergic. And I was going to swell and blacken out here, alone.

Footsteps. Jim was coming back, fast and purposeful, but looking strangely nonchalant – he was chewing something.

He was going to tell me to get a grip. Maybe slap me round the face a bit. I tried to bite my tears away. Alarmingly close, he snatched my hand up, his thumb pressed into my palm, still chewing. My hand appeared to be the most fascinating thing he'd ever seen. For a second I thought, deliriously, that he was going to kiss it.

And then he spat on me.

A load of soggy, dark-green gunk landed below my thumb and dribbled onto the sting. Warm and mulchy. Jesus. I tried to pull away but he was holding on tight with the hand he'd used to get the insides out of the hare. He spat again, to the side this time, a sound like a shuttlecock being thwacked, more green mess hitting the ground. Still gripping my hand in the air, as if about to whirl me around a dancefloor, he dug into his jeans pocket and pulled out a long scrap of grey-blue material. He pressed it over the gunk and wrapped it twice around my thumb and between my middle fingers, tying it tightly.

He put both hands in his pockets and we watched the cotton darken.

My thumb throbbed. The rag – and my hand – were sticky with hare-blood. 'What is that?' I said very quietly.

'Ribwort.' He looked at me. There was a tiny speck of it on the corner of his mouth. 'Should help a bit.'

I swallowed. 'Thanks.' I put the heel of my other hand to the side of one eye, wondering how much my make-up had run. My underarms were sweating like mad.

He dug the edge of a fingernail between two teeth, eyed it and blew a leaf-bit away. 'I'll drive you back. Should probably get some proper drugs in you all the same.'

Somehow, I didn't think he meant what I hoped he did.

We walked to the jeep, a strange little pulsing going in my damp thumb. Underneath the bottom of his jumper, his T-shirt was torn. Grey-blue.

Jim pulled up outside the shop. I really needed to calm down. High on pain-fuelled adrenaline, I'd jabbered on at him about the only time I'd broken a bone – shit retro pop night, massive rugby-playing dickwad, two fractured toes – and about my tooth. He hadn't said a word the whole time. Obviously.

'Do you smoke? Tobacco, or ... anything else?'

He shook his head. 'Not really.'

Damn. No blagging weed off him, then. It would have explained the monosyllabic vibe.

My hand wasn't burning so much now. 'I thought for a second that maybe I was properly allergic.'

'You'd have dropped dead by now,' he said, and smiled at me.

*

One antihistamine overdose and an ice-pack of frozen chips later, my heart was finally slowing in front of vanilla local news items involving broken-down ferries and debates about gas reserves.

I'd watched the pulpy ribwort drain away down the bathroom sink. Spit, *his* spit, and chewed-up plant. Witch doctor stuff. My palm still looked beefy, the hand of a strapping 1940s land girl, though the swelling had gone down a bit. Whether that was the gob-magic, or the medicine, or the chips, I wasn't sure.

The weather forecaster was a cheerful bastard for someone who brought endless news of rain. He'd worn that cheap suit the last three nights running.

165

I hadn't heard from Stef in forever. I messaged him. *How was ur party ting? X* PS Did we kill someone? Do you not feel the tiniest bit guilty? Have you forgotten all about it?

Hare-blood on my skirt was definitely a first, too. I'd scrubbed at the denim under the piping hot tap until it looked like a mud stain.

Haylo sweetness! Was EPIC. Snookerboyz r CUTE x

Stef had put on his second night in a snooker club, populated by proper grungy locals. Budget Polish lager and the smell of sweat and having to hover above the seat in the men's rancid loos.

Well jelz xx PS Cuter than Spanish boys? Are you off them now?

The forecaster looked extremely excited about the one hour of light cloud that we'd get tomorrow.

Awww ... how is ur lil kiltman? X

SHIT

The same for the day after and the day after that. Some rain, some cloud, about two minutes of sunshine if you smiled really nicely.

Nooo for true?

YUP ☹

Windchill. Coastal breezes. I imagined kicking the forecaster's gleaming teeth in.

Awww sorry luv. Need to get urself another 1 double quick

Did *you*? If he'd stayed, I would have stayed. I should have stayed.

There was a carved king and queen sitting on the coffee table. The king had blank eyes and a crude oblong of nose. I picked him up and immediately dropped him on my toe. Fuck.

I balanced the frozen chips on my foot.

Theres an older dude. With a beard. He's a LUMBERJACK & he's ok. I deleted it. I knew what Stef would say. Something like *U have official permission to get him prepped 4 me, fluffergirl.* And I'd say *in ur dreams, boyeee* and wait for his next response, which would never come.

There'd been the tiniest light in Jim's eye when I'd got out of the jeep.

Bear maybe. Wolf maybe. Not a squirrel.

*

I was halfway down the road into the white-hot centre of the village for fags and Diet Coke with Tyger on my tail when a car passed us, braking. Fraser's. I stopped, too, a few metres back. It rolled back down the road towards me.

The window came down. 'Hiya.' He was probably on his way to do a shift at the bar. And a spot of under-the-counter trading to pre-pubescents. No wonder he'd seemed so bloody popular.

'Hi.'

Tyger put his paws up on the front wheel.

'All right, mate,' Fraser said to him, before looking back up at me. 'Haven't seen you in a bit.'

The skin around his eye was still puffy and looked like it needed scrubbing. I stared past him up the hill.

He tried again. 'You've not been in for a drink.' He tapped his ear. I put my headphones round my neck and he repeated it. 'Do you fancy doing anything?'

I shook my head. My snare-beats were like someone spitting onto the road, over and over.

'Look, I'm sorry. About what happened. It's all fine now. I promise.'

Twat. 'You don't get it. I don't want to hang out with you. You were so shit up there, not just to me. To Finn and Becca.'

Tyger tried to high-jump the car door and scratched the paint with his claws.

Fraser faced forwards and clenched the steering wheel. 'They're talking to me, though.'

'Maybe they're nicer than me. Or more stupid. I don't know.'

His knuckles bleached further. 'I don't know why you can't just forget it.'

'You just want a shag.'

'I don't.' He cast a quick look at me, his dimple going. 'It was nice, though.'

I pulled my jacket in, stretching it tight around the back of my ribs. 'No, Fraser. I'm not seeing you, and I'm not having sex with you. Just go away.'

He crunched into gear. 'OK. Whatever.'

'At least your mum will be happy. And you can tell her I said that you were a shit kisser, too. A fucking octopus could do better. And you have a midget dick.' His head turned just slightly and I saw his eyes, a flash of hurt and surprise, as he drove off.

Tyger was in front of me, at the end of his lead, his tail shimmying. He barked, once.

'You're a slag,' I said to him.

One serving of dollopy, 100 per cent cocoa eyes, before he snuffled off to the verge and squatted down, looking effortful. I sighed, put my hand in my pocket for a plastic bag, and tilted my face up to the sky, eyes closed.

Stupid shitty attempts at sunshine. Stupid shitty attempts at manhood.

Something landed on the tip of my nose. Tiny, cold. I carefully lifted it off with my nail, and there, for a split second, before it disappeared into a translucent droplet that spread down the contours of my fingertip, was something that shouldn't have been there. Something that made absolutely no sense.

A snowflake.

Another night of reading non-feminist chick-shit, custard creams stacked by my head. Tyger was on my lap, the hairiest hot water bottle ever, sorting out my period pain.

I was just being stubborn. I knew that I was probably shooting myself in the foot, ridding myself of a boy who was *up* for stuff. But he'd been so spineless.

Lottie's phone shone on the arm of the chair. I picked it up, shouted the message from my uncle to her in the kitchen, and kept it under my thumbs. Jim had said he'd phoned the number on Tyger's collar when he'd found him. I scrolled through until I found the right date and the only unrecognised number, with Bev's before it. Lottie had probably been wailing to her when he'd tried to call. I guess he hadn't left a message, seeing as speaking wasn't exactly his favourite hobby.

I copied the number into my phone and stared at it. What was I going to say? *Hi, fancy spitting on me again?* Yeah, maybe not.

I gathered Tyger's cheeks in my palms. 'Wanna see your knight in shining armour?'

One generous mouthful of dog.

He came in useful sometimes. The next day, after reading forums about freak Scottish climate-events, I pimped him out

169

to get me a ride, holding him in my arms and looking lost and forlorn. He got extra biscuits for that, and a couple more to tempt him up and down the track. Today the view came courtesy of a drunk watercolour painter. The hills were the texture of damp flannel.

There was no answer when I knocked. I ambled round to the side of the house, dragging Tyger, wondering if I could make him a Crufts-style assault course out of the planks of wood and other detritus, train him up into a prize-winning mutt, get him a rosette the size of his head. There was a soft click of the door. I let the lead go and Tyger ran back, standing on his hind legs to lean on Jim's calves. He'd always win the trophy for Most Sappy Dog.

'Hey, me and Tyger thought we'd come and see if you were massacring any fluffy—' My voice dwindled.

Jim looked haunted, darker lines than before etched in charcoal on his forehead and under his eyes. I could see him make a tired attempt to dispel them but they held firm, like his skin was being tugged from the inside. He bent down and lifted Tyger off him.

Something wasn't right. The cheeriness I'd felt sauntering down the track fizzed away. I hiked my thumb over my shoulder. 'I was just—'

'It's not … I'm not up to it right now. Sorry.' One hand was in a fist, held a bit like Finn's littler one, tucked in by his thigh.

'Yeah, no, of course. It's cool.' I turned to go. 'I'll see you, then.'

'Polly.' I stopped and faced him. 'Another time. Just …' There was a long pause, as if the rest of the sentence had drifted out to sea. 'Not today.' As he put his hands in his pockets, I glimpsed a flash of colour. Dark red, on his knuckles.

'OK,' I said, quietly enough that he might not have heard it, and began the slow tramp back, Tyger moping alongside me, hoping that I looked breezy and super fit and perfectly stoked about having to walk straight back up that fucking hill.

I nicked a glance over my shoulder after quarter of a mile. He'd gone inside. Smoke wound up from the chimney, a question mark. I was so not going back there again. Talk about a slap in the face.

Killer-thorns brushed my shin. Everything was so prickly here – gorse, thistles, baby holly at ankle-height. All waiting to get you.

It started to rain.

Your look always darkened, rain on stone, when you spoke of your mother. She never liked me. I knew it even from afar, by the way your voice sounded like it was caught on barbed wire.

I met her only once. We went on the train to a grand building with a long private driveway and thick, sticky air inside. A lot of woolly looks from the other residents.

When she was still at home, you told me, she would have strange fits in her sleep. Clutching the bedclothes, arching up, cries like foxes in the night. There were things you couldn't explain. Eggshells, floating in milk. A thimble full of dull grey powder, finer than chalk. You once walked with her past a row of moles hanging by their noses from a wire fence, and she'd sent you back for a teacup and a knife and refused to say why. Crystals – you brought me one and I didn't recognise it. It wasn't local.

In her room, I sat on a chair so she could get a better look at me. There were dried leaves on a saucer, a spider in a jar. Her stare was as sharp as a glugful of whisky.

After that, I felt like she was always watching. I imagined her eyes on us as we walked. I saw her stitch her lips up tight at my laugh, which was loud, a barnacle goose overhead. The hiss of disapproval in the oak leaves. The tut of branches in the wind.

She was everywhere.

I hear her still. My own haunting. She is in my bones. I think I understand the darkness in her more than you do now. How someone can pull another to them, can move them like liquid silver.

As the light stays longer in each day, I can feel it in me.

The rain was even worse when I came out of the shop, three packets of Jaffa Cakes tucked under one arm and a soggy dishcloth version of Tyger hooked over the other. I'd carried him most of the way up the track before getting a lift with a guy whose car was filled with empty crisp packets, baby bottles and chewed-on plastic toys.

I propped a fag in the corner of my mouth and waited in the porch, reading the notices. Maybe the rain would stop, peel back like a theatre curtain. Kayaking courses. Mobile cinema – showing some Pixar movie this month. A ceilidh. Shoot me.

'Shall I spark up that wee one for you, lassie?'

The old guy with the wine-stain birthmark had just emerged, a high sheen on his forehead that might have been sweat or rain. He carried a canvas bag of groceries and was already bringing a lighter out of the inside pocket of his mac.

I put my fingers to my roll-up. 'Thanks.'

He stretched his shoulders back in a grand movement, his chest coming out as if he was about to yodel, and faced the sheets of rain.

Tyger, still crooked over my elbow, made a sudden jerking movement towards the guy and nipped him on the arm.

'Tyger! What the fuck?'

The man raised his eyebrows at him and they were like hats being chivalrously lifted by two country gents.

'Jesus. I'm really sorry. He never does that. You *never* do that.' I dumped Tyger on the floor. He looked at me like I'd just told him that my heart lay with another dog.

'Ah, never mind. Perhaps he doesn't think my coat has enough holes in it already.' He plucked at a small, frayed tear on his sleeve.

'I'm really sorry. Say sorry.' I prodded Tyger with my toe. He turned away from me with very deliberate, shuffling motions and lay down, his head just past the paving stone, raindrops landing on his nose.

I took the baccy out of my pocket. 'Um, do you want one?'

He turned to me again, the colour on his cheek no less startling closer up. There was a large, dark mole in the middle of it, a black hole in a molten-red galaxy. 'That seems like a rather fine deal on my part.'

I shrugged and began rolling him one. Apart from the tear in his coat, he was impeccably dressed again, a sort of catalogue model for retired eccentrics – coils of dirty grey hair coming out of a green beret, checked shirt-collar, pale pink tie, mac. His shoes were super polished, though maybe that was just the weather again. Everything here looked buffed and brass-rubbed, all of the time.

We watched the rain bounce as it hit the pavement and the roofs of the few parked cars. My jacket was still stuck to my arms.

'Does it ever stop?' I said.

'When you least expect it.' He stubbed his cigarette out under a pointed toe that moved like Fred Astaire's. 'If the rain's what you meant.'

I glanced at him. 'Maybe.'

'Ah, don't blame the rain on your troubles. It just doesn't know how to fall upwards.' He clapped his hands and picked up his shopping bag. 'Right my dear, no point standing round here all day.' He whisked a huge golf umbrella from the corner by the door of the shop.

'Is that yours?'

He winked at me. 'Let's say so.'

*

His name was Johnny and the spiky gold badge on his beret was for the Scots Guards – or The Kiddies, he said, with a flamboyant sort of affection. He told me about the Persian Gulf, his first posting, wide dry skies and palm trees and no women anywhere. And other places, too – he'd been all over. How the hairs pricked up on the back of your neck in alleyways in Belfast. Football games and their own radio station in West Germany. But he'd been back here a long old time, he said, since his leg had been damaged in a training exercise in Hong Kong.

'I'd only just stepped off that godforsaken boat.' It was as if the water had plumped up his voice as well as every inch of soil round here. He seemed to enjoy the sound and taste and smell of every word, rolling it around in his mouth like hefty swills of Rioja.

I took a step and a half for every bowling stride of his, keeping Tyger – giving me mega guilt-trip looks as he got more and more rained on – well away.

'And how are you finding our neck of the woods?'

'Oh, you know. It's definitely different.'

'Aye. It is that, I suppose.' There was a little more weight to his voice. The rain began hitting my calves as it bounced off the road. 'Arm?' He angled his elbow out.

'Um, OK.' I slotted my hand in. He smelled faintly of menthol cough sweets.

I wondered about that stone on the beach. The stone that had a shine on it like Johnny's shoes. Somehow, it didn't feel right to ask – he'd not been so garrulous when I passed him that day. As if he was happy to talk about the bright wide world out there, but would say nothing of this place. I prodded him about the Rhine again, and he was off, telling me about knowing the words to the German-language covers of Beatles songs, getting pissed on glasses of beer as thick as golden syrup, and being married to a chain-smoking girl called Hansi for two years.

'She'd gone down to the *Schwarzwald* by the time I came back. Callous woman. Left me a note. Her friend took the edge off the blow, though, as I recall. There you go.' Johnny tilted the umbrella back and showed me the sky. The rain had stopped. 'When you least expect it,' he said. 'And this, lassie, is where I disembark.'

A scrubby driveway led up to a bungalow. Dirty, streaked walls, sitting low in a well of damp grass. A battered, maroon-coloured car was parked next to it, a shade darker than his cheek. An old motorbike with no seat leant against the side of the house. None of it looked like him, with his polish and flair, inflated voice and gestures.

'Thank you for the cigarette,' he said, giving me a little bow. 'And the charming company.'

I almost sniggered.

He began to walk up the driveway, that slight lilt to his step, before turning and raising the folded umbrella as if a military baton. 'Another one for the collection.'

Kilt porn
Very gay. My fingers made tiny raindrops on the keyboard.
Loch porn
Full-on and in your face, literally, with a confusing lack of water until I translated the word into German.
Feminist porn
A lot of long articles that I should actually read, as well as some nice pictures of naked vegan people in parks and a menstruation porn site that somehow seemed scarier than everything else put together. God, I was bored.

I scrolled through mine and Fraser's messages, back when he'd been top of my limited Sex Order and not the worst contestant on a more savage version of *The Apprentice*. I was starting to think I shouldn't have been such a bitch until I got back down to the most recent ones, him asking how I was after I had bolted out into the night. If he'd really cared, he would have come after me.

Earth Porn pics of the day was good, if not exactly the crotch-diversion I'd been looking for. The lace-and-log-fire version of landscape photography – lurid trees over an obscenely blue lake that cascaded off an arcing shelf. I wondered if this place would ever make it on to that site. If you got the light right, or took a super-close-up of some grungy moss. Maybe it wasn't quite showy enough, hallucinatory enough. It was a bit subtler here, muted, like looking through the lenses they use to film Scandinavian crime dramas. The pale mustard and blasted green of the hills surrounding Jim's place. The bland sky.

Who had I been kidding? Jim wasn't my friend, or anything else. He was a stupid monolith with no social skills, and he didn't want me around. Which was fair enough. Why would you want me around?

I turned off the laptop. Turned off my phone. Lay on my bed feeling the chill of the duvet on my arms. The pillow that I normally stowed underneath a second, plumper one was feather-stuffed. I slammed my head down on it, rubbed my face in, feeling for the prickles and stabs. Sometimes I thought that my bones couldn't be dense and fibrous. That instead they were full of air, pea-shooters. Empty space where nothing sounded. The spines of feathers.

*

After an evening spent blowing bubbles into my warm white wine with a straw – Lottie drinking decaf coffee and reading a book on colour theory in her dressing gown – I went outside for a wander, my head frothy.

Twilights lasted twice as long here, as if refusing to give darkness its proper run. Tonight was another achingly slow osmosis, things just beginning to lose their edges.

This corner of the garden faced inland, where the distant end of the loch narrowed to a point. There was the dull grey gleam of two silver birches in front of me and a collapsed washing line next to them. Not a breath of wind, though cold enough for the bare skin of my arms to pebble.

It finally got dark. I'd never seen a night sky like this one. Like someone had flung up a sackful of cheap gold stud earrings. And the longer I looked, the more layers appeared. Stars and stars and stars. I tipped my chin up and stuck out my tongue. Maybe I'd catch one, the most insane acid tab you would ever have. It would taste like sherbet and champagne and those violet-coloured popping sweets and my head would explode. I waited for one to fall.

There was a noise that made my head snap back down. A wild, percussive sound, right in front of me.

The plastic covering over the washing line. I could just see it eddying from side to side in the wind. It went again, an abrasive slap of tarpaulin on pole, like enthusiastic hands on a wet arse. How could I be so freaked out by the dark? It was just the dark. Just—

I looked harder.

Next to the washing line, one of the silver birches seemed fatter in the middle. Like a snake swallowing down an antelope. And then something happened. The right hand side of the tree grew.

178

It grew. And swelled. It swelled and the tree *separated*, until there was a black space between the birch tree and the thing that had come off it.

Thin. Silvery-white. My height.

It stayed there, on the edge of the lawn. More than mist. More than cloud. Everything seemed to slow and grow a frost. My brain had cleaved in two, separated in a mirror image of the tree and the *thing*.

I backed away. Something pointed stabbed me in the shoulder and I let out a mangled gasp and scream and dashed into the house.

Door slam. Handle up. Key. I turned the garden light off.

'Polly?' Lottie walked into the kitchen. 'What are you doing in the dark?' She turned the kitchen light on and came over to me, tucking some hair behind my ear.

'There's something …' My teeth were rattling. I tried to slow my breathing and made myself face the back door again, then carefully pressed the light switch.

The garden flooded golden. Black shapes of the two trees and the washing line at the far end. The bird feeder and its sharp corners.

'There's Jane Austen on the telly,' said Lottie.

I nodded. Jane would sort it.

The orchid was a dark, curving shadow. I turned it round, pushed it to the furthest corner of the bedside table and hunched under the covers, imagining everything in the garden fattening and separating.

It had been like chalk dust, masses of it, collected in the air and formed into an indefinable shape, something with no edges. I'd wanted to make it come into focus. It had been grainy. Diaphanous. Gauze trying to become silk. Trying to become real.

There was a slow, spreading sensation in my stomach. Like warm peanut butter, clogging me up, binding sinews and bone and veins together.

I couldn't ignore it any longer. It wasn't unidentified sea life. Or freak weather.

Something was here.

9

Daytime was better. Surfaces were matte and real again.

Today I didn't even need a prod from Lottie. The sun was out and proud, the sky cloudless. Eggshell Blue. Wipe-clean Sky. Nowhere for any*thing* to hide. I could look it in the face. Even though there had been no face. No nothing, really. It was idiotic. It wasn't the Spanish boy. He was still alive, if being in a coma was still alive. I couldn't find any update online. I had drunk enough white wine to make my teeth feel as if they had rotted through to the gums. It had been the wine. Probably. Tonight I would drink only extremely calming herbal teas. Probably.

I was beginning to get off on the tight, dull throbbing along the sides of my thighs in the morning, and focused on stretching them out. Girl-power strides. The air was heavy with hot, musky smells, like a house party full of fourteen-year-olds, cheap body sprays mixed together. I walked on the verge of the road, crunching spiky weeds and little flowers the colour of Post-it notes and dip-dyed hair and Love Heart sweets – and a snail, accidentally – underfoot. The birdsong was layered like last night's stars. Best not to think about last night, or the stars, or anything. Daytime. Herbal teas.

A car slammed by, shitty house music lumping out. I wondered what would happen if I hitched and went wherever the driver was going, to the middle of nowhere or maybe some grey-arsed town. And stuck my thumb out again. A whimsical hitchhiking lottery, not having to make any decisions myself. I'd end up on a ferry to Ireland, or France, or as far as Russia, Mongolia, China. I could just keep going, a sort of snakes and ladders over the world map, drifting on the wind like hare-fluff. Chased by my own guilt.

For now, I had to drift on a smaller scale. I vowed to take the next right off the main road, no matter what. A brown signpost for a cave four miles away was my turning. I kicked at clumps of mushrooms that tore into strings of mozzarella, and weaved between the dark drops on the road.

Dark drops. New tar or engine oil, I'd thought. But the sun shone on a couple, and their edges reddened.

There was blood on the road.

I stopped and looked back. The drops trailed from the signpost at the corner, got bigger by my feet and continued past me. There was a bend in the road a quarter of a mile further on. Maybe Rocky was up there. He'd come back to get Fraser properly. And I was next.

Something on the verge up ahead. A dumped armchair cushion or a blanket or – no, something else. I walked very slowly.

Semi-camouflaged in the grass, large and still, lay a deer. A deep graze on its back and more blood swiped on the grass. Eyes open.

It blinked.

I let the weight of my boots power me back down to the main road and waited five minutes for a car, waving my arms madly when one came. It swerved and didn't stop. Almost three whole tunes had played before another approached.

I ran up to the window. 'Can you help? There's a deer up there. I think it was hit by a car.'

The moustachioed driver flipped up his sunglasses. 'Oh.' The woman next to him turned the radio down, argumentative voices smoothing to a murmur. 'Um, I wouldn't know. Can't you call the RSPCA or something?'

'Can you come and look at it? Or maybe put it in your boot? Take it to –' What, a vet? What the hell did you do with an injured Bambi?

'It's just ...' the woman leant over, a box of chocolate fingers on her lap. 'Sorry love, we're late for something. I would try the RSPCA. Or the police.'

The man gave me a watery, guileless smile and they drove off.

It knew I was there. Its belly rose when I stepped nearer, its neck shifting slightly in the grass. It was all the colours of curry spices, apart from where the fur had ruffled the opposite way, showing scrubby black-brown underneath. One of its back legs was bent the wrong way, like a broken umbrella spoke.

There was only one person.

A faint voice, careful. 'Hello?'

'It's Polly. I found a deer. It's injured. I don't know what to do.'

There was a long silence.

'Where are you?'

I told him as best I could.

'Does it have antlers?'

'No.'

'Is it moving?'

'Not really.'

A fuzzing noise in the background. 'I'm at work. Be there soon. Don't get too close.'

I sat down a few feet away. The deer bent its front legs and rubbed its cheek and ear into the grass, as if tired and trying to find the right position to fall asleep in. The back legs didn't move at all. Tiny tremblings ran along its neck and chest, something bubbling under the hide. A bird wheezed overhead.

This didn't quite feel real. The deer's fur was as short and uneven as carpet in a student house, and its ears were wisped, the ears of a much older animal. It raised a slender front leg, trying to touch something in the air above it, and brought it down again carefully.

No cars passed. Two or three snarled along the main road like distant drills. The sun was ironing out my forehead. I had water in my bag – maybe I could dribble some into its mouth. As I brought my rucksack slowly over one shoulder, the deer moved again, its chest rising, and a sound came tightly out, a slow-motion sound from very far away, coming closer.

A long, curving *broo-oo-oo-ooeeee*, broken up. Desperate. Almost human.

The bird stopped. The air seemed to stall and thicken. All I could hear were the deer's exhalations, grey and regular. I pushed myself up off the grass with my hands, just enough to move closer. There was a small, pale patch under its eye like a tear. I wanted to put my fingers out, touch the raised bone above its nose.

Eyelashes like pine needle fur encircled the rubbery eye-rim, with fine, long hairs winding out. I dared to lean over. The brown iris had a corduroy pattern – and something else. A white misting, like the reflection of a cloud. But then the mist travelled *across* the eye, and formed a shape.

Like in the garden.

A tightness in my throat, someone pinching the skin inside and twisting it. The shape wavered, a slight bend in the centre of it. I didn't breathe. The black bar of the pupil swivelled up to me and suddenly the deer jolted and kicked out, catching my shin.

I jerked back, a thin, slicing pain in my leg, like being caught by the edge of a hotplate. A line two inches across began to pink, the blood seeping up. I should have moved, got out of its eyesight, but something made me stay. That sound it had made – its mourning. It felt right to be bleeding. I would stay. Bleed with it. Rolling back to where I'd been sitting, I slowly put my hand in the air above its neck.

The jeep came humming up the road. A *scritch* of the handbrake.

'Polly, get back from there.'

I wanted to protest but his voice was so dark, and dense as oil. I removed my hovering hand and shuffled away on my arse, my palms rashing on nettles.

Jim walked over very quietly and stood by the deer's head. It made a sudden, alarming bucking, a small movement full of furious energy, as though it were being electrocuted. Or as if, in its mind, it were leaping away from him, tearing over the hills. It blurted, a dry, open sound. Its eye rolled.

For a moment everything seemed suspended. He and the deer, eyeing each other. A still life.

185

In one swift movement, Jim pulled out a knife from his back pocket, crouched down and, holding the deer by an ear and at the back of its skull, slit its throat.

'No,' I said.

The deer twisted and barked, a sound like stones being scraped on a road. Jim put his knee on its chest. More garbled, choking sounds. The front legs flailed. I stumbled onto the tarmac, clutched my elbows. Jim stayed on top of it, squatting, his hand between its ears. His knuckles were inky, scabbed.

The deer had stopped moving. A pool of blood like a silk scarf.

There was a hum and a car came the other way, slowing as it passed, a small girl with heart-shaped sunglasses open-mouthed against the window.

He wiped the knife on the grass and straightened. 'You're bleeding.'

There was a little trail down my leg, welling where the sock bunched at my ankle. 'I don't care.'

Jim opened the boot of the jeep and spread a plastic sheet out. He stood over the deer for a second, placed his hands underneath its belly and hauled it onto his shoulder, clasping the front ankles together in one hand. Its head hung down at his thigh. The pointillist painting in the garden that first morning reduced to something garish, ludicrous. As he turned, I saw the flank that had been lying against the grass, a near-perfect circle of exposed flesh, like the hide had been meticulously snipped away. Jim manoeuvred the deer into the jeep, working the body off his shoulder, the hooves catching on the frame, and bent its head to fit it in.

I saw the lolling, grey-pink tongue before he shut the door. 'You like killing things, don't you?'

He stiffened and tucked his chin down to his chest for a moment before turning around slowly and looking me straight in the eye. Flakes of bark clung to his jumper. 'Think I shouldn't have done that?'

I couldn't answer. I just shook my head, my lips clamped shut.

'Let's see to your leg.'

I shook my head again and stared past him up the road.

He took a breath in and put his hands flat on the front of his jeans. 'Just – we should just stop it bleeding.'

'Fuck *off*,' I said, tightly, stupidly. My palms stung. 'You just want to eat it.'

'I will eat it. Some of it.'

I lowered my eyebrows down against a thumb and middle finger.

'You called me,' he said.

'I thought you were going to rescue it.' My voice was stretched taut.

'She was dying.'

She. That made it so much worse. 'You – it's not fair.'

He just looked at me, patiently. Waiting.

*

Lottie stared at me, pushing her glasses up into her hair. 'By a deer?'

'It's dead now.' I walked to the kitchen and downed a pint of water, feeling my stomach swell and her eyes on my back.

'Did you ...'

'Yes, I kickboxed a killer deer to death.' Glass on table. 'It's fine.'

She was looking at me like she had a million things to say and wasn't sure which one to start with. Instead, she came and picked up my wrist, her thumb on my cuts. 'You don't have to be so gung-ho. You're going to really hurt yourself.'

'Don't I?' I gestured vaguely out of the window above the sink. 'Look at where we are.'

She stroked my skin. 'Still OK for later?'

I drank another half pint and nodded.

*

'So this is Douglas fir, and these are all softwood. All locally sourced. Being a good guy.'

Adam was giving us the tour of a house he'd designed a couple of villages down. It still had that show-home glossiness, choice pieces of unblemished furniture, no TV. Cobalt-blue window frames and a Scandinavian vibe.

He was doing his best offhand, all-in-a-day's-work voice. 'Underfloor heating, and the Rayburn keeps everything toasty.'

Lottie was putting her palms on the plaster, her eyes rainbowing with colour schemes, her brain switching the furniture around. 'There's so much scope here. So much *light*.'

Adam hummed non-committally and followed her up the stairs.

My forehead hurt. The sunburn felt like something of a stamp of pride. Branded by the weather. I went to the back door. A stream gave off dirty laughs a few feet away and the midges zinged around it.

I couldn't get that sound out of my head. The eeriest thing I'd ever heard. Would ever hear. All the world's heartache drawn out in one, long note from its throat.

Jim had waited while I'd stood there on the road, unwinding my anger and looking anywhere but at him. He'd wrapped a grubby J-cloth round my lower leg to staunch the bleeding and yanked a fistful of leaves from the bank for my nettle-stung hands. Just past my driveway, I had looked at the deer, prostrate on the back seat, and at the purple stain on Jim's shoulder.

He'd been staring at the roof of the cottage as if trying to see through it before he turned to me. 'I'm sorry about – before.' He hadn't meant the deer. 'Come and see me again. If you like.'

'Polly, are you coming to have a look?'

I trailed up the stairs. It smelled like the forest in here, roasted and sticky.

Adam was saying something about solar panels and breathing walls, Lottie nodding earnestly. I went to the window and looked down at the stream again.

'What do you think?' she said to me.

I shrugged. 'Yeah, it's cool.' I stared pointedly at Adam. 'Do you bring lots of people up here, then?' Secret shags with his secretary on plastic sheet-covered sofas, the smell of sex overpowered by pinewood flooring and his repellent aftershave.

'Not really.' He half winked at Lottie. 'You two are special.' She blew him a kiss. I felt like hurling. 'Anyway.' He looked at me, his smile not quite making it to his eyes. 'Shall we go have a drink?'

*

Adam and Bev's own house, which I'd managed to avoid so far, was a converted barn in the village proper. It had a lofty main

189

room, beams and several slightly amateur, swirly paintings on the walls that made me think of being on a fairground ride when I was little. They owned a completely bizarre lizard with a saggy neck and a gleefully demonic expression that was sitting frozen in a glass tank in the hallway. I'd thought it was a Damien Hirst rip-off until the tissue paper eyelid had come down.

Bev had made a massive casserole packed with herbs from their garden, loads of plant in with the meat.

'Have you ever cooked with ribwort?' I asked her, while Adam's artsy jazz-wank darted round in the background.

'Ribwort?' She looked into the middle distance. 'I'm not sure you can eat that. Just a weed, isn't it?' She looked at Adam. He pursed his lips and shrugged.

I sawed through the flesh of a sausage, pronged it on my fork and eyed it. Deer intestine. Hare guts. Fish heads. I stuffed in a gobful.

The evening degenerated into gossip and drinking port on the sofas. An old-school chill-out track came on and Lottie and Bev made big cooing sighs, reminiscing about some dawn rave in a field a thousand years ago. I pictured Lottie with limp daisies in her hair, twirling her blotchy, tie-dyed skirts, sparklers going in her eyes. God, I so wanted some weed.

Bev pulled Lottie up and they flung arms round each other and swayed. Adam was looking at me from the opposite sofa, his ankles crossed, that maddening semi-arranged expression on his face. I imagined digging my thumbs into his eyes.

'You two as well, then,' said Lottie dreamily, burying her face in Bev's circus-coloured cardigan.

His eyes changed then, focusing sharply, though his voice stayed deadpan. 'I don't expect Polly'd be too keen.'

190

I was still sulking over losing a heated argument to him about the threat of fascism in middle England, where I'd ended up shouting and wanting to catapult lumps of vanilla pod ice cream into his smug fucking face.

I stood up. 'Yeah, come on then.'

A vein swelled in his temple like a river after rain and his smile looked the most unhappy I'd ever seen it. Brilliant.

The music swirled, jellified beats and washes of sound, the sort you just melt into in your own little universe of one and is completely impossible to dance to. Still, it was totally worth it for Adam's extreme discomfort. He had one hand lightly on my waist, the other holding mine, as if we were waltzing and not moving to the musical equivalent of a lava lamp.

I gave him a look that I hoped said *Go on then, put your hand on my arse. Dare you.* He kept flitting his eyes down to my neck, or over the top of my head, his smile a thin line, looking fantastically self-conscious.

Lottie and Bev flopped back onto the sofa, Siamese twins joined at the head, eyes half closed, blissed out on nostalgia and a lot of dessert wine. They smiled up at us both as if we were a couple of puppies getting stuck in on YouTube.

The tune stopped and Adam stepped back. I could practically smell his relief. 'Time for coffee,' he said.

Their bookshelves showed off a pretty good mix of everything – classic and contemporary fiction, colour-coded spines, lots of reference books on architecture and art. There was some card-bound local history stuff and a book on Scottish myths and traditions. I pulled it out. Maybe my *thing*, whatever the hell it was, would be in here. On the inside cover was a dodgy engraving of women in bonnets pushing at some material with their bare feet. I opened it at a page about people with second sight foretelling events by looking at a sheep bone.

Adam came to my shoulder with a little handleless cup covered in navy-blue flowers.

'Can I borrow this?' I said.

'Wouldn't have thought you went in for that sort of thing, Polly.'

'Why not?'

He put his lips together and gave a half-amused shake of his head.

'Is it any good?'

'I've just dipped in and out. Think we were given it.' He seemed slightly chastened by the enforced dance number.

I looked at the back cover again. 'Is there anything from round here in it?'

Adam angled his head over to read the jacket blurb. 'Not as far as I know. But the stories are pretty universal I should think.'

'What do you mean?'

He sipped his coffee. 'Oh, you know, they're all the same aren't they, really? Doesn't matter what part of the world they come from. Fear. Loss. Love. Lust.' A faintly traced smile. 'The usual.' His face smoothed itself out. 'They might have the bonfire in there, though.'

I looked at him.

'A tradition. Bonfires on Midsummer's Eve. They do it up here.' He put a little extra breath in his voice, eyebrows raised. 'To keep the ghosties away.'

'I think someone's staying the night tonight,' Bev said dreamily from behind us.

192

Lottie was out cold, her neck bent awkwardly, her cheek on the arm of the sofa, mouth just wide enough to slot coins into.

Bev looked at Adam. 'We've had too much to drive. You'll stay, Polly?'

'It's all right,' I said, tucking the book into the back of my shorts.

'There's plenty of space,' she said. 'You can have a room each.'

The thought of Adam creeping over the landing with an erection nosing through his boxer shorts was not appealing. 'Yeah, it's OK, I'll head back.'

'I'll walk you,' said Adam.

I glared at him. 'It's fine. Honestly. Just lend me a torch.'

'She's a big girl,' said Bev.

The lizard was still catatonically plotting its world takeover in the hallway as Adam fished a small red torch out of a sideboard drawer. 'Get back safe.'

It was a mile back to ours, first through the dimly lit village before the road flexed out into the night, dark trees on either side. I striped the branches with my torch. This was nothing. I'd been in those fucking terror hills. It was like walking down a high street in comparison. I was basically Wonder Woman spliced with Ripley from *Alien*. Half boiler suit, half extremely impractical glitzy corset.

God, I'd never felt more alive than right now. Everything in me was primed, working its arse off – eyes, ears, tastebuds. The smell of nettles and the salt of the loch. My rubber soles on the road. I put my torch up into the night and all the stars shrunk away.

A faint crunch. I stopped, listened. There – a sound like grit moving very slowly under a swivelling boot.

'Adam?' My ears felt heavy, lined in lead. I shone the torch back. Maybe he'd decided to see me home after all.

For a second I thought I saw him, but the thin shadow was just a tree, cut at with blunt scissors and leaning into the road. My wine bravado was rapidly evaporating.

I kept moving, same speed. I wasn't going to go faster when there was nothing to fear. The cold plastic of the book squeaked against my spine. It was a weapon, like the Bible against vampires. Wonder Woman and Ripley and Buffy. Katniss. A breeze coasted over me.

It was fine for it to be Adam. I'd tongue him if it meant being back within four walls and my heart shuffling back down behind my ribs.

Another wash of breeze, stronger and warmer.

Something seemed to be collecting in the torchlight in front of me. Forming. Forming into pale, laddered lines. Moving forwards. The wind was blowing towards me with faint chalk lines in it. Chalk lines, or – something splintered, feathers or fine bones.

'No!' I shouted, and ran straight for it, taking the book out from my waistband.

I ran into darkness. The lines dissolved as I reached them, the book aloft in my hand. There was nothing to hit with it. Just a gentle buffeting sound deep in my ear, sea shell echoes, and the trees around me.

'Well, fuck you, then,' I said.

*

I woke up on the sofa in the morning with dank rosé-breath and one cheek on the open book. My tongue hurt as if I'd chomped on it. Someone was gushing about spring onions. I turned the TV off.

Fear was exhausting. I had shut the front door, turned on all the lights in the house and whacked the telly up, loud. A soft-focus detective drama – wedding hats and Victoria sponge filling and churches – had sent me to sleep.

That and reading about water horses who turn themselves into fit boys in order to seduce some totally gullible girl who should know better, especially when he has weeds in his hair. I'd also found stories about burying healthy babies or feeding them huge lumps of butter and stupid misogynist stuff about crossing yourself when a woman approaches. Whatever. Thank God I didn't have dark-red hair. There were plenty of mentions of spirits, all with unpronounceable names. Maybe mine was the *glaistig*, or the *caoineag*, or the *beanshith*. Maybe I needed to grow the fuck up.

My leg was itching like mad. I had a look. A near-perfect circle of small red midge-bites, like an anklet.

You made me things. An anklet of grey ribbon and cowrie shells that you strung above my boot. A headdress of pheasant feathers, with the longest, darkest ones in the middle. You once tied twigs together so that they criss-crossed into a star and wound wool round it, a dense spiderweb.

I was always better at harder, more solid things – the rocks, sometimes sanded down into smooth orbs, or just rubbed on my skirt and given to you. Metals, too. My uncle would let me use his tools, though they were too big for the things I wanted to make. Pendants. Bracelets. Hearts.

You said I should be a silversmith. That I had the hands for it, the eye. I dreamt of silver turning to liquid, liquid moulding into the shapes of leaves, snakes, pebbles. Adding tourmaline, dendrite opal, angel-hair quartz.

Silver into liquid into a new shape. Not knowing that it would happen to me.

One evening, a real keepsake. You held a bird's egg in your palm, bid me lift off the top. It had been broken so carefully that not a scrap of shell was missing.

And inside – inside was a ring.

The jeep was bumping up the track as I came out of the trees. I parked my arse on a lumpy bit of ground to wait for it. Tyger wasn't with me this time. I worried he was a shaggy bad-luck charm.

'All right,' Jim said, his elbow on the window frame.

I wondered if it still smelled of dead deer inside. 'Are you off somewhere?'

'No, just saw you coming.' He nodded at my acid-pink T-shirt. 'I was thinking about' – he pulled a face, a mixture of irritated and perplexed – 'going fishing.' His eyes flickered to my face and at my neatly bandaged leg for a nanosecond before looking past my shoulder at what I could only guess must have been an extremely diverting spike of gorse.

I split the bit of grass I'd been holding into separate strips. 'I'll be no bother. If that's what you're wondering.'

The inside of his eyebrows ended abruptly in two short, vertical lines like bookends. He was probably wondering if me not being a bother was even possible. Then he swiped the plastic bag and ragged envelopes off the seat next to him and opened the passenger door.

'Do you not wear a lifejacket or anything?'

Jim shook his head, folding up another square of tin foil.

Flat, tarpaulin water. I was gripping both sides of the boat as if they were the railings at the top of the Eiffel Tower. 'What if it, like, capsizes?'

'It won't.'

'But what if I just fall in?'

He sat back and looked at me like I was a total wimp. Which I was. 'Can you swim?'

Friday nights swimming with Dad. Fish and chips afterwards in the car, listening to his post-punk compilations, him

197

hamming up the knifey air guitars in Gang of Four and Magazine tunes while I used chips as drumsticks and the heat and vinegar soaked through to my knees.

'Yeah. I guess.' I eyed the bright water, stretching the length of an Olympic-sized swimming pool on either side of me. 'But not in *there*.'

Jim shrugged. 'Better not fall in, then.' He spiked the foil onto a hook.

Road trip. He had driven us up past the lead mines into a sky the colour of old milk, tipping over the top of the mountain and down into forest again, almost at a right angle. He'd said that this stretch was nicknamed the Burma Road, I guess due to it being World War Two-levels of bastard. Down below us was a small, squashed loch, the land puckered up around it.

The boat – small and dull blue-green – had lain upturned on a floor of matted pine needles. He'd dragged it to the edge, twigs gathering in an arrow-shape underneath it, right next to a sign that said NO FISHING.

So many goddamned midges. Ignoring them, Jim had dumped his bag in, held the end of the boat while I'd wobbled in, and pushed us off.

There was no one for miles. We'd passed a small stone building surrounded by barbed wire and pylons, and some sort of deserted army lodge, but civilisation felt very far away.

Once in the middle of the loch, Jim slotted the oars into their rusted locks and got to work. There were, thankfully, no rancid fish heads or tubs of pearly maggots, just a long, crude-looking rod, the end of which he lodged against his seat.

'So, now we just wait?'

He nodded, a smile hanging on one side of his mouth.

The hills wore the pine trees like a pelt. I imagined rolling it off as easily as the hare's skin. If you looked at the water long enough, it turned into old-school television interference. I crossed my eyes at it and went a bit dizzy.

'How's the leg?' I swear he glanced at my wrist as well.

I pulled the cuffs of my jacket down. 'Fine. Thanks.'

The water could have been sky, the sky water. We drifted, slowly, as if someone underneath had the boat in their palm and was marvelling at us. I looked for the kelpies and the selkies from Adam's book and imagined the rod arcing, Jim wrestling with a tangled white mass like sheep's wool, but the water was reflective and shiny and gave nothing away. It seemed safer, somehow, with him. I leant back a bit and drummed my fingers on the sides.

'Fish don't get morse code, you know,' he said.

I stuck my hands between my knees. 'Sorry.' I looked at the sky. 'Do you really just sit here?'

'Aye.'

Lots of thinking time, then. Time to form grand philosophies and plan world takeovers. I should probably write my essays out here. I'd nail them like a demon.

'Or I read,' he said.

I swapped him. His was quite a classy spy book set in Istanbul, monochrome turrets on the front. He was holding my Gilman – still shoved in at the bottom of my bag – like it was some medieval illustrated manuscript you should only touch wearing surgical gloves. I blathered on about gender-based economics and division of labour and fourth-wave feminism and how I was never going to have children, probably talking way too loudly and scaring the fish off, but he didn't seem to mind.

'You've had company.' Jim nodded at my bite-riddled leg. I had a line going up my calf as well, like the seam on some retro tights. Super sexy.

I crossed the other one over it. 'I'm English. They don't like me.'

He gave me a wry grin. 'They don't discriminate. And you're wrong. They *really* like you.'

I raised my eyebrows at him. 'Don't you get bitten, then?'

'I'm too tough for them. Thick skin.' He sniffed and shut one eye up at the sky. 'Trick for someone like you is to smoke. All the time. Pipes are good.'

I nodded, mock-considering. 'I could totally rock a pipe.'

'Here we go,' Jim said, sitting up a bit.

He picked up the rod, his concentration suddenly honed on the point where the line met the water. My breath caught on its own little hook as something slim and pale loomed up. Out it came, not a white thing but a half silver, half black fish, sleek as lycra, and he grabbed the line and brought it in. A wet dart with a slash-mouth.

It bounced around crazily in the bottom of the boat and I yelped and lifted my feet up, just about resisting the urge to chuck myself over the side. There'd only be more fish in there, after all. It made slick, flapping sounds, like Hannibal Lecter thinking about fava beans.

'Grab us that.' He pinned the fish between his knees and nodded at my feet.

I handed him the blunt wooden pole as long as my forearm and he promptly bashed the fish on the head with it. Demented death dance over.

'Ow.'

'Man's got to eat.' He worked the hook out of its mouth.

200

'Man can go to Sainsbury's.'

He breathed a little laugh through his nose.

We walked back to the jeep. My hands smelled of fish.

'Do you want to keep my book? I mean, borrow it?'

'Don't you need it?'

'Plenty more I can be getting on with. They're short stories, won't take you long. Or you can just read one.'

'All right.' He glanced down at his bucket. 'Want some dinner?'

*

'Where did you get those?'

I had the two mackerel out on a chopping board and was trying to watch a YouTube video on filleting fish, feeling like Gordon Ramsay only more sweary. 'Got given them. By a fisherman.'

Lottie put the kettle on. 'You're a charmer.'

'Aye,' I said, taking a gulp of air, holding it, and pulling off the second fish head.

*

The book had just been an excuse, really. The next day I got up early, smashed together all of Lottie's remaining baking ingredients and left Jim a message to say that I needed it back after all.

In the garden I put my hand to the silver birch.

Just a tree. Dashed all over with those little horizontal markings – you could imagine that twenty children had scratched in their ever-increasing heights. I tugged at a curling edge. The inside of the bark was pale beige, with slightly darker strokes. I kept peeling, meticulously, using both hands to pass the strips round, unwrapping it like a bandage. The thing had grown from right here. From *right here.* I'd not found anything about tree spirits in Adam's book.

There was a tingling on my leg. Fucking midges. Never thought I could hate something so small so much. I whacked my calf, hard, and kept tugging at the tree. Another tingle, as if several were guzzling on my skin. I couldn't see any. Now I was being tickled from my ankle up to the inside crease of my knee. I scratched like mad and swore for every last damned bastard hell midge I couldn't see.

Lottie called my name and stuck her arm out the back door, holding my phone. I could smell baked oats and honey.

My fingers were syrupy, a burnt red.

*

'Want one?'

Jim stepped over a tree root and looked back at the open tub of biscuits.

'You know, just for some variety in your diet of fish and hare and twigs and mud or whatever.'

After the birch abuse and some seriously OCD hand washing, I'd met him at the end of the village in the late afternoon to get my book back and had persuaded him to come for a walk. Everything in the oakwoods had a density to it today, sweat pouring off it like when you're four hours into a club and the walls are slippery and you slide down them as you get off with a third year you don't fancy.

'Can you eat those?' I pointed to some mushrooms shelving along a pine-trunk, their undersides the colour of parchment, the tops dark and dripping.

'Best not.'

'Why not?'

'They'd do you in.'

'In a good way?' I smiled at him in a manner that I hoped was devilish.

Jim looked at me like he was examining something under a microscope. 'No.'

'Shame.'

He held up his biscuit. 'Very nice.'

'I know,' I said, like a champion.

We sat down at the crest of a hill.

I plunged my finger into the acid-green beanbag next to me. 'What's this?' There were mini-forests of it all over the place.

Jim snapped a twig in two. A tiny ping. 'Moss.'

No shit. 'I know it's moss. What sort?'

He hardly glanced at it. 'Great Goldilocks.'

'What? You're kidding.'

He looked sidelong at me.

I reached over to another rock, covered with flatter stuff, the texture of the gross old dressing gown that Dad used to schlep around in on Sundays, his hairy calves out. 'What about that one?'

'Mouse-tail moss.'

I snorted. 'You're making them up.'

Jim raised his eyebrows, scrunched his mouth up and gave the slightest shake of his head.

'Yeah, and that's' – I pointed up at some jigsaw pieces hanging off the slim tree next to me. 'Blurty-tongue moss, and that one' – waving my finger towards another tree – 'is called, I don't know, Wizened cock tree.'

It was ridiculous how nice it felt to make him laugh a bit, even if it was just those spiked breaths from his nose. 'I'm not,' he said.

'Go on then, tell me some more.'

Jim leant back and made a sigh that sounded like he was up for the challenge. 'Have to give you the best ones now.' He looked around with a frowning grin. 'They're not here, but if you want good names ...' He gazed in front of him. 'Devil's-bit scabious. Scottish beard moss. Mountain everlasting.'

'Bollocks.'

He smiled at his feet. 'Nope.'

'How do you know them all?'

He was still holding the two bits of twig in his hands, like cutlery. 'It's like knowing all the names of the roads or the buses where you live. We don't have many buses. Or roads.'

'Did someone teach them to you?'

'My mother. She knew them all. I've forgotten half of it.'

That was about as monumental an offering as him ripping his lungs out and thrusting them at me. Thinking about someone else being attached to him made him more human. He was just a guy. With a mum. He hadn't said her name with much of a misty eye, though.

'Where's she now?' I carefully asked the tree next to me.

A long silence. 'Gone.'

'Do you – have any brothers or sisters?'

'I've a brother in Australia.'

'Oh, cool. Have you been out there?'

Another pause, in which branches scraped and you could hear the wind lifting up blades of grass like it had lost something.

Jim got up. 'No.'

I watched him wander off, dropping the pieces of twig. One, then the other.

He was lonely, then. No family around. I hadn't dared ask after his dad, but I couldn't quite see him popping up the road to his pa with a homemade cake in a Tupperware box under his arm – and he'd not talked of friends. I felt sure I was annoying, following him around, making him show me stuff, but – I liked hanging out with him. I didn't feel as if I had anything to prove. I could just be me, stupid me. And he didn't seem to mind.

On the track back down, Jim stopped suddenly. He was staring at the tiny, almost-empty car park at the bottom of the hill, shrouded by pines.

There was a man by his jeep.

I recognised him, even from this distance. The long mac, the antler stick. 'Oh, it's Johnny.'

We watched him. He was standing strangely at an angle to the front window of the jeep, as if he might be hanging around for a bus, but kept craning his head back to peer inside.

'You know him?' Jim's voice was opaque.

'Yeah, I talked to him the other day.'

His jaw was tight, his eyes fixed on Johnny, who was now ambling along the side of the vehicle, his walking stick trailing, making a great show of sauntering by even though there was no one around.

'I don't think he's trying to break into your jeep,' I said.

Jim didn't seem convinced, in which case I wondered why he wasn't steaming down there, batting him away. He was almost rigid and I could sense something simmering in him.

Johnny had done a full circle of the jeep, his body language a mixture of watchful and insouciant. Finally he walked off down the path towards the village, lifting the point of his stick as I'd seen him do before, stately, his other hand in his pocket.

Jim didn't move until Johnny had turned the corner and was masked by trees. Then he put a hand to the back of his head, digging a finger in with a slow, deep scratch, looking pensive and faintly angry.

'Shall we?' I said.

He lowered his arm, still caught up in a thought I couldn't quite read, nodded, and walked ahead of me.

10

Lottie persuaded me to have another fun-time trip to Fort William, winner of Crap Town of the Year three years running. A half-arsed high street and dour buildings and signs in florid italics and nowhere selling anything worth buying. Lottie dawdled at windows while I stuffed a pasty into my face and stared at the mountains, wondering if I was fit enough to climb them yet. Yeah, right. I'd probably have a panic-attack-slash-cardiac-arrest a quarter of the way up and have to be stretchered into a helicopter by mountain rescue.

I managed to lose Lottie for a bit to have a fag and steal into a bank to ask about loans. No one was free to see me, though, so I came away with a handful of useless leaflets and tried not to think about how fucking broke I was.

We missed the second bus, and – the next one being in about two years' time – Lottie expertly extinguished the prospect of a twelve-mile walk by using her best pleading voice on the phone to Bev.

We sat on a bench and watched the cars trundle onto the ferry, the metal ramp clunking.

She put her hand on mine. 'It's nice to have you up here. Even if I never see you.' She looked at me. 'Where do you go?'

I tucked my hair into my jacket. 'Oh, you know. Around.' I nodded at the mountains over on the other side of the loch. 'Into it.' She'd think it weird, me hanging out with Jim. It probably was weird.

The ferry arrived at the opposite slipway, a line of cars ready and waiting. Lottie drifted on to the list of things she would do when she got home to Surrey – more Benji-time, more discerning choice of clients, Italian lessons, Alexander technique. I tried not to think about what I would do. Get some shit cleaning job to try and claw back a scrap of my overdraft. Bore myself to death on Redhill High Street. Take up heroin to distract from guilt. Cry.

There was a double-beep like a goose honking behind us, and Bev waved through the window.

*

I woke up thinking I was freezing cold, only to find the bedsheet tacky with sweat. I was sure I'd heard something.

I'd just about got used to the stifling vacuum of silence up here. But now, wide awake in the dark, my blood humming, I found myself praying for raucous rat-arsed students, police sirens, a toddler shouting the same word over and over. Sounds that meant *people*. Real, fleshy, lovely muscle-and-fat-filled people.

A rustling noise. Coming from behind the curtains. My ears went hot. The window was open – I could just see the metal arm poking at the material like a long finger.

There it was again. The sound of someone rubbing two padded envelopes together. It seemed so audacious, so rudely penetrating.

I didn't breathe. My lips had completely dried up.

Rustle.

I lay with my hands flat on my stomach, like a corpse, daring it to happen again, dreading that it would. Every time it came, it had a different rhythm. Two rubs. Silence. Three, a gap, and one more.

It was playing. It was taking the piss.

I stared up into aubergine-coloured darkness – an aubergine rapidly spotting with mould, my eyes dancing, the mould multiplying. White-grey mould, a galaxy of it, descending on me. And one single, deliberate creak. Shitting hellfuck. I thrust my head under the duvet, put an arm out to pull in my phone and my headphones, and whacked on the squelchiest trash-dance I could find, praying that no one was there, trying with every fibre of my being to transport myself to a sweaty, strobey superclub complete with dilated pupils and shoving and drinks spilling on my feet. Superclub. Superclub.

In the morning, the plastic band of the headphones was digging into my jaw. Working them off, I felt something under the back of my hand.

There was a long, white feather on my pillow.

'Thanks for the present,' I said to Lottie in the conservatory.

She looked up from her book. 'What, darling?'

It was a swan feather. Or a goose's. One and a half times as long as my hand, and startlingly white. Surely not the feather of a proper bird – birds would get grubby, flying about, bombing into the woods, lording it in the loch. The barbs

209

were slightly shorter on one side and tightly pleated, the spine a shade darker. In bed I had run it along my lips. Moleskin, or velvet.

'The present. On my pillow.' Her piece of marmalade-laden toast hovered in the air. 'The feather,' I said.

She gave me an odd look. 'I didn't …'

'Oh. My bad.'

'Do you want some—'

I was already out of the room.

I sat Tyger down on the sofa and tapped his nose with the end of the feather. It was as delicate as a pair of fifteen-denier tights.

'So, this is your doing, is it?'

Tyger blinked and coughed.

I grabbed the lamp from the table and held it above his head, narrowing my eyes at him. 'Can you catch birds? Have you been pretending to be a cushion all this time when in fact you're a cunning huntsman? A hunning cuntsman?' Tyger did a quick-fire lick of his nose with the tip of his tongue, a little *thhp*. I leant back on my elbows with a sigh. 'That's a no, then.'

My phone buzzed in my pocket. Maybe it was Jim.

Heyo

Stef. It was the first time he'd started a conversation since I'd left London.

Hey you ok? x

Nope

Of course. He'd only get in touch with me when he was feeling sorry for him-fucking-self. He was probably in love with some boy he'd met three minutes ago who had already dumped him.

Whats up?

I stared at my phone, watching the dots as he typed.

A link came through. Facebook. The Metropolitan Police page. A post asking for help identifying a young man in hospital. And a photo.

*

In the forest on Jim's side of the loch I kicked at a tree stump and it crumbled, spilling everywhere. At one edge, there was a beetle stuck halfway out of a beetle-sized cavity. I crouched down to look.

'What have you got?' Jim asked.

'I don't know.' I pointed. It was edging two spindled legs out of its hole.

He picked it up carefully and held his palm right up to me. The beetle was doing a graceful, unhurried dance that made me think of those dreamy kung fu action sequences in Chinese movies. Green wings shimmering in the afternoon light.

It had been the heart of that tree, the king of it. And I'd gone and bashed its home in. Maybe its slow movement was actually agonised grieving. It twitched and I saw the Spanish boy, fitting.

I walked to the edge of the loch and sat down, sick as a dog. That photo of him on the police page – he'd looked asleep, apart from the plaster over the side of his nose, the tube on the pillow. I'd typed the hospital number into my phone and then deleted it.

Jim sat down a couple of metres away, letting the beetle slide onto a leaf. 'You all right?'

'I shouldn't have kicked that tree in.' I put my head in my hands, before looking sidelong at him through my fingers.

He chewed on the corner of his thumbnail and looked at it. 'OK.'

Rough semblances of trees, clouds, were sketched on the water. 'Have you ever fucked up something you couldn't undo?'

His thumb stayed near his mouth. Nothing breathed. 'Aye.'

I hadn't replied to Stef. What could either of us say now?

'I just …' I couldn't tell him. 'What do you do? When you can't make it better?'

There was the sound of leaves, brushing up against each other. He looked at his palm. 'Sit it out.'

I didn't even know the guy's name. He'd shouted it but the music was crashing in our ears and he'd had a strong accent. Stef had thought it sounded like Bottom, which made us both screech hysterically. A name to suit both the gayboy and the English student.

Sometimes I wished I could just swap myself, be someone else entirely. A new skin, like the selkies in the book. You'd shed your old, claggy one and come out slick and fresh-speckled.

'I don't know what I'm doing. I mean' – I looked over at him – 'in general.'

Jim picked at some heather. 'Do you need to know just yet?'

'Other people do. Other people have direction. I'm just …' I leant back. 'A fuck-up.'

A squirrel lolloped into view.

'No one knows,' he said. 'Things change.'

The squirrel looped about, trying to decide what punctuation mark to be.

'You might think you know, but –' he stared ahead and gave a sudden shake of his head, 'it's not always in our hands.'

The squirrel saw us and darted away.

212

I tried to wrestle myself out of the dark. 'What did you want to be? When you were my age?'

He righted himself slowly and looked at the loch. 'Up to my knees in mud and pheasants. Gamekeeping, ranging maybe.' He plucked a sprig of gorse and examined it. 'And married.' He said it so quietly that it almost got lost.

I hadn't expected that. 'What happened there, then?' I asked, very carefully.

His eyes clouded a little. He took a breath in but didn't speak. Then he got up, shreds of gorse-flower falling off his jeans. 'Things change.' He looked like he was going to walk away.

Of course. That's what he did. Went moody and fucked off.

But he put his hand out. 'Come on. Show you something nice.'

I followed him up a hill through the pines. He veered off the track and into a clearing surrounded by heftier trees, where a little sculpture hung from a protruding branch on a length of bright-green wire. Two horizontal oblongs of rough, mottled wood with semicircles topping and tailing them.

Jim sat down at the foot of a tree with leaves the shape of gingerbread men. He crossed his legs out in front of him, clasped his fingers on his thighs and smiled faintly up at me. His eyes moved to the ground next to him. It looked damp.

I slid down between two roots and leant carefully against the tree's ridges. 'What are we—'

He put a finger a foot away from his lips. 'Best not talk,' he said in a voice that was part-wind and mud.

The bottom of his earlobe had a tiny hole in it. A piercing, long since closed.

A root dug into the small of my back. He looked so comfortable and still. If you cut him open, maybe he'd be ringed inside and he'd give off that sharp, lacquered smell that was everywhere round here. Above us, the sky was a pale, silvery blue, the fright wigs of the trees against it.

I put my hand in the dank leaves and pine needles. It came away sticky, the PVA glue we used to coat our skin with in primary school, just to peel it off again. And moss was everywhere, dense and lacy and spearmint-coloured, or as darkly curled as kale. Probably with names like Wondrous Bathmat Moss and Wet-look Sex Leaf.

Jim gently nudged my elbow. He was looking straight ahead. A little bird with a peachy breast and a slate-blue helmet was perched on a branch, its neck angled, beak pointed at the sculpture. It flew forward, twisted and zipped back to the tree. Then it did the same thing again, before finally gripping onto the green wire with its talons. Tiny, furious jabbings, like I used to do with a compass around my fingers, trying to impress the boys. Of course, what a freaking idiot – it wasn't a sculpture. It was a bird feeder.

'Chaffinch.' Jim hardly moved his lips.

After a minute, another bird came down, smaller, puffed-up, with two Winehouse slicks of black on its head.

'Coal tit.'

The chaffinch again, and a brown bird, tail cocked.

'Wren.'

Two more chaffinches and a super-cute blue and lemon and lime one – a blue tit, even I knew that – joined in. Their wings purred as they bounced on the air, stopping at the feeder for a mad guzzle and whizzing off again.

My foot was tilted towards his knee, just touching. We watched them for ages, neither of us moving an inch, and it

214

never got boring. Two got into a little bitch fight, a blur of feathers and high chirping that probably meant they were enraged but sounded insanely sweet. One landed on the tip of Jim's boot just for a second, its movements like a finely made toy's, before taking off again.

It was like he was bloody Snow White or something.

'Did you make that?' I asked under my breath.

He nodded, still watching them.

'How often do you come up here?'

'On and off.'

'Have you brought anyone else here before?'

Jim's eyes were the colour of the kelp on my edge of the loch, when the sun was on it. He shook his head.

We walked back to the jeep. There was the mushroomy smell of rain coming.

'I thought maybe you didn't like birds,' I said.

Jim stopped short, his hands in his pockets. 'Why did you think that?'

'I don't know. When I first saw you ...'

He flushed and kicked at a root, started walking again.

*

In the conservatory, book redundant on my lap, I crunched a biscuit and startled myself with its loudness. Dust motes turned in the air around me, and outside midges and bits of leaves spun like snow.

Jim hadn't said another word on the way back, just nodded, his knuckles whitening on the steering wheel, when I said bye at the end of his road. He was like the weather, a thin skin of pale sunshine then three days of bastard rain. Whenever I felt I was getting somewhere he'd retreat back into his stupid Neanderthal self.

I went outside with a cup of tea in my hands. The pile of bark I'd peeled off the other day looked like the remains of a bird that had smashed into the tree. The evening sun was so intense, splaying out from over on the opposite hill. It coated the left-hand side of the plants and the fence posts in silver-white, and everything seemed astonished into silence.

The back of my leg itched like a motherfucker. I'd smothered every inch of myself in that cream again – the midges couldn't be biting me, unless they were some super-mutant strain. I pictured myself in a pair of protective visors, wielding a blowtorch like an Uzi, fag hanging louchely from my mouth. A deep American film trailer-voice introducing me, my name in splashy letters. There was a prickling sensation on my neck, at the bottom of my hairline.

This time I stayed still.

It wasn't a bite at all. It was as if someone were exploring me with very soft nails, a child who's just been in the bath. I went to stone. The tickling trailed up the side of my neck, behind my earlobe. I was welded to the grass, couldn't move even if I'd wanted to.

'Polly?'

I turned around, slowly, in my silver-white skin.

'I've been calling you,' said Lottie, looking at me curiously. 'Didn't you hear?'

I stared at her blankly.

She wrapped her cardigan round herself, her eyebrows coming up in exasperation. The oven fan grumbled behind her. 'Dinner.'

*

On the way to the hotel for a drink, Lottie and I passed Johnny sitting on a bench facing the loch. The hills on the other side of the water were going buttery yellow. I shouted a hello and he lifted his beret up as if it were a top hat.

'Who's that?' said Lottie.

By the time we got inside I'd filled her in on his whole life story. Fraser had his elbows on the bar, chatting to Becca and a guy with a leather jacket from the wrong decade, and he straightened up when I came over. Pastel colours still daubed round his eye. He'd probably told his mum that I'd whacked him. Wished I had.

'Double vodka and Diet Coke. And a tomato juice. Please.'

He looked at me as if I hadn't finished my sentence.

'What?' I said, keeping the word flat.

His eyes bruised. I gave him dead ones back and he did a small, curt shrug and shake of his head at the same time. Becca looked like she was trying to decide which bit of me to cut off first. I handed the money over in silence.

A bundle of limbs crashed into the bar next to me. 'All right, Pollth, fanthy getting thkinned alive?' Finn was giving me a braces-filled beam.

'Jesus. What happened to you?'

'I'm now offithially part robot. Come on, you know you want to. I'll play nithe.'

Lottie had her chin on her fist, gazing at me in wonder. 'How do you know everyone?'

I shrugged. 'It's just my way. I'm like a magnet. Two minutes. I'll be back.'

*

217

Three demolitions at the pool table and five double vodkas later I stepped out into the dusk. Lottie had gone ahead, pleading tiredness, and I'd fought the urge to tug on her hand and make her stay so I didn't have to walk home on my own. Drunken oblivion would make it better. It was ridiculous. It was nothing. Nothing but clouds and wind and twilight and my imagination.

The jeep was parked over the road. I stood still for a moment, watching it, then walked over, trying my best to stay in a straight line.

Jim opened the door, the light coming on.

I wasn't sure what to say or whether to smile.

He swivelled in the driver's seat, his feet on the frame, woolly hat jammed down to his eyebrows. 'I'm' – a small cough – 'sorry about ...' He clamped his hands between his knees. 'I'm just not very good at ...'

He'd been waiting here for me. Waiting to apologise.

'It's cool,' I said, quickly. 'Wanna come in for a drink?' He glanced past me to the hotel. 'I've got three pounds to my name. That's enough for one and a half beers. Or a double vodka, no mixer.' I nodded very expertly.

Jim's shoulders relaxed. 'No, you're fine. But' – he scratched the bridge of his nose – 'do you want to come by tomorrow?' He seemed to want to say something else, but if he did, he chewed down on it.

'*Sure*,' I said, with vodka-loudness.

I ran myself another pond-water bath, having managed to successfully make it home unmolested and fright-free. The air had been as cool and clean as all the vodka I'd drunk, no cobwebby, feathery distractions. I imagined giving birth to one now, a pale tangle trailing out from between my legs, curdling in the water.

When Jim had said to come over, I'd had to blink away an image of him taking off his clothes, and mine, and bending me over his home-made table. He'd showed me those birds, trying to cheer me up – before he cavemanned. I liked being with him, a lot, except it was hard to know what he was thinking, and hard to know when he was going to disappear into himself again.

Fraser had looked hopeful for a second at the bar, though less so with every drink I'd bought. How he couldn't see that Becca would sit on top of him in a flash, all her bones rattling like loose change, if he blinked nicely at her I had no idea. That look she'd given me tonight. Maybe she'd nicked my keys. The last place I'd definitely had them was at the bothy when I'd been fighting with my jacket on the bottom bunk, trying to get my kit off. She'd been making like a wolf outside, plotting my demise. No – if Becca had come into the house I'd probably be dead already. Fraser, then. I thought of him creeping round my bedroom, leaving me feathers. Jesus.

The patch of mould in the corner of the ceiling looked almost artfully painted on. Spreading. The steam rolled from me, my own mist-skin, and I closed my eyes.

Mist, slipping like shoulder-straps. Mist like earmuffs. Mist and mist and snow and clouds and skin and—

Feathers. Feathers on me.

I jerked awake, the fan as loud as rioting football hordes in my ears. For a second I could have sworn that I was in a bath of wet, white feathers. I shot out and turned round in front of the steamed-up bathroom mirror, more than once, checking that none were stuck to my back.

I am the wind and the white. Bones and feathers.

Why will she not tell you? I feel her story and mine, the twinned crystal, a different light on the stone depending on how you turn it.

Stories. There are so many stories here, others I never knew before.

Can you imagine a time when wolves still lived in these hills? The last wolf killed Maggie Cameron as she walked from her mother's over the pass, its jaws on her neck, a growl of heat and blood.

Brandon McDuffie was carried off by an eagle. He sat in a nest and cried until the eagle came back and tore his skin, his sinews snapping. The little girl Morag Leitch, having fallen, drowned in a burn no higher than her calves. Flora Cameron, dragged to the edge of a cave and her knees lifted next to her ears, cheek against gorse.

Some had places named after them, after their deaths. Clac Alasdair Oig. Allt mo Nionag. An Geata Lady. Glac Uamh Nigh'n Alasdair.

I don't know if anyone has named my place. Where the loch laps at the stones like a cat at milk.

The place where the bullet hit.

It was only the second time I'd actually been inside his house. I pottered around while he did things to the generator outside. It wasn't any tidier, that was for sure.

I was a lot more sober this time, though, and took more in. Mugs hung on thick, smoothed twigs under one of the cupboard shelves. Knives were in a jar next to a hand-carved wooden spoon. Old loose-tea tins were stacked along one side of the sink, the metal dull and dented. He obviously liked lining things up – jars, plates, books, a row of short nails sticking upwards above the fire. Like Benji. Except Benji would do it his own way, arranging our shoes in the hallway, or placing tomatoes in order of size on top of the fridge, going mental at me if I took one from the middle.

Clothes, in resolutely workmanlike colours, were kept in a couple of plastic boxes under the mezzanine. There was a musty smell, thick and antique. Everything seemed to have a very fine layer of dust on it.

Jim was leaning against the doorway, hands in his back pockets, seeming mildly discomfited. 'Wanted you to see something.'

Cut to me kneeling in front of him, examining his cock through a pair of pince-nez, giving it the big thumbs-up. God, Polly, stop it.

He was looking at the table. There were two largish folded pieces of paper on it. Maybe they were maps to hidden treasure and we'd find it together and I'd be minted and could stab the student loan people in the eyes with rolled-up fifties.

They weren't maps. They were drawings. Studies in fine black pen of birds' wings. On one, individual wings were isolated as if floating in a pale sky, dense shading for the shorter feathers, the strokes whisper-thin. The other showed a bird in flight viewed from the back, its long wings outstretched. Underneath it were sketchier versions of separate parts of the same bird – a whole underside of feathers, a single one, a tuft of tail, and the whole bird again in a few simple lines, like a wooden frame.

I thought of Leonardo da Vinci's drawings of flying machines and mills and tanks. It was as if Jim were inventing a bird for the first time. As if birds didn't yet exist.

'I just like to know how they work.' He sounded guarded.

'You're really good.' He didn't say anything, just took a step to the side, still in the open doorway, and back again. 'Did you train as an artist, then?'

'No. Just – started.' He took his woolly hat off. 'Kept doing it.'

I chucked a grin his way. 'Wanna draw me?'

'I don't do people.' His hair was sticking up, a raven who'd just shaken itself out after falling headfirst into a puddle.

'Why not? I bet you'd be good.'

He pushed himself off the door frame. 'People move.' It wasn't said unkindly.

'I can stay still.'

'Oh, aye,' he said, as if I'd just announced that I was the Queen or had been to the moon, and put the kettle on.

A deer skull rested on one windowsill, the antlers asymmetrically curving upwards, tips pointy enough to pick your teeth with. I thought of the deer I'd found on the road coming back to life, fur appearing over the bone, its graceful dancer legs and peat-brown eyes.

Jim cleared his throat behind me. 'Got you something.' He nodded vaguely at the table again.

I hadn't looked any further than the drawings. There was a pile of damp old newspapers that had fused together. A large pair of rusty scissors. An empty milk carton. A pipe.

I picked it up. It had a horizontal stripe around the well, which was a rich brown-red, its bottom deliberately pock-marked. A straight neck and a black mouthpiece that curved downwards.

'For the mozzies.' He had a hand on the back of his neck and was looking somewhere near my knees.

'Did you make it?'

'No.'

He'd gone to a shop and actually bought me something. I clamped the pipe between my teeth and chomped on it, jutting my lower jaw out, Popeye-style. Jim gave a slow grin.

I looked at the end I'd chewed. 'I don't have anything to put in it.'

He dug in his back pocket and slung me a pack of tobacco.

'Got anything stronger?'

Jim shook his head with half a smile and unhooked a couple of mugs.

I sat cross-legged on the floor with my tea and leant towards the pile of books by the fireplace. Retro-looking Lonely Planets and Rough Guides were interspersed with more novels. 'Have you been to all these places?'

He leant back in the armchair and shook his head. 'I haven't been out of Scotland.'

'What? That's insane. Really? But—' I stopped myself saying *But you're, like, forty.* I ventured on more gently. 'Why not?'

He scratched his beard and did that cloudy-eyed thing.

I pushed on, quickly. 'I want to go everywhere. The Far East, Australia, South America, Russia, well maybe not Russia, but *everywhere.*'

'You're here, though.'

'There are reasons.' I sighed. 'Money, for one. In that I have none. And' – I stopped. He glanced at me. I pushed my fist into the concrete floor. The sugar was kicking in. 'I was supposed to go on holiday. A proper holiday. I mean, not travelling, but you know, sun, sea, sand and – all that, with a friend. But I messed it up.'

Jim didn't say anything.

'I messed everything up.'

He was gazing towards the open door, cradling the underside of his mug.

'I might have killed someone.'

Anyone else would have leapt up, shaken my shoulders, said *What the absolute fuck, Polly.* Jim did the opposite. He went very still. Blinked at the doorway, before turning his head very slowly. 'How do you mean?' His voice was low, neutral.

'I was in London. With a mate. And we picked a guy up, sort of, and I mean, everyone takes stuff. Everyone does. It's just part of it. We thought he was just being shy, or polite, or that maybe he thought we were trying to sell it to him.' I tried not to let my voice crack. 'But he took it and it was all cool until we were waiting for the bus, we were going to go home together—'

I remembered Stef, whispering idiotically about spit roasts and Eiffel Towers and me smacking him in the mouth and telling him he'd be the only one getting roasted. The guy looking at us, smiling nervously, and a police car going by and Stef miming a blow job at it and whooping.

'And, yeah. He collapsed and was sort of fitting and it must have been the E and we …' I stared at the wall. 'Ran away. And left him. On the street.'

I snuck a look at Jim, whose eyes were on the floor. He had done that thing again. Where he asked a question and my answer was ten times as long and he just sat there, letting my words spill out. And he'd just absorb it, like nothing was a big deal. I could tell him I'd sawn off someone's face and eaten it as part of a five-course meal and he'd sit there, nodding sagely. Not judging.

I wished he would say something now, though. Anything.

'Do you know he's dead?' he said eventually.

I shook my head. 'He's in a coma.' I saw the plump bottom lip in the photo again, the sleepy slump of his head.

'Then' – he eyed his cup – 'he's not dead.' Spoken as if it was the final word.

Not dead *yet*. I told him about the wallet, about not really knowing his name. 'Do you think I should call the police?'

Another painfully long pause. 'No.' He took a slow breath in. 'There's nothing you can do.'

I wished I knew what his look meant. It wasn't blame, or disgust, or – it wasn't anything I understood.

I let out a shuddering breath. I felt like I'd been probed with a knife. 'Anyway,' I said, getting up, holding the pipe. What more was there to say? 'Um. Nice cactus.'

The one I had bought him sat with his others at the far end of the table, part of the little spiketastic family. Looking at it now, it seemed alarmingly phallic. God.

He turned his head towards the table and stared at it for ages. Then he tipped his cup up, finished it, and nodded at my hand. 'Gonna give that a whirl, then?'

We sat at the edge of the river.

'Eat shit, midgefuckers,' I said, pipe in teeth.

Jim breathed a laugh and flicked one off his eyelash. He hadn't said another word yet. Maybe he didn't want to speak to me again. Was just waiting this one out, waiting for me to get the hell away from him so that he could phone the Met and grass me up.

I looked at the cushioned cleft of the hills, the clouds pushing themselves between them. The giraffe-patches of heather. 'Where were you before this?' I still felt really fucking shaky. Needed to talk about anything else.

'Not far away.'

Wow. A whole life spent up here. Though he wasn't exactly brimming over with joy about it. 'What do you like best?'

'Best?'

I took the pipe out, feeling like a Victorian gentleman. 'What's the best thing about being here?'

A line deepened in his forehead. 'I'll show you if you like.' There was the edge of a challenge in his voice again, like with the lobster, and the hare. The Lobster and the Hare. Sounded like a really posh country gastropub.

'Yeah. OK.'

'Not now. Stuff to do. Tomorrow.' He stood up and wiped his hands against each other. 'It'll—' He stopped and I squinted up at him. 'It'll be all right.' His eyes were solid, full of earth.

I moved my hair out of my face and nodded. I wanted to believe him more than anything.

Jim glanced about as if he weren't sure which direction to walk in. 'And you'll get there.' He looked at me again and his voice was as soft as the water up here. 'You'll get to all those places.'

'Yeah. Maybe.' I wondered why he hadn't.

*

226

'What're you doing with him?'

I'd asked Jim to drop me off in the village so I could replenish dwindling Diet Coke and biscuit supplies. Fraser had been chucking bottles into the big recycling bins over the road. The waterfalling clinks had stopped as we'd passed, and I had studiously ignored him. When I emerged from the shop he was on the porch reading the notices.

'What's it to you?' I said.

Fraser was looking at me incredulously. 'Are you *shagging* him?'

I started to walk away. 'Fuck off, Fraser.'

He called after me. 'He's dangerous.'

Jim's dark look, next to the jeep, blood and feathers on his hands. The hare, dripping. I turned back round. 'Whatever, it's no big deal.'

He gave me an odd look. Definitely no dimples for me today. 'Are you serious?' Jesus, how little he knew. *I* was dangerous, not Jim.

'It's just poaching.' Hares and illegal fishing was not exactly terrifying stuff. Maybe other people had seen him taking birds apart, too.

The sun caught his face and there was a glint in his eye. 'Right.'

He was actually jealous. 'Have you got something of mine?' I said.

An aloof frown. 'No.'

'You haven't got anything of mine?'

'Like what? No.' Fraser dug into his pocket and I waited for the jingle of my keys. He produced a ten-pack of fags and plucked one out furiously.

I began to walk again.

'Polly.' Spoken with fag in mouth.

227

I stopped, but kept facing the bay.

'You should be careful.'

'You're a dick,' I flung back at him over my shoulder, hoping my arse was looking excellent.

*

I was lying on my back, my arms heavy at my side. Snow was falling.

It was falling onto me. Cold, wet kisses, dissolving quickly. Each flake was perfectly templated to slot into the gaps of other flakes, a complex jigsaw being constructed.

There was snow on my eyelids, awkward false lashes that I couldn't blink away. Flakes fizzed on my lips. My face numbed. Soon it had risen up around me, as high as my shoulders – I was part of a landscape of snow, a system of low hills, snow layering around and on top of me. It filled my ears and compressed, heavy as stone.

It kept coming. A fountain of snow. And I couldn't move.

11

Lottie was frowning at herself in the mirror in the hallway, her stomach sucked in slightly.

I put my hands round her waist from behind. '*I'd* do you.'

She put her palms on my knuckles. 'Um. Thank you. What do you smell of?'

Fags. A little drop of mid-afternoon booze. I heard the faint rasp of an engine outside and kissed her cheek. Earl grey tea on her breath. 'Off out.'

Her look said *again*? 'Where?'

'Just out. See you.'

*

We were walking in the sky.

It was so empty. I was probably leaving footprints where no human had before – apart from Jim, of course, striding through it like he personally knew every sprig of gorse, like every tree-root had a name. Which it probably did. A ridiculous one.

Late afternoon. Overhead a single bird wheeled high up, watching us move over the tops of the hills. Some sort of eagle, giving a cry like a raver's whistle at a festival in the morning, long after everyone else has stopped. Every shade of green was on display – Pepperskin, Wine Bottle, Wasabi

Bite, Squeeze of Lime. Seventies colours, all bright against a sky so wide it made my ribs hurt.

Jim said that come autumn, the turn of the heather would spread quickly. I pictured it, a purple blot at my feet, bruising outwards from me, all the way to the horizon. *Past* the horizon. Maybe it would keep going, not stopping at the outskirts of villages but bleeding onto pavements, under fences, up walls, keep bleeding.

The air had a brisk edge to it, but for once some heat came off the stones, which had the look of being pencil-sketched and not quite finished.

Jim turned round. 'Almost there.' He looked part of all this, like he had risen up, crackling, from the bracken. Part heather, part bark, part stone. His arms swung, blunt fingers brushing the fern.

I heard it before I saw it. Faint radio static, turned up slowly.

He stopped and I almost clattered into him. There was a gully and a bridge – if you could call it that. It looked like something a geeky kid could put together out of Meccano in about thirty seconds, just metal poles and wooden planks with big spaces in between. It didn't seem fixed to anything, just slung over the gap. Several metres below, water convulsed, cruising from a corner behind us and bashing itself over rocks before falling away into nothingness. A waterfall.

I raised my eyebrows at him. And then he took my hand and was pulling me across before I could even think about it and I hurtled over, not daring to yank back or look down. He hopped off, me next. The bridge gave a wobble and a sort of hum.

'Bastard!' I shoved him a little in the chest.

He gave me a gentle grin before walking to a shallow, sloping ledge.

'There?' It looked pretty bloody precarious.

'Scared of heights?'

I crossed my arms, tight. 'Scared of breaking both my legs and my neck and my head and being a dribbling vegetable for the rest of my life.' Like *him*, I thought, my blood stinging suddenly.

Jim was already moving past me. 'You'll be all right.'

He climbed easily down the rock face, soil loosening and falling, and I followed, negotiating stone shelves, the edges grazing my knees. The last time I'd done anything like this was in my final year of primary school, with a bright-yellow helmet on. And ropes. Lots of ropes.

At the bottom there was a coppery circle of water with curved walls almost enclosing us. The falls, not really so high now, barrelled down into the pool, like a big frilly Regency skirt being smoothed out.

'Right then,' Jim said.

I looked at him. 'What?'

He nodded at the water. 'You've got to go in.'

'I'm not going in. You never said anything about going in.' He didn't reply. I dropped my shoulders and tipped my head to the side. 'It's lovely. Thank you for bringing me here.'

'Chicken.' He was staring at the pool, a front tooth just tugging his bottom lip in, the corners of his eyes crinkling like ferns.

'You can't expect me to. It'll be freezing.'

He shrugged, nonchalant. 'I go in all the time.'

A few tiny, poster paint-green leaves were floating on the surface. There was a vinegary smell. The spray prickled my skin, just a little.

'*Fine.*' I tugged my boots off, staggering into the rock wall as I did so.

He eyed me sidelong with a smile and started unbuttoning his shirt.

Oh my God, it was so cold.

He went in first, having taken off all his clothes save for his boxers. I was pretending not to look at him, doing my own thing, but he was right *there*. In his pants. I saw a lean freckled back, a tiny bit of belly, both much whiter than his arms, and lots of hair on his thighs. But I couldn't look for long as suddenly he was in the water, ducking under and shooting back up with a big out-breath like someone had kicked him in the gut, and then he just hung in the water, facing me.

I was standing on the flat slab of rock in my clothes still, thinking, T-shirt on, T-shirt off, is he going to jump me, do I care, do I *want* him to, yes I sort of do so fuck it, and I whipped off my T-shirt and got out of my shorts with extreme speed, and had gone to the edge in my bra and pants, wishing I'd worn matching ones but glad at least that it was my bright blue bra that pushed my breasts up, holding my stomach in, my arms clenched by my side.

'You're a bastard,' I said.

He grinned, and one, two – just because I couldn't stand there in front of him practically naked any longer – I'd leapt in, and oh God, oh *God*, it was cold. Stupid, someone-biting-your-feet, someone-slapping-your-skin, gunshot-wound-in-the-face cold. The pool was deep enough for me to go right under, my toes just touching the stones at the bottom, and I'd come up, let out a tangled mix of scream and gurgle and thrashed around in a tiny circle. And I'd said it to him again, loudly, gleefully, hearing my voice bounce off the walls.

Jim just laughed quietly at me before turning and breast-stroking as lazily as if he'd been in a steaming spa pool. I was left to wrestle with the cold, gulping a couple of mouthfuls, it tasting lovely, actually – an iced vodka-gin-Listerine cocktail – and tried to get used to it, my breath coming like I was in a massive huff, lungs working like crazy. Short rock cliffs hemmed us in, the plants hanging on for dear life above us. I felt like some ruddy-faced medieval girl who had to trek here every so often to wash before going back to her life milking Highland cattle and churning cheese and singing boring old songs with fifty verses and no chorus.

I swam towards the waterfall and clambered onto the rock shelf, not really caring any more what I looked like and that he was going to get an eyeful of my arse. There was just enough space to squeeze behind it. I sidestepped along the rock and half crouched, laughing uncontrollably as the water pelted down in front of me on fast forward. It sounded powerful enough to behead me. I shuffled back onto the shelf, my toes gripping hard.

Jim was swimming on his back. His beard looked all springy. 'Thought you'd been eaten.'

There was a thin, delicate offshoot of water behind me, a silver chain. I stood under it, facing him, my hair plastered to my head, wondering how many porn scenes were set in a West Highlands waterfall. Probably loads. I lobbed myself back into the pool.

After a few more minutes of trying to catch those little insects on skates, dunking my head under and basically reverting to being nine years old, my feet were pinching.

I swam to the edge. 'I have to get out.'

Jim followed. 'Aye. Me too.'

*

On the rocks I began shivering like an idiot, hopping up and down and stamping each heel on top of the other foot. My toenails had gone blue. Jim gave me a towel to dry off with and disappeared behind a rock that stuck out like a half-open wing. I dressed incredibly quickly, a theatre actor between scenes, and he came back with his jeans and shirt on, sleeves rolled up, damp T-shirt crushed in his hand. When he saw me jiggling about he produced a hip flask from his bag and the burn of the brandy was the most perfect thing in the world.

We sat there for ages, the falls a mix of white and yellow solvent paint – Butt-Numbing Scottish Waterfall – and the sound blurry. I felt like my brain had been scrubbed. Goosepimples peppered my legs and my hair had gone as soft as anything. A glow spreading like warm butter on my skin.

'You did all right, there.' He was leaning back on his hands, his legs stretched out, bare feet crossed at the ankles.

I could see the corner of his boxer shorts that he'd crumpled up and stuffed in his pocket. I almost blushed, then. I should have done the same – my pants were soaking through my shorts, my skin going clammy.

I peeled a little weed off my arm. '*You're* a bloody otter or something.'

'Just used to it.' He passed me the flask again and brought his knees up, resting his elbows on them. 'The cold and wet's part of us up here, is all.'

'Is that why you're all so fucking miserable?'

'Aye, probably.' He breathed a tiny laugh through his nose. 'Cheeky get.' The water had scoured him clean, too. His limbs seemed to have loosened.

The long white scar I had seen on his wrist stretched all the way along his forearm, widening in the middle and going right up to the point of his elbow. 'How did you get that?'

Jim's look was pensive, ominous. 'A fight.'

My heart clunked slightly, thinking of Fraser. 'Yeah?'

He narrowed his eyes at me. 'With a tree.'

'Bad tree,' I said.

'Got my own back.' And he winked.

By the time we climbed up again – the bridge wasn't any less terrifying, though I ran over it first this time – clouds were loitering over the far hills. The brandy had infused my bones and I powered ahead of him, following the trail we'd made before. I probably had massive dark patches on my arse. I turned round and walked backwards. Jim was watching the horizon, frowning slightly into the sun.

One end of the sky was beginning to look vague and heavy. 'Is that coming our way?'

'Aye.'

I listened to the rhythmic rasp and crunch of my boots on the heather and to my shorts rubbing together, like a broom on concrete. My breath, too. I stopped dead. Everything else was so still, as if it had been shushed, forever the moment before everyone yells *Surprise!*

Jim caught up and followed my eyes to the mountains.

'Don't you ever get lost out here?' I said.

'I know it pretty well.'

That wasn't what I meant. I tried again. 'How is this here?'

A thoughtful pause. 'A glacier.' He lifted his arm. 'Coming right down—'

I hadn't meant that either. How are you here? I'd wanted to say, and me, standing in this place where you could hear grass, a single blade broken halfway down the stem, creaking.

But I let him tell me, because thinking of glaciers melting over millennia made me feel impossibly small, a speck of chalk dust, and it was better, somehow. Because maybe none of it mattered – what I'd done, all the rest of my failings – and we'd be flattened soon enough, crushed and hardened and mixing with mud and river and moss and other bones and becoming the base of a mountain. I could waft over the face of it all, turn in the light like a dust mote, catch it if I wanted to, find a fold of gloom if I didn't. It should have made me feel hopeless. But it made me feel free.

There was a strange, low roar in the valley. It sounded like a motorway, or a military plane doing a fly-past.

'What's that?' I said.

Jim cocked his head. 'Wind.'

We kept walking, light skimming the grass. Dark clouds scratched over, and there was a sudden, startling flush of sunshine just in front of us. Everything became floodlit and unreal.

And then the rain came down.

'Fucking hell,' I said.

The windows in the jeep had steamed up. The rain was making a sound on the roof like twenty people at a how-many-crisps-can-you-eat competition.

It wasn't quite night yet, but it felt like it. We'd walked as quickly as we could back to the jeep, still getting totally lashed by the rain, the wind smacking us about. The sky was a series of paint swatches smudged over and over – Duck Egg, Velvet Mushroom, Dove Grey. Black.

'Sorry. The heat's not up to much in this thing.' Jim tapped a dial near my leg.

'It's fine.' I began doodling on my window. 'That was very lovely. The waterfall.' I looked across at him. It was like we were back there again, the two of us, the sound of tons of river pounding on our heads. 'Thank you.'

He scratched his skull behind his ear for far too long, peering out. 'You're fine.'

The rain and the wind gave us something to concentrate on. I sighed, loudly, wondering why he hadn't turned the engine on yet. Not that I minded. I was perfectly happy sitting here with him, even if I probably did smell like a team of post-match football players.

He had both hands on the wheel and was staring straight ahead. Maybe he was thinking about putting the seat back and giving me what for. I'd drawn a heart on my window without realising and quickly splodged it out before leaning both forearms on the dashboard and looking over at him.

He caught my eye and cleared his throat. 'Let's run you back, then.'

Maybe not. He'd seen me in my undies now, after all.

I'd needed to pee for ages, and the sound of the rain coming at us like axe-wielding Vikings didn't really help.

'Can you stop?' I said, above the noise.

'You OK?'

'Just stop. Sorry.'

Jim understood, I thought, and pulled over.

I took a deep breath. 'Back in a sec. If I don't drown.'

I had to really push at the jeep door to open it. The storm had come from nowhere, someone up above us stirring, furiously, wondering why the wind and the rain wasn't all mixing together properly. I dashed into the trees at the side of the road, trying to find somewhere he wouldn't be able to see me, though it was getting darker by the minute. A weird howling, like Becca at the bothy. Fifty Beccas. As I squatted down I started to laugh. This was ridiculous.

I stumbled back to the road and stood behind the jeep for a moment longer, letting the rain coat me like the silver skin in the garden. I was drenched anyway. My arms out, my head back. I think I might have yelled a bit.

Jim was looking at me like I was an escaped mental patient.

I smoothed my hair down and squeezed out the ends. 'Done,' I said.

We braked suddenly and I slammed into my seat belt.

'Ow.'

'Sorry.' Ahead of us a massive tree was lying straight across the road, jagged in the headlights. In the darkness you could only just see where it had ripped from its base, torn like a big chunk of farmhouse loaf.

'Oh,' I said. 'Shit.'

He got out and walked up to it, hands in his pockets. In the headlights he was a big silhouette, the rain spiking down on him lit gold.

The whole road was blocked, the main road down to the head of the loch, to my village. You couldn't steer round it – the verge shot up steeply to the right, and tipped straight downwards into a precarious bank of dense trees on the left. I thought of the jeep rolling over and over with me rattling around in it, screaming. Or of making a ramp out of planks of wood, haring up it into the air and crashing down on the other side, action-movie style.

Jim got back in and sat there, chewing a nail. 'Don't think that'll get sorted till morning.'

'Oh. OK.'

There was a silence.

He swiped a hand over his face. 'I could walk you.'

It was miles. 'What, in this? And then walk all the way back? I mean, you could stay ...' I realised how much I didn't want to introduce him to Lottie. 'Can I stay with you?' I glanced over at him. 'I'll be no bother.'

Jim looked at his fingers. 'Aye, you keep saying that.'

My stomach sagged a little. We sat there, the rain terrorising the roof. The windscreen was starting to fog up again. Leaning forward, he rubbed his sleeve on it, turned the ignition and put the jeep into reverse. The gears sounded like a house falling down.

'I hope you like whisky,' he said.

Too much good whisky is barely enough, my uncle would say.

He had got worse as I'd got older. I would sit on his lap and he'd crush me round the waist until I couldn't breathe for laughing. He had a way of charming everyone, was always up to something, the police over more than once, always getting away with it.

He was all hands and I'd never minded, before. But his looks changed the taller I got, looks with a glaze on them. Once he pressed me against the sink when I was peeling potatoes, his whisky breath right on my neck. And one day I went over to return a screwdriver and he tucked my hair behind my ear and said something he shouldn't ever say, not to me, and I felt sick and ran all the way home.

I shouldn't have told you. Your knuckles rose almost through the skin, your jaw tightened. I don't know what you said to him, but after that my uncle's hands stayed by his sides.

It had been easy to say yes when you gave me the ring, to not even think about it. You protected me.

I thought on that as I sat under the holly and the hazel bush, as the rain came down, on the night when everything changed.

It felt very different bumping down the track to Jim's place in the almost-dark, the headlights jerking, puddles everywhere. It also felt very different inside the house. The air was weighted down. I stood in the middle of the room, my clothes clinging to me, making a lot of unnecessary sighs to paper over the silence while Jim fiddled about with oil lamps and got the fire going.

He passed me a big towel with loose threads hanging off it. 'You're probably starving.'

'I could definitely eat something.' I took my head out of the towel. 'I could make you something.' Jim's eyebrows drifted to the middle of his forehead. 'Just because I'm a student doesn't mean I'm a shit cook. I'm a *ninja*.'

He looked into a far corner of the house. 'I don't have much in.'

'What about the deer?'

He blinked, surprised. 'Do you want to eat that?'

I shrugged. 'It's dead, isn't it?'

Jim went to get the deer from the river. The rain was still battering the house and even listening to it made me shiver. I wondered about borrowing some of his clothes, but having him come back to find me lost in one of his jumpers seemed somehow a step too far. I looked in his cupboard instead and tried to think what the hell to make with deer and the contents of his shelves, which mostly held tinned tomatoes, Tabasco sauce, coffee and a tub of St John's wort tablets. This wasn't going to win me any prizes.

The door pounded into the wall and ricocheted back halfway. I went to close it and looked out into hissing, furious darkness. My own rain globe. Maybe the house would be

241

drummed into the sodden ground until you could only see the roof.

'Christ,' said Jim, stooping in the doorway with a torch in hand, rain dripping from his beard. 'That's not getting any friendlier.'

After dinner – not exactly my proudest culinary moment, but at least containing meat sourced by myself – I sat on the snowshoe chair, looking at the blank space at the top of my phone screen. I'd completely forgotten to message Lottie. Jim had relaxed and told me about the house and how he'd fixed it up, before going quiet again and staring into the fire as if it was one of the harder bits of *Ulysses*, clutching his whisky glass.

I'd been with him for hours. 'Do you never listen to music?'

He looked up. 'Got a radio. But you can't get much on it. Lots of people whinging mostly. And I've tapes in the Land Rover.'

'*Tapes?*'

He widened his eyes at me. 'Aye.'

I sniggered a little before making myself look very serious. 'They're coming back, you know. Tapes. Bands release stuff just on cassette now. Not big bands, but you're their perfect market.' I pointed a finger at him and nodded very definitely.

He eyed me wryly. 'What do you listen to, then?'

'All sorts.'

'Go on, then. Give us a blast of something.'

I scrolled through my music, choosing a band I'd seen play when I was staying with Stef, before everything went wrong. Nasty, heavy rock, spartan and punky, not normally my thing but their ferocity had made me laugh hysterically, and the singer had hurled himself into the front rows, narrowly avoiding my head, slammed to the ground and puked everywhere. Stef had declared himself completely in love.

Feeling bolshy, the whisky burning a hole in my stomach, I perched on the armrest of Jim's chair and put my headphones on his head. The band blitzed out, all tinny thrashing guitars and snare drum and hi-hats. He sat very still, his hands clasped and palms upwards, looking into the middle distance. I propped my chin on a hand and looked at the fire.

There was a weird little charge in the room. My feet were jammed next to his thigh, which was dead warm. After a minute, I glanced at him. He was looking sidelong at me. I raised my eyebrows as a prompt and he just raised his back, his forehead wrinkling. I screwed up my face and did some deranged, chair-based head-banging. He watched me with another one of his lazy half-smiles and didn't move a muscle.

The song was over in two and a bit minutes. He gave me back my headphones.

'So?' I said.

Jim gave me a shrug which might have meant that he quite liked it, or that he thought it was quite rubbish. 'It's all right.'

'You can't say it's all right. You have to say you love it. Or you *hate* it.'

He just chewed his bottom lip at me again.

'*Fine*,' I said, and shoved my headphones on my ears, getting off the chair. I played it again, grabbing my whisky and head-banging, not caring what I looked like, starting to jump around, singing along.

When I opened my eyes he was saying something to me, with the same dark, careful smile. I took a headphone off.

'What's your tattoo of?'

I stopped dancing. It sat just below my pelvis bone. And had been covered up since we'd swum.

'Oh,' I said. 'A bird.'

'What sort of bird?'

I lifted my shoulders and hid one of my ankles behind the other. 'Just a bird.'

That made me feel so stupid. It wasn't really any sort, just an anonymous, winged – *bird*. Probably should have thought about that when I'd had it done. Me and Lena had got them together in town – she had got stars on the inside of her wrist. Someone else would have made fun of me then, not knowing whether it was a sparrow or a – I don't know, a fucking thrush or something, but he didn't.

He folded his arms and the lines appeared between his eyebrows again. 'Don't mind me.'

I suddenly felt extremely self-conscious. 'Not if you're just going to sit there.' I put my hand out. He looked at it and breathed a laugh through his nose and shook his head. 'Are you going to dance with me?' I said, like I was his primary school teacher.

'No.' The word had a little upward scoop to it.

'Go on.'

'Your music's on headphones,' he said, looking at me like I was slightly mad.

'I'll play it from my phone.' I pulled the lead out.

Jim laughed silently again and stretched, putting his thumb and fingers on his forehead and gathering the skin together as if he had a headache. 'Do you want another drink?' He didn't wait for my answer, getting up and moving to the sink.

I crashed down in front of the fire. It worked grabby fingers under the slowly blackening logs. Splinters of flame streamed off and up with hissing bursts every time the wood snapped.

They drew me in. Right into the lungs of them. The more I looked, the more the flames became white and separated into feathers. I shivered.

'That's supposed to make you *warm*,' he said, next to me.

I took the whisky from him, remembering the sugary tea he'd brought out in front of his house that time. His own glass hung from his fingers. Large lines were appearing in the logs, like a pavement splitting during an earthquake. The darkness seemed to be falling in around them.

Jim squatted down and put two more blocks of wood on top. The fire considered them for a second, having a good sniff, before it pounced and up came the feathers again. He sat down to face it, his bones softly clicking, and put his elbows on his knees, not quite touching me. The heat was starting to press down on my forehead.

'Do you ever' – I spoke slowly and quietly to the fire – 'see things?'

The logs made a sound like someone grinding their teeth. The feathers flailed. Fire White.

'What do you mean?'

I put my nose to my glass and got a hit of sweet leather. 'I don't know. Out here. Do you see anything?' The wind chucked a few fistfuls of rain at the window. 'Anything strange?'

He drew his eyebrows in. 'Plenty.' I couldn't tell where the rain stopped and the crackling of the fire started. 'A sea eagle with an otter in its claws, for one. A dead stag drowned in a hill loch, just its antlers sticking out.' His voice was low and thick. 'I once saw a man burying something. Something quite big. He dug out chunks of mud and put a bin bag in there, patted it all down with a spade and crossed himself.' He sounded like he was reading the last pages of a children's story to a nearly asleep toddler. 'The northern lights, just over the hill. And once—'

I took my face out of my glass. The fire had turned his eyes into little video screens. It was the longest he'd ever spoken without me interrupting.

Jim took a big breath in. 'I'd been out early, just clearing my head. Too much of this.' He tilted his glass at me. The whisky slanted, a shallow triangle of molten gold. 'I was walking back and I saw something up on the hill.' A chill spread through me. 'Coming down towards the house. Sort of staggering, lurching around. And it – I don't know, I didn't like it. It floated round the side of the house and was looking in the window, and I thought it was some crazy sprite come to eat me, and it had pink bits—'

I shoved him, hard. 'Fuck off.'

He rocked back towards me, clutching at his arm and grinning. 'You're vicious.'

'You're a bastard.'

'So you keep telling me.' Jim put his chin on his arm and looked across at my legs, and at me. His eyelashes were little spiky shadows on his cheek. I thought about leaning over. He didn't move, his gaze whittling me down. God. He was – he made my skin hot. Not the fire.

Drunk. Drunkdrunkdrunk. I breathed in the whisky and wood smoke. Maybe I could spur things on a bit. 'I think I need to – lie down.'

His smile disappeared. I could swear there was a blush in with the glow of the fire. He looked awkward, then matter-of-fact. 'Aye.' He swallowed. 'You can sleep up there.'

'What about you?'

He jerked his head back a little. 'Chair.'

You don't have to, said a tiny child's voice in my head.

Jim drained his whisky in one gulp and got up. He moved to the corner of the kitchen, coming back with a pan, and stood with his head craned up at the ceiling. 'Rain's coming in.'

He held the pan up in mid-air, as if he was about to toss a pancake, and moved it slowly until it gave a click. He took my glass and picked up the plates, putting them in a new pile nearer the sink. I realised what he was doing. Making himself busy until I went up.

I stood, my face cool now it was out of the fire, and took a very long time moving my still-wet boots to a corner, picking up my bag, willing him to come back over. He kept finding things to do, turning the taps on, shaking a towel out.

'Goodnight, then.' I hovered.

He partly turned, but didn't look at me. ''Night.'

A drop of rain fell into the pan every half a minute. I kept waiting for the next one. It sounded like the last corn popping, the pan already brimful of yellow clouds. The wind was going insane. A dull brown-orange glow on the walls from the shushing fire. I had listened to Jim changing his clothes before settling in the armchair, which gave off little crunches of static, and then – nothing.

I lay totally still for a while under the cold duvet, looking up at the ceiling, realising how much I wanted something to happen. He wasn't like anyone else I knew. He was so *quiet*, but calm, too. Nothing fazed him. He was like the loch, just reflecting what was around him.

The more I lay there, the more the darkness grew heavy above me, stretching and pulling, something elastic. Maybe it was the whisky. The whisky wasn't keeping me warm, though. I put my hands under my armpits and curled up into a ball. I rubbed one foot on the other. My nose had turned into an ice cube. I was never going to sleep.

I carefully let out a jagged exhalation, just loud enough, I thought, to be heard. I imagined it zigzagging outwards, minutely seesawing on all the draughts through the house, finding its way into the far corners. Jim didn't make a sound.

More dramatic, then. I sat up suddenly, with an inrush of breath.

'You all right?' His voice in the darkness.

'I'm just – it's cold.' I gave a shudder, only half put-on. 'Do you have another blanket or something?'

There was a silence, and the sound of him scratching his beard. 'Sorry.'

I stayed sitting up, thinking, go on, just *ask*. Go on, Polly. 'Do you fancy – maybe you could come up here?'

The rain tumbled just above my head like peppercorns. The wind seemed to have grown long false nails and was trying to prise the ends of the roof off. He thought I was a massive slut. I *was* a massive slut. Then he made a sound, very formal, like he was about to make a speech. I opened my mouth to say, it doesn't matter, I almost said it, when there was a creak and two steps, and the top of the ladder scraped against the side of the bed.

His blanket was dumped on top of my calves. I wriggled over and he got in beside me and arranged it over the bottom half of the bed. I lay, rigid, trying to remember the words to Larkin's 'An Arundel Tomb'.

He moved onto his side towards me. 'Turn around, then.' He spoke as if it was obvious, but really gently, a sigh of leaves.

I twisted to face the wall, and he moved up to me and put his arm on my waist, just below my ribs. I waited for him to shift a little closer, start kissing my ear or something, but we just lay there, clothes on. He didn't say another word. I could feel his breath blotting my neck.

His arm was so hot. My own breathing was shallow, as if I were trapped in a box and had to ration it. I made myself inhale more deeply, my ribs lifting his arm up just a little, and down again. Up, and down. I listened to the wind, and the rain.

12

Oh, the wind and the rain. I remember it, that night.

It can change in seconds. A bright day can be shrouded in sleet as you blink, the mountain opening every vein, and the paths become rivers, and then the sun comes out again and everything is newly minted.

There's the rain that begins to crystallise in the cold. Tiny, laced worlds. The wind that heaps voice upon voice, low roars and pipe shrieks, like someone is pressing their elbow into it, making it wheeze and sing.

The kind that binds skirts to skin to hair to feathers.

It rains when the sun shines, as it did on the night when everything changed. Making it sparkle, even as it fell. I caught it in my hands, danced in it. You'd asked me to marry you, a ring in a fine-broken egg, and I'd shouted yes, in your ears, in your mouth, to the hills.

Everything can change in seconds. Rain and sun. Girls and not-girls.

I woke up with my face in his back, forehead touching his T-shirt, my nose numb. Everything was a vague, grey colour. He smelled sort of oaty. His breath whirred in his throat like one of those little hand fans you'd never need up here. I pulled the covers over my head and let the air get fuggy. A leather belt had strapped itself around my skull. Whisky brain.

Jim stopped breathing for a second, as if someone had pinched his nose, and began to roll over onto his back. I got out of the way just in time. Eyes still closed, he put a palm over his face and rubbed his temple with his thumb. He swallowed and the gurgle rattled past his ribs.

He turned his face to me. 'All right?' His eyes were stuck together at the edges.

I nodded.

He exhaled heavily and tipped his chin up. 'Storm's off.'

'Yeah.'

'Did you sleep?' His voice was scratchy.

'Yeah.' I grinned sheepishly. 'Thanks.'

He smiled at the ceiling and moved his arm under my neck, gathering me to his side, my hands scrunched up next to him.

We just lay there like that for a while. I could picture his heat creeping onto me, spreading like an oil spill. He seemed as casual and unaffected as anything, as if I'd always been there, his hill wife, chopping wood by his side, peeling the fur from rabbits, letting my leg hair grow. I thought I could hear tiny raindrops again, but it was him, blinking.

'How old are you, Polly?'

'Old enough.'

More raindrops. 'Old enough for what?'

'Whatever you were thinking about.'

He breathed a short laugh. No harm in trying. I mean, surely he wanted to? He was right *there*.

Jim turned suddenly and looked at me so intently that I felt like he was trying to melt me down.

'What?' I said, petulantly. Trying to mask my nerves.

He just kept looking, his arm underneath my ear, and I didn't dare say anything else and just stared back. He put his other hand at my waist, hooking a finger underneath my T-shirt, and when I didn't move, went up over my lower ribs and back down over my stomach. His palm was boiling, as if he'd been holding it over a gas ring. I tilted onto my back so that my stomach flattened a bit. And then he was kissing me, a few quick ones, and some longer.

I pulled away. 'I need to clean my teeth.'

He had a smile and a frown mixed up together. 'No you don't.'

'My mouth tastes gross.'

He kissed me again and pursed his lips mock-seriously, squinting into the air above my head. 'Tastes fine to me.'

I'd never kissed anyone with a beard before. I kept getting mouthfuls of moustache along with lips and teeth and tongue. Scottish Beard moss.

Jim pushed my T-shirt and bra up with his knuckles. Fucking hell.

He pulled back at my sharp in-breath and looked at me carefully. 'Too much?'

I shook my head.

'Sure?'

I nodded.

He cupped my breast and kissed the other and his hand was on my hip, which I hoped seemed bony, and he was pulling my knee towards him and rolling over between my legs and I got my hands at his waistband and I stopped. He froze, too.

252

'Do you ... have a condom?' Tongue in tooth. 'I'm not – sorry – I'm not on the pill.'

He shook his head, a small movement. 'Do you not?'

I shook mine. Nice one, Polly, way to kill it stone dead.

He hovered above me, a dark shadow. 'I'll come out.'

I looked at him for what was probably too long. Fuck it. I nodded.

It was nice. It was definitely nice. Pretty quick I guess, but in a dirty, urgent sort of way. I felt all candle-waxy and I liked the way his beard scratched against my cheek.

Jim lay next to me, breathing loudly through his nose. My pants were still around one knee. His heart sounded like a horse galloping away.

He put a palm on my inner thigh, high up.

'It's OK,' I said. My hangover was seeping back along my forehead.

He gave me a gentle frown. 'Yeah?'

'Mmm-hmm.'

He gazed at me for a bit longer, then reached down under the covers, brought one of his socks up and wiped my belly with it.

'Um,' I said.

'What?' He looked at me with a lazy grin, bunching the sock up and slinging it off the side of the bed. 'I'm not getting up.' And he pulled me to him again.

I brought my bra and T-shirt down and settled in. He was a proper hot water bottle.

Jim suddenly put his hand between my legs. 'What's this, anyway?'

I angled my head awkwardly. 'What?'

'This.' He pressed down more firmly.

'What do you mean? What's wrong with it?'

'Nothing's wrong with it. It's just – where's your hair?'

Jesus. I shifted up the bed to make a gap between me and his hand. 'Isn't that – it's what girls do now.'

A pause. 'All girls?'

Where had he been living for the last ten years? 'I don't know.' I stared up at the ceiling. 'Men like it.'

'Do they?'

'Yes.'

'Must be old-fashioned, then.'

'Old, maybe.'

He laughed through his nose at me. 'You're like a girl I used to know.'

That was new. The girl who'd left him, the one he'd wanted to marry? 'Yeah?' I said, quite vaguely, trying not to sound too interested. 'In what way?'

He blinked slowly and sniffed. 'Long hair. Sparky. Bit rude.'

I opened my eyes wide in not entirely unfeigned indignation. 'Thanks.' I looked at him. 'Am I?'

'A bit.' He gave a slow smile. 'S'all right, I can take it.' He put his forearm under my nose. 'Thick skin, remember?'

I liked how we didn't have to talk. I had a leg hooked over one of his and my ear was pressed flat on his shoulder. When he scratched his chest it sounded like a saw tearing at wood. I wondered if Lottie was up yet and whether she'd seen that I wasn't home.

The urge to pee couldn't wait any longer. I dragged my pants up and clambered over him, and he gave a sort of sleepy groan. I put his puffer jacket on, slid my feet into his boots and went outside.

Afterwards, I faced the hills behind the house. They looked like – friends. Great brooding giant guards. If anyone came by that Jim didn't like, they'd just stretch up some more, do a silent sideswipe and fling the invader a few miles away. They were *his* hills.

I walked to the river and knelt down. My fingers looked swollen in the water – pale, uncooked sausages. I picked up a rock, smooth and slick, and balanced it on top of another one. Fraser was such a wanker, trying to freak me out. What the hell was his problem?

A loud slosh behind me. Jim was tipping the rainwater out of the pan. I stood up and he looked at my legs, a long, slow smile coming on one side of his face. Mud was stuck to my knees. I stomped back, flicked river water into his eyes, and carried on past him into the house.

The coffee jar was out on the table.

'Do you want some breakfast?' he said behind me.

I thought about staying here all day, pinning him down underneath the duvet. He'd totally let me. And I thought of Lottie, guiltily. 'I should get home.'

He looked at me, tugging his bottom lip into his teeth a bit.

'You've got no reception. My mum will be – she'll think I've drowned in a ditch.'

Jim smiled. 'I'll run you back, then. Give us a minute.'

He went outside and I looked at his books on the big shelves, my head on one side to read the titles. A stack of papers, individually folded, sat on top of some hardbacks.

More drawings. I pulled one out. It was more of the same, except – not quite. Part of a human skeleton – pelvis, curved spine, ribcage – with feathered wings. It was beautiful, eerie, and a bit strange for someone who said they didn't draw people. My eyes travelled ahead, and – I saw them, at the end of the shelf.

My keys.

They were definitely mine. Broadly toothed and silver, the little green-rimmed plastic keyring, the perfectly coiling writing of the cottage address. I filed the paper away and picked them up, thinking of the feather on my pillow. My heart made a sound like a lock turning.

Jim stopped when he saw them dangling from my forefinger. 'Meant to give them back to you.'

I didn't say anything.

'Those are yours, right?'

I looked at them.

'Reckon maybe on – that first night? The *other* time you were in my bed,' he said, a little slyness sliding in.

'Yeah,' I said, in a voice not quite my own.

Jim walked to the sink, his back to me. He'd had them all this time. That was weird.

He wiped his hands on his jeans and reached into his pocket, his own keys making a muffled jingle. 'Shall we, then?'

I got into the jeep. Jim had disappeared round the corner of the house. He'd had my keys for ages. Why hadn't he returned them? He suddenly loomed in the wing mirror and I almost had a panic attack. There was a chainsaw in his hands.

The door opened behind me, and he chucked it into the boot.

When he got in, I was staring at him. He looked back at the chainsaw. 'In case I need to have a go at that tree.'

He didn't. The road was clear, the tree sliced into discs by the verge, pine needles scattered. The air was humid with our silence. Jim glanced over a few times as if waiting for me to say something, and fixed his eyes back on the road when I didn't. My mind was jangling. I wondered if he could hear it. Maybe it had been him. I mean, he'd taken my book. That hadn't seemed too bad, on its own. He'd wanted to read it, it was quite cute, really. But a swan feather on my pillow? Fraser had said—

Jim looked over again and I realised that I was shaking my head in a small, furious movement. I put my hand in my fringe and feigned a headache, giving him a blurry grin, and he smiled back, that diagonal line appearing on his forehead, his seaweedy eyes crinkling up.

Fuck it. Fuck what Fraser had said.

He braked outside the gate. 'Polly.' He was looking at me as if trying to get me to focus. 'Are you OK? You're not – that was all right?'

I nodded. It had been. It'd been lovely.

'Give us a kiss, then,' he said, dead gentle.

I leant over and kissed him lightly. He tasted of coffee. I got out of the jeep.

Lottie was in the hallway.

'I'm really sorry. Phone died.'

'God, Polly, please stop doing this. I just need to know where you are.'

'I just said. My phone died. I was at Fraser's.'

'I thought you two had fallen out. Why didn't you use his phone?'

'The storm fucked the mobile receptions. And the landline. Was yours working, then?'

Lottie glared at me and crossed her arms. '*Yes*. And I hate it when you swear.'

*

I woke up with grooves along my palm from the keys, like I'd been attacked by a chihuahua. I put them by the orchid pot and pushed the duvet to the bottom of the bed with my feet. There were scratches on my knees from climbing down to the waterfall, faint, raised lines. A crust of salt on my stomach.

Dangerous. I didn't know him that well. I had to keep telling myself that. I didn't know him at all. Maybe Fraser hadn't meant the hare-trapping and the bird-exploring, the unnerving vibes he gave off. But I didn't want to ask Fraser.

Another orchid had flowered. White, pale tongues. Overlapping.

*

Adam's face went through several fleeting scene-changes – surprised to wary to arch to wary to surprised again.

'Can I come in?' I didn't give him the chance to answer.

Abstract music came from upstairs and the smell of proper coffee was thick in the air. Adam joined me in the living room and crossed his arms. He had a pencil behind his ear.

'Is Bev here?'

He took a breath, shut his mouth, and didn't say anything for five seconds. 'She's not. As it happens.'

I kicked my toe into the rug. 'I don't know who else to ask.'

I could hear his brain ticking. His eyebrows couldn't decide which way to go and just sort of wiggled about. He nodded at the sofa. I plonked myself down, crossing my legs and facing him as he joined me. A coat of whisky still needed stripping from the inside of my head.

'How long have you been living here?'

Adam looked faintly relieved. He put his elbow on the arm of the sofa. 'Eight years now.'

'Have you ever – has anything ever happened round here?' I couldn't quite believe I was even thinking about this. 'Like, bad things?'

An inscrutable look. 'What sort of things?'

'I don't know.' I gripped the underside of my sofa cushion. 'Something dark. Some crime.'

He regarded me like I was an earnest Year 10 pupil doing a local geography project. 'Not much. I'm not quite sure what you mean.'

I wasn't either. 'Doing stuff to animals, or maybe stalking or assaults or something.'

'There's a spot of theft occasionally. Domestic abuse perhaps, if you're lucky.' I didn't return his smile and it disappeared behind a mildly curious frown. 'It's a pretty safe place, Polly. The police mostly have to deal with motorbike accidents and lambs going astray and people losing their keys.'

I put my cheeks in both palms.

'Can I get you anything, Polly? You don't seem quite—' He went to put a hand on my knee. I raised my face and we both watched it suspended in the air. I felt strangely blank, neutral. He drew it back and rubbed his thigh self-consciously. 'There's coffee on.'

Adam came back with some posh little cups. 'There was something that happened a long time ago here, if you're really keen. Before we moved up. Not animals, mind.'

I took one from him. Bitter, old earth smells. It needed sugar. 'What?'

'I'd have to look it up. A murder, I think. Twenty years ago or so.' He smiled at me. 'It probably made the police station's decade.'

*

Jim

Actors, comedians, high heels. The cursor blinked.

Jim murder

Madonna, The Doors. This was ridiculous.

James murder

I added the name of the village. The loch.

Assassinations and revenge killings in the sixteenth century. Clan history. King James IV. Death-row stuff on Wikipedia. More genealogy on the second search page. I clicked on *Images* and saw snapshots of the village – the swings, the shop on a sunny day and the loch, surprisingly blue. Maps, old church records, and—

Something clotted in my throat. I sat up on my bed.

A blurred shot, hair floppier and no beard, but definitely him. The same deep pencil marks between his eyes. I put the cursor at the side of his mouth, on his lips. He looked pained, harassed – more than I'd ever seen him – and the strangest thing was what he was wearing.

He was wearing a suit.

It linked to a STV news site. The headline, in artless, bland type: *Murderer released after fifteen years in prison.*

I was sick onto the carpet.

I opened the laptop again, not wanting to look at it. Having to look. Hoping my powers of reading would fail me, that the words would just be strange shapes, untranslatable. I didn't read the whole thing through, just swept over the short paragraphs.

He'd murdered his girlfriend. He'd murdered a girl called Molly Bawn and been sentenced to life in prison. The article was dated five years ago.

James Randall. His name was James Randall. Not just Jim, a name that seemed as simple as the life he led, as short as his sentences.

My stomach felt like it had been hole punched. His fluid, my fluid, the bitter-copper river, the dirty white waterfall, the storm rain, the blood from the hare, the blood from the deer, the ribwort mulch, pouring out of me, viscous.

I made it to the toilet, just.

Lottie found me with my head against the base of the sink. 'Polly, it smells of—'

I retched again. My tongue was coated in tree-resin.

Hands sweeping my hair away. 'Come on. Bed.'

She stopped short in the doorway, seeing the floor. 'God, Polly, what on earth have you been eating? Or drinking?' A despairing glance. 'I'll get the mop.'

The night sky was a split fig.

My skull was empty but sleep was very far away, as distant as somewhere with traffic lights and late-night chippies and

261

evangelical churches. Lottie had cleaned up my vomit while I'd lain there, facing the ceiling. She'd drawn the curtains and I had listened to the little firework-bursts of the adverts from the TV for hours. When they finally stopped and the hallway lights clicked off, I'd put on my hoodie and gone outside.

I hadn't needed a torch. The moon was alight, clouds like three giant, interlocked snowflakes behind it, and bright enough for me to stumble down by the stream and out onto the stones, to stare at the loch and the wide, starred sky.

The loch slopped, the flesh of someone very heavy walking.

Mångata. Moon street. That's the word Adam had said ages ago, the Swedish one.

It couldn't be. Jim. How could someone so gentle have done that? I thought of him pulling me apart, bone by bone, my chest broken open, head tipped back.

I felt fragmented, my limbs leaden and not quite attached. Like someone above me was in control, tiny hooks worked into my shoulder blades. I waited for them to lift the strings, pull me off the stone and into the black-blue air, along the moon street, my toes dragging the loch into fine lines, like two pluming wings.

A rushing sound by my ear.

I ducked. Something swung over my head like a bell. Weight and heat, the slight prickling of something skimming the top of my ear as it passed. Straightening, I saw a large, dark shadow, wings, moving over the loch to the hills opposite.

There was a cry. Grainy, small and furious. Shrinking as the shape disappeared.

That midsummer night there was a crackle in the air. As if the pylons were buzzing too loudly. The sky had been so strange, rain and sun mixed up together. A sky like a wound.

The bonfire was early with the forecast rain, and everyone came out, drunk on beer and wine and whisky. The girls from the village. My uncle.

I made my way to our special place as the light started to fall away, but the rain was so heavy. I sat under hazel and holly bushes, listening to it, thinking over and over of you and of what we'd do together.

Married.

You had gone to tell her. Your mother. To tell her you'd asked me. Saying you didn't care what she said, but I knew you did, a little. Anger in your voice on the phone afterwards, a fissure vein.

I was made strong on that midsummer night. I feel it now, tightening in me like a hunger. And I know it's my one chance to make this girl see. Her story draws nearer to mine as the changeling light comes in with the rain.

How can you explain, when you don't have words? How can you explain that there had been dreams and tumblings and—

And he shot me and killed me by the setting of the sun.

The next day passed in a fog. Thick cloud and falling snow.

I looked at my phone. Looked at it again.

Afterwards, his come had welled into a jellyfish on my stomach, like one I'd seen on Finn's beach.

I kept my laptop shut for most of the day. A briefcase containing all the world's secrets. All the world's secrets and only one that mattered.

He'd put his thumb on my lip like I had something hidden in there.

And he'd said I was like her.

After a while I made myself lift the screen up. I found an older photo on another news report, one from twenty years ago. Jim, smooth-faced, his hair down past his ears.

And his girlfriend. The girl he'd killed. There was a picture of her, the same one used in the three articles I found. It was taken side-on but her face was turned to the camera, shiny-cheeked family members behind her and a slight misting on the lens. Reddish shoulders and pale blonde hair down her back. A silver bar pierced through the top of her ear. Her grin was slightly uncomfortable, like she'd just had her name called by the photographer.

He'd shot her, with a rifle, further up the loch.

I went down to the loch again to look for the bird from last night, but found only hell-clouds of midges and the wasting sun.

I sat for ages.

He'd chopped up the deer thigh for me, leant over to get the knife. The sure, tearing sound of red flesh.

There was a putrid smell coming from the water.

He hadn't made a sound, just held my hip, his hand over my tattoo. His breath had been dense. Chalky.

There was golden, silvering, white light on the loch instead of the sky. Stripes of it and bigger patches expanding, taking over, and it was everywhere, it was the whole loch and I staggered back until I reached the house.

Lottie found me with my cheek pressed against wicker in the conservatory, my arm drooping. 'Come for a drink. A soft one. To settle your stomach.'

Tyger tried to wriggle free. I grabbed him tighter and hummed a no.

She sighed, disappearing, and I fished out the port bottle from underneath the chair.

Port. A quarter of a bottle of white wine left in the fridge. Kahlúa. Something that tasted of mint and furniture polish. I had it all and more, soaked up with biscuits. Tyger was lumped on the floor, his head on his paws, looking up at me.

Fuck it. Maybe I would go out.

Fraser wasn't behind the bar, thank God. But he was there.

Jim. And Lottie.

'You should come,' Lottie was saying to him, running her hand through her hair.

Jim had his forearms on the bar and his face turned towards her, shoulders relaxed. 'Aye, all right, we'll see.'

Lottie saw me standing there. Her face was bright, everything pulled wide and high. 'Hello, darling. You came.'

I couldn't say anything. Jim glanced over his shoulder and when he saw me his smile caught, just for a second, before he made it casual again, swivelling round in his seat towards me.

Lottie was trying to sound offhand, her best champagne voice. 'Polly, this is Jim.' She looked at him meaningfully, as if they'd just been talking about me. 'This is my daughter.'

Jim clasped his fingers together, his eyes on me, little flints sparking in them. 'We've met, actually.' He saw my eyes widen and scratched his beard, easy as anything. 'I found your dog.'

'That was you?' Lottie put a hand on his arm. 'Oh my God, you sweetheart, *thank* you. He's a nightmare sometimes, he just follows his nose, to the nearest ditch, or drain, or bog, or – lucky we had you to rescue him, aren't we, Polly?'

I still didn't move. Or speak. The rainbow of spirits sloshed around my brain. Lottie gave me the subtlest of glares. I ignored her and kept staring at Jim, who was looking at me with a mixture of lazy smile and faint puzzlement. The way he *always* looked at me.

Lottie stretched over-dramatically. 'I am going to powder my nose.' She slid off her stool, faced Jim and gave him a sort of bow-curtsey combo. 'Excuse me.' As she passed, she squeezed my arm, whispered '*Be. Nice.*' and floated off to the far corner.

I was left flat-footed in front of Jim. The room was beginning to curl at the edges.

'She's nice, your ma,' he said. When I didn't say anything, he furrowed his eyebrows, still smiling. 'You all right?'

My voice came out as taut as a wire. 'Can I talk to you, please?'

His smile became less certain, by only a whisper, but he answered lightly. 'Aye.' He threw his eyes to Lottie's stool.

I shook my head, a small, tight movement. 'Somewhere else.'

His Adam's apple bobbed in his throat as he nodded, his face open.

*

266

Once I was outside, I had to keep going. The bar door rattled behind me as I put both fists under my elbows and took off down the road, really quickly, the way Olympic walkers do. I couldn't decide if I was trying to pull Jim away to talk to him properly, or if I was just trying to get *away*, full stop. I could hear him padding behind me, a few metres back.

'Polly.'

I kept going.

'Polly.' His footsteps got heavier and quicker.

I started to run. I heard him say something under his breath and knew that he'd started jogging. The damp air hit the back of my throat. I veered off the road and towards the loch, onto grass and mud. Feet squelched behind me. I got to the rocks and turned round.

He stopped too, a metre away. 'Polly, what' – his voice lowered. 'What are you doing?'

I gulped the air. 'Stay away from her.'

His shoulders dropped and he almost grinned. 'Don't be daft. I didn't know she was your ma. And even if I did—'

'No, you don't under—just stay away from her.' I faced the loch again. Jutting rocks lurked in the water. Everything was beginning to be washed in dark blue, heavier brushstrokes for the hills. Denim Dusk.

'OK,' he said.

'You don't like the hotel.'

'I don't. I didn't.' He spoke gently. 'Thought I should get out more.'

I didn't know how to speak to him, not now, not now I knew. I took a step closer to the water. My toe was at the edge, where the rock fell away sharply.

'Christ.' Jim darted forward and grabbed my elbow. I yelped as he pulled me towards him. 'You're really pissed.' His grip softened, but he didn't let go. 'And high, or' – he peered at me and went to touch my hair. I whipped my face to the side and he brought his hand back. 'All right.' He sounded like he was trying to pacify a wild dog or a spooked horse.

The sky made him a murky shape, but I could see his eyes well enough. 'I know what you are,' I said.

His eyebrows came down and there was a tiny, sideways movement of his head before his face changed. It changed in an instant, every pore suddenly closing up. A standing stone. He knew. He knew what I meant.

'Oh, aye.' He carefully let go of my elbow. 'What am I, then?'

My breath juddered out. I felt like I might need to jump into the loch at any second, into the dark, glistening water. I wondered how cold it would be, if the salt would make my lips sting, if you'd hear me after it closed over my head.

'Why didn't you tell me?' The words were all glued together. I'd told *him*. I'd told him about me. But that was nothing. Not compared to this.

Leaves shifted in the tree behind us.

'When?' Jim's voice was a small, flat stone. 'When I gave you your dog back?' I could hear the breeze lifting the grass, and the sop of the water on the seaweed. 'When you were off your head and falling asleep on my bed?' He looked at me. 'When you knocked on my door? When I was fucking coming on—'

He shut his mouth abruptly and closed his eyes, slamming the heel of his hand up to his forehead like he'd had a lightning flash of pain. 'Sorry.' I heard him inhale, a breath dredged up from the bottom of the loch, and he sat down, bringing his knees up and leaning both elbows on them. 'Sit down.'

I shook my head.

He looked out to the water again. Whale shadows just under the surface. The moon was hiding half its face.

'Why did you keep my keys for so long?'

'What?'

'My keys. You had them for two weeks before you gave them back.' I corrected myself. 'You didn't even give them back. I found them.'

He spoke to the loch. 'Found them the other day – a couple of days ago maybe. Down the side of the bed.' He looked up at me with a mixture of alarm and anger. 'For fuck's—' He almost moved towards me, but stopped when I flinched. 'You think I'd – what – *break into her house?*'

'Whose house?'

His shoulders slumped, violently. 'Your house.'

There was gravel in my throat. I let my question out suddenly. 'Who knows?'

He jerked his head up, almost annoyed. 'Everyone knows,' he said, as if it was obvious.

'When did … Why did—'

'Don't. Just, don't.' He put a finger and thumb to his temples.

I had to ask. I had to. 'Why did you …' My voice shrank to almost nothing. 'Kill her?'

He stayed very still. 'I did my time, Polly. I did—' It was as if his body was winding down. 'I did my time, and then some.'

'I just—'

'Just fuck off, all right? Leave me be.'

I stood rooted for a few seconds, then carefully picked my way over the rocks. When I got to the grass, he was still sitting there, crouched over his knees, a shadow. From the road I could hardly see him. He'd been inked over. He had dissolved into the loch.

*

269

'I come back and you've both vanished into thin air. I looked like a right Billy No-Mates.' Lottie leant on the frame of the kitchen door, a glass of water in her hand, bafflement in her voice.

My blood was as heavy as mercury. 'Felt dodgy. Came back here.'

'Where did he go, then?'

'Don't know.' I scraped at a spot of dried ketchup on the kitchen top.

She looked slightly wistfully at her glass. 'He was nice.'

It was like being stabbed in the gut with a penknife. 'Fuck.'

'Polly.' Lottie's voice was sharp. 'What's going on? Are you actually ill? Not just—' She looked exasperated. 'You get too drunk too often. It's not ...' She put her hand out towards my hair.

'Please, really. Fucking – fuck. I just need to sleep.' I stumbled out to the hallway.

I didn't understand. He didn't seem sorry that I hadn't known. He didn't even seem sorry about – God, I couldn't even *think* the words again, it was too exhausting. He'd been in jail. For fifteen years. He'd shot someone. Someone who – I touched my laptop keyboard and forced myself to look at the article again.

Molly Bawn. My age, just under. And I realised something else, then.

Her name rhymed with mine.

Midsummer's eve. I'd woken up with the sunrise prising itself metallically under my eyelids at a time when everything should still have been dark. I wandered outside as the birds began to string their songs together, my feet licked with dew, looking

270

for *bauchans* and horse-demons and the Ghillie Dubh, before going back to bed mid-morning. Tyger kept popping his head round the door, like a nurse checking in on a patient. I'd eaten nothing but biscuits for a day, and the sugary mulch was the putty holding my insides together.

Lottie was sitting on my bed. It was the afternoon. Rain tickling the window like an annoying child pestering a cat. 'I don't know what's wrong with you.'

'Everything's wrong with me.'

She was holding a headband with fake leaves spiralled round it on her lap. 'I know you've been struggling a bit this year, but – I thought you were having a good time here.'

'I've fucked up,' I said, through a mouthful of duvet.

'Polly. You're getting ahead with your work, and—'

'I failed the year.'

'What?'

I lifted my head a little. 'I failed my exams and have to rewrite my essays. If I don't pass everything in September I have to redo the year. Which costs nine grand extra. Or leave.' I pictured myself strung up, punchbag-style. 'And I'm still paying rent on my room. I slept with Lena's boyfriend. Dan. I moved out early because they all fucking hate me.'

A long, bewildered pause. 'Right.'

Or her taking me back to the daughter shop, exchanging me for a better one. 'And me and Stef …' I stared ahead.

'You and Stef what?'

I might have killed someone. I shook my head.

Lottie looked out of the window, before making a sound like air coming out of a tyre. 'We're going to the bonfire later. I'd like to see you there.'

I nodded, looking at the wall.

271

She put the headband on the bedside table and rested a hand on my leg over the covers, just for a second. 'And for goodness' sake, have a shower.'

Lottie had gone to Bev and Adam's for a pre-bonfire dinner. I ghosted around the house, lifting things up – the retro cameras in the cabinet, the bulbous plastic lamp, salt and pepper shakers on the dining room table. Checking I was still real. The stray minerals dissolved on my tongue like tiny bee stings. Wasp stings.

I picked up my phone and dialled a number I'd found ages ago.

An automated message about a switchboard. I pressed a couple of keys, my fingers looking like they belonged to someone else.

A man with a thick African accent answered.

'Yeah,' I said. 'Hi. Um. I'm wondering about a patient you have there? He's ...' I didn't know his name. A tiny drum began thudding in my ribs.

'OK, what's the name, please?'

'Um.' I mumbled the word *bottom*. Tried to make it sound Spanish.

'Is that the surname?' He sounded so far away.

'First name. He's from Barcelona.' I realised that they might not know that, if he hadn't woken up. If his wallet had been stolen. 'Tall, dark hair, early twenties. He was found in Dalston. On Shacklewell Lane. A few weeks ago.'

'OK, my love. Give me a tic.' Tinny music. A classical string quartet playing from under the sea loch.

A rustle, a loud sitting-down-again sigh, and the man came back on. 'OK, I'm not clear if you're family. Did you know him?'

Did.

'Hello?' the receptionist was saying. Other words.

I dropped my phone on the floor. The man was still speaking.

Did I know him.

I lay down on the carpet. Not breathing.

Did I know him. Did. Dead.

I saw Stef again, his arm slung over the boy's shoulders, pulling him down to shout in his ear. Licking the pill and putting it in his mouth. Me cheering as the boy swallowed. He did that. I did that. I would lie here forever. I wouldn't move. Blink. I would make my own permanent blackout.

There was a dull sound that wasn't my heart. Hollow, rounded. I stared at the ceiling. The sound again.

I sat up. I couldn't quite work out where it was coming from. It sounded like someone in a flat three floors down was installing a bathroom. Except there was nothing three floors down but mud and stone and the crushed splinterings of humans, hundreds, thousands of years old.

Three definite, solid taps at the back of the house. I hauled myself up and went through the kitchen, opened the door. Against the luminous green of the garden were two white, curved shapes, flat and tapered. At first I thought they might be made of cake icing. I walked over.

They were wings. Swan wings.

I sat down, drew them onto my knees. The feathers had the delicacy of pressed flowers and overlapped perfectly. I walked my fingers up the near-translucent spines.

They were so large. They looked real.

The way the wings bent looked like my own elbow joint. Tucked underneath the hem of fine down was the pearled sheen of bone. It had the smoothness of a seashell. At either end of the bone, small slits had been made and rough brown twine threaded through. The longest feathers at the bottom were tied with the same twine so that each wing was closed, the shape of a large pocket.

They were meant to be worn.

13

There were lights all over the village. Not electric lights but candles, the flames dancing in old jam-jars on the porches or on saucers in the front gardens. Small, grounded stars. Some of the houses had placed a log horizontally above their front door. On one house nearer the road, I saw it more clearly. A silver birch bough.

The bonfire had already been lit. It was outside the village, up a side road and in a sloping field overlooking the loch. Traces of music doodled on the darkening sky – a fiddle, other indefinable instruments. People were clumped around in groups of four or five, their talk and laughter bubbling, standing near but not too near it, the way crowds do at the scene of an accident.

I climbed the short hill, my shoulders already hurting. The sun was lowering, the sky broad orange and grimy pink, clouds laddering like a pair of cheap tights. My head felt chlorinated, swilling with the kamikaze cocktail I'd downed before I left.

The bonfire was a criss-cross of crates and planks. One by one, people would advance and add their own offering. Logs, long thin branches, a couple of picture frames – someone dragged a chair with the spindles coming away and chucked it on. A muted cheer as the wood took.

Faces began to bleed into familiarity. Haimie, the landlord at the hotel bar, standing next to a barrel of beer on a wonky plastic table, shooing away the younger kids as if they were pigeons. Gray, the accordion player, was next to him, arms on belly, wearing massive sunglasses and a red cowboy hat. The little boy from the swings, his face painted in amber and white stripes, ran round and round the fire, his own determinedly dizzy ritual.

Fraser was further up the field, playing tunes with two guys on guitars. Becca stood next to them, hands jammed in the pockets of her trench coat. Finn and his pool mates were in a huddle nearby, beatboxing ineptly while Fraser told them to fuck off, his chin still gripping his fiddle.

You could never sum up a sunset like this in pithy paint swatch names. It was all the colours you'd ever known and all the ones you'd never dreamt of, swiped across the sky, bleaching as it rose, thickening at the horizon.

'I've got wings, too.'

The little girl with the pale blonde hair was standing next to me in a raincoat with insects printed on it. Small wings were strapped to her back, the elastic crossing over her chest. White, synthetic gauze stretched over plastic frames.

I touched the fluffy edge of one. 'They're lovely. Did you make them?'

'Jeannie did.' Her voice was small, scurrying. I could see Jeannie Robertson on the other side of the fire, her fingernails glowing a deep sea blue. A man – Fraser's dad, maybe – was next to her, smoking, a camera slung round his neck. 'She helped me. Did she help you make yours?'

A few strands of gauze came away in my fingers and floated towards the fire. I watched them whirl upwards, staying just abreast of the flames. 'I don't know.'

276

Ash caught in my throat. I plucked up the girl's hand. She resisted but I held firm, her fingers gathered, and she let her arm go doll-limp and hang there, standing awkwardly with me. It was as if we'd always been here, two swan-girls together.

A youngish woman in a leather coat half-heartedly called out 'Davy', over and over again, while the girl's big brother continued to buzz round the flames, a boy-tiger-moth. Smoke was coming off the fire like the morning mist off the mountains. It did a slow, billowing dance, a seal rolling, or a white skirt underwater.

'Good Lord, darling, where did you get those?' Lottie was wearing fox-ears. The little girl sensed her moment and wriggled her fingers free, dashing off.

'Present,' I said.

Bev came whirling up in a long velvet cape, her hair piled high on her head. She was making a sound like an electrical toy low on battery and drawing bright holes in the air with a sparkler. 'We're banishing the spirits, Polly, every one of them!' She made the sounds again.

The fire stirred itself into the sky, into a sun that was orgasming like I never had. The musky clouds were a sleek, long-beaked flock of birds.

Adam was by my shoulder. He wasn't wearing a costume, of course. He handed me a slim, chrome flask cup. 'Mulled wine. The Bev special.'

I gulped some down, burning my lips. 'Do swans fly at night?'

'I've no idea,' he said in a mulled voice. 'Thinking of trying it?' A hit of ginger on the back of my throat. 'I don't think there are swans here, anyway,' he said. 'Apart from you. Herons, they're pretty statuesque. Though I can't say I've seen many at night. Turning all ornithologist, are we?' I shook my head and handed back the empty cup. 'Well, I've never seen one anyway. You must be specia—'

I was already wandering off.

Shards of flame appeared higher up in the sky, not attached to the bonfire, like unruly kites.

I was in front of Jim's fire again. The low whisky-burn of his words.

'You all right, darls?' A zombie was looking at me.

I stared at him and felt my knees collapse. My arse met the ground very suddenly. Wet grass. 'God, Finn,' I said.

He sat down and put his better arm round my shoulder. It hung there in an amateur fashion. I wanted to wail, shove my face in his warm neck, tell him to just gnaw the flesh off my bones and be done with it.

Finn-the-zombie gave the thumbs up to his two mates, who were by the keg, trying to scab beer off Haimie. They sniggered back and made creatively graphic hand gestures. 'Do you want a beer? I'll get you a beer.'

'Yes,' I said. 'I want a beer.'

He patted my shoulder over-demonstratively and jumped up, hovering in front of me. 'Do you actually want one? If I say I'm getting it for you, he'll let me have it.'

I could see Becca lurking, giving me death stares. I fingered the small bottle of ouzo in my pocket. 'Have it. Have it on me.'

'You're magic, Polly.'

Someone had opened their car doors and was playing rocka-billy – yowling male voices, guitars sounding like they had been recorded in a tin bath. Lottie and Bev were dancing, hands slicing the air. The strobing light on people's bodies was the colour of the lobster from the loch.

278

A shudder from the bonfire and a million tiny flecks, bright orange pencil-flicks, hit the sky to a collective sigh. There was a constant patter of clapping and stamping from its centre, the fire demanding its own encore.

Lottie was talking to Johnny, who leant benignly towards her, his hands folded behind his back. I trailed over, my ankle twisting as I misjudged a mound of grass.

One glance at my shoulders and back and his mouth fell open. 'Right. Well.' He turned abruptly and moved away with the preciseness of a soldier's drill.

Lottie looked at me, puzzled.

Everyone hated me.

I began to see the torched skeleton of the fire. Black spines and fingers, houses. The frames of hospital beds.

Dark scratches, frown lines and eyebrows.

'Nice wings.' Fraser was standing behind me watching the bonfire, arms folded.

Becca stood next to him, flexing her fingers repeatedly.

'Where's your man, then?' he said. The fire made his face pale red, as if someone had just drawn a knife over his hairline, his blood washing down.

'He's not my man.'

'You got bored of him too?'

I began to walk away. 'Fuck off, Fraser.'

Becca stepped in front of me. 'Don't talk to him like that.' Her voice was like a fairy demon who had just drunk poison.

I stopped. 'Oh what, she actually speaks? Doesn't just howl at the moon or bleat through a fucking tin whistle? I mean, who the hell plays that anyway? It's like the aborted foetus of

279

a primary school recorder.' I was faintly aware that Lottie was standing a few metres away.

Becca bared her teeth at me. She was wearing glow-in-the-dark fangs.

'You're fucking mental,' Fraser said.

'She. Wants. To. Bang. You. Have *her*. She'll probably stick two fingers down her throat afterwards but she'll give it a good go first.'

Becca lunged at me, her hands outstretched. I grabbed one wrist and slapped her cheek.

It might as well have been a bolt of lightning. Her pointed chin dropped, before she shut her eyes and shrieked. 'Stay away from him! Stay away from Finn! Stay away!'

I lurched back towards the fire, a satisfying burn on my palm, the alcohol puddling between my ears. People around us had hushed and Fraser's muttering came through, conciliatory and filled with disgust. The words 'Bitch' and 'Crazy.'

The fire was one great mass, arching up, shape-shifting. I moved closer. There was a boat in the flames, then a hill, then a great slick object that moved as if through water. And there were dresses and hands and feathers, looming closer, and I waited for them to rise, come out of the flames and stuff themselves in my mouth, plumping up in my lungs, wings expanding out and filling every inch of me.

Closer.

'Easy there.' Adam's voice in my ear, warm and spiced, his hands pulling me firmly backwards. 'Probably best not to actually roast yourself to death.'

'Polly,' Lottie was hissing. 'What are you doing?' She and Adam were looking at me.

My cheeks were melting. 'I just ... the fire. There's stuff in it.'

After telling Lottie I was going home, I wandered away down the field, the heat still prickling my skin, the wings heavy on my back. Only one bird-shaped cloud was left in the sky, its body thinning until the wings had gone and it was all neck, then just beak and bone, then nothing but bone. The wind was getting up, and maybe there was rain, or it might have been midges, speckling my nose. Or feathers. I didn't know any more. I didn't know anything any more.

The rain and the sunset. The day and the night. Just like before.
They always said that on the night when the light was longest, the dark things were strongest, hanging like a cloak on your back. I am the dark thing now, the dark and the white.
She must see me. She must tell you.

I took the road away from the village, the colder air sliding over me. The sky was vast and purple-blue. I wanted to fall right into it. Fly.

The mountains were reduced to their simplest state in this lack of light, all their detail gone. I kept walking, the ouzo blazing a clean line down my throat, until the trees crowded in again.

Drops of rain, sure of themselves. Rain and sun.

And a sound. Like a giant's bone breaking.

A sound that made every other sound stop dead. That made me stop dead. A sound with a powdery echo.

My breath curled out. It had come from above me, or beside me. The tinny music from the car in the field filtered back in.

Again. Nearer. A rock hitting another rock in the air.

No. A gunshot. Near me. *At* me.

I began to run.

*

With a bullet, the sound doesn't come after the pain, nor the pain come before the sound. They happen exactly as one. The time it takes to click a finger, to take a breath. I remember it.

Our stories, coming together. Twinned.

Three more gunshots, each with the weight of great birds. Huge gulfs between them, caves of silence, apart from my breath and my boots as I ran. I waited for one to hit me, a dark, sharp punch in the shoulder, in my neck, my back. I waited to be smashed into the road.

A bullet is a pain that deafens. A sound that hurts. A pain-sound that is in one finely honed place and everywhere, up against each bit of skin, bone.

There had been the sound of my blood, stopping. The pain of my heart, becoming a loch. I feel it again now.

I looked behind me and there was a light.

A light, fringed and spiked. A shimmering mist. A light that looked almost like a girl.

No words came. I kept running.

A girl and another girl, on the road. Wings. She and I.

See who I am. See what I was.

There was someone in front of me.

I didn't have time to stop. Hands around my arms. I let out a scream.

Jim's eyes, glowing white.

'No, please don't. Please don't—' Dead. I was dead.

Whisky on his breath. He was shaking me but looking past my head, back down the road. I felt his grip harden, fingers on my elbows, before he shoved me onto the verge. I staggered into the ditch, knee first.

Not dead.

I wanted to throw up. Blood was whirlpooling in my skull. Voices – Jim's, mixed in with others, male and female, one quite high, pinched. I pushed myself up, waited for the road to stop undulating and let my boots lead me back the way I'd come, ducking erratically, wondering where the bullet might sing in from.

'Oh, come on, just having a bit of fun.'

Fraser.

Jim's voice was quiet and knotted. 'That's fun, is it?'

'I was never that close.'

'You like taking potshots at people?' No answer. 'What's she done to you?'

They were right in the middle of the road, Fraser and Jim and Becca. A few metres away.

'You can talk, you fucking psycho.'

Jim's voice dropped further. I could hardly hear him. 'Oh aye, I'm a real fucking psycho. I'll come for you.'

One of Fraser's hands was underneath the butt of his rifle, the other under its slim neck. Half angled towards Jim. 'Yeah? Do it. You're just going to get banged up again. Back where you fucking belong. You shouldn't be here. You shouldn't be near people.'

A sliver of silence. Every bit of air in me plummeted to the soles of my feet. A sense of waiting, almost polite.

Jim moved. There was a moment of concentrated sound – a scuffle, exerted breaths, gravel scratching on the tarmac – before a crack, wood against bone. An owl scream from Becca.

Fraser crumpled.

Jim was holding the rifle at the barrel end. 'Get.'

Becca seemed to be levitating, dancing an inch above the ground, unsure as to whether to fly at Jim or go to Fraser.

Jim nudged Fraser's leg with his boot. '*Get.*'

Fraser rose, very slowly, an oiled shadow peeling itself off the road. He lifted his hand to his head and looked at it. Becca stepped to him, tugged on his arm. They turned and walked back to the village and the glowing field.

'You're dead.' Becca flung the words back, frail and barbed.

'Oh aye,' said Jim, low enough under his breath that she wouldn't have heard. He was holding the gun in both hands as if midway through an oar stroke.

Between the trees, the loch glimmered, something secretive. The sky was an underwater blue. Thin shouts from the field like pathetic fireworks going off.

Jim suddenly seemed to come to and walked to the side of the road, placing the rifle on the verge. He stalked towards me, stopping a metre away. 'How did you know?'

The shots were still ringing in my ears. 'Know?'

He grabbed my arms. '*Polly.*' His thumbs dug in.

I tried to focus. The trees had deranged, drunken poses. 'You're hurting me.'

'How did you know about that?' His eyes were black.

I'd never seen him look like that before. 'About what?' I twisted and tried to get the swan wings off my back.

Jim got there first. He turned me round and yanked at them. 'This isn't a game. I'm not your fucking—'

The twine cut into my shoulders. I was almost laughing. 'What are you doing? I don't know what—'

He pulled me round again. I stumbled and his hand was there, slapping me hard, just below my eye, as if trying to wake an unconscious person. I reeled back but he still had me by the other elbow.

'What *are* you?' he said.

I tried to wriggle free. 'Please – please don't hurt me.' My voice had broken up.

He dropped my elbow. 'Fuck,' he said, very quietly, and turned and walked away.

There was a warm, dull pain smouldering across my cheek-bone, white as fire.

White. Everything had been white. I waited for my own clouds, mists, shapes to appear, just to fuck with me some more. In the sky, in the loch, in front of my nose. But there was only the snipped-out moon on the dense, finally-dark sky.

*

The front door went. The sound of stamping the mud out on the mat. I could hear Lottie wait, compose herself in the hallway.

She walked to the sink. I didn't turn round from my position on the back step, staring out into the night. The tap was turned on. Kettle. Mug. Sugar out. Milk out. She sat down next to me.

As she turned, she exhaled a sigh like she was getting ready to unleash hell on me. A pause. 'What's happened to you?'

My knee was patched with mud, a bit of blood. My face streaked. 'Nothing.'

'Did you get into a *fight*?'

'No.' I couldn't stop shaking.

'I *saw* you slap that girl.'

The rifle had been heavy, the metal tartly cold. I'd carried it back to the field and put it wordlessly into the hands of

285

the man who I assumed was Fraser's dad and stumbled away again. The wings were left splayed on the road, where Jim had pulled them off me.

Lottie put her hands in her hair. 'Polly. This was supposed to be a holiday. For *me* as well as you. Half the time I've spent worrying about you, where you are, how much you're drinking.' Her hands came down and she looked at me, tired and furious. 'You reek of drink, or cigarettes, or *ganja*' – the last word said with a sort of incredulous reverence. 'Now you tell me about your studies, and everything else, when all this time I've been under the impression that – I've been *proud* of you. And tonight ...' she shook her head and looked out at the garden. 'I don't know what to say.'

Then don't say anything, I thought. Though part of me wanted her to keep it coming. Bruise me.

She was still shaking her head. 'And I don't know what you said to Jim in the hotel, I'd asked him to come along tonight, and he'd said he would, maybe, and—'

I dumped my head in my palm.

'Are you even listening? For God's sake, Polly, you're an adult. Please let me be one, too.' She took the fag packet and lighter from my lap and sparked one up. 'Sometimes I don't know how to help, darling, but it's all I want to do.'

'You *do* help. I promise.' I looked at her. 'I don't have any friends, Mum.' The sentence soared down, wound itself up tight.

Lottie took my hand. 'I'm your friend.'

I did the only thing left. The only thing I hadn't done properly up here. I burst into tears.

14

More orchids had flowered. They looked like wings of a bird landing on water, many wings, the yellow centres speckled red, like a fine spray of blood.

Everything seemed different this morning. Not that I could quite think straight, with a hangover the size of Europe concreted in my head. Jim had been furious – I'd never seen him like that. I wondered what Molly had done to anger him so much. To make him want to do that. The reports hadn't said what his reasons were, just pummelled straight through to the facts. The words were written in neon on my brain. *Cold blood. Confession.*

Confession. Something that I needed to do.

He'd stopped Fraser, though. Knight in tarnished armour stuff, sort of. Before he'd hit me. I didn't think he meant to hit me, not really. Something about me dressing up had made him so mad – it didn't make sense. Didn't hang together.

Lottie was in the hallway.

'I'm going out for a bit,' I said. 'To see someone I met before. I won't be gone all day.'

She opened the sides of her dressing gown and gathered me up to her. A warm, crumpled hug that smelled of scrambled eggs.

*

287

'Why did you say I'd been here before?'

Finn was easy to bribe. Half a bottle of banana schnapps had been enough to get him to take me to his beach again. I'd stapled my head to his shoulder and listened to him yelling back at me about dog races and different types of electric guitars as we grizzled past the low hills. Gran-gran had given me a shrewd frown and put a pan with worn plastic handles in her grandson's hands, commanding him to collect mussels, to which Finn had flexed his arm and said he had plenty, thanks.

Gran-gran made a sound like a creaky chair as she sat down. 'It was a feeling I had.' She looked at me. Her expression was burrowing, curious. 'If not that, then part of your story's up here at least.'

The caravan smelled of seaweed and warm, wet wool. I tucked my foot up underneath my thigh on the seat by the longest window. 'You said everyone has a story.'

'Aye. They do.'

'Finn says you know everything that's happened here. I thought you might know about – a murder. Twenty years ago? A guy' – it hurt to say it out loud. 'Shot his girlfriend.'

She didn't look the slightest bit surprised. 'Oh, aye.' Her voice was cashmere, a blanket over my shoulders. 'Everyone has their own version of that one, I expect.' She didn't elaborate, simply wrapping her hands around her cup. Her veins marbled her knuckles.

'So ... ?' I said.

'Well, if you've heard about it, what do you want to know from me?'

'I don't know, I thought, maybe – I just didn't understand it.'

She looked at me for a long time. 'Every story has another, hidden away. Maybe more than one. Who's to say what the

288

real one is. People say I've got a few screws loose, for living the way I do.'

'But you just like it?'

'Well, I've got very used to it. I've been here thirty years.'

I felt like I could swim down into her eyes, find seahorses and squid and those fish with serious underbites and antennae that glow in the dark. I waited. And she told me her story.

She had always lived here, in this corner of the Highlands, but once she'd had a proper house, where she'd brought up her kids. She showed me a photograph of her husband, a small, stout man who looked like he had a hot water bottle stashed under his shirt. He was standing on a moor with two small children under each arm – one of them Finn and Becca's mum – like lambs or baby pigs he was rescuing, and his grin was as broad as the sky behind him.

Sandy had worked on submarines further south, she said, and would often be away. He would return with oil still under his nails and a smell of the sea, but not the normal smell – something ingrained, speaking of depths and darkness. It sweated out of him. She didn't even swim.

One night, his submarine – on a training exercise somewhere off the west coast – had never come back up. Reports had been mixed, even though she and other wives had camped outside the base and raged for days, weeks. Almost certainly an accident, flooding or a weapons explosion. Gran-gran said that when subs failed, they sank to their crush depth – words that sounded soft and muffled but were surely anything but. Skulls caving in like the metal of the hull. I imagined the dented sub lodged awkwardly in sand and rock at the bottom of the sea, a giant version of one of Benji's old bath-time toys. The skeletons of men eroding there in the water. Human coral.

One night, she'd woken up with a fever dried on her like sea salt and got into her car in her nightgown. Driven miles and miles to this beach and stood, facing outwards, with the wind all over her like fingers. Goosing her good, she said to me, a distant lighthouse flash in her eyes. And she'd looked out at the booming, hushing darkness and – I shivered – he'd been there. A feeling of weight next to her, calm and smelling of oil and cigars, and she could hear his words, woven in with the wind.

He had said that he would see her again on this shore some day, before the feeling and the scent whipped away like sea spray.

She sold her house, she said, and packed the kids – teenagers by then – off to her brother's. People grumbled. She bought this caravan, had it moved here by a haulage truck, and had lived here ever since. And every day, morning and night, she walked on this beach, in case it was the day he would return.

'One day he will, probably when I can hardly stand upright.'

There was a clock made of driftwood leaning on the kitchen top. It ticked loudly every other second, like it had a limp. Outside, I could see Finn jumping off a rock, a foot landing in the pan, small black shapes scattering.

'I'm sorry,' I said.

She let out a melodic sigh, as if she'd been for a long, satisfying walk and had just got home. 'No need for you to be sorry. It's the way of it. Most people would say I'm crackers. Pining this long. But I know what happened that night. I see things.' Another unblinking look, but kind, half-smiling. 'Like you do.'

My skin pin-pricked all over.

'You should look again at the story you think you know.'

I took a breath, felt it swell and move seawards. 'Do you mean – it wasn't him?'

She cupped one palm in the other, her thumbs slotting together. 'I just know that he was a good boy. He doted on that wee lassie.'

*

I'll see you again on this shore some day. Her words had been like the end of a simple song. They fluttered in my skull as we headed back, Finn's boy-angst music streaming along with us. I wanted to believe what Gran-gran had said about Jim. Maybe there was more to it. I tried to think who else might have been here that long, far back enough to tell me something more.

I squeezed Finn's sides when we'd passed through the centre of the village. 'Can you drop me?'

He swerved alarmingly, did an emergency brake and craned his head round. 'Your wish, my command.'

'Thank you.'

Finn tapped his cheek with one finger. I kissed it and slid off. He gave me the brightest, most filthy of grins as he looped round and chugged away.

Johnny's house looked as if it cried mascara tears. There were long, dark swipes on the outside walls, dusty windows, and a motley collection of umbrellas in a plastic bucket by the front door. The doorbell had an old-fashioned clang.

No answer. I peeked through the kitchen windows and walked round to the patio doors, wisps of dandelion fluff breaking up and joining the midges. With my forehead to the glass, I could see a grand, sunken sofa, old-fashioned zigzaggy wallpaper, a line of glossy rocks on the mantelpiece above a gas fire. Next to it, framed photos of boats and groups of soldiers, a girl – maybe his German sweetheart. I cupped both hands tightly around my face to block out the light and stopped breathing.

The photo. Long blonde hair. Uneasy grin. Something silver and shiny at the top of her ear.

It was Molly.

I walked back home very quickly. When we'd seen Johnny snooping around the jeep, I had thought that Jim didn't know him. But maybe he did. Maybe he knew him well.

Back on my laptop, I found the photo of Molly the press had used. I had only really looked at *her* before, seen the smile she would always have, the freckles on her shoulder. Behind her were three people. Two of them were looking at the camera too, big greasy grins on their faces. The third had his back to the camera but was looking round. You could only see a bit of his face, the side that wasn't too birthmarked. But it was definitely there – a splash of wine-red on his temple.

I did my time, Jim had said. *And more.* As if he hadn't deserved to be in prison that long.

Or as if he hadn't deserved to be there at all.

I went to the courtroom that bleak, quiet day, found my way in, weaved past shoulders. I wanted to speak, to defend you, to say to everyone, it's not what you think. I'd thought that I had my old voice still. I hadn't known. Not really. And you didn't see me, and you never knew.

You'd never worn anything but jeans and boots and T-shirts. Your shoulders were clothes-hanger stiff. You hardly ever looked up.

Everything was thin, cheap-looking. The opposite of the sandstone columns outside, the great stamp on the wall. Plain tables and office chairs. The smell of varnish and starched shirt collars. Sweat. Words were ironed flat.

Your brother – I'd met him, twice, an even taller version of you, with a deep, dirty-dishcloth laugh – leaning forwards on the railing, hands clasped, listening to the edges of every answer. Paler than I'd remembered. Next to him an aunt of yours, maybe.

My da and my ma and my brother, lined up against the wall outside, smoking like they needed cancer to come on, fast.

I miss them, of course. I don't even know where they moved to. One day I went to our house and they had gone.

But I had to stay. Here, where it all happened. Dark woods and water hush. Rain and caves. Waiting for you to come back.

My uncle was there, at the courtroom. He didn't say anything either. I was trying to make him, but he wouldn't.

I waited outside the village, thumb out. The sun flared a path along the water, doubling my hangover. It was wearing black clouds like a vintage fur coat. By the time I was dropped at the end of Jim's track – by two lean gay guys in their fifties who'd been sea swimming, their wetsuits steaming up the back windows – it was as if each bit of crusty old fur up there were dropping off in a long, spiky streak of rain.

I tried to be Scottish. To ignore it. Focus on talking to Jim, finding out what really happened. He couldn't have done it. The more I thought about it, the more I had a feeling that there was something missing in this story.

The door was locked, though the jeep was there. My T-shirt stuck to my back with sweat and rain; I looked like I'd been licked by a big dog. I thought about sheltering under his wheelbarrow, but if he found me there like that, he'd think I was even more unhinged than he already did. So I sat on a pile of splintered logs, letting the rain soak in, running a hand up my one-day stubble. Leg-logs.

My shivers were coming thick and fast by the time I spotted Jim a mile or so along the valley, a single vertical charcoal stroke. He filled out as he came nearer; shoulders next to his ears, hands in his pockets. Wearing the rain as a cloak. And I knew exactly the point at which he saw me – his pace wound almost to a halt and he walked twice as slowly towards the house.

He stopped a few metres away. 'What do you want?' His voice was grainy. The line between his eyes had deepened and set like dried, cracked mud.

I'd waited all this time and I didn't know what to say. He stood still. A raindrop fell off my nose.

294

'Fine,' Jim said, brittle, and unlocked his door. He shut it behind him.

The rain crumbled over the far hills and kept coming. I tipped my head back, opened my mouth. Rain on my tongue, the back of my throat, my lungs. I wanted it to fill me up, seep through my bones until I was nothing but water, until I melted into the grass. Evaporating, falling again. Rising, falling.

I heard a click behind me. The door was open an inch.

He was sitting at the table, scratching the wood and looking fixedly at his fingernail. I stood in the middle of the room, rain falling off my hair onto the floor. It smelled of burnt toast in here.

'Turn around,' he said.

Pins shot down my legs and into the concrete. His expression was locked down. I swivelled around on the spot very slowly to face the fireplace, my breath sewn up.

This was it, then. I almost *willed* it, for my neck to be met with the cold edge of a knife, the imprint of a rifle barrel, to prove my stupid hopes wrong. Because I deserved it. I deserved everything I got. But when he stood and stepped closer behind me, he did something else entirely.

He took off my jacket, peeling it from my arms. The hem of my top lifted up, my back exposed to the air. Fingers at the hooks of my bra, which loosened just slightly at the front as he undid it. Christ. I hadn't been expecting this, now.

A thumb at the inner point of my left shoulder blade. He pushed it, not exactly gently, and I let out the tiniest of breaths. The thumb moved around the bone, first at the base, then in towards my spine and working up to my shoulder, as if testing it for dirt. He held onto me there, under my top, and his other thumb mirrored the movement he'd just made on the right hand side. Like he was massaging me. The least likely time for a back-rub ever.

I stayed very still. My skin felt as if it were lined, a rind of something. There wasn't a single sound – I couldn't be totally sure that he was breathing. A fingernail traced down my spine, fine as a pen-tip.

His hands fell away and my bra was being re-fastened, my top lowered. The lightness of his touch almost stung. I heard him step away, sit down. He was staring at the floor. I had no idea what had just happened. The seduction seemed to be over before it had properly begun.

Jim glanced at me and nodded at the towel on the snowshoe chair.

I pressed it to my head and hid for a moment, wondering if he'd lost his nerve and was going to come and have another go. Nothing.

Clutching it around my shoulders, I took a deep breath. 'I wanted to thank you for – I don't know what Fraser was doing.'

He didn't say anything.

'I don't know what I did to upset you. I mean' – him sitting with his back to me at the lochside in the dark-blue light. 'I know what I did before, but—'

'Why were you wearing those?' He sounded like he hadn't slept in days.

'The – the wings?' He stared at me flatly. 'For the bonfire … everybody dresses up.'

'Why *those*, Polly.'

'They were given to me. Left for me. I thought maybe it – it was you.' It sounded ridiculous even as I said it.

He turned to me slowly, his face blank. 'Why would I do that?'

I just swallowed and shook my head.

Whatever I'd said seemed to change something. Jim rose and stood in front of me, putting a knuckle under my jaw and tilting my cheek up, his nail on my neck. Looking for a bruise. He took a small, jerking breath in and dropped his hand. 'I'm sorry.'

'I've had worse.' I bared my teeth and tapped my finger on the chipped one.

'No.' It came out as a sigh. He shook his head and kept shaking it. 'You shouldn't be here. You shouldn't be spending time with someone like me.'

I hugged my towel around me. 'I liked spending time with you.'

'*Liked*,' he said, sounding unsurprised.

'Like.' I shivered.

He was still shaking his head, almost imperceptibly.

Jim made me a cup of tea and sat at the table again. I let the steam redden my cheeks.

He spoke quietly. 'Who gave you those wings?'

I looked up. 'I don't know. And what is it about them?'

His eyes darted around the table.

'Why were you there?' I said. 'On the road?'

He bit down on a fingernail and spoke to it. 'Thought you might be there. Thought I would ...' He didn't seem to want to finish his sentence. 'Try and' – he shook his head and his hand fell onto his thigh – 'talk to you.'

I had to ask him. 'What happened? With Molly?' It was the first time I'd said her name out loud. The name that rhymed. I wondered how else I rhymed with her. 'I know there's something – I know you didn't do it.' My voice came out louder than I'd meant it to. 'You covered up for someone, didn't you?'

Jim went very still. I waited for him to tell me. To tell me it was Johnny. There was a crack in the wall next to the doorframe. Four faint little patches of deep red. His knuckles.

He brought his head up. 'No.' I heard the tap drip, just a notch louder than the rain. Once, twice. 'It was me. Sorry to disappoint you.' The words were plain, lean, sad.

There was a large stone pressing against my chest, without malice, pushing me slowly into the wall. Pushing further. 'Something happened, though, didn't it?'

He ground his wrist into his forehead. 'Look, you don't know me. No one does. And if I can't explain it then …' His arm thunked down on the table and he looked at me properly for the first time that day. 'How can anyone else?'

God, why did he have to be so opaque? 'You don't know me either. I see – weird shit happens to me. *I* can't explain it.'

'What do you mean?'

'Things following me around.' I put my face behind my palms, swiped them to my temples. *Like you do*, Gran-gran had said.

Jim chewed at his bottom lip. 'What things?'

'Half the time I think it's just the weed and that. I don't know what's real and what's not. I don't know where the line is. But …' I might as well come out with it all. Everything else had fallen apart. 'Clouds in the water, and mist, and shapes coming out of trees, or on the horizon, walking or floating, I can never tell, and the orchid petal falling, now that I think about it. There was a light, when I was lost after

298

the bothy, following me. And feathers. A swan feather. On my pillow. I thought you might have left that, and the wings, but now I don't know, it sounds stupid but maybe that was the thing as well. And last night—'

I stopped. He was looking at me, his jaw hanging open. His eyes travelled the room. His breathing was the breathing of someone on their death-bed.

He leant back very slowly in his chair, the wood popping. 'You should go now.'

I hadn't resolved anything. He hadn't told me anything. 'But wait, I—'

Jim stood up.

He hadn't offered me a lift. I walked back up in the rain, long waterfalls of it. No cars passed. I held my jacket over my head, covering my phone, waiting for a bar to appear. Lottie didn't pick up. The bar wavered. Finn neither. Or Bev.

'Christ. You look like a drowned dog. What are you doing out here?' Adam had the passenger window wound down halfway.

'I don't know.' I got in next to him and stared straight ahead. My hair was wallpaper-pasted to my cheeks.

'Did you get lost?'

I turned his radio off.

He seemed to understand that now wasn't the time for flirting, or talking, or anything, and did a swift, smooth U-turn. 'Let's get you home.'

I felt like I was going into meltdown again. She'd been killed, by him. But there was something else. There *was*. Even he'd said so. How could I know if he didn't tell me?

Seaweed collected in my brain, crackling pods rubbing against each other as I lay awake. He thought I was mental. I probably was mental. The room felt moist, as if it were drizzling inside. A darkness that would last only a few hours.

I waited for it to come. To rustle, to draw stinging lines on my neck, to morph and move into something I finally wanted to understand.

It never did. I woke up at half four, the day already coming, the birds going off like every type of alarm clock possible.

The orchid had lost all its petals. They lay, scattered wings.

Wings and white.

It's hard to describe what happens, when you turn from one thing into another.

As I sat watching the rain that night, I felt translucent. As if lights were shining inside me. Making me glow, cold and glimmery. Each raindrop sparked another. I was illuminated. I thought, I should start walking again, get up there, to you, never mind this weather. It's just weather. And then—
  The gloaming.
  I looked it up once, that word, though the 'o' and the 'a' were mixed up in my head. A dark, shimmering word. A sound like a moon. Like the moon, lamenting.
  Silver into liquid into a new shape.
  My spine began to burn. A prickle all over, thistles under the skin. My mouth hardened, amber-coloured. I wanted to moan with the pain of it and the beauty of it, and nothing came out. My neck soared. I was frozen into a heart-shape.
  And I flew.

This girl doesn't fly, the one on the road, the one who is sad. She doesn't turn from one thing into another. She hasn't understood, not quite. But perhaps she has said enough.

Day into night. Sun into rain. Girl into bird.

15

'One more for your collection,' I said, dumping Lottie's umbrella in the bucket.

Johnny was holding the door open as if it were the gate to a royal palace. He'd done so only after peering oddly at my face and over my shoulders. If Jim wouldn't tell me, I would find someone else who would, and at the bonfire, Johnny had looked almost as disturbed by my wings as Jim had. And there was a photo of Molly on his wall.

I pushed in past him. The sofa and armchair were uphol-stered in a sinuous olive brown and had wide, polished wooden arms. There was a serving hatch in the wall and a ceiling light with a fan on, as if he might be living in a tropical country. A boiled vegetable smell that almost made me gag hung in the air.

'Welcome to my humble abode,' he said, ambling in behind me. 'It's not much, but it does—'

'I don't care,' I said and crossed my arms. He raised his eyebrows in a show of gallant surprise, and I watched them see-saw down again. 'How do you know Jim?'

He blinked, once, and looked out the window. 'Jim?' His voice was trying ignorance on for size.

'You were at his jeep. In the car park by the woods.'

Something passed over his face – puzzlement, suspicion, *guilt*. Cut to the chase. I lifted the photo of Molly off the wall, leaving a rectangle of anaemic wallpaper underneath, and heard a measured intake of breath behind me.

She was a bit younger than the press photos – maybe sixteen – and you could just see a strip of loch behind her head. Strands of her hair were plaited into two thin braids in the folds of blonde on one side. Strappy black vest top. A rash of freckles on her nose. Holding the picture – something physical, as opposed to those I'd seen on my laptop screen – felt as palpable as if I were holding *her*, hands wedged under her shoulders, while she looked back up at me, trying to work me out.

'Was she your daughter?'

It was like I'd just headbutted him in the stomach. Johnny sat down all at once, his large hands gripping the arms of the chair, and took a couple of deep, chugging breaths. 'My niece.' A little of the courtliness in his voice had eroded.

'Did you kill her?'

'No, I did *not*.' Extra emphasis on the last word, and spoken as if answering a prosecution lawyer. Far less outrage than there should have been.

'I know you know something,' I said.

He frowned at the floor, examined the tip of his shoe.

I pressed on. 'Why were you scared of me? At the bonfire?'

He tried to twinkle his eyes at me. 'Not scared. Just remembering.'

Remembering what? '*Tell* me. Please.'

A pause as vast as the loch. 'No, lassie,' he said. 'It's old water now.'

'It's not. It's not *old*. Tell me.'

He sighed, a sound that swirled in his throat. 'It's twenty years gone. I've not told – it feels peculiar to …' He seemed to be gathering himself, as if he were getting dressed to go out, shrugging a heavy greatcoat on. 'I've never quite believed it myself. The years, they start playing tricks on you, dancing in front of your eyes when you're trying to walk straight. Or as straight as I can.' He looked at me, his eyes a little watery. I didn't believe him. 'Have some tea with me.'

I wanted to run at him and shake him till his teeth rattled out of his head. But I was just getting somewhere. 'Tell me where everything is. I'll make it.'

Johnny had proper teacups and saucers, little silver spoons with flying ducks on them. He insisted that I put chocolate bourbons out on a plate. Whole milk in a jug.

He bit a corner, the crumbs dusting the air in front of him. 'I went out last thing, after the bonfire. The light was just starting to go. A sunset too, even with the terrible weather, which was unusual. It was when I was still drinking a lot. Too much. And being outside'd always see me right, rain or no. Right enough, anyway.'

Get on with it, you hoary old bastard, I thought, but nodded and sipped my tea.

'I remember seeing Jimmie up on the ridge and thinking, it's a bit late in the day for him. And I knew his shotgun too, twelve-gauge, yoked over his shoulders.'

Fucking come on.

'After a time, I'd come down to the loch. I remember I was sitting having a wee fag and there was a crack and then a flash of white to my right. This whooper swan was coming over, higher than usual – they normally keep quite close to the water.' He balanced the saucer on his knee and moved his hand flat through the air as if stroking it. The large, dull gold ring on his middle finger caught in the light. 'Bright yellow beak, black tip. Have you seen those seaplanes?'

I shook my head.

'Oh, but you know what I mean. That's what it looked like. Like a seaplane with a cranky engine, veering all over the place. And it was calling out.'

He made a yelping cry like a trumpeter being strangled.

'And as it came back overland to my left ... I don't know. It all happened very fast. And I thought, good Christ, Jimmie, what the hell are you doing, shooting a *swan*? They can put you away for that. Swan meat doesn't even taste any good, they say. Like pond water, and chewy as anything. But, here's the thing. The echo from the gunshot fell away, and the bird pitched, and it' – he stopped, frozen for a moment in the memory – 'it *grew*. Expanded outwards.' He gave a slow sniff. 'It was like a coat, a pile of laundry – no, there was a skirt in the air.'

My heart gave one, swelling throb.

'Legs – flailing – blonde hair, tumbling fast and down, down, and then it was in the grass. *She* was in the grass. Not a bird at all, not any more.'

The teacup was burning my thigh.

'And there was an odd sound.' He looked into the middle distance. 'I swear to God I can still hear it.' He focused again. 'Like a snared badger, and Jimmie was running, running down the hill, and holding her up, and I knew. I knew it was Molly. My firecracker. I was shown a police photo of her afterwards and she'd looked, oh just as she always did, pale as winter, but her eyes – I'll never forget them. And' – he put two closed fingers onto his chest – 'a bloom of blood below her neck. Like a flower.'

It was her. It had been her all along.

'Why didn't you say anything?' My voice had gone to shreds.

'Say what? I didn't want trouble again.' He caught my look and smiled ruefully. 'I've taken more than umbrellas in my time.'

Swans and girls and bones and—

Johnny was still talking. 'How would I have helped, anyway, saying what I'd seen? It made no sense. A swan becoming a girl? I might have – if he'd said. Jimmie. But he didn't, you see.'

I prised the cup off my leg. A red circle. 'Why wouldn't he have done?'

He took the cup from me. 'Say what he saw? 'Cause they'd have deemed him mad, lass.'

Bones and feathers and—

'Wouldn't that have been … better?'

'No.' The word came out low and long. 'His ma was away on the winds for years, lassie. Institutionalised. I don't think he wanted to end up like her.'

Feathers and clouds and mists and—

'He wasn't good enough for Molly. Not by a long shot.'

Swans and girls and bones and feathers and clouds and mists and—

I was under the hazel and then I was in the sky.

She changed me. Your mother. How could you have known?
    My shoulder blades stretched taut and angled, hooks under the skin. My head was too far away from my body. A heaviness in my chest like stones weighted there.
    There was a shadow underneath me, a small slick of oil slipping fast over the water, and I watched it, and I realised that it was me. A swan. Not a girl.
    And then – I fell.

I didn't see you. See the shotgun. Your anger at your mother, at her refusal of us, the anger that made you lift it to your shoulder when you saw a swan. Instinctive, or maybe more than that. Maybe her curse on me had cursed your blood, too.

Your face above me. Full of bright pain, before it gathered every shadow that had ever been.
    It was the last thing I saw. It will always be the last thing.
    And I will be the first thing you see when you come to me.

It was all her. All Molly. Molly, or some sort of strange, halfling, Instagram-filtered version of her.

I walked back with my gut churning, Gran-gran's words clumping up together again like flotsam. *I'll see you again on this shore some day.*

I tried phoning him. No answer, though that was hardly unusual seeing as there was basically a non-reception force field around his house. Or maybe he was looking at my name flashing up, willing it to go away.

I'll see you again on this shore.

The look he'd given me when I'd started talking about what I'd seen. He'd known. What it was. Who she was. He'd known before I had.

The morning after the waterfall and the storm. His hand curling round my shoulder blade, my bra all wonky. Clearing away my hair to put the prickle of his beard there. My gluey stomach.

I tried again. Maybe he was up in a forest manning a harvester, stoically ignoring me. It went to answerphone. 'It's m— It's Polly. I know why you looked at me like that. I'm sorry. I didn't know. Please call back.'

Brilliant. Most cryptic message ever. I poked in another number.

*

I loitered outside the secondary school, a long, bland building next to a lime-green field, and bit down on a roll-up.

Finn loped out, his head swiftly moving from side to side as if he was doing a world-saving drop for MI6. He wheeled his moped over to me and fished out his keys. 'Seriously, though, can you drive it on your own?'

'Just remind me again.'

He pulled out a bit of chewing gum from his mouth and let it pop back in. 'What's up, anyway?'

'Finn, I haven't got time. Please.'

He talked me through it, putting his hand over mine to get me using the clutch on the extended handle at the same time as changing the only gear with my foot. The bike made a sound like a really annoyed giant bluebottle. I jolted forward two feet, stalled, and started again, doing a wobbly circuit around the car park.

He watched me with an uneasy smirk, scratching his head. I drove back to where he was standing.

'What do I get?' he said. 'For lending you my bike? You could write my baby off. My da'll end me.'

I could write *me* off. 'I'll try not to. Whatever you want.'

He flashed me a ludicrously suggestive grin, a grin that said I would be stripping down to my pants and licking him like a Calippo while gyrating to all his favourite whiny dirge shit. 'Yeah?'

Whatever. 'Yeah.'

He beamed, the gum poking out from his teeth. 'Knew you'd come round eventually.'

A bald man in white shirtsleeves came out, hands on his hips. 'Finbar Mackay, this is lesson time, you little shit. Get back inside.'

Finn put his hand up casually, not turning to face him. 'Yeah, yeah, right, keep your slaphead on, old man.'

'I'll get it back to you later,' I said.

The man shouted his name again in the manner of a small, vicious dog about to do serious ankle damage.

Finn put his good hand in his pocket and began to do a funny, sideways jog back to the main entrance. 'Don't fall off,' he yelled back at me, waving.

*

309

Fuck, it was harder without him behind me. Hurling Lottie's car through the glittering streets of Redhill after a couple of sneaky drinks felt way safer than being on this sack of shit. I stuttered and blurted away from the village to the head of the loch and round, trying to get the revving right. The moped took one look at the main hill and cried. I had to horsewhip its arse up there. Two guys littered shouts out of their windows at me as their car overtook me. I gave them the finger and almost came off.

I hurtled down Jim's track, seeing fresh versions of my own death with every bump, bird's eye views of me and the moped in swastika poses in the grass. The jeep wasn't there.

The door was unlocked. Hopefully he wouldn't mind me waiting here. I left it ajar, just to warn him.

There was a stillness inside. Everything seemed to be holding its breath – the furniture, the books, the firewood – and watching me carefully. I tapped the surfaces of things loudly, trying to feel normal. I picked out a book from the big shelf. *Arabian Sands.* A Bedouin guy casting a long, thin shadow on a sculpted dune. Written on the first page proper, in green biro: *To Jimmie. One day we will go here, and there, and every-hwere ... Molly x x x x*

My heart capsized.

She had written in four others, books with far-flung bits of the world on the covers. A similar message in each one. Circles above the 'i's. The weird misspelling. Four kisses. I felt a crushing, guilty sadness. I'd called him a murderer. To his face.

With one of the books still in my hand, I realised why it felt odd in the house. It was *tidy.* No pile of crusty dishes by the sink. No bottles. Everything had been neatened, ordered. I put my head out the door. His tools had all been

310

stacked against the front wall. Back inside, his drawings were in a pile on the table, pinned with a dull metal paperweight shaped like antlers. On top was the last one I'd seen. The human ribcage and the wings. I felt the ghosts of his thumbs on my spine.

Why had he come back here, to where it had all happened? Why hadn't he gone to India or Bali or Argentina? All the places he read about, that they'd dreamed about.

I'll see you again on—

Because he'd been waiting. To see her. Except he never had. *I* had.

And I'd told him.

Maybe that's what Gran-gran had meant, really. That if she saw Sandy again, she'd go with him. And going with him meant—

I whisper on the wind to you but you never hear. I whisper don't forget me and I whisper I know it wasn't you and all you hear is the wind.

I whisper come to me. And I touch your neck and all you feel is the wind.

But she sees. The first night in the wood I moved in the bracken to get a closer look and she became still and willow-straight and I thought — she heard me. The light just poured into her. I could see her bones.

My crystal twin. My story sharer.

That night I whirled and spun over the hills, a moon dance, knowing what to do.

She can't hear my words on the wind. No one can. So I talked to her in the water, in the air, with the only colour I know now. With the only sounds I can make now.

And, finally, you know that I am here.

I drove the moped back up the track and down the other side of the long, steep hill, the wind grabbing at my knees. Back to the loch, to the village. Back to the forest path I'd taken days and days ago, when I'd lain in the moss, got stoned and lost and passed Johnny coming the other way. Back to the beach.

Jim had to be there.

The beach was empty. The news reports said it had happened on the north side of the loch, a mile east of the village. I dumped the moped and hobbled over the slick stones.

The half-sun made blazing silver blotches on the water. There was a boat further out.

This was where it had happened. I tried to imagine it – *her* – flying across, the rude smack of the gunshot, Johnny further down out of sight. A girl in the grass. Jim running down to her.

Here. The smooth, polished stone, upright and facing the loch. Its two fine, pale curves, meeting in the middle like swan wings. And I knew then that Jim hadn't put it there. Johnny had. He'd made it for his niece. A gravestone.

My insides were tied like the end of a balloon. He wasn't here. I tried to picture the Ordnance Survey map and track everywhere I'd been with Jim. The lobster cages. The birds. The waterfall – oh God, I'd never be able to get back there.

As I clambered back over the stones, I thought of Johnny. The smooth, blunt antlers on his walking stick handle. And the other antlers I'd seen, less than an hour earlier, paper-weighting Jim's drawings. And I remembered where I'd seen something in that pallid, hand-beaten metal before.

*

313

When you went away I walked and wandered and swam and flew. And when you came back you'd been hollowed. A bone chime sounding only grief.

You made this home and lifted your shoulders up, away from people. My once-laughing boy.

You looked for answers. You picked up birds, took them apart, their struts and trusses, looking for me. You sat with feathers and bones spreading around you like petals. As if you hadn't punished yourself enough.

This girl makes you laugh a little. It is hard to watch but I know it will not be for long.

My love. I love you still. With the winter beginning to shiver in your hair and the years forging paths on your face.

I want you to come now.

It wasn't your fault. That's all I've ever wanted to tell you.

I want you to walk with me on the brows of these hills. Come drink with me under the cold moon's silk. The glass lid. The deep death.

Water and air, that's all we are.

No vodka dares this time. The padlock was already in the dirt by the wall, the gate open a notch. I left the moped next to the jeep.

I stepped inside the tunnel, blocking out most of the day. The chill was immediate.

The first turn was just a few paces away. I didn't have a torch. I didn't need one.

Ahead, there was a whisper of light.

Someone was in the chamber. Sitting on the ground, legs out, a torch angled upwards. The metal heart that hung from the ceiling cradled in its beam.

'Jim?'

No answer.

I said his name again and thought I heard something, very faint, a sound that could have come from way under the rock, hundreds of metres down. There was a heavy, sweet smell, almost like tree sap. I inched closer, my fingers against the cold wall.

'Is it you?' His voice was strange, molten.

I leant down, picked up the torch and shone it on him.

Jim's palm was facing up. Arm and hand dark with blood.

'No.' I dropped the torch, scrabbled for it, swore.

Snapshots of him in the light. Head hanging to one side. Legs crossed, almost casual. Hunting knife. Bottle of whisky on its side by his thigh, a shallow well of amber left. Other arm resting limp in his lap. And red. Creeping puddles of red.

'No,' I said again, kneeling, lifting his arm by the elbow. Blood pulsed from his wrist. 'Fuck.' It came out as a juddering whimper.

315

Jim squinted at me and shut one eye, as if he'd just woken up. 'What are you doing here?' He hardly moved his mouth.

'I know what happened,' I said.

'No.' The word was slow, tired.

'Listen to me. I know what happened. I know it was an accident. The swan. You never meant to. I'm sorry – I'm sorry.' I swore again, digging my phone out. My hand was shaking. The light gave Jim's cheek a blue glow.

No bars.

I heard him lick his lips with agonising effort. 'You shouldn't be here,' he said. 'Should you?' There was a slight upward inflection at the end. The whole cave smelled of whisky.

There was so much blood. A buzzing in my ears. I pulled at the laces of my boots, stood up and kicked them off, unbuttoning my shorts at the same time. The torch was shining on my ankles. 'Yes, I should.' I stepped out of the shorts and yanked my tights off.

'You're nice.' A sleepy voice from the darkness.

The knife was by his far boot. I leant over, trying to avoid touching him, my nose running like mad. Pinning the torch between both knees, I sawed at the crotch of my tights. The material squeaked. I wrapped one of the legs tightly around his wrist, feeling the moisture soak in, trying not to cry. I could see the underside of some of his skin.

'It's too late,' he said.

'No, it's not. Shut up.'

I sat on his legs, facing him, trying to slide the second piece of fabric under his arm, stretching the material as much as I could, tying the ends in a tense knot. His jeans were sticky. My breaths were the loudest thing. I couldn't hear his.

'It's not. *Is* it,' I said like a teacher. I put my hand on his chest. A long, slow thump. Thunder, very far off. '*Jim.*' He

316

didn't answer, his eyes shut. I touched his beard, got blood on his cheek. 'Jim.' My voice was small, lost in the darkness.

I stood up in a rush, kicking the knife away to the corner. The whisky, too. It rolled, an alarmingly loud sound, like a tower of bells being rung all at once.

'Don't go.' Jim began to lift the arm on his lap before dropping it again. He sighed. 'I'm coming with you.' The words were waves overlapping.

And I realised that he wasn't talking to me, not really.

I ran out barefoot into the bright, bright day, onto the gravel path and the grass, phone in my bloody hand and shorts in the other, breathing cool hill air.

Hoping.

*

Simple things were best.

Packing. Bed-making. A note saying *Sorry* placed in the desk drawer along with twenty quid, totally not enough to cover all that weed. Saving my work on a memory stick. Simple things.

'Polly.' Lottie was at the door of my room holding two brown bananas. Her glance was gently weathered, like it had been out in the rain too long. 'There's someone outside for you.'

Fraser was talking to Adam by the open car boot. He practically flinched when he saw me, a cowed-dog look better than Tyger could ever pull off.

Adam glanced at us both and disappeared inside with an unconvincing cough. Tyger stood firm.

I pulled my hoodie around me, an unnecessary reflex action from spending a month up here – it was actually quite hot this morning and the air felt thick enough to clot my throat.

Fraser stood at a right angle to me, his hands in his pockets. 'Yeah. I'm ...'

I imagined his face blooming with bruises, all coming up to the surface at different times, like spring filmed on fast forward.

'I'm sorry,' he said. 'About the other night. I was just – having a laugh. I was a bit high. And pissed. Pissed off. I'm – yeah. I'm sorry.'

There wasn't much to say. I nodded.

'I heard about what happened,' he said. Five words like soap bubbles, curved with light, filled with the world, disappearing.

I felt blank. If someone pressed their fingers into me, hard, they wouldn't even leave a mark. Not for a second.

He was looking at me. 'Yeah. Right. OK. So I'll –' he hiked his thumb over to his car.

Adam came out with our suitcases as Fraser's car jerked away. His look carried a sliver of curiosity, Sherlocky, too polite to ask. He knew, too.

He opened the back passenger door. 'Go on, critter.' Tyger half hurdled, half long-jumped into the back seat. I climbed in, gathered him into my lap.

Lottie followed, full of end-of-holiday sighs and a nod for Adam, who turned back round and started the car.

I watched the roof be swallowed up by the palm trees, the loch recede. The double-greenness of everything.

Lottie's smile was careful. 'We'll take it nice and slow when we get back. Perhaps it will be a bit easier to work at home. Less ...' she blinked her words away.

Tyger smelled muddy. Maybe he'd had a final roll around, just to bring something back with him. I had taken a last look at the loch this morning. Picked up a stone, a really flat one, and put it down again.

'Sweetheart.' Lottie put a hand on top of mine. A paler, freckled version, the skin thinner, the veins a little higher, but the shapes the same. She waited until my eyes lifted to hers. 'It wasn't your fault.'

I found the feather in my pocket, the first one I'd picked up on the road. I ran my nail along it, only one way.

As we rolled through the village a black crow unfolded itself on one of the swings, rising from the seat. Becca. Wrapping an elbow around one of the chains, she rocked, a slight pendulum, and very slowly, deliberately, raised her middle finger.

It wasn't your bullet that killed me, not truly. I died the moment I turned into a swan. She did it, your mother, tricks broiled deep in her blood, in the mosses that grew in her brain. I'd felt it, her hatred of me, felt something dark and furred on my tongue, in my ears, before the feathers came. She killed us both.

We'll be two swansouls, you and me. The rise and fall of our breath, the rise and fall of the sea.

16

Another train. This time everything was bare and bruised, just as he had once said it would be. The mountains had exposed jawbones. Leafless trees among the firs. Crows. Deer. And so much water.

It took me a while to pluck up the courage – the other side of the summer and more. I couldn't phone, or even text. Couldn't do it. So I wrote. I wrote a letter, on actual paper with a pen, like it was the nineteenth century, and addressed it to the village Post Office.

It was another month before I heard anything back.

There was a space behind my ribs, as if I were a plum with the stone removed. I stared out the window. The train was making an old-fashioned rattle as it climbed into the mountains, nothing but bleak hill on either side, stretching to the end of the world.

'Hello,' I said.

He was standing in front of the jeep, his hands by his sides, looking like he didn't know where to put them. 'All right.' He had a real coat on, with tons of pockets and buttons. And the woolly hat, obviously.

We stood a couple of feet from each other. The wind had a blunt edge to it.

'You changed your hair,' he said.

'Yeah.' As soon as I had got home – *proper* home, home to Lottie's – I'd gone into town and had it all chopped off, super short. I'd looked at all the faded pink draped on the floor, lots of brown mixed up with it, and felt nothing at all. Benji cried and ran away in terror when he saw me.

Jim took my bag from me. I tried not to look at his hands, his wrists.

We were both quiet as he drove out of Fort William, its loch a slab of breeze block. A thousand blind butterflies were headbutting each other in my throat.

I didn't know how long he'd been in hospital for. Finn had messaged me, mostly in skull and alien emojis, to say that Gran-gran had dropped in on him after a week. That he was still on suicide watch.

Jim stopped in a garage before the ferry and slightly turned to me, his hands on the steering wheel. I could just see the tapered end of a scar, diagonal, straying onto the pad of his palm.

'I wasn't sure if … Were you wanting to stay with me?' he said. 'I could sort you a B & B somewhere.' Each word sounded like it was blinking into the light after a long hibernation.

Fuck. I had probably got this all wrong. A couple of butterflies escaped. 'No, I – if that's cool.' I glanced at him. 'To stay.'

'Aye. Of course.' His voice drifted, like he was half asleep. He swallowed and shifted abruptly, leaning towards me to pull

322

out his wallet. 'Do you fancy getting some food? I didn't know – get whatever you like.' He handed me two twenties.

I folded them lengthways. 'I can feed us for two weeks on that.' A line appeared in his forehead. I held up the notes and made eye contact for the first time since we'd been in the jeep. 'Student.'

It was dark by the time we took the turning to his. Those late, light nights – somehow, I'd thought it would always be that way up here, the clouds rolling on to their backs way past ten.

When we got inside, he made himself busy – starting a fire, unloading the shopping, not commenting on the fact that I'd totally lied about my frugal skills and spent almost all of his money on black olives, red wine and steak. I sat cross-legged on his armchair and watched the flames begin to take.

Eventually, when he couldn't find anything else to do, he stood in front of me. 'Polly, I'm …' he looked at the fire as if it might be able to spit up the rest of the sentence for him. 'I'm sorry you found me like that.'

'I'm not,' I said.

Jim took a breath in and his chin dropped to his chest.

'But, I mean—' It was my turn to look into the fire. 'A lot of me's been thinking. Worrying that—' I'd hardly thought of anything else this whole time. My voice went salty. 'Do you mind that I did? Find you?' I was practically whispering. 'You did that for a reason.' I could feel a tiny lochan tear forming.

Jim squatted down in front of me, his fingers clasped. 'I don't mind. That you did.' He bent his neck to try and catch my eye. I looked as far as his earlobe. 'I'm glad you did.'

The lochan spilled, ran down to the corner of my jaw and onto my chin.

He reached out and blotted it with his thumb. 'I'll get you some wine.'

We didn't talk about it any more. My throat grew hot from the wine and the fire. I talked for a while about uni – I'd spent more time reading in the last three months than I had in the whole of my second year. Passed my retakes. Got my brain on.

Jim told me what he'd been doing to the house, repairing the window frame where it had started to crumble with damp, making a clothes rack, getting a better system for water drainage. He told me which forests he'd been working in and I wondered when he'd started again, and if people had looked at him strangely, or asked him questions. I wondered whether his arms hurt when he manned the harvester. I wondered what he thought about.

I shivered and put my elbows on the table. 'Can we keep the fire on all night?'

He looked at it, and back at me. 'It's not plugged in, you know.'

'Oh. Yeah.'

'If you get up a few times, you can. Keep it on.' There was the trace of a smile. Almost.

'I'm an idiot.' I shook my head at myself and put one finger in a wine drop on the table.

'I won't want you to get up.'

Bang. My skin crackled, or the fire did. Jim sat very still, the lines in his forehead nearly smoothed away. He reached over and tucked his forefinger under all of mine, and pulled my hand over the table, and my arm with it, and kept gently pulling until I was out of my seat and standing with my knees pressed against his, and until I had to put my hand on his shoulder to balance, and until he'd kissed me.

'How can you be cold?' he said.

Nothing of me touched the floor. I was lying on top of him in front of the fire leaning my chin on my hands, which were resting on his chest, which glistened slightly.

'I am. My toes have fallen off.' I put my cheek on his neck. A pulse thrummed against my ear. I thought of the blood throbbing from his wrist. 'I was supposed to cook you a steak.' I tried to sound extremely sad. 'I've failed.'

'I don't call what just went on failing.' He touched my nose. 'I've eaten now, anyway.'

I pushed myself up to look at him and he slung his eyes from the ceiling to me with a slow smile, the first I'd seen since the evening at the bar, with Lottie. His bottom lip was stained purple and had a faint, buttery sheen.

I hit him.

I was wrapped in a blanket and the blanket was under the duvet. The quiet up here was something I hadn't realised I'd missed.

I looked up at him. 'What was it like? In jail?'

He put a hand in my hair, just above my ear. There was a tiny squeak as his lips rubbed together just once. It must have been a minute before he answered. 'Depends which one you mean.'

I'd not even thought of that. I had just assumed that he had been in the same place the whole time. 'How many were you at?' I tried not to sound too probing. To let him know that he didn't have to answer, if he didn't want to.

'Five.'

Five. Was that better or worse? No one likes moving house. It probably hadn't been like moving house.

His nail softly scratched my skull, right at the top of my spine. 'Maximum security. For two years. With the worst sort. On your own most of the time. High security. For a long time. Medium. Then open, for the last two. Where you can go out a bit.'

He didn't sound angry, or anguished. Just – that's what it was. Fifteen years of his life, told in ten seconds.

I touched the inside of his wrist. Thick, glazed cuts crossed over his older forestry scar. They would always be there, now. He stayed very still.

'What do you think happened?' I asked.

Jim knew what I meant. The breath he took in was as big as the whole house, bigger, taking in air from the far hills. 'My mother.'

The words grew wings, stretched out, flew. I opened my eyes wide at him and took my fingers away from his arm.

His gaze was a hill tarn on a dark day. 'She didn't like her. She had ways. I still can't tell you how.'

He didn't say, 'But I know it's crazy.' I didn't say, 'That is not possible.'

He told me more about his time inside, after I'd teased him about how quiet he was in bed. He'd said that you had to keep it pretty under wraps in prison, and I'd wanted to die for being so thoughtless.

He spoke, patiently, of the endless boredom. The routine he had to keep, meetings with psychologists, workshops he hated. Of trying to keep fit, once he was allowed to move about more. Doing his best to avoid all of the politics, the cliques. Crap meals on plastic trays. A massive chunk of his life that was not a video but a sketch with a soft HB pencil, page after page of the same thing.

And no trees. No hills.

'What does your ma say about you coming up here?' he said in the morning.

I screwed up my face and tried to look exceptionally cute and wholesome.

'Does she not know?'

I bit my lip and shook my head in slow motion.

His frown was faintly headmastery. 'Does anyone know you're up here?'

'A friend. My next-door neighbour in halls.'

Flora. Really, really posh – she had freaking rowing medals and played the bassoon. She listened to my story while eating toffee popcorn, like she was watching a movie heavy on the swanky visual effects, and she didn't tell me I was mad. In fact, the next day, she'd presented me with a book on transmogrification and taken me to see this clairvoyant woman who'd put her fingers on my temples and told me that I'd be a great traveller and that my many sisters missed me.

'Why?' I asked.

'Just – you know.' He put his nose in my hair. 'I don't want it to seem like, I don't know, like I've foxed you into coming up here.'

'*Foxed* me?' Old-school.

'I don't know.' He almost blushed.

'What, like you've kidnapped me?'

'No, it's just, I'm too – you're just ...' the way he cleared his throat made it sound as if there were a bumble bee trapped in there. 'It's probably not very good for you to be here.'

I tried to assume a very pensive, professorial demeanour, then shrugged. 'Never mind.' I put my finger in his mouth.

'Aye,' he said, trying to speak around it. 'Right.' And he slid his hand under the blanket.

We walked. We walked in the empty hills through leached colours. Jim lent me his hat and I pulled it down to the bottom of my ears. We drank coffee and whisky and drove to the coast to look at the islands, far off. I told him how I had rung the police in London, told them I had information on the Spanish coma victim. I'd searched on a baby names site – Bartho, I thought it must have been. I had gone to the red-brick station on the high street near where we'd left him, been interviewed, shitting myself the entire time. The police had seemed bored, taken notes, said that they'd be in touch, and I'd never heard back from them. They didn't tell me whether he was alive or not. There hadn't been any more reports of anything online and I'd began to wonder if he'd just been moved when I'd phoned the hospital. My dead-not-dead boy.

When I finished speaking Jim stared at the islands for a long time before turning to me. 'Even if it was the worst that you think – it wasn't your fault.'

I hugged my arms around myself. 'It wasn't yours, either.'

He looked out to sea again. An almost imperceptible nod.

I never mentioned Stef to the police. He sent me messages once I was back but I couldn't face replying. The longer I left it, the easier it was to not see him. To make new friends.

Flora and I went on marches and got kettled like bosses, sat in cafes working and making our mochas last all day, did dodgy faux-burlesque on the little stage in the main student club, became a team. She got fed up with me talking endlessly about promoting bands and made me put a night on, booking a pub. I was terrified, but I did it. It was cool.

I eventually told her about Bartho, too. We made a little shrine – a crap drawing of him, Spanish beer bottle labels, candles and beads.

Fuck Stef.

The next night I woke up and found Jim looking right at me, very close. I could just make out the glisten of his pupils, like the curve of the dew on the morning I found him here.

When he spoke, the words only half came out. 'Have you seen her?'

He meant since I'd been up here, these last two days. I shook my head. He blinked, the little dawn curves vanishing, reappearing.

'Maybe she's gone now,' I said. We lay there, not touching. 'Maybe she understood.'

His lips moved, a small, dry sound. Neither of us spoke for ages.

'Why did I never see her?' he said.

'I don't know.'

'Why did you?'

'I'm mixed up with her, somehow,' I said. He took in a weighted breath. 'You know I am.'

'How is that possible?'

'I don't know. Our names rhyme. And things happened, didn't they? Not quite the same way, but – the swan wings, and' – I swallowed, hardly daring to say it – 'the shooting, and everything.' Part of my story was up here, like Gran-gran had said.

'How did you know?' he said, with aching quietness. 'I never told anyone …' He still couldn't do it. Couldn't put what seemed so unreal into words. A swan, turning back into a girl.

'Johnny told me.'

He went very still. 'Johnny?'

'He saw it. He saw what happened. He never said anything to anyone.'

I could see his confusion and a slow fury mixed thickly in with it. He moved a hand over his forehead, as if to rub away what I'd just said.

I knew he wouldn't have it out with him. Because all those years ago Jim had wanted to hurt himself, to take the blame. Maybe Johnny testifying wouldn't have helped. It would have made it look like collusion.

I dared myself to ask. To draw away his anger. 'What was she like?'

It was a long time before he spoke, but when he did, his voice was low and unfogged. 'A dreamer.' He turned towards me, a distant look on his face, as if half of him was back there, twenty years ago. 'She liked stories, and making stuff, and thinking of all the places she'd go. She wanted to travel. Made me want to.' He shifted, put a hand on his stomach. 'She liked music, like you.'

She was just a girl, I told myself. She had just been a girl. 'The stuff I like?'

'Well, no. Maybe. Indie guitar stuff. The Stone Roses, people like that.'

'I like the Stone Roses.'

'There you go, then.'

I wondered if he'd told anyone about Molly, any of the guys in prison, the psychologists, or if all his thoughts of her had remained closed up, locked in that little metal heart, until now. 'How did you meet?'

Jim gazed at me, his eyes two dark pools that never got the sun. His ribs rose and fell, once, heavily. And I let him tell me their story.

Afterwards he seemed drained. A strange shiver – and he was never cold.

I folded my arms underneath me and rested my head on both hands. 'You should go. Away from here.'

I imagined my words sinking down inside him, looking for the bottom. 'Where,' he said. It didn't sound like a question.

'Anywhere. You could go anywhere you liked.' I didn't know if that was true. When you had a murder conviction.

'I've not been anywhere.'

'That doesn't mean that you can't. You can just leave. Nothing's stopping you.' I didn't know if that was true. Maybe it still was. Maybe it always would be. 'She's not here any more,' I said.

*

It had been two months since I'd gone up there. I was in halls, lying on my bed, when my phone lit up. Jim. He never called me, ever. He would text me little climate reports and I had to pretend I didn't have a shortcut to Lochaber's weather on my phone. I wrote to him again, a few times – got quite into it actually, even though my handwriting was entirely amateur, like a seven-year-old's. He made me a case out of

331

maple for my smashed-up phone, sending it in a padded envelope with a tiny note.

'Hello,' I said.

'Hello.' He sounded like he was calling from a cave. 'You all right?'

'Yeah.'

'Have I woken you up?'

'No, no.' My voice had gone all wispy. I was a pathetic, useless, wilting *girl*. 'Are you?'

'Aye. Yeah. I ...' I could hear him take in one breath, then another. 'I wanted to tell you. I'm going to go. Like you said.'

I lay back on my pillow. 'No way. Where?'

'Not so far. Further in. My boss put in a good word for me over on a conservation site. Trees still. Just south of Loch Ness.'

'Monsters and shit,' I said, like a complete idiot.

'Aye, maybe. I'll keep an eye out.'

'I'm proud of you.' It wasn't moving to the other side of the world, but I knew it was a big deal for him. A first step.

He exhaled a little puff of air that sounded like a mini explosion very far away. Neither of us spoke for half a minute, at least. 'Will you come and see me sometime?' he said.

'Yeah,' I said. 'I guess I could squeeze you in.'

*

I did. More than once. With his brother's help, he managed to buy a dilapidated bungalow, and when he wasn't chopping down old trees and planting baby ones for work, he was generally slicing them to bits for his own place. It wasn't exactly in a metropolis, but it was at least at the edge of a village. He knew the names of his neighbours. Got a dog.

I found some time in between exams, when I definitely should have only been reading and revising my arse off in a corner, and snuck up north again for a weekend in early May. Jim made me study, bringing endless cups of tea and sitting behind me, playing with the ends of my hair, which had grown back down to the nape of my neck.

'You're not helping.' I was sitting on a blanket on the half-built porch. The light had started to go and tea had been replaced with whisky.

'Sorry.'

I craned round. 'I didn't say stop.'

He stopped anyway, unfolding himself slowly and disappearing inside. The sound of a cupboard being opened. Bracken lifted his head up from his paws and looked at me. I pulled a face at him, African–American literary criticism careering round my skull, fighting for space with Simone de Beauvoir and queer theory. Who needed coke when you had five more exam-condition essays in the next two weeks. 'My brain is going to implode,' I said to him. 'Help me.'

A tiny, upside-down comma of a whistle from Jim and Bracken whipped past me into the kitchen.

'Whatever, fickle dog.' I tipped the bottle up. I was getting quite good at whisky.

The porch was at the back of the house, overlooking a matted garden and a tiny thread of stream, with woodland beyond. Midges were just starting to rub their evil little villain hands together.

'That's a very uncouth way to treat sixteen-year-old Macallan, you know.' Jim sat down next to me. He'd been scraping moss off the roof tiles all afternoon and his hands were stained and tacky.

'That is because I *am* extremely uncouth,' I said.

'Oh, aye.' His voice was almost the same colour as the sky. 'You and your English degree and your red wine and art films.'

'I haven't got my English degree yet. I still might colossally fail,' I said grandly, drinking from the bottle again.

'You won't.' Quietly, amused.

I didn't know what I was going to do, if I got it. When I got it. About anything, really. I eyed his bare feet and the two grey hairs that had recently appeared behind one ear.

One step at a time.

He'd talked of seeing his brother in Australia, meeting his two young nephews, once enough years had passed since his release. He said it carefully, as if it wouldn't come true if he spoke too loudly. I'd scrolled through images on my phone of amazing places that he could visit now, even with his conviction. He'd just nodded, as if trying to digest a statistic about light years or the size of supergiant stars.

Bracken came back out. He was the colour of dead ferns, with a white stripe between the bones of his forehead, and gave an acute bark only when absolutely necessary.

'You are the best dog in the entire world,' I said, putting my fingers in his warm chest as he sat down on his hind legs. 'I hereby declare Tyger to be silver-medal doggy to you. I basically totally love you.' Bracken gave me a full-frontal huff of appallingly stinky breath. I slid my eyes over to Jim.

He was staring into the milky light. A single midge was manically doodling in front of him.

'That last bit wasn't to Bracken,' I said, mostly into the dog's neck.

Jim took a small breath and still didn't look at me. Maybe I hadn't said that out loud. Or he was ignoring me. I was that midge.

'Anyway,' I said. 'Um. Right. Fuck.' I got up, swiftly, and power-walked into the trees.

Well, that was me told.

When I came back, having used a couple of trees as a vicious nail file and also punch bag, he was sitting in exactly the same position. I hovered in front of him, wondering if I could change my train ticket and whisk myself away from him first thing tomorrow, never return.

'Sorry,' I said.

He was looking at me with half a frown and half – something more delicate, vulnerable.

'I'm sorry,' I said again, even more hopelessly. Bracken gave a twine-thin yowl.

'What for?' His voice was thoughtful.

'Spoiling everything.'

Jim gave a tiny shake of his head and picked up the whisky bottle, cradling it in a palm, tossing it lightly to the other.

Behind me a bird burbled, maybe one of the pair of gold-crests that hung out here. Plump bullets with a lick of bright yellow on their heads. I knew them now.

I wasn't sure what to do. Whether to move or say anything else.

His teeth tugged at his bottom lip and he took a slow breath in. It seemed to energise him, just enough. He looked up at me properly. 'I've loved one girl my whole life. It's all I've known. And because of – everything that happened' – those words sent out on a fug of heavy air – 'it's all mixed up with grief, and guilt, and worse.'

335

I felt a desperate sadness. 'I know.' That was it. I could never compete with something so massive and so tragic. How can you be better than a ghost?

'No.' His voice was soft. 'I'm saying that ...' He stared at the trees for a moment before turning his head back. 'Because of that, it's a big deal for me. That's all.'

The bird stopped.

I understood. If he said it now, he wouldn't be saying it to me alone. He'd still be saying it to her. Just a little bit.

I sat down next to him, my elbows on my knees.

He handed me the whisky. 'I'm too old for you.' A dark, wry smile that was uncomfortable with itself.

'Don't care.'

He inhaled, long and measured. 'I just – I need for this not to be rushed.'

'OK,' I said.

Jim put his arm around me. 'Thank you for telling me.' His eyes were evergreen. Always the same colour, winter or summer.

We looked out into the dusk. The midge did a stone-skimming jump away from us, into the softly fading pines.

*

There was one thing I never told him, though. That I'd lied.

I saw Molly everywhere up there, that November when I'd first gone back to visit. A blur of wings and hair, white tangles in the bushes. Among the trees, trailing like a ribbon, or peeling off the silver birches, just as before. Once she was right outside the door as he shut it for the night.

And I heard her, too. A whirring sound, like someone rolling their tongue. A little snap, like twigs or small bones breaking. I heard it, and I looked right at him, and smiled and was just me. I kept on being just me.

Just Polly.

AUTHOR'S NOTE

Molly Bawn (Roud 166)

Also known as Molly Bán, Molly Bond, Molly Vaughan, Molly Van, Polly Vaughn, Polly Vaughan, Polly Von, The Shooting of His Dear, The Shooting of His Deer, As Jimmie Went A-Hunting, or The Fowler.

Molly Bán, or Maílí Bhán in Irish Gaelic, translates as 'Fair Mary'. Probably originating in the seventeenth century, it was found in many nineteenth-century broadsides, and is most likely of Irish origin, with other versions existing in Scotland, England, America, Canada and Australia. In some versions, Molly (or Polly) is turned into a deer rather than a swan, which is likely simply a mishearing of 'dear'. She does not always appear to Jimmie, or Johnnie Randell, Randall, Randle, or Reynolds, in court.

The ballad retains elements of more ancient supernatural beliefs and is thought to have its roots in the Swan Maiden myth, which is found in stories from Africa to Russia. The Norse Valkyrie could take the form of a swan and travel *rida lopt ok log* – 'through air and water'. The ballad has been likened to the classical myth of the death of Procris, and to Nepheles's killing of his lover in Ovid's *Metamorphoses*.

I came across a lesser-known version of this story when visiting Loch Sunart in the West Highlands. In 'The Salen Swan', the mother of Jimmie is so jealous of Molly that she turns her into a swan. As he shoots her, she falls out of her enchantment and he sees he has killed his lover. He wanders the loch distraught and thinks he can hear her calling to him, so throws himself into the water. And that, they say, is why there are no swans on Loch Sunart.

Recommended recordings:

Anne Briggs, 'Polly Vaughan'
Packie Manus Byrne, 'Molly Bawn'
Martin Carthy and Dave Swarbrick, 'The Fowler'
Shirley Collins, 'Polly Vaughan'
Alison Krauss, 'Molly Ban'
A. L. Lloyd, 'The Shooting of His Deer/Lord Bateman'
Mishaped Pearls, 'Jimmy'
The Furrow Collective, 'Polly Vaughan'
You Are Wolf aka Kerry Andrew, 'swansong'

Packie Manus Byrne sings 'Molly Bawn'

Come all you young fowlers that handle a gun
Beware of night rambling by the setting of the sun,

And beware of an accident that happened of late
To young Molly Bawn and sad was her fate.

She was going to her uncle's when a shower came on,
She went under a green bush the shower to shun.

With her white apron round her, he took her for a swan,
But a hush and a sigh, it was his own Molly Bawn.

340

He ran home to his father's with his gun in his hand,
Saying 'Father, dear Father, I have shot Molly Bawn.

'I have shot the fair damsel, I have taken the life
Of the one I intended to take as my wife.

'She was going to her uncle's when a shower came on,
She went under a green bush, the shower to shun.

'With her white apron round her, I took her for a swan
Oh Father, will I be forgiven for the loss of that swan?'

'Oh Johnnie, my Johnnie, do not run away,
Do not leave your own country 'til your trial day.

'Don't leave your own country 'til your trial comes on,
For you'll never be convicted for the loss of the swan.'

The night before Molly's funeral, her ghost did appear,
Saying 'Mother, dear mother, young Johnnie is clear.

'I was going to my uncle's, when a shower came on,
I went under a green bush, the shower to shun.

'With my white apron round me, he took me for a swan.
Won't you tell him he's forgiven by his own Molly Bawn?'

All the girls of this country are all very glad
Since the pride of Glen Alla, Molly Bawn, is now dead.

And the girls of this country, put them all in a row
Molly Bawn would shine above them like a mountain of snow.

ACKNOWLEDGEMENTS

Thanks to my agent, Louise Burns at Andrew Mann. To Robin Robertson, Ana Fletcher, Clare Bullock and Suzanne Dean at Jonathan Cape. To my first readers, Sue Myers, Daniel Andrew, Anna Snow, Dannie Price, Jamie Coleman, Marina McCarron and Jil Thiers. To Maureen and Stuart Crooks for introducing me to this part of the world. To Todd Dunaway for the hare help. To Dunlachlan Cottage and Cedar Cottage in Strontian. To the Faber Academy for kickstarting the writing. To my very first reader, Andrew Furlow: everything is for you, really.